Be charmed, teas...
playbo...

*H*er
CHRISTMAS
*T*emptation

They may not be looking for love...but
they just might find it!

Barbara Dunlop writes romantic stories while curled up in a log cabin in Canada's far north, where bears outnumber people and it snows six months of the year. Fortunately, she has a brawny husband and two teenage children to haul firewood and clear the driveway while she sips cocoa and muses about her upcoming chapters. Barbara loves to hear from readers. You can contact her through her website at www.barbaradunlop.com

Debbi Rawlins lives in central Utah, out in the country, surrounded by woods and deer and wild turkeys. It's quite a change for a city girl who didn't even know where the state of Utah was until four years ago. Of course, unfamiliarity never stopped her. Between her junior and senior years of college she spontaneously left home in Hawaii and bummed around Europe for five weeks by herself. And, much to her parents' delight, returned home with only a quarter in her wallet.

Cathy Yardley needs to get out more. When not writing, she is probably either cruising the internet or watching movies – those featuring pirate captains and those not. Her family is considering performing an intervention for her addiction to pop culture. She lives in California. Please visit her at www.cathyyardley.com.

Her
CHRISTMAS
Temptation

BARBARA DUNLOP
DEBBI RAWLINS
CATHY YARDLEY

M&B™ and M&B™ with the Rose Device
are trademarks of the publisher.
Harlequin Mills & Boon Limited, Eton House,
18-24 Paradise Road, Richmond, Surrey TW9 1SR

HER CHRISTMAS TEMPTATION
© by Harlequin Books S.A. 2008

The Billionaire Who Bought Christmas © Barbara Dunlop 2007
What She Really Wants for Christmas © Debbi Quattrone 2007
Baby, It's Cold Outside © Cathy Yardley 2007

ISBN: 978 0 263 86898 2

009-1208

Printed and bound in Spain
by Litografía Rosés S.A., Barcelona

The Billionaire Who Bought Christmas

BARBARA DUNLOP

For Jane Graves, author extraordinaire.
You know the rest.

CHAPTER ONE

JACK OSLAND peered through the window of his Gulfstream jet plane as an indistinct figure emerged in the scattered snow falling on the tarmac at JFK.

"Did I even *mention* the word *kidnap?*" he asked his cousin Hunter who was sitting in the opposite seat.

"I can tell you're thinking about it," said Hunter, turning to improve his view, the white leather creaking beneath him.

"You're clairvoyant now?" asked Jack.

"I've known you since you were two years old."

"You were a baby when I was two."

Hunter shrugged. "You've got that telltale twitch in your temple."

"That just means I'm ticked off." Jack's attention went back to the woman who was striding through the frozen swirls of white. *Ticked off* was an understatement, and he was watching the reason walk toward him.

A slim five and a half feet, her face was obscured by a fur-trimmed hat and the enormous collar of her matching, cream-colored coat.

"Maybe she'll say no," Hunter offered, a hopeful lilt to his voice.

"And maybe pigs fly," Jack responded.

The woman wasn't about to say no. Nobody ever did. When Jack and Hunter's billionaire grandfather Cleveland Osland asked a gold digging, trophy babe to marry him, it was a done deal.

"Well it looks like dogs fly," said Hunter with a nod toward the future Mrs. Osland.

Jack blinked.

A flash of red pulled his gaze to her high-heeled boots. Sure enough. There, prancing along at her feet, was a tiny, plaid-coated fur ball.

As the implication registered, Jack shot Hunter a triumphant look. "Am I right, or am I right?"

"Her dog doesn't mean a thing."

"It means she's not turning around and going home."

"They only loaded one suitcase."

"You don't think Gramps's first wedding gift will be a platinum card?"

"Well, you *still* can't kidnap her," said Hunter.

"I'm not kidnapping her." Jack was desperate, but he wasn't a fool. He had no desire to give up a Malibu Beach penthouse for an eight-by-eight cell with a lumpy mattress, a leaky toilet and a roommate with a skull tattoo.

He didn't know how he was going to stop her. But, whatever his plan, he'd have to come up with it before the jet made it to L.A.

"What exactly did your mom say to you?" asked Hunter.

"She said that Gramps was at it again, and the latest one was hitching a ride with us. That's all I got, because she was boarding a flight to Paris, and we lost the connection. She's on the plane now."

"Could she have meant something else?"

Jack gave his cousin a deadpan stare. "No. She could not

have meant something else. Gramps is getting remarried, and it's up to me to put a stop to it."

The future bride approached the aircraft, tipping her head to gaze at the fuselage. Jack caught a glimpse of straight, white teeth, burgundy lips, a smooth, flushed complexion and blue eyes that sparkled like jewels.

"Well, there's nothing wrong with Gramps's eyesight," muttered Hunter.

"I sure wish something would go wrong with his testosterone," Jack returned, giving the steward, Leonardo, a nod to open the cabin door.

"He doesn't sleep with them," said Hunter.

Jack stared at his cousin in disbelief.

"At least not until they're married. And then, well it sounded like sporadic attempts."

Jack was momentarily speechless. "You actually *asked* Moira and Gracie about their sex lives with Gramps?"

"Sure. Didn't you?"

"Of *course* not."

Hunter smirked. "You are such an easy mark. It was your mom who told me. I guess she asked them. She was worried about a possible pregnancy."

Jack wondered why his mother hadn't talked to him about her fears, instead of Hunter. Jack was her son, and the CEO of Osland International, the man whose job it was to protect the family interests.

Leonardo finished lowering the aircraft staircase, and the woman's quick footsteps echoed on metal stairs.

"You could try reasoning with her," Hunter suggested as they rose to their feet.

Jack snorted his disbelief.

But Hunter didn't give up. "Warn her that Gramps has done this before."

"She's a twentysomething trophy babe, dating an eighty-year-old man. You think there's a chance she'll be offended by his ethics?"

The woman in question rounded the corner in all her fur-trimmed, youth-dewy glory. The little dog barked once, but obeyed when she shushed it.

After a brief moment's hesitation, she smiled brightly at the two of them, leading with an outstretched, manicured hand. "Kristy Mahoney. I don't know if you heard, but I'm meeting with Cleveland and the Sierra Sanchez buying team on Monday. Cleveland said you wouldn't mind if I caught a ride?"

Her voice was as soft and husky as a lounge singer's. And she had an interesting flare of fashion—both for herself and the dog. In addition to the red plaid coat, the dog wore a collar that sparkled with rhinestones. After the single bark, it had stayed perfectly still, unblinking in her arms. It looked like a child's toy now, with wide glassy brown eyes and blow-dried fur.

Hunter was the first to step forward. "Hunter Osland. I'm one of Cleveland's grandsons. And of course we don't mind if you join us."

"A pleasure to meet you," she pulled off her white glove and gave his hand a graceful shake.

Then she turned to Jack and raised her finely sculpted eyebrows. Her face was porcelain-doll beautiful, with a tiny up-turned nose, a delicate chin and wide-set, thick-lashed eyes.

"Jack Osland," he said, his voice unexpectedly gruff as he reached for her hand.

"Mr. Osland," she responded, closing her delicate fingers around his.

Jack was distracted by the feel of her cool skin, and her mesmerizing beauty. He barely heard Hunter's voice.

"Call us Jack and Hunter. Please."

She smiled into Jack's eyes, as if all was right with the world. As if she wasn't a shameless hussy hoping to get her hands on the family fortune. Quite the little actress this one.

"Jack, then," she said.

The sound of his name somehow sensitized his skin. Her vaguely tropical scent surrounded him, and her blue-green gaze seemed to bore directly into his brain. For a split second, he empathized with his grandfather. But he ruthlessly shook off the feeling. Unlike Cleveland, he wasn't falling for azure eyes, full lips and long legs on a woman who could barely string together a coherent sentence.

Not that Kristy appeared to be struggling with the English language. But her two predecessors sure had.

Gracie, Gramps's first bimbo, thought the bottom line was caused by poor-fitting panties. She had designed jewelry so ugly it had to be melted down and sold for scrap. Moira had insisted on her own perfume label. R & D on that little venture had set the family back about a million bucks.

With Kristy, apparently it was fashion. And since Cleveland was the major shareholder in Osland International, and since Osland International owned the Sierra Sanchez chain of women's fashion stores, she had a whole lot to gain from the impending union.

Jack, on the other hand, had a whole lot to lose. Reminding himself of that important fact helped him will his brainwaves back to normal.

"Welcome aboard, Kristy," he said.

His voice was even as he released her hand, but his brain was scrambling for a way to neutralize her. In less than five hours they'd be in L.A. That gave him five hours to figure out a way to save his family several million dollars.

* * *

This trip was the opportunity of a lifetime for Kristy Mahoney. She was trying to play it cool, hoping Jack and Hunter hadn't noticed the tremor in her voice and the slight shaking of her hands. It was a combination of nerves, adrenaline and way too much caffeine.

She'd been riding a high for a week, ever since she'd wrangled an invitation to a fashion-week after-party at Rockefeller Square and met L.A. clothing-store mogul Cleveland Osland. When he'd admired her self-designed gown, she was more than flattered. Then she'd been stunned when he'd asked to see her sketches and samples.

When he'd asked her to meet with his buying team in L.A., she'd begun pinching herself every hour on the hour, waiting for the illusion to vaporize. Any second now, she expected to wake up in her SoHo loft with Dee Dee curled up at her feet. She was sure she'd be tangled up in sweaty sheets, because this was better than any sex dream.

"Your coat, ma'am?" asked the steward.

Kristy switched Dee Dee from one arm to the other as she removed her hat and coat and her other glove. The man named Jack took in her straight black skirt and the snug red sweater, laced up at the front. Then he glanced disapprovingly at Dee Dee. Kristy felt her spine stiffen. Cleveland had claimed to be a dog fanatic, and Dee Dee hated to be left alone. Besides, she helped keep Kristy calm.

A year ago, Kristy had found the Pomeranian in a dank alley a few blocks from her loft. Cute little Dee Dee had popped out from behind a Dumpster, looking sweet, pathetic and small. Kristy hadn't had the heart to leave her out in a gathering November storm. Nor did she have the heart to let her stay at the animal shelter when no one claimed her.

Now she subconsciously squeezed Dee Dee as the steward hung her coat in the compact closet and Hunter gestured to one of the thick white leather seats.

"Please," he said.

"Thank you." Kristy sat down and crossed her legs, settling Dee Dee on her lap. The little dog's warm body helped chase away the butterflies in her abdomen.

"May I offer you a cocktail?" asked the steward as Jack took the seat opposite Kristy and Hunter sat down across the narrow aisle from Jack.

"Some fruit juice would be nice," said Kristy. It was nearly five o'clock, but she wanted to stay sharp. With the time-zone change gaining them three hours, they were scheduled to land in California at seven.

"I was about to open a bottle of ninety-three Cristal," Jack interjected. "We're celebrating the opening of a new Sierra Sanchez store in France."

Kristy hesitated. She didn't want to be rude…

"I could make you a Mimosa," offered the steward. "With fresh-squeezed orange juice?"

Kristy breathed a sigh of relief at the compromise. "That would be perfect. Thank you."

"Perfect," Jack echoed, obviously pleased as he leaned back in his seat.

He was wearing a Reese Gerhart suit, a Stolde shirt and a gray, diamond-patterned, Macklin Vanier tie. His studied, casual pose, along with the shock of dark hair that curled rakishly across his forehead, reminded her that she'd seen him mentioned in both *Business Week* and *GQ* in the past six months. Jack Osland—entrepreneur extraordinaire, heir apparent to Osland International, a man to see and to be seen with.

Beneath Dee Dee's sleeping body, Kristy surreptitiously pinched herself once more. Last year he'd made the list of the top twenty hottest male executives in America. Though, from her current vantage point, it could easily have been a list of one.

The jet engines whined, and the aircraft jerked to rolling, turning sharply to make its way to the runway. While they waited their turn in the lineup, the steward served the drinks—champagne for Jack and Hunter, and the mimosa for Kristy.

Jack immediately raised his glass. "To successful ventures."

Hunter coughed.

Kristy followed Jack's lead, toasting then taking a sip of the tart, effervescent concoction.

"SO, TELL US about your business, Kristy," said Jack, about three hours into the flight.

She placed her second mimosa on the burnished cherry-wood table between them. Then she took a deep breath, organizing her well-rehearsed pitch. "We're a fashion design company—"

"We?" asked Jack, cocking his head.

"Me," Kristy admitted, slightly rattled by the swift interruption. "It's a sole proprietorship."

Jack nodded.

When he remained silent, she picked up the thread of her pitch. "A fashion design company specializing in high-end ladies wear, specifically evening gown—"

"And what was your bottom line last quarter?"

Kristy hesitated. She'd hoped to gloss over her order volume and income, along with the modest size of her company. Although she'd been fighting for years to break into the New York fashion establishment, she'd yet to secure a retail contract, and her private sales were a whole lot less than stellar.

"I'm looking forward to the opportunities Cleveland can offer," she said, instead of answering directly.

"I'll bet you are," said Jack.

"Excuse my cousin," said Hunter. "He doesn't know when to stop talking business."

"I'm just asking—"

"Do you like basketball, Kristy?" asked Hunter.

Kristy turned to him and blinked. "Basketball?"

He nodded, taking a sip of his champagne.

"I…uh…don't know much about it."

"Cleveland loves basketball," Jack put in.

Kristy turned her attention back to Jack. "I'm afraid I don't watch sports."

"Hmm," Jack nodded sagely, his brow furrowing.

"Is that a problem?" She glanced at Hunter and then Jack, trying to read their expressions. Was it like corporate golf? Was Osland family business conducted at a basketball court?

"Would you recommend…" she paused. "I mean, should I learn something about basketball?"

"I would," said Jack.

"Jack," said Hunter.

"Well, I *would*."

Kristy took a big swallow of her mimosa. Okay. Basketball. She sure wished she'd known about this earlier. She could have taken in a game, watched some ESPN or read a sports magazine.

Then she had an idea. "I don't suppose you two would share…"

Jack grinned. "Sure. He's a Lakers fan. And I wouldn't mention the Clippers if I was you."

Hunter jumped in. "I have tickets to the Lakers Sonics game on Friday, if you'd like—"

"Bud Reynolds is his favorite player," said Jack, shooting Hunter a glare. Then his more normal expression quickly returned as his attention shifted to Kristy. "The Budster is up for player of the year. He's ten for thirteen on threes from the straight away."

"And seventeen for thirty-five from downtown," said Hunter. "You should really join me at—"

"Kristy doesn't like basketball," said Jack.

She fought a moment of panic. "I never said I didn't—"

"She might change her mind," Hunter put in.

"I could learn," Kristy offered. If basketball truly was the golf game of the Osland corporate world, she was more than willing to give it a try.

Jack's mouth thinned as he spoke to Hunter. "Dating Kristy is not the answer."

Dating? She glanced from one man to the other. *Dating?* What had she missed?

"It's nothing but a basketball game," said Hunter.

"Drop it," said Jack.

Then a voice interrupted from the plane's intercom. "Mr. Osland?"

Jack pressed a button on his armrest. "Yes, Simon."

"Just to let you know, we're reading an indicator light up here."

A muscle in Jack's temple twitched, and everything inside Kristy went still.

"I'll be right up," he said.

"No need," Simon responded with a static crackle through the small speaker. "I'd like to have air traffic control divert us to Las Vegas to check it out."

Jack shot Hunter a glance.

Kristy tried to interpret his expression. Were they out of gas? Out of oil? Losing an engine?

He pushed the intercom button. "Your call, Simon."

"Roger that, sir." The intercom went silent, and Kristy's throat turned paper-dry.

Neither of the men spoke.

"An indicator light?" she rasped.

"I'm sure it's nothing to worry about," said Jack.

Kristy waited, expecting him to say more.

"That's *it?*" They were at thirty thousand feet, and something was wrong with the plane. She picked up her mimosa and took a healthy swallow.

"The jet is in perfect running order," said Hunter.

Her voice rose. "Except for the *indicator light.*"

Her thoughts flashed to her sister. Sinclair had begged her to postpone the trip until after the holidays. But Kristy hadn't wanted to risk losing Cleveland's interest. So she'd insisted on rushing to California.

If only she'd listened. If only dreams of fame and fortune hadn't clouded her brain.

Then she wouldn't be here. She'd be home and safe, instead of facing... She stared up at Jack. "Can you at least ask him what the light was indicating?"

"Kristy—"

She nodded to the intercom button. It was *her* life at stake, too. "Will you *ask* him?"

Jack heaved an exaggerated sigh. "Trust the pilot. He's a professional. And if it was serious, Simon wouldn't be chatting about contacting air traffic control. He'd be declaring an emergency and taking us down."

Kristy peered out her window at the last orange sun rays in a darkening sky. She didn't see a fire, didn't hear any metal twisting, and the aircraft wasn't losing altitude or bouncing around. Then the steward appeared, looking calm and collected as he cleared away the drinks.

She supposed there would be a few more signs of panic if a fiery death was imminent.

"Relax," said Jack.

"It'll be fine," said Hunter.

But both men were on alert.

Then something banged on the airframe. The plane lurched sideways, and the steward nearly fell over.

"Buckle up," Jack commanded.

The man nodded, his face instantly pale. He slipped into the nearest seat and clipped on the belt.

There was relative silence for a few minutes. No more banging, and the plane stayed smooth, the engines purring normally.

"Ever been to Vegas?" Jack asked into the steady hum.

Kristy blinked at him.

"Ever been to Vegas, Kristy?"

She shook her head, stroking Dee Dee with a trembling hand. She wished now she'd left the little dog at home. At least then Dee Dee would be safe. Sinclair would have adopted her, Kristy was sure of that.

She blinked away a burning in her eyes. Sinclair. What if she never saw her sister again? Or her parents? What if her family was forced to watch the twisted, fiery wreckage of the jet on the evening news, knowing—

"Kristy?"

She glanced up to see Jack's expression soften with sympathy. "Everything's going to be just—"

The plane banged again, this time taking a sudden drop in altitude and leaving her stomach behind.

"Simon is the best in the business," Jack bravely carried on.

"That's reassuring, but it's the plane that's the problem," Kristy reminded him.

"It's just an indicator light."

"Well, it is indicating *something*."

Her fear morphed into anger. She knew it didn't make sense to be mad at Jack. It wasn't his fault they were all about to die. But he was the one arguing with her, and she couldn't seem to bring herself to think logically.

The intercom crackled to life. "Mr. Osland?"

Jack was quick to respond. "Yes, Simon?"

"It's the hydraulics on the right aileron. But we're compensating. And we're cleared to land. I don't want anybody back there to panic."

"We're not panicking," Jack responded.

"*I'm* panicking," Kristy hissed.

"He says he's compensating."

"What else is he going to say? That we should write our wills on a cocktail napkin?"

Hunter crossed to the seat beside Kristy. He belted himself in then took her hand in him. "If it was a serious danger, he'd be telling us to assume the crash position."

"Do we know the crash position?"

"Feet back, head down, hands behind your neck." Jack demonstrated.

Kristy tugged her hand from Hunter's and tried it, just in case, while the landing gear whined, and the wheels clunked into place.

Simon's voice came over the speaker once again. "Relax, everybody. Make sure your seat belts are tight. I'm not expecting anything but a slightly bumpy landing."

Kristy clasped Dee Dee to her chest, glancing out the window, trying desperately to quell the churning in her stomach.

She could see the outskirts of the city. The houses loomed large against the desert landscape. The strip rose up in the distance, glaringly brilliant and really quite beautiful from this angle. She'd give a lot to see the inside of a bright, clanking, smoky casino or even an Elvis chapel before she died.

"Kristy?"

"What?"

Jack reached for her hand across the table. "Look at me."

She glanced up as his warm palm closed over hers. She wondered vaguely how his hand could be warm at a time like this. Hers felt like ice.

"What the dog's name?" he asked softly.

"Dee Dee."

"Dee Dee's going to be okay," he said.

His eyes locked onto hers, and his deep voice rumbled through her body. "You're going to be okay. And I'm going to be okay. An hour from now, we'll all be laughing about this over wine and grilled lobster on the Strip."

Kristy didn't really believe him, but he seemed to be waiting for an answer. So she gave the barest of nods, and he squeezed her hand in response.

"Just keep looking at me, Kristy. I swear it'll be all right."

She held his gaze, and she started to feel hope.

The runway rushed up to meet them. The plane lurched to one side. Red emergency lights flashed in her peripheral vision. But for some ridiculous reason, Kristy kept her faith in Jack.

CHAPTER TWO

As THE Gulfstream finally coasted to a halt at the far end of the runway, Jack quickly rose from his seat. There was no reason for anyone to be hurt, but he wanted to make sure.

True to Simon's word, it had only been a bumpy landing, followed by a long stretch of deceleration. Even now, the emergency vehicles were struggling to catch up.

Still holding her hand, Jack went to Kristy first. "Okay?" he asked, peering into her eyes.

She gave him a series of swift nods, one hand stroking the little dog.

He smiled at her, let go of her hand and moved forward to where Leonardo was belted in. The man looked pale, but otherwise perfectly fine. Jack strode past the small closet and pulled open the flimsy cockpit door. "Simon?"

"All's well," Simon confirmed.

The copilot gave Jack a thumbs up.

There was a loud banging on the cabin door, and Jack quickly released the latch and lowered the staircase.

"Everybody okay?" shouted the fireman standing closest to the stairs. He was flanked by two others in their turnout gear. Behind the trio was a lights-flashing fire engine, an ambulance and two paramedics on the rain-spattered runway.

"We're all fine," said Jack as an airport security car pulled up, yellow lights adding to the show.

Simon appeared next to Jack's shoulder.

"A hydraulic problem," he told the emergency workers. "I'll meet you inside to fill out the paperwork."

"You need me for anything?" asked Jack.

Simon shook his head. "I'll take care of it. But you'll have a few hours to kill."

Jack nodded then turned to find Hunter and Leonardo both on their feet. Leonardo was helping Kristy into her coat, balancing the little dog in his arms while he tried to be of assistance in the narrow aisle.

"We might as well go inside," Jack said to them. "It'll take some time to do the incident report and look at repairs."

"Can I be of assistance?" asked Leonardo.

"Don't worry about us," said Jack. "Simon or I will call you when we know anything."

"Thanks," said Leonardo, handing the dog back to Kristy and giving it a pat on the head.

Jack gestured for Kristy to be first out of the aircraft, and one of the firemen came partway up the stairs to take her hand.

"I'm fine," she protested.

"It's slippery from the rain, ma'am. If you follow me to the car, security will take you to the terminal."

Jack shrugged into his overcoat and followed them down the stairs. Hunter was right behind him, and the three hitched a ride in the back seat of the sedan to the main terminal at McCarran International.

As the glass doors of the terminal glided open, he

breathed a sigh of relief. Everyone was safe, and the plane was intact. But, as soon as those facts were neatly filed away, his pragmatic brain began calculating the silver lining. At the very least, he'd bought himself three or four hours. Because, despite his connection with Kristy during the emergency landing, his mission hadn't changed. And he now had some extra time to figure out how to stop her wedding to his grandfather.

The doors swooshed shut, and the noise and confusion of the main terminal engulfed them. They joined the crowd snaking its way past the luggage carousels and rental-car booths, and Jack fought an urge to put an arm around her shoulders and keep her close to his side. Ridiculous, he told himself. She'd had a bit of a scare, sure. But she was from New York City. This crowd certainly wasn't going to rattle her.

He raised his voice so that Hunter and Kristy would hear him over the din. "I say we head for Bellagio's." He couldn't see hanging around an airport for three or four hours. Not when Le Cirque was so close by.

"I'm going to grab a commercial flight," said Hunter, slowing down and stepping out of the main pedestrian stream. The escalator next to him stretched up to the departures level. "I've got a golf date with Milo and Harrison in the morning," he finished.

Jack glanced at Kristy, worried she might hop on a commercial plane, as well. But he quickly realized she wouldn't want to pay full price for a same-day ticket.

"I guess it's just you and me," he put in, before it occurred to her to call Cleveland and ask for his credit-card number.

Kristy glanced around the crowded terminal. "You go ahead. I can wait here."

Was she masochistic?

"My treat," he clarified, in case money was stopping her. He would have paid for her dinner in any case. It was his plane. She was his guest.

She started to back away. "I'm sure you have plenty to do without me hanging around."

"Like eat a steak and drink a martini?"

She smiled at that, and it was hard to imagine she was a gold-digging opportunist.

"Reports to read?" she asked. "Phone calls to return?"

It was nice of her to offer. Really it was. But didn't she know enough to shut up and take the free dinner? Besides, he had no intention of letting her out of his sight.

"I'm honestly only planning to eat," was his answer. And conspire against her, of course. But he didn't think it was necessary to divulge that bit of information.

She gave him a look that said she didn't believe him. "What about Dee Dee?"

"The hotel will take care of her. You won't be the first celebrity to show up with a pet."

"I'm not a celebrity."

"Yeah, but they won't know that. I'll get us a really long limo, and I guarantee the concierge will find a solution."

He could see she was still hesitating, so Jack brought out the big guns. "Do you really think my grandfather would ever forgive me if I abandoned you in an airport?"

Her eye twitched, and he knew he had her.

He knew he had her even before she opened her mouth.

"Okay," she finally said with a nod. "We don't want to upset your grandfather."

"That's right. We don't."

Hunter gestured to the up escalator with a jab of his thumb. "You two kids have fun. I'm off to find another ride."

Kristy gave Hunter a brilliant smile and moved gracefully toward him, her hand outstretched. "It was a pleasure
to meet you."

Hunter reached for the hand, a goofy grin growing on
his face. "Me, too. I'm sorry I have to leave you here."

"Don't be silly. You obviously have things to do. Me, I'm
clear for the rest of the weekend."

"Really?"

Jack could see Hunter rethinking his golf game with
Milo and Harrison.

"If you want to come along," Hunter said to Kristy. "We
can probably catch something on United."

Jack wasn't about to let that happen. "Kristy's not interested in being stuffed in a last-minute back seat of a com-
muter jet."

"How do you know?" asked Hunter.

"Because she has a brain," said Jack, shifting in front of
Kristy, squaring his shoulders and giving his cousin a crys-
tal-clear *back off* glare. How was he supposed to save the
family fortune if Kristy was off flirting with Hunter?

Hunter shrugged his capitulation. "Catch you next
week, then."

"Yeah," Jack returned. "Next week."

With a wave, Hunter stepped onto the escalator.

Taking Kristy on a date. Of all the crazy, lame-ass plans.
Did Hunter think he could dazzle her with his good looks
and charm and make her forget all about Cleveland's billion-dollar offer?

Kristy didn't want a relationship. She wanted a sugar
daddy. She wanted a besotted rich old man who would indulge her every whim.

Jack stilled.

Wait a minute.

What was he thinking?

Kristy didn't want a besotted, rich *old* man. She simply wanted a besotted rich man. She'd probably take a young one just as quickly. In fact, she might prefer a young one.

He stole a sidelong glance to where she was cooing at Dee Dee.

They were stuck together in Vegas. The land of glitz and glamour and fantasy. Where better to fall head over heels for a rich young man? Where better to have a rich young man fall head over heels for you?

And Jack was a rich young man—at least he was comparatively young. When you put him up against Cleveland.

Cleveland. What better way to make sure his family's reputation and fortune didn't take another hit, he'd get Kristy to marry him instead. And keep their money out of her hands.

Of course, he'd have to work fast.

Simon would lie for him about the jet repair, buy him tonight, maybe part of tomorrow. But eventually Kristy would get tired of waiting. She'd bite the bullet and buy a ticket on a commercial airline.

Until then, however…

He offered his arm and gave her a genuine smile. "Ever tried the tasting menu at Le Cirque?"

She shook her head, hesitating then taking his arm.

"Then you're in for a treat. Come on." He gently urged her forward. "Let's go find ourselves a really flashy limo."

FORTUNATELY, since Jack ordered the tasting menu, Kristy didn't get a chance to look at it. If she had, she suspected the prices would have given her a heart attack. Everything about Le Cirque reeked of wealth and privilege.

The tables were covered in white linen, well-spaced,

with comfortable, padded chairs. The service was impeccable, and the decor spectacular. Bold burgundy carpets covered the floor, while padded, striped chairs surrounded the tables and spotlights shone on recessed circus murals.

They started almost immediately with chilled cocktails, then she savored course after course of exotic delicacies complemented by fine merlots and chardonnays.

Afterward, Jack didn't even glance at the bill before handing over his platinum card.

His cell phone rang.

"I'm sorry," he said, reaching for his inside breast pocket.

Kristy shook her head. "Don't worry about me." She settled into the overstuffed chair, sighing as she gazed around the softly glowing room. The ceiling was draped with bright silk—yellow and orange and ivory fluttering like a tent dome around a central chandelier. It was dark outside, and the dancing lights of the fountains beyond the windows added to the intimacy of the restaurant.

"What time?" Jack asked into the phone.

Kristy took another sip from her wineglass, letting the tart, woodsy flavor ease over her tongue, as the room's ambiance seeped in and relaxed her.

"If that's the best you can do," he said, catching Kristy's gaze and giving her a smile that warmed her blood. "I understand. Okay."

He flipped the phone shut.

"Everything okay?" she asked, truly not caring for the moment. As long as nobody had gone bankrupt or died, she was going to enjoy her stolen evening with a handsome, intelligent and interesting man.

Things like this simply didn't happen to women like Kristy. Her last dinner out had been the bistro down the block. She and her date had split the bill. It hadn't been expensive. But watching him calculate the charges, add the tip and count out change had definitely taken any romance out of the evening.

"Simon's waiting for parts," said Jack.

Well, that didn't sound too dire. "What does that mean?"

"It means we're stuck here for the night."

Okay. That burst Kristy's little bubble. Cash-flow alert. She'd planned on finding a small family-style motel outside of L.A. Her travel budget didn't include Bellagio rates. Not even for one night.

"Don't worry about it," said Jack.

"About what?"

He reached for her hand, stroking his tapered fingers over her knuckles. "Whatever it is that made you frown. Don't worry about it."

"I have to worry about it."

"Says who?"

"My accountant and my credit card company."

He grinned. "Oh, that. Don't worry. I won't let you go bankrupt before morning."

She frowned at him. "Dinner was great, but you're not paying for my hotel room."

"Why not?"

"Because I have self-respect."

"You're my guest."

"I'm your fellow strandee."

"It was my plane."

"And you let me ride on it for free."

Jack sighed, and she could feel him regrouping.

He opened his mouth.

"No," she jumped in.

"You don't even know what I was going to say."

"Yes, I do."

"No, you don't." He got to his feet. "Come on. I'm going to show you something fun."

"You keep your platinum card right where it is."

He grinned, his eyes glowing in the candlelight. "Cross my heart."

She nodded. "Okay. That's better." She bunched her linen napkin on the table and rose with him. "So, what is it?"

He shook his head. "It's a surprise. It won't hurt a bit. But that's all I'm telling you."

"Will it be embarrassing?"

"Not in the least."

"Will I hate myself in the morning?"

His gray gaze went smoky, sizzling into hers for a split second, clenching her stomach, tripping her heartbeat. "I certainly hope not," he said.

"Jack—"

The sizzle evaporated. "Grab a sense of humor, Kristy. I'm not propositioning you"

She felt like a fool. "Sorry."

He held out his hand, the dare clear in his smirk.

She took a deep breath. Then she told herself to chill and curled her fingers into his palm.

His hand was strong, warm and dry, just the way she remembered. There was something about the texture of his skin, or maybe it was the way his fingers wrapped confidently around hers. It was the way it had been on the plane. She felt safe in his hands, as though he was in control of the planet, and all she needed to do was hang on for the ride.

It was probably a lingering emotion from the turmoil of the airplane landing, but it felt nice all the same.

THEY MADE their way across the patterned carpet of the casino. Machines flashed and chimed on all sides, while muted lighting showed yellow through draped fabric valences. Kristy tucked in behind Jack as he naturally cleared a path in front of him while he strode confidently through the crowd.

Above the buzz of conversation, a woman whooped in delight, and applause broke out around one of the craps tables.

The throng thinned, and they approached the casino cage where a neatly uniformed woman greeted Jack with a smile.

"Fifty thousand," said Jack, tossing his credit card on the counter.

Kristy turned to blink up at him like an owl. "That was a joke, right?"

He glanced down and gave her a wink and a mischievous grin.

"Seriously," she prompted.

But he didn't answer. Instead, he turned back to the clerk who handed him a receipt and a stack of bills.

Kristy focused on the money, trying to figure out if fifty thousand was casino lingo for some other amount. Maybe he'd meant fifty dollars or five hundred.

But those were thousand-dollar bills. And there were a lot of them. She'd never even seen a thousand-dollar bill.

Feeling panicky at the thought of him walking around with that much money, she pulled up on her toes and hissed in his ear. "This is nuts."

He leaned down to whisper back. "How so?"

"You can't blow all *that*." She was practically hyperventilating just looking at it.

He smirked. "I'm not blowing it. They'll give it back to me when I cash in the chips."

Like that was a reasonable answer. "Only if you *don't lose it*."

He shook his head. "Have a little faith. I'm not going to lose it."

"You can't know that."

He tucked the bills into his inside pocket. "Sure I can."

She resisted an urge to sock him in the arm. "Do you have a gambling problem?" Was she an enabler in all this? Should she try to drag him out of the casino? Maybe call Hunter for help?

Jack grinned, turning to walk away from the cashier. "It's not a problem at all."

She moved up beside him. "Seriously, Jack. Should we leave?"

"I told you. This is going to be fun." He stopped in the middle of the casino and took a look around. "Okay, what are you up for?"

"A drink," she said, suddenly inspired. "We should go back to the lobby bar instead."

"They'll bring you free drinks at the table. Ever played roulette?"

He started to move again, and she scrambled to keep up. "No. Of course not. I don't gamble." Like she could afford to on her budget.

"Really?" he asked.

"Really."

"That's too bad." He stopped in front of a green numbered table and a shiny roulette wheel.

"Hop up," he said, putting the stack of bills down on the edge of the green felt.

She stared at the money, a sick feeling growing in the pit of her stomach. "No way."

He pulled out one of the high chairs. "Don't spoil the party."

"Jack, really—" Then she realized they were attracting

attention from the dealer and the other players, so she lifted her heel to the crossbar and jumped up into the chair.

"That a girl," Jack murmured approvingly.

The dealer took his money and replaced it with a clear plastic tray of color-rimmed chips.

Jack took the seat next to her. "There you go. Now pick a number."

She glared at him.

"Care for a drink?" a female voice said from behind her.

"Glenlivet," said Jack. "One ice cube." He looked at Kristy. "A Cosmopolitan?" That was the drink she'd had before dinner.

She considered saying no. But two minutes ago she'd claimed to want a drink. She didn't want to look like a fool. So she nodded, and the woman jotted it down.

"Did you pick a number?" asked Jack.

"Twenty-seven," she said, giving up the fight with an exasperated sigh.

He nodded at the table. "Well, put some chips on it."

She picked up a single hundred-dollar chip and leaned over to the twenty-seven square.

"That's it?" he asked with obvious disappointment.

"You might be sure you're not going to lose," she said, as the dealer spun the wheel. "But I'm not."

"I never said you weren't going to lose."

"There you go."

He sat back in his seat. "What I said was, *I'm* not going to lose. And that's because I'm not going to play."

The wheel stopped on thirty, and the dealer cleared away her chip.

"See what you made me do?"

"Pick another one," he said, eyes dancing. "And this time live a little."

"Is this voyeurism for gambling addicts?"

He laughed at that. "I thought you said you wanted a room?"

"What does this have to do with getting a room?"

"You'll see."

"And it was *you* who wanted a room. I'm happy to wait at the airport with Dee Dee."

"All night?"

To save several hundred dollars? "Yes."

The dealer tossed in the small white ball.

Jack nodded to the wheel. "You missed that one."

She swiveled the chair to the side. "Can we leave now?"

"We've got drinks coming."

The ball stopped, and a sequin-covered woman next to Kristy gave a cry of joy.

"Play a number," said Jack.

"You're insane."

He lifted a stack of chips and placed them in her palm. "If you want to play it safe, take red or evens. Or, see that? If you put it on the line, you can cover two numbers."

Kristy squinted at another man's stack of chips sitting on the line halfway between two numbers. "Really?"

"Swear to God."

Kristy had to admit, that seemed like a pretty good deal. She put a stack on the line between seventeen and twenty. She refused to count the chips to see how much she was gambling.

Jack placed his arm across the back of her chair and leaned in. "Now don't let it rattle you if you lose. You're going to win some, and you're going to lose some. But we'll be fine in the end."

Kristy held her breath as she watched the white ball bounce around the wheel. It rattled to a stop on the seventeen.

She blinked, sure she must be hallucinating.

"You won," said Jack.

"I did?"

"You want to let it ride?"

She watched the dealer add a stack of chips to her bet. "Ha. What are the odds of it hitting seventeen twice in a row?"

"Exactly the same as the odds of it hitting any other number."

Kristy eyed him skeptically.

"Seriously," he said.

That couldn't be right. She reached out and moved her winnings to twenty-nine and thirty.

Then she reconsidered and cut the stack in half.

Jack sighed, leaning in to mumble in her ear. "We'll be here all night at this rate."

She ignored the warm puff of his breath on her skin. "I don't want to lose it all at once."

The dealer spun the wheel and tossed in the ball.

"There's plenty more where that came from," said Jack, tapping his finger on the plastic tray that held his chips.

"I can't believe you're so cavalier with your money."

"I can't believe you're so cautious with my money."

The ball bounced to a stop.

Kristy had lost.

"See?"

The waitress arrived with their drinks. Chatter ebbed and flowed around them as the sequined woman next to Kristy wriggled off her seat and slid to the floor.

A thirty-something man in a dark suit took her place.

He smiled a friendly greeting at Kristy. Jack reacted by leaning closer to her, closing the space between them.

She struggled not to grin at his posturing. They were about as far away as you could get from dating, yet some anthropological instinct had obviously kicked in.

"Make a bigger bet," said Jack, the fabric of his suit brushing against her bare forearm.

"Fine," she said, scooping a long round of chips and placing them on number four.

"Wow," he breathed, and she shot him a worried look.

But he was grinning. "Just messin' with you."

"You're a jerk. You know that?"

"Yeah," he chuckled.

She lost again.

"I don't like this game." It didn't matter that it wasn't her money. She was stressing out over losing it anyway.

"You're doing fine," he said.

"Can we do something else?"

"One more time."

She gave a hard sigh. "Fine."

Following the lead of the man sitting next to her, she placed a smaller stack of chips on the cross between four numbers. Then she took a bracing swallow of her cosmo.

The ball clattered around the wheel, settling on twelve, one of Kristy's numbers.

The dealer added a couple of chips to her stack.

"Low risk, low payoff," said Jack. He grabbed two stacks of chips and set them on number twenty-two. "Incidentally, that's also the way things work in real life."

"I know," said Kristy, watching in morbid fascination as the wheel spun around again.

"Do you?" he asked.

"Why do you think I'm going to L.A.?"

Astonishingly, with that much money riding, Jack turned away from the wheel to stare at her instead. "Is it?"

She nodded, not taking her gaze off the ball. "For the chance at a big payoff. I left my sister, my holiday shopping and my baking behind."

He kept his gaze glued to her profile. "Well, if this works out, you'll be able to do all the shopping you want."

"I suppose that's true." Then her eyes widened and her stomach clenched with the thrill. "You won!"

Jack stared at her a split second longer. Then he glanced at the roulette wheel. "I guess I did."

"Do it again," she urged. Clearly he understood the game better than she did.

His shoulders relaxed. "It's your turn."

"You're better."

He split his bet between number eighteen and the red zone. Then he pushed a stack of chips onto the line between eight and nine.

"Wow," said Kristy.

"What?"

"You must have a secret system."

He shook his head. "You pick numbers. It's completely random. Help me out here."

Scooting forward in her chair, Kristy gamely pushed a couple more stacks onto the board.

"Now we're talking," said Jack.

"That's a pretty rich bet," said the man next to her.

She felt Jack still.

Then the man glanced past her to Jack. His expression sobered, and he turned his attention to the table.

The ball hit the wheel.

Kristy doubled her money on two, and her bet also paid out on black. Several spins later, with her Cosmo glass empty and a new player at her elbow, they were up several thousand dollars. A man in a navy suit and a red tie approached them.

He introduced himself as the casino manager and asked if they'd care for another drink.

Kristy was pretty much done with alcohol. Besides, it was getting late. She hoped she'd won enough to pay for a hotel room because, now that she was tired, an airport waiting area didn't sound all that appealing.

To her surprise, the manager held out a key card to Jack. "Please accept the Ruby Suite with our compliments."

Jack gave Kristy a sparkling-eyed look. "Interested in a suite?"

"Two bedrooms?" she asked. It occurred to her that this could be a setup. Jack had been a perfect gentleman so far—maybe too much of a gentleman to be trusted.

He raised an eyebrow in the manager's direction.

Without missing a beat, the man pocketed the key and retrieved his cell phone.

"This is Raymond Jones. Can you bring me a key for the Diamond Suite?" He paused. "The roulette tables. Thank you."

He flipped the phone shut. "Two bedrooms," he said.

"And my dog?" Kristy asked.

"Not a problem," said Raymond.

"Then, thank you," she said with a nod and a smile. A free suite definitely solved her accommodation problem.

"Anything else we can do to be of service?" asked Raymond.

Jack glanced at Kristy. "I can't think of anything? Can you?"

Kristy shook her head.

Another man appeared at Raymond's elbow and provided a new room key.

Jack accepted it with a thank you, while Raymond gestured to the expanse of the casino. "Please. Enjoy the rest of the evening."

"We will," said Jack. "Thank you very much."

As Raymond and the other man walked away, Kristy turned to Jack. "So, did you pay him to do that?"

"Nope."

"Come on."

"I didn't have to pay him. The room's free."

"I don't get it."

"That's what happens when you bet big."

"They give you a free room?"

Jack placed his hand in the small of her back, gently steering her toward the cage.

There was something about that hand...

"If you're losing," he said. "They want you to stick around and keep doing it. And if you're winning, they want you to stick around long enough to lose it back to them."

"Is that what we're going to do?"

"Nope. Not unless you want to."

"I don't want to lose."

"Then I vote we cash out and enjoy our free room."

A free room with Jack.

Correction, a free suite with Jack. Two rooms, really.

She glanced up at his handsome face, and her stomach fluttered at the thought of such an intimate setting with such a sexy man.

Two bedrooms, she reminded herself.

Still. It was a hotel suite. And they were in Vegas. And she'd be a bald-faced liar if she didn't admit her mind was jumping to the possibilities.

CHAPTER THREE

KRISTY MAHONEY was quite possibly the most perplexing person Jack had ever met. She admitted she was marrying his grandfather for money, yet he practically had to twist her arm to get her to gamble. They'd walked past designer fashions, fur coats and numerous jewelry displays in the hotel lobby, and she hadn't so much as sent a covetous look at the merchandise, never mind suggesting she needed a few things to tide her over until morning.

Any gold digger worth her salt should be demanding Cleveland send a new private jet by now or dressing herself to the nines on Jack's credit card. Instead, she was gazing around the luxury hotel suite in what appeared to be awe.

"It's huge," she muttered, her heels echoing on the marble floor of the foyer, Dee Dee's claws ticked along at her side as they stepped into the living room.

Jack shut the suite door behind them. "You were the one who insisted on two bedrooms."

She turned. "Did I foil your plans?"

He tensed for a split second before realizing she was referring to any plans he might have had to sleep with her. "I have no plans." At least not to make love with her. At least not tonight.

Though, if she'd agreed to one bedroom and hopped into a king-sized bed, he would have eagerly followed.

"Let me guess," she purred. "Other women generally fall for your 'come on up to my free hotel suite. Oh—'" she dramatically raised her hand to her lips, mimicking his voice "—look, there's only one great big bed.'"

He couldn't help but grin at her exaggeration. Yet, somehow her opinion pricked his pride. It seemed she felt he had no honor, and had to resort to trickery to attract women.

He found himself crossing the foyer to gaze down at her. "Kristy," he began in his own defense. "I'm a thirty-two-year-old man who works out five mornings a week and is in control of a billion-dollar conglomerate. What have I done to make you think I can't get women?"

She didn't miss a beat. "You're only thirty-two?"

God, she was spunky. "Ouch."

"And I thought it was Cleveland who was in charge of Osland International."

Ahhh. This one definitely had a better brain than the last two gold diggers.

"He's the major shareholder," said Jack. "I'm the CEO."

She shrugged. "I don't even know the difference."

Like heck she didn't.

"But, whatever," she continued. "I'm still not sleeping with you."

"Kristy, Kristy, Kristy." He didn't want her to sleep with him.

Okay, yeah, he did. Obviously. Since she was stunningly sexy, and he did have a pulse. But what he really wanted was for her to fall for him.

Which meant he should probably stop yanking her chain.

But it was so much fun to tease her. And the woman could definitely give as good as she got.

"I'm sure you get women all the time," she conceded.

"Now you make me sound like a player."

"Are you?"

"No." He wasn't. He dated women occasionally. And he slept with women occasionally. But he was very discriminating. And he never led them on.

She moved to the middle of the living room, checking out the rest of the suite. "Got a girlfriend?"

"Not at the moment."

Her perfume left a trace in the air. It was nice. More than nice, actually. It wasn't fruity, yet it wasn't floral…

"Did she break up with you, or did you break up with her?"

Jack blinked. "Who?"

"Your last girlfriend."

"It wasn't a serious relationship."

Kristy turned back and nodded. "Ahhh."

"What's with the ahhhs?"

Was she accusing him of something?

"I know your type. Love 'em and leave 'em."

There was something in her eyes, not hurt exactly, but something. Had somebody left her? Was that why she was willing to settle for money instead of love?

Now he was curious, but he didn't want to bring up the subject of her love life. Because that would invariably lead to his grandfather, and Jack wanted her to forget all about Cleveland for tonight.

"I can hardly love you and leave you in forty-eight hours, can I?" he said instead.

"Forty-eight?"

Oops. "Twenty-four," Jack corrected himself. "I meant twenty-four."

"You scared me there for a minute."

He gave her his most congenial smile. "Wouldn't want to do that." Then he nodded to the glass balcony door and the view beyond. "How about a swim?"

She turned to follow his gaze.

He crossed the room to open the doors, implicitly bidding her to follow him onto the wide veranda. "Take a look down there."

She joined him to lean on the rail, between a pair of twin loungers at one end of the veranda and an umbrella table set up for four at the other.

He heard her suck in a breath as she gazed at the Mediterranean-style courtyard. The lighted pool was embraced by pillared fountains, terra-cotta tiles, tropical trees and sculpted shrubbery. It was peaceful and deserted this time of night, and the patterned pool bottom wavered through the mist rising from the heated water.

"It's almost midnight," Kristy whispered. "Are we allowed?"

He shrugged. "We're high-rollers in a complimentary suite. You think they'll stop us from taking a swim?"

"My swimsuit's still in the plane."

Had the woman never heard of shopping? Had she never heard of butler service? As if a tiny thing like a swimsuit would stop them. There was a phone on the table between the two loungers, so Jack picked it up and pressed zero.

The voice on the other end was prompt. "Yes, Mr. Osland?"

"Any chance we can get a couple of swimsuits up here?"

"Of course. I'll have the butler bring up a selection right away. The sizes?"

Jack covered the mouthpiece. "Size?" he asked Kristy.

Her eyes went a little wide. "Uh, four."

He nodded. "Women's four and men's thirty-two."

"Thank you, sir. Someone will be right up."

Jack replaced the receiver.

Kristy glanced at the phone. "Just like that?"

"Just like that," said Jack. Then he couldn't resist giving her an impish grin. "I'm hoping you get a bikini."

She eyed him up and down, a frown on her face that made him self-conscious. "I guess it's not quite the same for women."

"What do you mean?" Was it an insult?

She gave him an exaggerated shudder. "I mean, the thought of any man in Spandex."

He took a couple of steps toward her. "Did I mention I work out?"

"I'm sure you're perfectly gorgeous under that suit." Then she stilled as her own words obviously registered.

He was torn between making a joke and making a move. Deep down, he knew he shouldn't do either.

Still, he was suddenly aware of the way her eyes sparkled in the moonlight and her hair framed her face in gentle waves. That elusive perfume wafted through his senses once more. And everything inside him screamed at him to kiss her. Under normal circumstances, he'd definitely take the expression on her face as an invitation.

But these were not normal circumstances. He was on a mission. And he didn't dare scare her off.

He settled for brushing a wisp of her hair from her face. Her cheek was soft under his fingertips. Her lashes fluttered at the contact, and it was more than he could do to ignore the signal.

He subconsciously leaned forward, and she tipped her head to one side.

The knock on the door saved him.

Jack forced himself to pull away, his voice husky with

burgeoning desire. "Our suits are here," he stated unneces-sarily.

Kristy drew in a breath, and gave her head a quick shake. "Right."

He squeezed her hand gently, in silent acknowledgment of what they both knew had almost happened. Then he stepped into the suite and answered the door.

The butler handed him three women's and three men's suits on silk padded hangers. Jack tipped the man and sent him on his way.

Then he turned to find Kristy back inside the suite.

"Pick a bedroom," he invited, refusing to let himself look too deeply into her eyes as he handed her the women's suits.

She motioned to the closest door, the smaller of the two rooms. Again, Jack was surprised when her actions didn't fit his expectations. Either their almost-kiss had truly rat-tled her, or she didn't care about sleeping in the plush, four-poster bed in the main bedroom.

Either case was intriguing.

IN THE COOL evening air, the pool water was chilly against Kristy's legs. A sultry breeze blew over her aqua, one-piece suit as she gradually made her way down the sloping stairs.

Jack on the other hand, executed a neat dive into the deep end, his shimmering form moving swiftly underwater to-ward her. He broke the surface, coming to his feet and rak-ing back his dark hair with spread fingers.

"Feels good," he announced, looking slick and sexy in the diffuse garden lights.

"Feels cold," she responded, especially in comparison to the heat building inside her at she stared at his broad, bare chest.

He took a couple of steps forward. "Need help getting in?"

She reached out and gripped the handrail. "Don't you dare."

His grin was wide, showing straight, white teeth and bringing out a small dimple in his left cheek. His dark eyes sparkled. "It's easier if you do it fast."

She took a step down another stair. "I don't need your help, thank you very much."

She should have been worried about the cold water. And she was. But her mind also went immediately to Jack's slick, wet hands against her own bare skin, and her blood pressure took a jump.

She put her foot on the bottom of the pool, the water coming slightly past her waist.

He closed the distance between them. "My sister always screamed when I threw her in, but in the end she thanked me."

"I'm not your sister."

"You think I don't know that?" His gaze darkened as it dipped to take in her suit.

Her entire body clenched in reaction, reminding her all over again that he was sexy and smart and funny, and women around the world adored him. She definitely wasn't going to sleep with him. But that didn't mean she couldn't take advantage of the opportunity to flirt a little.

He shifted even closer in the waist-high water, and her mind waged a split-second war. Wrestling around in the pool at midnight was quite a ways past flirting. But then, he was only going to dunk her, not ravish her. Despite his joking innuendo, he had been a perfect gentleman all evening.

Still, they'd almost kissed on the balcony. And Kristy

wasn't a complete fool. So, just before his fingertips brushed her skin, she did a surface dive, scissoring her feet, propelling her body away from him and into the deeper water.

"Chicken," he mocked as she came up for air.

"I prefer to take care of things myself," she responded, pushing her wet hair back from her face.

His forehead creased for a microsecond, and she thought he was about to say something. But then his expression smoothed out. "Where I like to help out as much as possible."

She kicked her legs to keep herself afloat. "You're such an altruist."

He gave a dramatic, self-effacing sigh. "This is true."

"*And* an egomaniac."

He swam closer. "Well, you're a tease."

"I am not." But she paused, reevaluating her behavior so far. "How do you mean?"

"Batting those come-dunk-me eyes, and then spoiling my fun."

She splashed at him. "Poor baby."

He grinned, then dove under.

Before she could react, his hand wrapped around her ankle. He tugged just hard enough to pull her below, then he instantly let her go, and she bobbed back up.

"Not fair," she sputtered, kicking over to where she could grab the edge.

He glided up beside her and rested his hand on the pool deck. "Who said anything about fair?"

He inched closer, his skin glistening with droplets of water, his hair nearly black in the shadow of the deck chairs. His eyes grew heavy with desire, and his voice vibrated her very core.

His thigh brushed hers, sending licks of energy across her skin. Her stomach contracted, and her lips went soft. She could feel an invisible pull compelling her forward.

"I've had some really bad ideas in my time…" she breathed.

He lifted her chin with his index finger. "And we're definitely going to talk about that someday."

She stared straight into his slate-gray eyes. Her chest went tight with emotion, and her body tingled with blatant sexual desire.

He tipped his head, light mist curling around his face as he leaned in. "But right now…"

Her body shifted forward, and she closed her eyes, savoring the sensation of his strong arms, his broad chest and his hard, hot thighs coming up against her own.

Their lips met.

His mouth was silky-soft, warm and mobile, with just the right combination of moisture and pressure.

She leaned in, bringing her breasts flush against him, wrapping her arms around his neck, letting him keep them both afloat in the deep water.

His hand splayed across her wet hair, holding her close, deepening the kiss. His hard thigh inched its way between hers and sensation burst through her body, coming out in a moan and a plea for more around their passionate kiss. She wanted to rip off her suit and rip off his suit and make wild wet love right here in the pool.

He broke off the kiss, moving to her neck, then outward, nudging the bathing suit strap out of the way to plant wet kisses on the tip of her shoulder.

She buried her face in the crook of his neck, inhaling deeply, flicking out her tongue to taste the salt of his skin. She threaded her fingers through his hair, tightening her arms, wanting to get closer, harder, tighter. Her legs went around his body, pulling him intimately between her thighs.

He slid his free hand up the tight suit, resting on her ribs, his thumb creeping along the underside of her breast.

She held her breath, as it circled higher and closer. When it rasped its way over her nipple, she groaned in his ear.

He swore in return.

Then he stilled, and slowly drew back, resting his forehead against hers.

"A little too public here," he breathed.

When her world settled back on its axis, she nodded in agreement, even as she tried to put some context around the experience. "That was…"

"Unexpected," he said.

She nodded again.

"Better make that surprising," he continued. Then he paused. "No. Better make that astounding."

He was right. On all counts.

"Tell you what," he began, his voice growing stronger.

She fought an urge to melt against him again. She didn't know what was happening here, but there was no denying she wanted more of it. They were both adults. And this was Vegas. If she got a vote, she'd vote they find someplace more private—say their hotel suite—to see where this all went.

"We'll dry off," he said.

She liked the plan so far.

"Then we'll go somewhere very public."

She started to nod, but then his words registered. Wait. The plan was off the rails already.

He drew back even farther, and the water sloshing gently against her felt cold again.

"And have ourselves a very decadent dessert."

Did *dessert* mean what she thought it meant?

She gazed into his eyes to find out.

"Don't look at me like that," he growled.

"Why?"

"Because I'm trying to be a gentleman here."

"I mean why *dessert* in a public place?"

He smoothed her wet hair back from her forehead, and gave her a melancholy smile. "Because I really meant dessert. Like I said, I'm trying to be a gentleman here. You said you didn't want to make love with me."

"But—"

He put his index finger over her lips. "Truly, Kristy. I don't want you to regret anything in the morning."

She wasn't going to regret anything in the morning. She'd said no lovemaking earlier, before she knew him, before she understood the power of the electricity and passion between them. They owed it to themselves, to the rest of their lives, maybe to the entire universe, to see where this was going.

"Would *you* regret it in the morning?" she asked.

He searched her face. "Not a chance in hell."

"Then—"

"Dessert," he said, with a small shake of his head. "And then our respective bedrooms."

A small part of her knew he was right. But a much bigger part of her railed against logic. She wanted to throw caution to the wind and drown in Jack's arms, even if it was only for one night.

She wasn't normally an impulsive person. But he brought out something latent and wild inside her, and she feared if she stopped it now she'd never get this chance again.

Maybe she'd regret it later, and maybe she wouldn't. "I don't see—"

"But I do see. Trust me on this one." His look was deadly sober. "Because I'm right."

Finally, she nodded, telling herself it would seem like a good decision in the morning.

AT 7:00 A.M., with sunlight streaming through the window of the hotel bedroom, Jack wished he still thought tucking Kristy into her own bed had been the right decision.

He wasn't a man who normally questioned his actions. Once his decision was made, it was made. And for better or worse, he went forward from there. But at this particular moment, he was questioning. For one, he'd be in a lot less pain if he'd let last evening proceed to its natural conclusion. For another, she'd made no secret of wanting him.

And making love might have actually *helped* in his plan to romance her. He hadn't been dishonest about his feelings. Deliberately romancing her had been the furthest thing from his mind for most of the evening. He'd simply been enjoying himself with a bright, beautiful, funny woman.

Now, while the daytime traffic came to life on the city streets below—just past that eerie lull between five and seven while the gamblers and partygoers crawled into bed and the bakers and city workers ate breakfast—the right or wrong of his actions last night pounded uncharacteristically through his brain.

Following a private opening of the hotel boutique for slacks and T-shirts, he and Kristy had dried off and changed. Then they'd shared a sticky, sweet, chocolate volcano in the restaurant.

Watching her spoon the smooth, dark sauce into that pert mouth would have broken most mortal men. But not Jack.

He'd kept his hands to himself, all the way through dessert and all the way back to the suite.

There he'd behaved like a monk, and he'd been inordinately proud of himself at the time. Because her flushed cheeks and smoky sapphire eyes had transmitted the kind of invitation that made his body beg for mercy.

And it was still begging for mercy.

And she was in the next room. Probably still sleeping, since the traffic noise and the whirr of a far-off vacuum in the hotel hallway were the only sounds in the silent suite.

He toyed with the idea of waking her up.

There was nothing stopping him from crawling in next to her in the warm bed and picking up right where they'd left off.

The worst she could say was no.

The best she could say was…

Instead, Jack reached for the telephone next to his bed. Seven in the morning with no sleep and a raging hard-on was not the best time to be making logical decisions. He punched in Simon's cell phone number.

"Captain Reece here," came Simon's staccato but sleep-edged voice.

"Sorry," said Jack, feeling a twinge of guilt for unnecessarily waking the man up.

"No problem. You ready to go?"

"Not yet."

"Okay." To his credit, Simon didn't ask Jack why the hell he was calling this early.

"Can you buy me another day?"

"In Vegas?"

"Yeah."

Simon stifled a yawn. "Sure. Shipment delay on the parts?"

"That'll do it."

"Done. Just keep me posted."

Jack chuckled. "But maybe not at 7:00 a.m.?"

Simon's voice relaxed. "That'd be nice. But I'm on call whenever you need me."

"Am I screwing up anybody else's schedule?" Jack asked.

Cleveland had exclusive use of one of the Osland company jets, while Jack was the primary user of the other. But Jack didn't need his jet every day, and other Osland executives frequently booked it when he was in L.A.

"Hunter called a charter company. We're covered."

"Great. Thanks for your patience, Simon."

"No worries. I'm fine. I'll grab some tickets for a show tonight."

"Have a good time." Jack hung up the phone, his hand resting on the receiver for a moment. He'd wondered if Kristy might enjoy a show. Cirque du Soleil was playing.

He rolled out of bed.

He took a cold shower and brewed himself a cup of coffee in the in-room machine. Then he picked up the phone to call his assistant.

"Hey, Jack," came Lisa's voice on her cell phone.

"Morning," he responded. "Didn't wake you, did I?"

"It's seven o'clock," she responded. Lisa was a morning person extraordinaire.

"Been jogging yet?"

"Just putting on my shoes."

"Well, I'm stuck in Vegas."

"Really? How'd that happen?"

"Jet trouble. Simon's having it repaired."

"You okay?"

"Fine."

"Why don't you grab a flight?"

"I've got a passenger." It wasn't really an answer, since commercial airlines generally had more than one seat available on their flights.

But Lisa was too polite to ask any questions. "You need anything from me?"

"Did we hear from Neil Roberts on the Perkins project?"

"Let's see." Something rustled in the background. "He says escrow will close on the factory Friday. The union agreements are almost finished—some sticking point on pension transferability. And the tooling for the robotics hit a snag in Bombay, but he's dealing with it next week."

Jack jotted a couple of notes on the hotel stationary. "Does he need me to call?"

"Didn't say so."

"Okay. I'll touch base with him on Monday. Anything else?"

"Harry's retirement in the New Year. If you want the engraving done on time, we have to get the order in now. Gold or platinum."

"You've seen them both. You decide."

"He'll want the gold."

Jack shrugged in the suite. He'd have gone with the platinum. But Lisa knew their Western Regional Controller better than he did. "Go ahead then."

"You sure?"

"You're the expert."

He could hear the grin in her voice. "It's about time you—"

"Have a good run."

"I will. Have fun in Vegas."

Jack grunted something noncommittal before he hung up the phone. He wasn't in Vegas to have fun.

His gaze wandered to Kristy's bedroom door. But having fun was certainly turning into a huge temptation.

He left his notes on the small desk and crossed the room to her door, knocking lightly.

"Hmmff?" came a muffled reply.

He eased the door open. "You waking up?"

She rolled onto her back, her blond hair fanning out across the white pillow, and her creamy shoulders peeking out above the ivory duvet while Dee Dee resettled herself on the foot of the bed. "I am now."

"Not a morning person?" His hand tightened on the doorknob, and he forced his feet to stay glued to the carpet while he let himself wonder if she was naked under the sheets.

"Not when I stay up half the night eating chocolate and ice cream."

Jack's gut clenched once more at the memory of how she'd dug into the chocolate volcano, her tongue curling around the spoon, rescuing a drop of chocolate sauce that had dabbed on her lower lip. He wondered for the thousandth time how he'd had the strength to send her off to her own bedroom.

He forced his thoughts back to the present. "I have good news and bad news."

She sat up, trapping the sheet under her arms, bringing it tight against what he was now sure were her naked breasts. "The good news first."

It took him an inordinately long time to find his voice. "We have tickets to Cirque du Soleil."

"I guess I don't have to guess the bad news." But she didn't look overly distressed at the thought of staying in Vegas.

Jack clenched his teeth, redoubling his effort to stay on

this side of the room. "Simon's waiting on the parts shipment," he lied.

She nodded her acceptance of the explanation. "Any guesses as to when he'll get them?"

Jack mustered up a casual shrug, the words *Don't do it, Don't do it* turning into a mantra inside his head. He was proud of how normal his voice sounded. "Up in the air. We may have to do some more gambling to keep the room."

Kristy smiled at that, and the world shifted inside Jack. Her eyes turned the most incredible shades of blue. They sparkled like jewels when she was happy, then darkened to a smoky sky when she was aroused. He hadn't made her angry yet, but he'd bet anger had its own distinct shade.

For a split second he realized he was going to find out exactly how her anger looked come Monday. The thought clobbered him, until he shoved it aside.

She shifted to a more comfortable position on the bed, one delicate foot peeking out the side of the blanket. "You do know, don't you, that we could lose more gambling than the suite actually costs?"

He let his gaze rest on her perfect pink toes. "Law of averages says we won't."

"I thought the odds were on the side of the house."

"They are. But most people neither win nor lose big. And we'd have to lose pretty big to cover all this."

She glanced around. "True enough. If we're going to be stuck here, is there any chance we could get our suitcases from the plane?"

He forced his gaze from her bare foot and focused on the headboard behind her left ear, forcing himself to regroup and think logically about his plans. They could send for their suitcases, certainly. But that would undermine his efforts to make her feel like she was in a Cinderella fantasy. Clothes and jewelry were an important part of the package. She had to get completely caught up if he expected her to marry him by Sunday night.

"Don't you think it's more fun for me to take you shopping?" he asked.

She frowned. "I can't let you keep spending money on me."

He gave another shrug. "It's my fault you're stuck here."

She cocked her head to one side. "*You* broke the plane?"

"I own the plane."

She hesitated for a few seconds. "I guess you do, don't you?"

The question seemed rhetorical, so he didn't bother answering.

"This is all a bit surreal for me," she said.

Jack fought the urge to move farther into the room to reassure her. "Just go with it."

"Easy for you to say."

She was obviously worrying about Cleveland, and she'd think to call him soon if Jack didn't at least pretend to explore some alternatives.

He took a chance. "We could book commercial tickets, but that'll probably take just as long as waiting for Simon."

Then he held his breath and waited.

"I suppose," she ventured, clearly not convinced.

He tried to lighten the atmosphere. "We're marooned, Kristy. Think of it as being on a desert island."

She cocked her head, and he could tell his ploy was working. "A desert island that comes with a casino, chocolate volcanoes and Cirque du Soleil?"

"Hey, I had to pull a lot strings to get those tickets."

She gave a small, self-conscious smile. "Sorry. I'll stop complaining and lighten up."

"Yes. Do stop complaining. And do lighten up. We're marooned together until tomorrow, and there's nothing either of us can do about it."

She glanced around at the sumptuous furnishings and the rich curtains in the spacious bedroom. "I have to say, this is the best desert island ever."

Jack chuckled at that. "Come on, then. Let me show you the rest of it."

CHAPTER FOUR

KRISTY sat up straight and peered past the Eldorado Tours sign to a mass of bright yellow, blue and red fabric that billowed out across the packed desert sand.

"What's that?" she asked, bracing her hands on the dashboard as Jack bounced the rented SUV into a dirt parking spot next to the porch of a small, graying building.

"It's a hot air balloon." He smiled, clearly pleased with himself as he shoved his sunglasses above his forehead.

She blinked at his profile. "You told me we were going to see the Grand Canyon."

"We are."

"But—"

He killed the engine and set the hand brake. "Did you think we'd ride down the cliffs on burros?"

She angled her body to face him. "I thought we'd drive up to the edge and take a look over." She'd never been to the Grand Canyon, but she imagined there were any number of lookouts along the main road.

"This is way better," said Jack. "We'll cruise down between the cliffs and get a close-up of the river."

Kristy's stomach dipped at the thought of skimming

close to jagged rocks in something as fragile as a hot air balloon. "Is that safe?"

"It's safer than falling off a burro on a narrow trail."

She glanced back at the rapidly expanding balloon. "*That's* your benchmark for safety? Anything above falling off a burro?"

Chuckling, he opened the driver's door. "Don't be a wuss. You'll have a blast."

Taking a deep breath, Kristy reached for her own door handle, trying to remember if she'd ever heard reports of balloon fatalities in the Grand Canyon. She couldn't think of any, but that might simply mean the mathematical odds were catching up with them.

Jack rounded the hood and pulled on the top of her door, drawing it open the rest of the way.

"Have you ever ridden one?" she asked.

The roar of the balloon's gas burner echoed in the air as the huge balloon lifted from the ground, taking on a life of its own in a slight, desert breeze.

"A burro?"

She gave him an exasperated glare. "A hot air balloon."

"A couple of times."

"Really?"

"Sure."

She squinted at the bold yellow against the crackling blue sky. "How exactly do they steer?"

"They don't." He retrieved a small cooler from the back seat of the car. "You're pretty much at the whim of the wind."

"This is not reassuring, Jack."

He placed his free hand at the small of her back, urging her toward the gate. "The pilot's licensed."

"So? You just told me he can't steer."

"The Grand Canyon's a pretty big place. We're sure to

happen across some of it. Where's your sense of adventure?"

"I left it on the jet."

His face suddenly tightened with concern. "Hey, you're not still freaked out from that, are you?"

She shook her head. Then she stopped. Now that he mentioned it, it was sort of unsettling to be going back up in the air again.

"Good." He took her at her word, increasing their pace. "This is going to be fantastic."

FROM THE moment they lifted off the ground, Kristy had to admit, Jack was right.

The trip was better than fantastic. There was nothing quite like being above the ground, yet out in the open air. The balloon was slow and smooth. She was glad she'd worn a long-sleeved blouse, but with record high temperatures, the breeze was soft. Between the pilot's narrative and Jack's questions and jokes, she completely forgot to be frightened.

They soared the breadth of the canyon, dipping between layered cliffs of red, green and brown stone, nearly kissing the brittle, scrub-covered valley bottom, only to rise again and wend their way between spires of sculpted rock.

"With this wind, I can put you down at Narin Falls," said the pilot.

"Perfect," said Jack, giving Kristy's shoulders a squeeze. "Feel like a picnic?"

She nodded, relaxing back against him, content to be marooned and forget about the world for a while longer.

His arms wound briefly around her, his khaki-covered legs brushing against her new jeans, and the hard planes of his chest and stomach giving her a sense of security and certainty. She savored the feelings as long as she dared.

And then the balloon descended, following the steep drop of a cliff. It floated over a dusty plain until they came to a winding river with sprinkles of green lining either bank.

Then, in slow motion, the plain fell away. The river plummeted into a waterfall, burbling white and blue on its long drop to where it crashed into a turquoise pool surrounded by trees and shrubs and grass.

Kristy gasped at the sight.

"Hang on," said the pilot.

The balloon quickly lost altitude, the basket scraping along the sand, bumping to a stop several hundred feet from the oasis, the balloon canted over to one side.

Jack jumped out of the basket, steadying it with one hand, and all but lifting Kristy out with the other.

The pilot quickly handed him the cooler, then tossed a blanket over the side.

"We're clear," Jack called, his arm firmly around her waist, backing them both away.

The pilot poured on the heat, and the balloon reinflated.

"He's leaving," Kristy stated, trying to get her footing sorted out on the soft ground.

"He is," Jack agreed, keeping her clasped next to his side.

"How are we going to get out of here?" She'd seen the view from the air. They were miles and miles away from anything.

"He'll give the helicopter pilot our coordinates."

"We're getting picked up by helicopter?"

"Sure." Jack nodded, giving the pilot a final wave.

Kristy blinked up at him, the reality of the excursion suddenly hitting home. She was alone. Really, really alone with a man she'd only met yesterday.

She wasn't scared, exactly. What were the odds Jack had brought her by hot air balloon to a desert canyon to ravish or murder her? Plus, the balloon pilot was a witness. If Jack was a closet ax murderer, he'd be pretty stupid to let the only witness to the planned crime fly away.

Jack was a businessman, and an incredibly busy one at that. He was running an international conglomerate. She wondered, not for the first time, why he would take time out to entertain a virtual stranger. Taking her on an impromptu picnic didn't make any sense.

"I don't get it," she told him.

He glanced down at her. "What's to get? They'll send a helicopter. It's part of the tour."

"But—"

"Don't tell me we have to have the burro discussion again. Because I don't think they could even get burros in here. It's too far—"

"What I don't *get*—" she interrupted.

He snapped his mouth shut and gave her a chance to speak.

She took a breath. "Is why you're doing this."

"I'm doing this because I don't want to spend ten hours walking home after our picnic. We have tickets to Cirque du Soleil tonight, remember?"

The man was being deliberately obtuse.

"I mean all of it." He could easily have dumped her at the airport last night and gone about his business.

"All of what?"

Fine. She'd play along and spell it out for him. "Dinner. A balloon ride. A picnic?"

"Would you rather do something else?"

She pulled back from the arm that was still loosely around her waist. "You act like we're dating."

He let her go, fighting a grin. "Dating?"

"You know what I mean."

"Did I say we were dating?"

Okay, now she was embarrassed. "No, you didn't."

"Good. We're together on that at least."

She scowled at him. "You're wasting your time."

"No, I'm pretty sure I'm having a picnic."

"You should have left me at the airport."

"That would have been rude."

"I'm not your responsibility."

He glanced around. "Why are we discussing this now?"

"Because—" She paused, following his lead, giving a quick check on the desert around them. He made a good point. What was she hoping to accomplish by standing here arguing with him in the hot sun?

Answers, she supposed.

Like, what was he doing here? What was *she* doing here? She wasn't the kind of person to fall into adventures with rich, sexy, exciting men. Her life simply didn't work that way.

After a minute's silence, he lifted the blanket from the sand, gripping the cooler firmly in his other hand.

"We're here," he explained, "Because sightseeing is way more fun than hanging around an airport for two days. You know, you really have to lighten up, Kristy. You want to stand here and argue until we get sunstroke, or find some shade and break out the wine and sandwiches?"

At the mention of the food, Kristy realized she was starving. Her attention turned to the little cooler. "Sandwiches?"

He gave a sharp nod of approval and started for the oasis, tossing a final volley over his shoulder. "There. I knew you'd see things my way."

She scrambled to catch up, sand creeping into the crevices of her shoes. "I didn't see things your way."

"Sure you did. And that means I won the argument."

"There was no argument. And definitely no winner. We came to an amicable agreement involving shade, food and wine." She fell into step with him.

He slanted her a knowing grin. "You agreed to relax and enjoy the picnic."

"I did not."

He shrugged. "Okay."

"I merely accepted the fact that I'm trapped here with you for now."

"Poor baby."

She jabbed him with her elbow.

He hunched over to protect himself, but he was grinning. "Just make sure you don't have any fun. Otherwise, I'm the winner."

Kristy struggled not to laugh along with him. "Don't worry. I won't."

He glanced down. "You sure? 'Cause I think I see a smile in there."

She shook her head and pressed her lips together. "No, you don't."

"Liar."

She let herself grin, silently deciding to relax and take a breath. There really was nothing for her to worry about for the moment. Dee Dee was happy. She was having a great time with a concierge staffer named Randy and three other dogs staying at the hotel. A picnic beside a waterfall definitely beat an airport waiting room, even if it did mean Jack won the argument.

Maybe it didn't matter that today didn't reflect her real life. Fact was, it was happening to her. Against all odds and previous life experience, she was stranded in Vegas with a sexy billionaire who wanted to entertain her. She should enjoy it.

"What kind of wine?" she asked.

"Ha. Getting fussy are we?"

"No. I'm taking your advice and lightening up." On impulse, she covered his hand that held the cooler and gave it a squeeze. "This is incredibly nice of you, you know."

"I'm an incredibly nice guy."

"I'm serious."

"So am I."

She laughed, and then went silent as the ground turned from sand to sparse cacti, then to shrub brush and a few sparse pine trees. The roar of the waterfall intensified, and the spray cooled the air by several degrees. A brilliant glittering pool came into view amongst the rocks and willows.

"How did you know this was here?" she asked, glancing around in awe.

"The tour guy told me about it."

They came to a halt next to the pool, beside a small tangle of mesquite.

"We lucked out," said Jack. "Depending on the wind, we could have ended up at Lone Pine, Condor Point or Dead Man's Gulch."

He set the cooler down on the grass to spread the blanket.

Kristy kicked off her shoes. "Dead Man's Gulch? Now I'm picturing alkali residue and bleached cow skulls."

"Not exactly romantic."

She did a double take. "Why would we want romantic?" Then she immediately wished she'd kept her mouth shut. They weren't dating. They'd been particularly clear on that point a few minutes ago. She should have let the comment pass.

He bent over the cooler, swinging open the lid. "I mean in the generic sense."

There was a generic sense to romantic?

Nope. She wasn't going to ask.

He retrieved a bottle of wine. "Oh, look," he announced. "The hotel packed Chateau Le Comte merlot. Now that's hardly generic."

He gestured for her to sit down on the blanket then took a seat beside her. The wind waved its way through the mesquite trees, while birds twittered from branch to branch. Jack rustled through the cooler, retrieving two long-stemmed glasses, a corkscrew and a plastic-covered plat-ter of cheese and wafers. Making quick work of the cork, he poured them each a glass of the wine.

He smoothed back his dark hair and held his glass up for a toast. "To us," he said, his eyes going silver in the bril-liant sunshine. "In the generic sense."

Everything inside Kristy relaxed. There was something so reassuring about his expression. It told her they were okay. They could go ahead and goof around, drink wine, see the sights, and it didn't have to lead anywhere.

She clinked her glass against his. "You know, this is about the strangest thing I've ever done."

He took a sip. "Yeah? Well, for me, it's not even close."

She tasted the fragrant wine. It was smooth and light, the flavor bursting in her mouth. Then she eyed him up. "You do realize that absolutely begs the question…"

He grinned. "It does, doesn't it?"

She nodded encouragingly.

He thought for a moment. "Let's see. If I had to choose, I'd say it was the fire."

That definitely got her attention. "You lit something on fire?"

"Hunter lit something on fire. I was only along for the ride."

Kristy took another sip of the merlot. "It was Hunter's fault. Of course."

"It was definitely Hunter's fault. He was upset. Still, if it wasn't for the gypsy and the elephants, we'd have been fine."

"You're making this up."

"I swear it's true. We were maybe fourteen and fifteen. We all went to the circus. Dad being Dad, and Gramps being Gramps, we got a special pass to go behind the scenes.

"Hunter decided to get his fortune told. But special pass or not, the wrinkled old gypsy made us pay twenty bucks. Trouble was, back then, we weren't as grounded in reality as we are—"

Kristy scoffed, practically choking on her wine.

"What?"

"Grounded? Your private jet has mechanical trouble, so a helicopter is picking us up after a bottle of Chateau Le Comte at the Grand Canyon. You call that grounded in reality?"

His eyes narrowed. "You want to hear the story or not?"

"Absolutely. Sorry."

"At least now I know I have to pay for the helicopter and the jet," Jack muttered.

"You've made amazing progress," she allowed.

"I have. Anyway. I told Hunter to keep his money. But he wouldn't listen. He paid her, and the gypsy gave us the standard someone-close-to-you-has-suffered-a-loss spiel."

Kristy had seen con artists at work before, testing basic questions until the subject engaged with one of them. "It could be an economic loss or a personal loss," she mused aloud, attempting to put the right quavering note in her voice. "Or maybe 'he has dark…no, light hair.'"

Jack jumped back in. "'He's old…no young…no maybe middle-aged…'"

"'Wait a minute,'" Kristy cried. "'He might be a she!'"

"You definitely get the drift," said Jack. "But Hunter was pretty impressed. The gypsy 'saw' that he'd cheated on a test and stolen his father's Jamaican rum, and he was convinced she could tell the future."

Kristy leaned back on her elbow and took another sip of her wine, trying to picture Jack and Hunter as spoiled teenagers.

"Which would have been fine," said Jack, gesturing with his glass. "Except she laid out the tarot cards and told Hunter he was about to meet his destiny. Tragically for Hunter, his destiny wasn't to become a rock star, it was to marry a young redheaded girl who would give him twin daughters."

Kristy started to laugh, not sure whether to believe Jack or not.

"You laugh now," he said. "But Hunter was convinced it was in the cards. So he decided he needed to steal her cards to change his destiny. We waited until she left the tent, then snuck back in. He paused for effect. "And that's when the elephants showed up."

"In her tent?"

He shot her a look of censure. "Of *course* not."

Kristy made a small circle in the air with her wineglass. "Well, of course there were no elephants in the tent. Because there isn't anything weird at all about this story."

"The elephants were outside on the grounds. But they were heading somewhere, and they shook the ground when they passed. And then one of them trumpeted, and Hunter nearly wet his pants."

"I'm sure he appreciates you telling this story."

Jack snickered. "He knocked over an oil lamp, caught the table cloth on fire and burnt up the tarot cards, the table and the tent."

"I wonder what *that* did to his destiny."

"Nothing. Six years later, he met a redheaded girl."

"No way."

Jack nodded.

"Did she have twins?"

"Nope. They broke up."

"That's not a very good ending."

"My uncle paid the gypsy thirty-five thousand dollars for the tent."

"Now *that's* a good ending."

Jack stretched out his legs and propped himself on his elbow. "She thought so, too."

Kristy followed his lead, straightening her blouse and jeans, then removing the plastic cover to snag a triangle of gouda. "What about you? Did the gypsy tell you your fortune?"

"That she did."

"What was it?"

He shook his head. "Uh-uh. Your turn to share."

"My life's boring compared to yours. Did your fortune come true?"

"Not so far."

"Well, what *was* it?"

He helped himself to a slice of havarti and a small, round cracker. "What do I get in return?"

"Twins?"

"Ha!" He nearly choked on the cracker.

"What do you want?"

He stared at her intently for a moment, while the waterfall roared, the breeze waved the mesquite trees, and the birds continued to twitter amidst the big, empty desert.

Kristy grew hot, then cold, and then very confused by her intense desire to kiss him.

"I'll trade you for a secret," he finally said.

She swallowed. "I don't have any secrets."

"Everybody has secrets."

"Not me."

Except maybe the fact that she wanted to kiss him. She hadn't murdered anyone or knocked over a bank. She occasionally didn't answer the phone when she knew it was her mother—especially if it was a Friday night, and she had a sappy movie on DVD and a pint of triple fudge chunk in the freezer.

But he wasn't getting that one. No way.

Jack watched her expression for a long moment. "Your first lover," he said.

Her throat went tight, and her voice came out as a squeak. "What?"

"Tell me about your first lover."

She drained her wineglass, stalling for time. "I don't think so."

"How old were you?"

"How old were *you?*"

"Seventeen."

"Really?" Despite herself, her curiosity was piqued, as was her imagination. She closed her eyes and gave her head a shake.

"How old were you?" he asked again, his voice husky against the birds and the breeze.

Kristy sighed. Fine. "Twenty."

He reached behind him for the wine bottle and topped up both of their glasses. "Ah. Late bloomer."

"No. An absolutely perfect bloomer."

Jack grinned at her expression. "Who was he?"

"A boy I met in college. It was in his dorm room and completely unmemorable. Now, are you destined to cross oceans? Father many children? Fly to the moon?"

"Buy a golf course."

He looked completely serious.

"What the heck kind of a fortune is that?" For *this* she'd told him about her first lover?

"The gypsy was a fake, Kristy."

"She was right about Hunter."

"The law of averages was right about Hunter. He's dated a whole lot of women of varying hair colors."

"But a golf course? That was all she told you?"

Jack hesitated. His eyes twitched, and he got a funny, faraway look in them. "No," he said. "She also told me I was going to marry a woman I didn't trust."

"I suppose that's better than having twins."

It was Jack's turn to drain his glass. "I suppose. You want to swim?"

"It's too cold. And we don't have suits."

He came to his feet, placing the empty glass on the top of the plastic cooler. "There's nobody around for miles."

She stood with him. "You're around."

"I won't look."

"I might." The thought came out her mouth before she could censor it.

"There it is," he said softly.

"What?"

"Your secret."

CHAPTER FIVE

THEY didn't swim. But Jack had accomplished his mission. Kristy was getting to know him, and she was still attracted to him. He was halfway home.

The helicopter had picked them up and ferried them back to the hotel. In the interest of time, Jack had made arrangements for the rental car to be picked up at the hot air balloon base. That gave them time for a shopping spree before dinner and Cirque du Soleil.

He picked Addias Comte, a shop just off the strip in an exclusive mall.

At first, Kristy resisted the idea of him buying her clothes. But he insisted and prevailed. And, after trying on a few outfits, she got into the spirit of the adventure.

"I'm not even coming out in this one," she called from behind the door of the spacious changing room.

"You have to come out," he countered, sitting up straight in the leather armchair in the richly appointed alcove at the back of Addias Comte.

Silence.

"Kristy?"

"It's…"

"What?"

"Fine." The door opened, and Kristy marched defiantly out in an emerald-green satin cocktail dress. It was cut low, revealing a wide swath of skin between her breasts, the V dipping almost to her navel. The waist was gathered in a wide belt, with a circular rhinestone buckle that would have done Liberace proud. The way the fabric was gathered around the buckle made her look like the back of a chair at a big hotel wedding. The skirt was split up the front, revealing almost as much thigh as tummy.

Jack loved it. But she sure wasn't going out in public like that.

"Next," he said.

"See?" she retorted, turning to flounce back into the changing room.

Next was a plain black pinstripe, very straight, buttoned up the front with a mandarin collar and a leather belt.

"You look like you're going to a funeral," he said.

"Something softer?"

"Something a whole lot softer."

She turned back into the room.

While she was changing, Jack asked the clerk to bring some jewelry, purses and a few pairs of shoes. Once she found the right dress, he fully intended to accessorize it.

The next one was basic black. It was strapless, with a small lace fringe along the neckline and a skirt that draped to mid-thigh. It was sheer and frothy, and he absolutely wanted her to wear it for him later. But it wasn't right for tonight.

"Too short," she said.

He nodded his agreement, but after she returned to the changing room, he instructed the clerk to wrap it for them when Kristy was done.

The next time Kristy came out, he knew they'd found

the right dress. It was a snug-fitting, shimmering gold sheath. Sleeveless, with a scooped neck and a tight skirt that came almost to her knees, it was topped with a three-quarter sleeve, cropped, black satin jacket.

"You'll need your hair up," he said. And she'd need a diamond choker, black stockings and some spike-heeled shoes.

"You like it?" she asked, glancing down at herself.

"It's the one."

She stared at him in obvious surprise. "But, I'm—"

"It's the one," he repeated.

Just then the sales clerk arrived with the jewelry. He picked up a diamond-and-yellow-gold necklace and earring set and walked over to her.

She watched him closely, looking both worried and excited.

"Try it with these." He unfastened the clip and motioned for her to turn around.

Her hand went to her throat, fingering the rich jewels. "Are they real?"

"Don't worry about it."

"Jack—"

"I said, don't worry about it." He managed to get the delicate clasp fastened.

She turned, and her cheeks were delightfully rosy. "I can't let you—"

"Put these on." He handed her the earrings.

Biting down on her lip, she slipped them onto her ears.

The sales clerk appeared. "Pumps or open toes?" she asked Kristy, holding up two pairs of shoes.

Kristy glanced at Jack.

He pointed to the pumps, and the sales clerk produced a pair of sheer black stockings to go with them.

He backed up to sit down on the chair again. "So now let's see the whole thing."

Kristy took a deep breath, but she went back into the change room without complaint.

"We're at the Bellagio," Jack said to the sales clerk. "Could you see if their salon will have time to do her hair tonight?"

"Certainly," the sales clerk answered. "Anything else?"

Jack glanced around. "The black dress. A negligee—something elegant, soft, with some lace. And maybe an evening purse?"

The woman smiled. "Right away."

WHILE KRISTY had her hair done, Jack bought himself a requisite suit at one of the hotel shops. Then he sat through an exquisitely torturous evening, hearing her laugh, watching her smile and seeing her move beneath that shimmery gold dress.

At the end of it all, he handed her the package with the negligee and all but ran into his own room. He didn't know what it was, but something inside told him to keep his hands off for tonight. He used every ounce of his willpower to stay in his own bedroom instead of begging her to make love with him.

But then Sunday dawned, and she was wearing jeans, and it was much safer around her in the daylight. They joked their way through a tour of the Hoover Dam, then had a late lunch on the deck of a Lake Mead marina and took a sunset boat tour. By late evening, they were just off the Strip, walking hand in hand, absorbing the energy of tourists and partiers.

Suddenly Kristy stopped dead, tugging on Jack's hand. "Oh, my God."

He quickly scanned the crowds around them, looking for trouble. "What?"

"Over there. A gypsy fortune-teller."

Jack shook his head, and reflexively backed away from the sign where she was pointing. "Oh, no."

"Oh, yes." She pulled hard on his hand, dragging him toward the gaudy, flashing storefront. "We need an update on your golf course. And I've never done this before."

"And you don't need to do it now." Three was definitely a crowd. He didn't need any distractions tonight. He was trying to think of a quiet spot back in the hotel, rehearsing over and over in his brain how he'd propose.

Not that he expected her to say no. Well, he supposed she *could* say no, since she already had Cleveland's offer on the table. And wouldn't that suck for Jack's ego?

He shook that thought right out of his head. All things being equal, Kristy should prefer him over his grandfather. After all, she seemed to like hanging out with him, and she got all his jokes.

Still, he was unaccountably nervous at the thought of popping the question.

Luminitsa the Gypsy—Your Future Revealed, proclaimed the glass door.

"Kristy," Jack protested, but he couldn't bring himself to physically stop her.

Bells jingled as she pushed opened the door.

He blinked to adjust to the low light.

The room had an orange glow, candles flickered on most horizontal surfaces, and the walls were covered with tapestries, bright-colored scarves and Celtic drawings. A woman with huge earrings, eyelashes a mile long and a silk kerchief wrapped around her head, emerged from behind a beaded curtain.

"Come in. Come in." She motioned with wrinkled, ring-bedecked hands to a small, round table.

Kristy eagerly slipped into one of the folding chairs, while Jack hoped humoring her in this wouldn't take too long.

He glanced at the walls until he saw the gypsy's price list. Then he handed the woman a fifty for the shortest reading she offered.

She waved her silver rings at him. "You, too. Sit, please."

Jack clunked into the other chair with a sigh.

"You are a skeptic," she said, arching one brightly painted eyelid.

"You could say that," he agreed.

Kristy nudged him with an elbow. "Ignore him," she said to the woman.

Luminitsa nodded, jangling her hoop earrings with the motion.

She held out her hands, dramatically waving them over the crystal ball positioned in the middle of the table. A spotlight shone on it from above. As she moved her hands in a series of sweeping motions, the spotlight became brighter, making the ball glow.

"I see water," said Luminitsa. "Maybe a beach. It could be the ocean."

"We're going to California," said Kristy.

Jack shot her a censorious look. The least she could do was make it slightly harder for the con artist.

The woman shook her head. "No."

"We're not?"

"Not today."

"Tomorrow," said Kristy.

"Maybe," said the woman. She eyed Jack, then Kristy, then turned her attention to the ball.

The spotlight had gradually turned yellow, then orange, making the ball seem to have a life of its own.

The gypsy suddenly sat back. "There was a plane crash."

Kristy shot Jack a look of astonishment.

He remained unimpressed. Everybody knew something about a plane crash somewhere.

"No. Not a crash," said the woman. "But something…"

Kristy opened her mouth, but Jack grabbed her knee and squeezed.

She turned to give him an impish grin.

"What about the future?" he asked. "Kristy's future." The sooner they got to that, the sooner this would be over.

Luminitsa screwed up her wrinkled face, peering intently into the ball that was now bright red.

She jumped up. "Oh."

"What?" asked Kristy.

Luminitsa glanced from one to the other, a sly smile forming on her face. "Congratulations."

Jack and Kristy's gazes met.

Kristy mouthed the word *twins,* and Jack rolled his eyes.

He turned back to Luminitsa. "Congratulations on what?"

"On your wedding," she said.

Jack's entire body went still. Was there something in his eyes? Something about his posture?

"Wedding?" asked Kristy.

"Today's your wedding day."

"Which one of us?" asked Kristy.

"Both." She waggled her wrinkled finger back and forth between them.

Kristy's mouth dropped open. "To *each other?*"

Luminitsa nodded.

Jack grabbed Kristy by the hand. "That's it," he announced decisively, tugging her out of her chair and turning her to the exit.

The bells jangled again as they left.

"That was weird," said Kristy.

"We're in Vegas," he responded. "How many just-been-married or about-to-be-married couples do you suppose she sees every day?"

"I guess," said Kristy. "But that was weird."

For Jack, it wasn't so much weird as it was damned annoying. Luminitsa had just thrown a wrench in his carefully laid plans.

KRISTY SWAYED to the music of Yellow Silk, the jazz band playing in the Windward Lounge, as she rested her head against Jack's broad chest. She was trying to pretend that she didn't care that these were their last few hours together. Simon had promised the plane would be ready by ten, and they'd be in L.A. an hour after that. She was wearing the lacy black party dress Jack had secretly purchased at Addias Comte, along with the diamond necklace and earring set, and she couldn't help feeling like Cinderella.

Too bad the clock was about to strike midnight.

She knew she should be happy. Tomorrow morning she'd meet with Cleveland and the Sierra Sanchez buying team, and career-wise, she might just live happily ever after. Because if everything went her way, her life would turn on a dime. What she had dreamed of for years was suddenly within her grasp.

But melancholy overtook the joy in her heart. This was the end of such a beautiful fantasy.

The tempo slowed, and Jack gathered her close. She could feel the beat of his heart thudding rhythmically against her chest. His scent had become familiar. At some point, she'd started associating it with peace and safety, and she certainly felt that way now.

The fabric of the lacy black dress whispered against her legs. It clung to her breasts, nipped in at her waist, then flowed gently to midthigh. A Jacynthe Norman, from the winter collection in Paris, she knew it had to have cost Jack a fortune.

She'd have to leave it with him, along with the diamonds.

She wondered briefly if she'd ever see him again. If she was a supplier to the Osland Corporation, maybe they'd have a chance—

Then she stopped that thought in its tracks.

They'd spent a stolen weekend together. It was never going to be anything more than that. Their real lives were about as far apart as two people could get. He lived with the ultrarich in L.A. She lived with the struggling class in New York. Even if she did make a sale to Sierra Sanchez, they'd hardly be moving in the same social circles.

"You're so quiet," he murmured into her ear, his breath tickling her skin in a way that made her long for his lips to brush up against her. She itched for it. She ached for it.

"Just thinking," she said, splaying her hand over the taut muscles of his back.

"About?"

She tipped her head to look up at him. "Tomorrow."

He paused. "Really? I'm thinking about tonight."

"You worried about the plane?"

He shook his head, his eyes turning the color of thick smoke, as his hand slid up her ribcage, brushing purposefully against the side of her breast. "I'm not thinking quite that far in the future."

Her heart thudded in response to his caress. Her skin

prickled with anticipation. And her body convulsed with longing.

She swallowed, hardly able to form the words. "We still have the suite."

He stared at her, but didn't say a word. Then his arm tightened firmly around her waist, and he turned them both toward the nightclub door.

Outside, the air was sultry warm, thunderclouds had gathered above the skyscrapers, holding the daytime heat. Their forked lightning strikes sparked like lasers in the haze, faint thunder echoing after. Halfway down the block, the first raindrops splattered on the warm concrete, and Kristy and Jack joined the other tourists who scattered for shelter.

Damp and laughing, they made it to the Bellagio lobby.

Jack turned to look at her, taking in the rain-spattered dress, smoothing her damp hair back from her face. "You are so beautiful."

Kristy inhaled. "So are you."

He glanced at his watch. "We've only got a couple of hours." Then he looked into her eyes again, voice bedroom-husky. "I can't believe we put this off so long."

"What were we thinking?"

He took her hand and started across the lobby. "I don't know."

But instead of heading for the main elevator block which provided the more direct line to their room, he took a circuitous route past the shops. She wondered if they needed something from a store. Condoms, maybe? It wasn't the height of romance, but she supposed practical was practical.

But they carried on past the Essentials store, around the courtyard pool area.

"Did you rent us a cabana?" she asked. The suite was fine. The suite was wonderful. And, really, the clock was ticking.

Jack shook his head. He slowed, turning to look at her as they passed the grand balcony. "I don't want this to end."

"The walk to our room?"

His mouth curved in an ironic grin. He squeezed her hand while shaking his head. "You and me."

She peered at his expression. "I don't understand."

He nodded to a spot in front of them, and she followed his gaze. The East Chapel.

"Marry me, Kristy."

She stopped dead. "Huh?"

He held her gaze with his own. "Did something ever seem completely right to you?"

"What?" Had he lost his mind? Yeah, they were having a fantastic weekend. And yeah, she couldn't wait to get back to the suite and tear off his clothes. But this wasn't 1952. They could make love without getting married.

"This feels right," he repeated. "I know it's right."

She took a step toward him. "Jack. The fortune-teller was a fraud."

"This has nothing to do with the fortune-teller."

"Then what does it have to do with?"

"You and me."

"You and me are about to make love."

"Yeah," he nodded. "Over and over again if I have my way."

Kristy glanced at her own watch. "Not unless you're a whole lot faster at it than I've fantasized."

He drew back. "You've fantasized?"

"Yeah," she admitted. "Haven't you?"

"Oh, yeah." His eyes went softer still. He blinked. "Marry me, Kristy."

"No."

A group of partiers rounded the corner, their drunken shouts and laughter intruding on the moment.

Jack whisked Kristy to a glass door, opening it to steer her onto a pillared patio overlooking the pools. He closed the door behind them.

"Listen to me," he said.

"Jack," she sighed, fighting hard to hold her emotional ground.

Truth was, making love to Jack over and over again for the rest of her life sounded really good right now. And there was a deceptive intimacy to huddling in the sheltered darkness while the storm rumbled and flashed in the sky. Raindrops battered the waxy leaves of the potted tropical plants, while a film of steam rose from the pool decks and fountains, obscuring the pot lights, giving the entire garden an eerie glow.

He moved in close, his whisper tortured and husky. "I can't lose this chance. I can't let you go."

She squinted. Was he serious? Did he really want to see her again? Romantically?

She'd hardly dared hope.

No. Scratch that. She *wouldn't* dare hope.

His fingertips brushed her cheek. "This is something, Kristy."

Her chest contracted. She had to agree with him there. This was definitely something.

"Have you ever—" he breathed. Then he closed his eyes for a second, as if gathering his thoughts. "Have you ever, in your entire life, ever felt this way?"

She slowly shook her head. There were no words to describe how she felt about Jack—the passion, the admiration, the deep-down soul connection.

"We can't let it go," he said.

"We don't have to let it go." They could see each other again. He could come to New York. Heck, he had an office there, and his own jet plane. He could drop by and see her whenever he was in town.

He ran his hands up and down her arms. "How many people do you suppose say that?"

"Say they'll get together again?"

He nodded. "Hundreds, maybe thousands. And how many of them ever do?"

She shrugged. Not many, she'd suspect, and that gave her a hollow feeling in the pit of her stomach.

"We leave this hotel, Kristy, and you know as well as I do that'll be it."

Would it? Would they really walk away from a connection this strong?

"You'll go back to New York. I'll go to L.A. We'll e-mail, maybe call. But pretty soon, our memories will fade. We'll decide it couldn't have been as great as we thought. We'll write each other off as a weekend fling."

She found her voice. "We *are* a weekend fling."

"We don't have to be." His hands met her upper arms, his voice going earnest. "We can be better than that. Let me make it so we… So *I* have to be better than that."

She knew he was talking crazy. People didn't get married to guarantee a second date. She opened her mouth to tell him so, but he put an index finger across her lips.

His gaze bore directly into hers. "I think I'm falling in love with you, Kristy."

Her entire body convulsed with a wash of emotions and hormones. Love? Could this possibly be love?

"Don't let me walk away from you, Kristy. Don't let me be the man I know I'll be."

She wanted to say yes. In every fiber of her being, she longed to complete the fantasy.

Love.

She rolled the idea around in her brain.

She didn't know anything about romantic love, but she'd sure never felt this way about any man before. And if this was as good as it got... Well, it was pretty darn good—talking, laughing, touching. All Jack, all day, every day, for ever and ever.

"Marry me," he groaned, his hand tunneling into her damp hair, cupping her head, drawing her forward. "Make me come back to you."

And then he kissed her. His hot lips possessing and devouring her own. Raw passion permeated every breath, as the wind swirled around them, tearing at their clothes, rattling the broad leaves. The staccato beat of the rain matched the frantic melding of their hearts.

She clung to his shoulders, tipping her head to deepen the kiss, her spine bending as she leaned back, baring her neck and chest and body to him. He peppered kisses on the exposed flesh, cupping his hand over her breast where her nipple had puckered beneath the thin, damp fabric. Sparks flew off in all directions, lighting her brain, making her feel as though absolute clarity was within her grasp.

The world fell away until there was nothing but Jack. Their differences didn't matter. Geography didn't matter. Fashion, business, money and power. None of it mattered. There weren't two of them anymore, only one. And the universe would have to settle around that reality.

She anchored her hands in his thick hair, drawing him back, staring into his passion-clouded eyes.

"Yes," she said. "Yes, yes and yes."

He sighed. Then he entwined his fingers with hers, straightening until he faced her. "You have made me unbelievably happy."

Kristy smiled at him, everything inside her going calm. They'd make it work. She knew with an absolute certainty that she could put her faith in Jack.

Hand in hand, they floated down the hallway to the hotel chapel.

There, Kristy was given a delicate bouquet of white roses. They signed a bunch of papers. Jack asked the organist to play "At Last," and he chose plain gold bands, whispering promises of diamonds in her future.

But Kristy didn't need diamonds. She didn't need designer clothes or corporate jets or a high-end penthouse. All she needed was Jack. And, as the chaplain asked her to repeat the age-old vows of faith and fidelity, she knew she was getting Jack forever.

NEXT TO THE big four-poster bed, with Kristy in his arms, Jack ignored the heated accusations of betrayal and deceit that pounded away at his brain. Instead, he peeled away her silk dress, revealing her creamy, pink-tipped breasts, and honestly told himself he was the luckiest man in the world.

"Beautiful," he murmured more to himself than to her. "So beautiful." Then he placed a soft kiss on one tip and then the other.

Kristy drew in a gasp of pleasure, her fingers curling into his hair.

"I love you," she gasped, and a knife twisted deep inside his heart.

"And I'm about to love you," he growled in return, hating that he had to fudge the phrase. She deserved better.

"For just as long as you'll let me," he finished.

Then he tugged her dress down to her ankles and gently pushed her back on the bed to stare at smooth stomach, her lacy black panties and the creamy thighs that twitched ever so slightly in anticipation of his touch. He'd pay for this one, that was for sure. But no power on heaven or earth could stop him from making love to her tonight.

She reached for him, and he caught her hand, staring into her eyes as he kissed each one of her fingers.

"I want you so bad," he told her truthfully. "Like I've never wanted anything in my life."

She smiled up at him, blinking a sheen of moisture from her eyes. He stripped off his shirt, tearing most of the buttons. Then he yanked off his pants, and her eyes went wide at his naked body.

"It's been…"

He waited.

"A while," she finished.

A feeling of primal possessiveness welled up inside him. He reached for the delicate wisp of her panties and discovered his hand was shaking.

She covered his blunt fingers with her small, manicured hand.

"Nervous?" she asked.

Hell no. "Trying to take it slow," he managed.

She hooked her thumbs into the lace strips at her hip bones and pulled downward. "Why?"

He blinked, transfixed by the light downy curls covering her innermost secrets. The rampage of lust that slammed into him almost knocked him over. He grasped her panties and finished the job for her. "Damned if I know."

Then he eased down atop her, kissing her deeply, urging her mouth open, capturing her tongue, while his hand worked its way down her smooth skin. He thrummed one nipple, rolling it to a peak, encouraged by the groans and moans and the wriggle of her small body under his thighs. He followed her ribcage, dipping into her navel, teasing her soft curls, feeling the puffs of her gasping breath against his ear.

Then her hands went on a journey of their own, along his side, her thumbs grazing his flat nipples, her fingertips digging into his back, just hard enough to ratchet up his desire. Then they trailed over his buttocks, to the backs of his thighs, her nails grazing his skin, circling in, starting a familiar pulse at the base of his brain.

In an act of self-preservation, he grasped her hands, dragging them up, pinning them firmly to the mattress on either side of her head. She tried to protest, but he kissed it away. He used his knee to nudge her thighs apart. Then he pulled back, ever so slightly, watching her expression as he eased his way inside.

Her lips parted, rounding in an "Oh," while her hips flexed against him. He gritted his teeth, refusing to rush, letting her heat and moisture envelope him. Though his brain screamed at him to hurry, and his hormones battled his muscles for control, he forced himself to stop, to regroup, then to carry on one centimeter at a time.

Kristy thrashed her head from side to side. She drew up her knees and pushed her hips forward. But he drew back with her, controlling the pace, holding them both on the edge of exquisite torture.

His muscles turned to molten steel, and her pleas for mercy scalded what was left of his self-control. But he didn't give in…didn't give in…didn't give—

A pithy swear word leaped from his soul, and he lunged forward, burying himself to the hilt.

She freed her hands, and her arms wrapped tight around his neck. Her lips and tongue planted hot, wet kisses along his shoulder.

His mouth was jealous, so he cupped her chin, lining her up for a carnal kiss as his body found its rhythm. He teased her tongue, sucked on her lips, tasted the sweet nectar of her mouth.

Her hands squeezed tight on his biceps, her fingernails denting his skin. Sweat formed between them, slicking their skin, adding to the eroticism of their joining. He cupped her buttocks, drawing her tight against him, tighter, tighter, as he pumped harder and faster. He could feel her muscles tense. Her mewls of desire grew higher pitched, louder against his ear.

This was it. He was losing it.

He held on, held on, held on.

Then her keening cry and the convulsions of her body sent him crashing over the edge. Waves of release washed over him as he held her, reveling in the warm buzzing glow of satiation.

Reality was going to hit them like a freight train, he knew. But, for now, nothing mattered except the small sporadic twitches that told him Kristy was resting on the same plane of satisfaction as him. He inhaled the scent of her hair, stroked his hand over her full breast, tasted the salt of her skin.

Her breathing gradually relaxed, and he eased her sleeping body into a spoon against his own. Then he reached for his cell, and sent a quick text message to Simon.

No need to head for L.A. now. Jack had accomplished his mission.

He swallowed a sudden lump in his throat, his usual self-righteousness was battling an unfamiliar and unsettling slither of guilt. He told himself it had to be done. The family was his responsibility. And, anyway, Kristy had brought it on herself.

She had.

He hadn't been given a choice.

Then she wriggled her bare bottom against him, and his arm spontaneously tightened around her. She turned her head to look up at him and smiled like an angel, even as the unmistakable glow of desire rose in her blue eyes.

He chuckled softly, brushing a lock of hair from her flushed cheek. "Again?"

She nodded, and he immediately kissed her swollen mouth.

His body sprang to attention. He flipped her onto her back, pressing her warmth and softness into the big, wide mattress. Just a little longer, he promised himself as desire and passion licked at the corners of his soul. Just a few more hours in paradise.

He'd be burning in hell soon enough.

CHAPTER SIX

JACK WAS awakened by Kristy's cry of shock. She scooted out of his arms, flipping back the covers and letting in a blast of cold air.

He blinked his blurry eyes to see her leap from the bed and rush naked into the en suite.

"What?" he called out, sitting up and ruffling his hands through his messy hair. He could see her naked profile at the sink as she scrambled for the toothpaste. They'd made love into the early-morning hours, then slept soundly in each other's arms. She couldn't be shocked to find herself naked in his bed this morning.

She marched from the bathroom, a white robe draped around her shoulders, open in front, a toothbrush protruding from her mouth. She unceremoniously uncovered him. "We're late!"

Jack rolled out of bed, slipping his arms into the other robe as a concrete block settled firmly in his stomach. They weren't late, because they weren't going to her meeting in California, and it was time for him to 'fess up. He couldn't postpone it any longer.

She trotted back to the sink, spitting out the toothpaste and rinsing her mouth. "Call Simon," she commanded, above the sound of the running water. "Tell him to warm up the engines or something."

Jack tried to frame up his confession, but he couldn't find the correct words. Hell, he could barely command his vocal chords to work.

"Kristy," he finally rasped.

She turned. "Why are you still standing there?"

His hands involuntarily closed into fists. "Because there's no point in going to L.A."

Her glance shot to the clock on the bedside table. It showed eight-fifteen, and her voice went hollow. "We could call Cleveland and explain."

Jack jerked backward, his guilt turning to shock. "*Explain* that we got married?"

She nodded.

"And you think he'll still want to see you?"

Her eyes went wide, giving her face a sweet, vulnerable look that almost got to him. But he ruthlessly reminded himself who she was and what she'd planned, and that she'd married him under as many false pretenses as he'd married her.

"He values punctuality that much?"

Jack shook his head, giving a dry chuckle. "I think he values fidelity that much."

"Huh?"

"Kristy, you married me." Jack jammed his thumb against the center of his chest. "*Me,* not him."

She blinked, and her voice dropped to a confused whisper. "What are you talking about?"

Man, she was good. Sometimes he couldn't believe just how good she was. He also couldn't believe she'd keep the dumb act up for this long. What was the point?

He grabbed his slacks from the chair where he'd tossed

them last night. He stuffed in one leg and then the other, watching her with a fatalistic curiosity.

"The jig is up, babe. You can't get your hands on Cleveland's money if you're already married to me. And you can't get your hands on mine because, one of those papers you signed last night was a pre-nup. And it'll hold up in court."

Kristy staggered back. For a second there, he thought her knees might give out beneath her. *"What?"*

"What?" he mimicked, sarcastically even as he fought the urge to pull her into his arms and offer comfort.

He hated himself for that weakness. And because of his inner battle, the response came out harsher than he intended. "You're caught. You're not going to be Mrs. Trophy-Wife-Cleveland-Osland-Number-Three. You'll have to find another scheme to hawk those rags you call a spring collection."

Her face turned pure white, and she groped to steady herself on the back of a chair.

Then his cell phone jangled on the table. He snagged it, hoping it was an emergency that would get him out of here and away from his unreasonable guilt.

"Yeah?" he barked.

"Where the hell are you?" his grandfather's voice boomed.

Perfect. Could the moment get any worse?

"Vegas," Jack answered, while Kristy blinked at him with big, round, accusatory, blue eyes. He was tempted to turn away from her censure. But he was in the right. She was the one who'd hatched the plan to get his family's money.

He held his ground.

"Hunter tells me you've got Kristy."

"Yeah," said Jack, holding her gaze. "The two of us got married last night."

"Well, get your asses to California. I've got seven people sitting around the boardroom table waiting for her."

Gramps reaction threw Jack. "Didn't you hear me? We *got married* last night."

"Bully for you. Nanette and I bought a Ferrari last night."

"Who's Nanette."

"My fiancée."

The sensation of being sucker-punched was so strong that Jack actually flinched.

He stared at Kristy in horror as she held the oversized robe around her for protection—her confused eyes, her sleep-mussed hair, her over-kissed lips.

What had he done?

What *had* he done?

Stupid question.

He'd married the wrong woman.

HEARING JACK'S explanation, and listening to his side of the telephone conversation with Cleveland, it took Kristy about thirty seconds to put the pieces together. The whole thing was a fraud. Jack hadn't been falling in love with her this weekend. He'd been making a preemptive strike against her.

Her feelings of hurt, confusion and embarrassment were quickly replaced by anger. What kind of a cold, calculating snake did it take to fake a romance, marry a woman and then make love to her, not once, not twice, but *three times?*

Jack snapped his phone shut, and they stared at each other in silence for a long second.

"We'll get a divorce," he pronounced.

"You bet your life we'll get a divorce." She yanked the belt tight on the robe. "Although keeping your hands to yourself last night and leaving open the option for an annulment would have been a nice touch."

"I couldn't take that chance."

Her bark of laughter came out a little high-pitched. "Of course you couldn't take that chance, what with me being a sleazy gold digger and all. *Any* reasonable man would have had sex with me so I couldn't get an annulment."

"Kristy—"

"Don't you *dare* try to defend yourself."

"It's happened before."

She looked him up and down. "What? You've married other women who were engaged to your grandfather?"

"No! I mean he—"

"I don't want to hear about it."

"He's married bimbos—"

"Stop."

"—before!" Jack shouted over her protest.

A *bimbo?* That's what he thought of her?

She coughed out a harsh laugh. It was either that or cry.

"Well, in that case, Jack. You came up with a great plan. I mean, if you take away morals and ethics and, well, every scrap of reasonable humanity. It was a great plan."

"I thought you were—"

"A bimbo. Uh-huh. You've made that clear. So, is my meeting in L.A. still on or what?"

"This afternoon."

"Good." She stomped back to her own room, intending to call an airline and book a commercial flight. If she never saw Jack Osland again, it would be far too soon.

"You take the jet." His voice was directly behind her.

"Get out of my bedroom."

"You take the jet," he repeated. "Simon is ready. I'll make other arrangements."

"Don't do me any favors."

"It's the least I can do."

"Under the circumstances, there is no least you can do."

"It's the only way for you to get there on time."

She sucked in a breath between her clenched teeth. He was probably right, and maybe she was a fool to strive for any scrap of dignity at this point anyway. The man had kissed every inch of her body last night. And she'd told him she loved him.

A sharp pain pierced her chest.

She truly thought she had.

"Fine," she bit out. "I'll take the damn jet. But only as long as you're not on it." Then she turned away from him to jerk open a dresser drawer and plucked out the skirt and sweater she'd arrived in.

"Don't take this the wrong way, Jack" she said. "No. Actually. Go ahead and take it the wrong way if you like. But I never want to see you again."

"Understandable," he muttered.

She twisted around to look at him. "Gee, thanks."

"I had my reasons," he said.

"It was a great plan," she mocked. "You must be really disappointed that it failed."

ONE LOOK at the expressions on the Sierra Sanchez buying team told Kristy she was going to fail.

Her sketches littered the top of the polished mahogany boardroom table, with swatches and samples draped on racks around them.

"The lines are technically strong," said one of the men. She thought his name was Bernard.

"The fabric works, but it'll be a challenge for the skirt to stand out in a crowd." Irene Compton was the lead buyer for the chain.

"Overall," said the one named James, sifting through her sketches like greeting cards. "The collection is...competent."

Kristy felt herself shrinking in the luxurious armchair. Competent. Thousands and thousands of budding designers were competent. She didn't have a hope unless she was outstanding.

"Hmm," Irene nodded. "Maybe we could think about testing it in Value-Shoppe?" She named a European discount chain.

Value-Shoppe? Kristy had to bite down on her tongue to keep from protesting out loud.

The room went silent, while each of the team members contemplated the drawings. Bright yellow sunshine streamed through the window. Car horns honked a dozen stories below, and a mist of clouds gathered in the distance over the bay. The world outside was still spinning, even while her dreams were being dashed.

"Well, *I* think she shows promise," said Cleveland.

Six jaws snapped shut, and everyone's attention flew to the older man sitting at the head of the table.

Seconds of silence ticked by before Cleveland spoke again. "I was thinking about the Breakout Designer category at the Matte Fashion Event."

Adrenaline hit Kristy's system in a rush at the mere mention of the prestigious London fashion show. A designer couldn't even enter the Breakout Designer Contest without a powerhouse retailer behind her. Even in her wildest dreams...

"Perhaps if we mix and match some of the ideas," Irene

offered slowly, glancing at a patterned skirt and a white lace blouse.

Cleveland nodded his approval. "Now you're getting creative."

Kristy didn't want Cleveland's charity. But the *Breakout Designer category?* She swallowed her common sense, and let the conversation carry on around her.

Bernard jumped in. "This neckline is unique. And we can certainly scallop the hem and slim down the line."

"We'd need at least a half-dozen new or revamped pieces for the contest," James warned.

Cleveland brought the flat of his palms down on the tabletop. "That's fine. Since we're all on board, you can talk through the details later." His attention turned to Kristy. "Right now, Kristy is joining me for a drink."

She glanced at the buying team, bracing herself for narrow-eyed glares and sidelong expressions of condemnation. They might all think the way Jack did—that Kristy was Cleveland's floozy. Why else would he overrule their judgment on her behalf?

But, to her surprise, everyone was smiling.

Irene rose from her chair and offered her hand. "We're looking forward to working with you, Kristy."

The other team members nodded and murmured agreement.

Kristy stood up to shake hands with Irene. "Uh. Thank you."

Cleveland opened the boardroom door. "This way, young lady."

She nodded her thanks to the rest of the team, then preceded Cleveland into the wide, bright, plant-adorned hallway.

"You didn't have to do that," she said as they made their way to the bank of elevators.

"Do what?"

She motioned behind them, torn between being polite and shutting the heck up. "Back there. Give me special—"

"You think I pulled rank because I like you?"

"Well…"

He pressed the elevator button with a wrinkled finger. "Kristy, I've made a whole lot of money in my life by seeing things that other people miss. You have something. It's raw, but I think it's there.

"I'll work with you," he continued. "And I'll buy your collection when and if it's good enough. But that back there wasn't altruism and it wasn't nepotism."

A flutter of excitement rolled through Kristy's stomach. Cleveland actually thought her fashions had a chance?

"It's going to take a lot of work and dedication."

She eagerly nodded. She'd work as hard as it took for a chance to fly to London and compete in the Breakout Designer Contest.

"Are you prepared for that?"

"Of course."

"We have until December thirtieth."

Kristy quickly did the math in her head. That was less than three days per outfit. Impossible. But she'd have to do it anyway. "Right."

"Your staff is available over the holidays?" he asked.

Kristy hesitated. Not because her staff might not be available, but because she didn't actually have any staff.

"Kristy?"

The elevator pinged, and the doors slid open.

She took a step forward. "Don't worry. I'll manage."

"Kristy."

She didn't look up at him. "Yes?"

"How many people work for you?"

She swallowed as the doors glided shut.

Cleveland waited.

"Just me," she finally squeaked.

There was a long silence as the car glided downward and floor numbers flashed red.

"You've got guts," said Cleveland. "I'll give you that. But if this is going to work, you must be completely honest with me."

"Sorry."

"How big is your workshop?"

"It takes up most of my loft."

He raised a gray, bushy eyebrow. "Don't be evasive."

"It's six hundred square feet."

The elevator eased to a stop.

"Well that's definitely not going to do it," said Cleveland, gesturing for her to move ahead of him into the lobby.

As they walked across the polished marble floor, past statues and paintings, skirting a central waterfall encircled by bench seats, Kristy could feel the deal of a lifetime slipping from her grasp. She couldn't really blame Cleveland. Six outfits in three weeks was nearly impossible under the best of conditions. But it seemed downright cruel of fate to bring her this close, to tantalize her with the brass ring, only to unceremoniously yank it away from her.

"You'll come work at the mansion," said Cleveland decisively.

Kristy stopped in her tracks. What mansion? *His* mansion? The Osland family mansion?

He halted and turned back, a sly smile coming over his wrinkled face. "Really. You're married to Jack now. You have every right to spend the holidays with his family. We have a lovely estate in Vermont, near Manchester."

Kristy didn't even know where to start. She wasn't married to Jack. Well, she was. But she wasn't. At least not in any real sense. And she never wanted to see him again. She sure wasn't about to arrive on his doorstep for the holidays.

"That's insane," she finally managed.

"Excuse me?" said Cleveland, his bushy eyebrows slanting in an expression of surprise.

Whoops. For a minute she'd forgotten who she was speaking to.

"Sorry," she offered.

He gave her a sharp nod. "There's a workshop. Plenty of room for you to spread out. And we can bring in machines, materials and staff."

Kristy hesitated, worried about making him angry. But they had to get the matter at hand out in the open.

"You *do* know why Jack married me, right?" She might be embarrassed about being duped, but she had promised Cleveland she'd be completely honest with him. And, on this, she definitely needed to be honest.

"Certainly I know why he married you. They think because I'm eighty, I'm losing my marbles."

His bluntness surprised her.

"Are you?" she dared to ask.

He sobered, and the sound of the indoor waterfall filled the silence around them.

"No," he said. "I'm running out of time. I like beautiful young women. And I'm running out of time."

Her stomach clenched with worry. "Are you…ill?"

He shook his head and smiled. "Just old." Then he straightened, taking command once again. "But I'm still the major shareholder. This is your choice, young lady. You can work through the holidays in Vermont, or I can find someone else to sponsor for the Breakout Designer Contest."

"And Jack?"

A twinkle came into Cleveland's eyes. "You're worried Jack won't want to see you?"

She was more worried that she didn't want to see him. But the other had certainly crossed her mind. She and Jack had parted with some pretty harsh words. Still, it didn't mean she'd let him ruin her career.

Watching the play of emotions across her face, Cleveland patted her shoulder reassuringly. "I think my grandson deserves to reap the consequences of his actions, don't you?"

And then she got it, she understood Cleveland's motivation for inviting her to the family mansion. "I'm your revenge on Jack."

"Nice little twist, isn't it?"

"He was trying to protect you, you know." Even as the words popped out, Kristy couldn't believe she was defending the man. He'd manipulated, hurt and humiliated her for his own ends. He was a cold-hearted snake, nothing more.

"And what makes you think I'm not trying to help him?" asked Cleveland.

"Because there's nothing about me being in Vermont that will help Jack."

"Well then, what about becoming a successful fashion designer and winning this year at the Matte Fashion Show?"

Kristy paused. "And I should do everything in my power to make sure that happens, shouldn't I?"

"If you have a single brain cell in your pretty head, then yes."

"I do," she said.

"Then we understand each other."

She couldn't help but smile in admiration. "Your marbles are fully intact, aren't they?"

"That they are. But it suits me sometimes to let people

think otherwise." He gestured towards the glass doors leading to the street. "Shall we get that drink now?"

Kristy started walking. "You know what I think?"

"What do you think?"

"That Jack learned everything he knows from you."

"Let's hope you're wrong about that."

"So I GUESS we got it wrong," said Hunter, looking more amused than worried as he teed off on the first hole at Lost Links. He watched as the ball arced down the fairway, bouncing to rest just shy of the horseshoe-shaped sand trap and a small grove of oaks.

"We damn sure got it wrong," said Jack, accepting the one wood from his caddy. His mood had been foul for two days now. "And I blame *you* for the screw-up."

"Me?"

"It was your brilliant idea to date her."

"I wanted to date her because she was hot, not in some Machiavellian attempt to thwart Gramps's wedding."

"Don't knock Machiavelli." Planning and strategy were the watchwords of every executive.

"I noticed you didn't deny she was hot."

"All right, she's hot. But she was dating our grandfather."

"No, she wasn't."

"Well, she could have been." Jack pushed his tee into the turf then straightened. He'd gone over and over his weekend in Vegas, wondering why he'd never once questioned Kristy's identity. Even with all the little inconsistencies in her behavior, he'd never once asked himself that pivotal question. He hated making mistakes.

"If she had been dating him," he felt compelled to point out to Hunter. "It would have been a good plan."

Hunter peered down the sunny fairway. "With a solid

plan like that, it's almost hard to believe anything went wrong."

"Yeah," Jack agreed as he lined up to tee off.

He thwacked the ball dead on, and it sailed over the tree-tops, bouncing into the center on the fairway only a few feet short of the green.

Hunter waited for Jack to hand over the club to his caddy. "So, explain to me why we'll lose less money with you married to her instead of Gramps."

"Because I had her sign a prenup. You think I'm stupid?"

"You really want me to answer that today?"

"Get stuffed." Jack pulled off his white leather glove and turned to head down the fairway. He'd spend years living this one down.

Hunter fell into step beside him, the two caddies staying several paces behind. "Let me make sure I'm understanding this. In a haze of passion, on a lark, at the hotel chapel, she agrees to marry you, and you pull out a prenup. She didn't find that odd?"

Jack was trying hard not to think about the hotel chapel, nor the lies he'd told her to get her there. "There were other things to sign. And she wasn't paying all that much attention to the details."

"Because you're irresistible to women?"

Yeah, right. "It's a curse."

Hunter's laughter rumbled across the quiet golf course. "My sympathies. So, what now?"

Jack shrugged. "Now we get divorced."

"Just like that?"

"I suspect she's called her lawyer already."

"You don't think she's going to sue your ass?"

"Based on what? Showing poor judgment in Vegas? If that was grounds for action, our legal system would be gridlocked into the next century." No, Jack was pretty sure he was safe on the financial front.

Hunter stopped next to his ball, sizing up the lay of the course and checking the direction of the wind rustling through the palm fronds. "So, that's that?" he asked Jack, then glanced at his caddy with his brow raised.

"Six iron," the young man suggested.

"Not exactly," said Jack. "Gramps is still engaged to Nanette."

"Well, you can't marry them all," said Hunter.

Jack's marrying days were definitely over. "I wasn't thinking about me."

Hunter lined up his shot. "Look into my eyes," he said matter of factly, with a swing and follow through. He went to stand directly in front of Jack. "Not with a gun to my head."

"I'm sure she's a knockout."

"And I'm sure you've lost your mind." Hunter handed the club back to his caddy, and they all started for the spot where Jack's ball lay.

"You got a better plan?" asked Jack.

"I've got a thousand of them. And none of them involve me marrying anybody."

"He marries Nanette, it'll cost us."

"There are more important things in life than money."

As they made their way over the fine-trimmed grass, Jack pondered the relative value of money and emotional health. He'd never really thought about it before because money had always been paramount. But if his wakefulness the last two nights was anything to go by, money had some serious competition. He wished he'd put Kristy on a commercial plane the minute they hit Vegas.

He didn't need the stress of worrying about how she was

feeling, nor of his conflicted memories, nor of dwelling on the prediction of a long-ago gypsy. Which, by the way, was beginning to feel like a curse.

The curse of the midnight gypsy. It would make a good movie title. Hunter could be the hero. Jack the villain. Kristy would get rich, and the redheaded girl would be adored by fans around the world.

He lined up on the ball, chipping it up onto the green, less than ten feet from the hole.

"So, whatever happened to Vivian?"

Hunter glanced up sharply. "Huh?"

"She was the redhead, right?"

Hunter stared at Jack as if he'd lost his mind.

"A couple of years ago. You dated that redhead who beat the crap out of you at golf."

"Only because she used the ladies' tee."

"So, you do remember."

Hunter shrugged, snagging his putter and walking onto the green. "Sure."

"Where is she now?"

Hunter crouched down on one knee, eyeing the slope of the terrain. "Why do you care?"

"You remember when you burned down the gypsy's tent?"

Hunter stood up. "You mind if I play golf now?"

"Seriously," said Jack.

"No. I've forgotten the rampaging elephants, the fire department and the lawsuit that grounded me for a month."

Jack grinned, his mood lightening for the first time in forty-eight hours.

"You remember what she said?"

"How did this get to be about me?"

"She said a redheaded girl would give you twins."

Hunter shook his head in disgust and turned to address the ball.

Jack held his tongue while Hunter swung the putter.

The caddy lifted the flag, and the ball plunked into the hole.

"She also said I would marry a woman I didn't trust," said Jack. "Think about it, Hunter. What were the odds?"

Hunter slid the putter through his grip, handing it upside down to his caddy. "Please don't let the shareholders hear you talking like this. They'll have you impeached."

Jack stared hard at his cousin. "You remember what else she said."

"That you'd buy a golf course." Hunter glanced around. "You bring your checkbook?"

"Don't play dumb."

Hunter snorted. "I don't need to. You're doing a fine job of that all by yourself. You're a logical man, Jack. I didn't marry Vivian. There are no twins. And gypsies can't predict the future."

Maybe not consistently, but the two Jack had talked to were sporting pretty good averages. And the first one had also predicted Jack and Hunter would blow the family fortune. "Are we over-leveraged on anything?"

"No. Now hit the ball."

"Nothing out there that can bite us in the ass?"

"Not unless Kristy signed the lamest prenup ever."

Jack took a deep breath, running the cool shaft of his putter across his palm and settling his grip on the black, perforated rubber. Hunter was right. The prenup was fine. Kristy took away what she brought to the marriage, and Jack took away what he brought. Which was exactly the way he wanted it.

He took a few swings, testing the weight of the putter. Then he tapped the ball.

It followed the contour of the green, arcing up the high side then veering at the last second to hit the hole. *Exactly* the way he wanted it.

CHAPTER SEVEN

As SHE marched up the impossibly imposing brick steps at the Osland mansion outside Manchester, Dee Dee trotting along on her leash, Kristy reminded herself that nothing had changed. Recognition and success in the fashion world were still her dream.

She'd already had plenty of other setbacks over the years. And every time, she'd picked herself up, dusted herself off and redoubled her effort to bring her fashions to the attention of the industry.

Now, gazing up at the sprawling, three-story, snow-covered Colonial, she assured herself this was no different. She'd pick herself up one more time. Marrying Jack was merely a blip on her road to success, and a year from now she'd be laughing at the absurdity of thinking she was in love after only two days. Nobody fell in love that fast. She'd been swept off her feet by a man who'd set out to trap her. That was all.

Of *course* he'd seemed like the perfect man. Anybody could pretend to be perfect for two days. He'd laughed at her jokes, pretended to admire her intelligence, professed to like the same wines and catered to her every whim.

But it had all been a lie, a sham. And as soon as he'd

shifted to the real Jack, she hadn't liked him at all. In fact, she'd hated him then. She still did. And that was why showing up on his doorstep and cornering him with his fake marriage was going to be so easy.

In the back of the limo, halfway between the airport and the Osland estate, she'd realized she wasn't simply getting revenge for Cleveland. She was also doing it for herself. Jack was in line for a comeuppance, and her success would show him a thing or two about judging people.

"And it will be his own darn fault," she pointed out to Dee Dee as she reached to ring the bell.

It chimed a musical tune, echoing inside the huge house.

A dark-haired, middle-aged woman opened the door. She wore a blue-and-white tunic with slim gray slacks. Her glance flicked to Dee Dee then returned to Kristy.

"Can I help you, ma'am?" she asked pleasantly.

"I'm here to see Jack Osland."

The woman stepped back, opening the door wide. "Mr. Osland is expecting you?"

Kristy shook her head.

The woman's smile faltered for a scant second. "Who shall I tell him is calling?"

Kristy stepped over the threshold. Dee Dee followed, her trimmed nails making muted clicks on the black-and-white tile.

"His wife," said Kristy.

The woman's brown eyes went round for a moment. "I'm sorry?"

Kristy nodded in confirmation of what the woman had just heard. "You can tell him his wife is…home."

"Fine." With admirable aplomb, the woman gestured to a gilt settee along one oak wall of the bright, octagonal room. "Please, do have a seat."

"Thank you," said Kristy, as the woman exited down a long hallway. She walked over to the settee with Dee Dee trotting along beside her. Instead of sitting down, she scooped the dog into her arms, straightening Dee Dee's blue, satin-lined coat. It was made of fleece, with a discreet appliqué sewn at the collar. She gave the dog a reassuring pat, snuggling it close to her chest.

It took about thirty seconds for swift, masculine footsteps to sound on the hardwood floor of the hallway.

Kristy took a deep breath, squaring her shoulders as Jack rounded the corner.

When he saw her, he came to an abrupt halt. Sunbeams from the beveled windows shone in his dark eyes, highlighted the uncompromising planes and angles of his clean-shaven face.

"Is this a joke?" he demanded.

She kept her voice light and airy by sheer force of will. "Hello, honey."

His square jaw clenched in the booming silence that followed her words.

"I'm home," she finished.

He advanced warily, as if Dee Dee might bite. Which was ridiculous.

"This isn't your home," he stated.

"I'm your wife."

"In name only."

"Actually, if you'll recall, your name was pretty much the only thing I didn't take."

"What do you want?"

"Domestic bliss."

"I'm serious."

"So am I."

"If this is about money—"

"This is about fashion."

He rolled his eyes and made a sound of disbelief deep in his chest.

Another figure emerged from the hallway. "*There* you are." Cleveland strode across the foyer, his hands outstretched.

Jack jerked back in reaction.

"We were getting worried," said Cleveland, scooping Dee Dee out of Kristy's arms and planting a dry kiss on Kristy's cheek.

"Gramps," Jack interrupted.

"Did I forget to mention Kristy was coming?" the old man asked Jack, his face a picture of innocence. Kristy didn't buy it for a second.

Then all of Cleveland's attention turned to Dee Dee. "There's my sweet Pookie," he cooed, holding the dog aloft and letting her lick his nose. To Jack he said, "Don't just stand there, my boy. Get the suitcases."

"She's not staying," Jack quickly put in.

"She is. She's your wife."

"This isn't a joking matter. If she moves in—"

"I've offered Kristy the use of the workshop above the garage."

Kristy watched Jack's eyes narrow, small creases appearing in the corners. "Why?"

"To prepare for the Breakout Designer Contest at the Matte Fashion Event in London. Sierra Sanchez is sponsoring her."

Jack shot Kristy an accusatory glare.

The man could certainly be intimidating, but she refused to back down. She wouldn't, not after coming this far. Still, she didn't want to fight in front of Cleveland. So she arranged her features in a picture of naïveté. "Would you mind showing me to my room?" she asked Jack.

"Great idea," said Cleveland, tucking Dee Dee into his arm like a football. "By the way, Nanette and I have called it quits. She's keeping the ring. And the Ferrari as a matter of fact."

With that, the older man strode from the foyer.

Jack's dark gaze bore into Kristy. "How did you do it?"

She couldn't resist. "The same way Nanette did it?"

"Kristy," he growled.

"I showed him my clothes, Jack. Not that it's any of your business."

"This family is my business."

Okay. She wasn't going to do this. He was one powerful and sexy man, and he clearly wasn't used to being crossed.

Not that she was crossing him. Quite the contrary. He was the one who'd crossed her. But she suspected it would be a cold day in hell before he'd admit it.

She tipped up her chin. "I think I'll check out the workshop. I've got a lot to do."

"This is about revenge, isn't it?"

She barked out a cold laugh. "Don't flatter yourself. If not for the career opportunity, I wouldn't have given you another thought for the rest of my life."

She was lying. She'd lain awake four nights running remembering him.

THE WORKSHOP was a dream come true. Kristy had been expecting something dark and dusty, since it was above the garage, which was separate from the house. Instead, the room was bright and sparkling, with high ceilings and freshly painted white walls. A bank of windows lined one wall of the huge, rectangular room, while fluorescent lights gleamed off the hardwood floor. It had five oversized, white-topped tables, at least a dozen utility chairs, several padded stools and a long bank of closets stretching from one end to the other.

While she struggled to keep her jaw from dropping open, Jack crossed his arms over his chest. "Tell me again how this isn't about revenge."

She snapped herself back to reality. "I don't have to explain myself to you."

"I'm the one footing your bill."

"Your grandfather's footing my bill. He's also the one getting revenge."

Jack drew back in surprise. "You're Gramps's revenge on me?"

"Either that or I'm a brilliant fashion designer. Take your pick."

Jack gave a snort of disbelief.

"Thanks so much for the vote of confidence."

"I'm going with the mathematical odds."

"Well, I'd give it a thousand to one that I'm staying."

"You can't stay."

"Oh, yes I can." She was planting her butt in this dream of a workshop and getting ready for the most prestigious fashion contest in the world.

"My mother will be here tomorrow."

"So?"

"So, I am *not* about to explain a wife over the garage."

"I take it she doesn't know about your preemptive marriage?"

"Of course she doesn't know."

"Then you might want to come up with a cover story." Kristy turned away, running her fingers over the smooth tabletop, meandering her way through the room.

"I get it," said Jack with a frustrated sigh. "Go ahead. Tell me what it'll take?"

"For me to disappear?"

"Of course."

"Nothing."

"Really?"

"I mean there's nothing you can offer. Nothing I want." Other than what she had here. She had exactly what she wanted right here. Except for Jack's oppressive presence, obviously.

"Everybody wants something," he said.

"Maybe. But I've already got it."

"Do you want an apology? Is that it?"

She turned back. "An apology would have been nice four days ago."

"Okay, I'm sorry. I'm sorry I misjudged you. I'm sorry I married you."

"What you mean is that you're sorry you're stuck with me."

"Can you be reasonable for a minute?"

"I don't think so."

Jack gave a hard sigh.

"You made your bed," she pointed out.

"And I made a pretty damn fine bed for you while I was at it."

"And I'm lying in it."

His jaw tightened, and they stared at each other in crackling silence.

But, despite her best efforts, her sympathies were engaged. She had a mother, too.

"You don't have to tell her we're married," she finally suggested.

"You announced it to the staff," he reminded her.

"Oh, yeah." She paused. "Bad luck."

"That makes this partly your fault."

"*That's* the tack you want to take?"

He'd had her there for a second, but he was quickly losing the advantage. This wasn't her problem. It was his. And she didn't need to feel any obligation to solve it for him.

But then he had the grace to look sheepish, and she felt bad again. And his motives, after all, were honorable. He was trying to help his grandfather. Kristy had merely been collateral damage.

"We could tell her the truth," she offered. "We had a whirlwind relationship in Vegas."

"And how do I explain that you're in the guest room?"

"I didn't work out? We had a fight?"

He advanced on her. "That'll just raise more questions."

"Well, we're running out of options here." She was trying to be helpful, but he wasn't making it easy.

"Not quite."

"What do you mean?"

"We pretend we're happily married. Then we pretend we divorce in a month or so."

Kristy shook her head. That sounded like way too much Jack, and way too often. "I don't think so."

He glanced around the big room. "Name your price."

"I already told you, I don't have a price."

"Fabric? Notions? Sewing machines?"

"Cleveland beat you to it."

"A staff?" Jack continued. "An unlimited budget."

"No."

"Do you have any idea what an unlimited budget means in my world?"

"You mean the world where you own private jets and rent helicopters?"

He nodded. "That world."

She wasn't sure if it was his apology, the expression in

his eyes or the thought of an unlimited budget. But, she hesitated.

"Do you want to win the contest?" asked Jack.

Sure, she wanted to win. Her life would change overnight if she won.

His voice dropped to a conspiratorial level. "I can make that happen."

"You can't bribe the judges." What kind of a victory would that be?

Jack rolled his eyes. "I'm not bribing anybody. I can get you silk from the Orient, wool from Kashmir, lace from France, and I can fly you to the corners of the earth to pick it all out."

Kristy was human enough to be tempted.

And Jack was smart enough to seize the moment. He held out his hand.

She narrowed her eyes, wanting to make sure their cards were on the table. "And I'd have to…?"

"Smile at parties, sip champagne, wrap a few gifts and skate on the pond." Then his gaze went dark and his voice turned husky. "And sleep in my bed, of course."

A rush of heat burst in her chest.

"Purely platonic, I promise," he quickly added.

"You've lied to me before," she pointed out.

"True enough." He inched closer. "But I'm not lying this time. I'll keep my hands off, and the world is yours for the taking."

Kristy's instincts screamed at her to say yes. She was probably crazy. In fact, she was sure she was crazy. But he'd apologized, and he didn't really seem like a bad guy. And the things she could do with an unlimited budget….

Fate was smiling on her.

In fact, fate was flat-out grinning at her.

"Deal," she said, before she could change her mind. Then she reached out to shake his hand.

LATER THAT evening, Jack stopped in the open door of Cleveland's study. "You," he said to his grandfather, "are a scheming and manipulative old man."

Cleveland glanced up from where he was cooing at the goofy little dog. "Unlike you?"

"You brought her here on purpose."

"I brought her here to design clothing."

Jack shook his head, advancing into the room, past the leather sofa, the grandfather clock and the stone fireplace, to get to the mahogany bar, which jutted out from an oak-paneled wall. "You did not. And this fashion contest is going to be a total embarrassment for Sierra Sanchez."

"Not necessarily," said Cleveland.

"Yes, necessarily," Jack countered. Plucking a gorgeous woman out of obscurity and throwing her onto the world fashion stage had about a million-to-one chance of being successful.

"Well, *I* really like her," said Cleveland.

"You really like all hot women under the age of thirty-five."

Cleveland smiled. "At least I don't marry them."

Jack poured himself a snifter of brandy. "Actually, Gramps, you do."

"As usual, you're exaggerating. All Nanette got was a sports car, a mink coat and a diamond ring." Cleveland ruffled the fur between the dog's ears. "Wasn't that all she got, Pookie?"

Jack took a seat in a leather armchair, frowning at the dog. His grandfather had always had a soft spot for animals. Though Jack had never seen him quite this attached to one before.

"You should make a go of it with Kristy," said Cleveland. "She's a great girl."

Jack coughed out a laugh. "That's a perfect idea. Because we've obviously set such a good foundation for a long-term relationship."

A telltale twinkle came into Cleveland's eyes. "So, have you decided what you're going to tell your mother?"

Jack gave him a smug smirk in return. "That it was a whirlwind romance. Kristy's agreed to play along."

"Really." Cleveland looked surprised.

Jack nodded his answer, swirling the amber liquid against his warm palm.

"And what did that cost you?"

Jack paused. "More than Nanette's sports car. Less than the condo you bought for Opal."

"I knew I liked that girl."

"Irene Compton says she's mediocre."

Cleveland shrugged. "What does Irene know? I have a feel for these things."

"No you do not have a feel for these things." What Cleveland had a feel for was his libido. He might not have been dating Kristy, but he couldn't have missed the fact that she was a knockout. "Irene, on the other hand, has been in the fashion business for thirty years."

"Everybody's wrong sometime," said Cleveland.

While that might be true, Jack knew experts were right a whole lot more often than they were wrong. That's why he hired them, and that's why he paid them so well.

Irene was an expert. And since Kristy was, by Irene's account, a mediocre designer, there was a good chance she'd crash and burn at the Breakout Designer Contest.

Bad for Sierra Sanchez, and bad for Kristy. Jack frowned at both of those thoughts and took a swig of his brandy.

Hunter appeared in the doorway. "You two kids playing nice?"

"Jack's a bit snippy," said Cleveland.

"Gramps is busy playing God."

"Not God," said Gramps. Then he paused. "Yeah, okay. God it is."

Hunter chuckled and shook his head, sauntering over to the bar. "You know there are three huge vans out in the driveway?"

"I called earlier to express a few things over for Kristy," said Jack.

"Ahh, the blushing bride," said Hunter as he followed Jack's lead and poured himself a brandy.

Jack gestured to the two men with his glass. "You two remember, for the holiday season, she *is* the blushing bride."

Hunter held up his hands. "Hey, I'm not about to tell our moms what you did."

Cleveland nodded. "And I'm not about to tell them why you did it."

"Just so we're clear," said Jack. "I'll announce an amicable divorce in January."

"And Kristy's going along with this because?" asked Hunter.

"Because of the three huge vans in the driveway," replied Jack.

"See how easy it is?" asked Cleveland.

"Funny," said Hunter. "She didn't strike me as the mercenary type."

"Everybody has their price," Jack repeated.

Not that he held it against her. Kristy recognized a good thing when she saw it was all. And Jack could respect that. It wasn't as if he was buying her a sports car or a five-carat diamond she could turn around and hawk. It was in everybody's best interest for her to do well at the Breakout Designer Contest.

Cleveland rose from his chair. "So, now that the fun's over, Pookie and I are off to bed."

"You'll remember about Kristy?" asked Jack.

"Yes, I'll remember about Kristy," Cleveland harrumphed. "You think I'm going senile?"

Jack looked at Hunter, and Hunter looked at Jack.

Cleveland shook a wrinkled finger in their direction. "Don't you forget whose brain it was that built this company. An empty warehouse and a corner store. That's what I started with."

"And the family seat at the stock exchange," Hunter pointed out.

"Wasn't worth a dime in the thirties," Cleveland countered, scratching Dee Dee on the head. "Insolent young pups," he muttered. Then he left the room, his footsteps echoing down the hallway.

"He seem okay to you?" Hunter asked, folding himself into the armchair opposite Jack.

"Mostly," replied Jack. He always thought his grandfather was absentminded only when it suited him. But Jack wondered how much of it was an act, and how much of it was a sign of a failing memory.

"He broke up with Nanette," said Jack. "So, that's a plus."

"And you marrying Kristy?" Hunter asked with a self-satisfied grin. "That a plus, too?"

"That," said Jack, swirling his brandy again, "is an inconvenience."

"A gorgeous woman pretending to be your wife. Yeah, I'd call that an inconvenience, all right."

"She's not pretending," Jack corrected. For better or worse, Kristy actually was his wife.

"So, you'll be sleeping with her?" asked Hunter.

"In a manner of speaking." Jack shifted in his chair.

Hunter gave a knowing chuckle. "Now *that,* cousin, is an inconvenience."

Jack polished off his drink. "Speaking of which." He rose to his feet. "I'd better make sure she can find the towels."

"You poor, pathetic thing," laughed Hunter.

"What?"

"It's only ten-thirty."

Jack refused to react. So it was early. So he was looking forward to climbing into bed with Kristy. So sue him.

CHAPTER EIGHT

In Jack's big bedroom, Kristy gave herself a mental pep talk. Sleeping here wasn't going to be so bad. She could keep everything in perspective.

Sure, she was attracted to him. After all, he was a great-looking, sexy guy. But she was still annoyed with him for lying to her. And her annoyance would keep her from doing anything rash.

She eyed up the king-size bed. Then she checked out the love seat tucked in an alcove with a bay window that over-looked a pathway lined with winter-bare trees, each of them glowing with hundreds of white lights. In the distance, a giant evergreen rose above the garden, blinking with color, its crowning star golden against the black sky. The Oslands really went all out with Christmas decorations.

Back to the love seat. She could co-opt a pillow and blan-ket from Jack's bed. The love seat was on the short side, but she could make do. And it would be better than sharing the bed.

She sat on the cushions and bounced up and down. Not bad. She leaned over to lie down, turning on her side, bend-ing her knees in an effort to find a comfortable position.

Not perfect.

"You've got to be kidding," came Jack's voice from the doorway.

Kristy popped into a sitting position. "Just considering my options."

He clicked the door shut behind him. "You are not sleeping on the couch."

"Well, I'm not wild about sleeping in the bed."

"We're newlyweds."

She stood. "I've got news for you, Jack. The honeymoon's over."

"Not as far as my mother is concerned. And she'll be here any day."

"Your mother won't be in your bedroom."

"But the staff will be in *our* bedroom. And I have no desire to explain why my bride is sleeping on the couch."

"I'll fold up the blankets every morning."

"Not."

"Jack—"

"Me, you, bed." He punctuated his words by pointing with his index finger. "This is not optional."

"Women usually respond well to that tone, do they?"

"I don't know. I've never had to order a woman into my bed before."

Kristy moved toward him, putting some swagger into her step. "Is that what you're doing?"

"Yeah," said Jack, hot eyes following her progress. "That's what I'm doing."

She stopped in front of him. "Well, good luck with that."

"I'm not going to need luck."

"No?"

He scooped her into his arms. Before she could do anything more than gasp in surprise, he marched across the room and deposited her on top of the duvet.

"No luck required," he stated, staring down at her.

She propped herself on her elbows, trying to look af-fronted, even as a grin crept out. "You cheated."

He grinned in return. "Who cares? I won."

"And how much satisfaction is there in that if you cheated?"

He leaned down, bracing a hand on either side of her, bringing their faces close together. "Quite a bit, actually."

Kristy could feel an awareness humming through her body. "I will escape," she warned in a whisper.

He raised his eyebrows. "You think?"

"The minute you're asleep."

"Well, good luck with that," he parroted.

"I'm not going to need luck," she countered.

AN HOUR LATER, Kristy realized that what she really needed was a crowbar.

Jack's arm was latched firmly around her waist, anchor-ing her, spoon-fashion, to his body. His breathing was deep and even, so she was pretty sure he'd fallen asleep. But his grip hadn't slacked off one bit.

She was well covered, having passed over the filmy ivory and peach negligee Jack had secretly bought her in Las Vegas in favor of an oversized T-shirt. The shirt fell past her knees and was thicker than flannel. Still, Jack's fore-arm was warm and intimate against her stomach.

She wasn't uncomfortable. In fact, she could have eas-ily fallen asleep. But it was a matter of principle now. She couldn't let him win this particular war.

She wrapped her fingers around his thick wrist and pulled against his arm.

His response was to mutter in her ear and snuggle closer,

drawing her buttocks tight against the cradle of his thighs, his hand slipping lower, cupping her hip bone.

She froze, willing her body to ignore the sexual signals he was sending out in his sleep.

But goose bumps rose on her skin, and a thick pulse started deep in her abdomen. She squirmed, trying to get away from the sensations. But that only made things worse. Her nightgown rode up to midthigh, and the friction of Jack's hand through the fabric of her gown made the goose bumps tingle with desire.

She squirmed again, scrunching her eyes shut and biting down on her bottom lip. Desire throbbed freely now. Her toes curled and her muscles began to clench. Her nipples tightened as his breath fanned against the back of her neck.

She straightened her legs, but that brought the back of her thighs against his hot body. Skin on skin, inch after glorious inch. Her hands curled into fists. Oh, this was going to kill her.

His hand moved, and her hips flexed involuntarily backward as a gasp escaped from her lips.

He sucked in a tight breath, and she realized he was awake.

She stilled, expecting him to say something. She was embarrassed, but, more than that, she was completely aroused.

His body hardened against her.

He gave her a few moments to protest, but then his thumb drew a lazy circle around her navel. His fingertips were still snug against her hip. She knew she should say something, knew she should stop him. But cocooned by his warmth, with the Christmas lights twinkling through the big windows and his strong body enveloping her, she couldn't bring herself to break the moment.

His lips touched the back of her neck. They parted, turning the brush into a kiss.

She really had to stop him.

If she didn't stop him right this second…

Her fists curled tighter, nails biting into her palms.

His fingertips fanned their way down her thighs. They encountered bare skin. She held her breath as they trailed their way back up.

His kisses worked their way around her neck. He kissed her ear, her jawbone, her cheek, while his fingertips brushed her downy curls.

Then he drew another strangled breath. "For God's sake, tell me no."

She tried, but she couldn't form the word.

He kissed the corner of her mouth.

She turned her head to meet him, angling her body, tipping her chin.

His gaze caught hers in the blinking red and green glow. He gently found her center, and her hips flexed in reaction.

Then his mouth was on hers, kissing her passionately, his tongue delving deeply into her mouth as his finger entered her body.

She moaned, and her thighs twitched apart.

He stretched his leg over hers, pressing her into the mattress. His hand set up a rhythm, and the world shifted to the apex of her thighs.

She tried to hang on, but he hit all the right spots. She dragged in a breath, inhaling his scent. She flicked out her tongue, tasting sweet brandy on his lips. She twisted the comforter convulsively between her fingers.

He had to stop.

This was crazy.

She was out of control.

She opened her mouth, but her words turned into a cry, and sensation shattered around her.

He held her tight, slowed his kisses, whispered something that she couldn't begin to hear around the roaring in her ears. But it sounded nice. It sounded soothing. It sounded like she didn't have to worry that she'd just let go under his caress.

And then the lights blurred and the soft bed turned into a cloud, as a warm peace settled into her very bones.

IN THE MORNING, Jack hauled himself out of bed at 6:00 a.m. He'd nearly given in to temptation last night, and he didn't want to think about what he'd do if Kristy woke up sleepy and pliant in his arms. It could go one of two ways, neither of them good, and he owed it to her to at least try to keep his word from now on.

He left her sleeping and showered down the hall. Then he took coffee into the study. It was too early on the west coast even for Lisa, so he logged on to the Sierra Sanchez computer server and hunted around himself. It took nearly half an hour to find a number for Zenia Topaz.

Jack wanted to make contact with the one person who might be able to help him help Kristy. Zenia Topaz was a top fashion designer, and her contract with Sierra Sanchez gave Jack a little leverage. Plus, they'd grown to be friends over the years.

He'd already ordered what he could think of for Kristy last night from the Manchester area. But he didn't know anything about international fashion design. He had no idea what was in and what was out, what kinds of things Kristy would need to have a running chance at the Breakout Designer Contest. Hopefully, Zenia could give him some advice.

And he wasn't only doing this for Kristy, he assured

himself. He had the best interests of Sierra Sanchez in mind, as well.

"Topaz Fashion," came the cheerful answer.

"Zenia Topaz, please."

"She's expecting your call?"

"No. It's Jack Osland."

"One moment please, Mr. Osland. I'll see if she's available." The line clicked.

Jack listened to elevator music, tapping his fingers against the desktop as the minutes ticked by. He realized as he waited that he didn't spend very much of his life on hold. Other people must. Although he had to remember that Zenia hadn't been expecting his call.

The line clicked again. "Mr. Osland?" came the same voice, sounding a bit breathless and flustered this time.

"Yes?"

"Ms. Topaz will be right with you. I'm sorry, sir."

"No problem," said Jack.

Another click.

"Jack," Zenia's voice singsonged.

"Good morning, Zenia. How are things in New York?"

"Things are fabulous. The city's lit up. We've been out skating already. Are you in town?"

"I'm in Manchester. I was wondering if you could help me out."

"Absolutely, Jack. Whatever I can do."

"Sierra Sanchez is sponsoring a designer in the Breakout Designer Contest at Matte Fashion."

"Umm-hmm."

He swiveled his chair to face the window. "She's working here over the holidays, and I'd like to pick up a few things for her."

"What kind of things."

"That's the problem. I'm not sure."

"Okay…" Zenia's voice was searching.

"Fabric, notions, shoes, I don't know. I was hoping you'd have some ideas."

"Do you have her sketches?"

"Not really."

"Jack—"

"It was a last-minute thing. I think she might be building on something she has, or she might be coming up with something brand-new. Gramps met her—"

"Ahhh."

"Oh. No." Jack automatically shook his head. "It's not like that." Well it *was* kind of like that. "Listen, my jet is at your disposal, as is my credit card. Can you make a few calls to your suppliers? Just send one of everything."

Zenia gave a husky chuckle. "Who is this woman?"

Jack paused. "My wife."

"No way."

"It was a whirlwind courtship."

Zenia clucked her tongue. "Like grandfather, like—"

"No! Like I said, it's nothing like that."

"Sorry."

"That's all right. Can you help me out? I want to surprise her."

Kristy could buy anything else she wanted later, but Jack couldn't help thinking they'd do better with an expert like Zenia making the choices.

Zenia was silent for a minute. "You know she's only got two weeks."

"The jet is warming up on the tarmac."

Zenia took a breath. "Okay. Tell the pilot to file a flight plan to Paris then Milan. I'll send one of my assistants along to purchase what she'll need."

"You're a goddess," said Jack.

"Yes, I am. And I want to meet this woman when I'm at the show in London."

"Actually, I can suggest something even better…."

WAKING UP alone in Jack's bedroom was a mixed blessing. It saved her the embarrassment of facing him after last night. But now she had to spend the day dreading the moment she'd have to face him.

Did he think she was selfish? A tease? Did he think it was his turn next? Did he have expectations for tonight?

She paced the length of the workshop, giving her head a quick shake, forcing Jack from her thoughts.

She stopped herself at the drafting table, plunked down on the stool, opened the sketch pad and stared down at Irene's notes. The Sierra Sanchez team had liked the necklines. They'd liked some of the fabrics, too.

The team's biggest complaint had been the lack of sparkle and imagination. Kristy thought she understood. Unfortunately, now she wasn't so sure.

She closed her eyes, trying to think about sparkle, imagination, maybe passion.

Oops. There was Jack again.

She could see him in the hot air balloon this time, skimming over the desert against the bright-blue sky. The balloon was round, billowing out with primary colors, bright yellow, red and blue. The lines were soft, sand rippling off in the distance, rocks polished by the foaming water, curves on the river sweeping through the valley.

In the distance, the cliffs were jagged, painted with muted stripes of brown and rust and gold. A waterfall crashed over them, hurling spray high into the air, white water bubbled at the bottom of the falls. She heard Jack's rumbling voice, his laughter, his teasing suggestion they skinny-dip. She was hit with a new sense of desire, even while the foaming water turned into billowing crinoline and the stripes from the surrounding cliffs took the shape of a bodice.

Her eyes flew open. "Wow."

She grabbed her sketchbook and began bold pencil strokes across a blank page.

A wild and exotic dress grew before her eyes—a tight, sleeveless bodice, with stripes arching into a reverse, rounded neckline. She'd use some kind of metallic in the fabric, jazzing up the earth tones. She nipped in the waist, then filled out the skirt, widening the stripes as the fabric fell to midthigh. Then she penciled in the billowing crinoline, at least six inches showing below the skirt.

Dark stockings and spike heels would give the sensuality she was looking for. It was sassy and sexy and completely different from anything she'd conceived before.

She had a sudden vision of herself wearing it, curled up on the blanket in front of the waterfall, Jack's hot gaze traveling the length of her body.

She drew a deep, shuddering breath.

Then she came back to earth, blinking at the surprising creation. It didn't look like the kind of thing Irene would like. The woman's tastes had tended toward sleek and sophisticated.

But this dress was definitely passionate. And, for better or worse, Kristy was feeling passionate.

Maybe it was frustration. Or maybe it was repressed desire. Or maybe it was simply the opulence and excess of the Osland mansion. But Kristy definitely wanted to let herself go, to find her sensual side and bring it out in jazzy, extravagant clothing.

Of course, she couldn't.

She had a sponsor. And she had a job to do.

Enough fooling around. She flipped to Irene's notes on her original sketches. She'd start with her classic cocktail dress and take it from there.

WHEN KRISTY entered the mansion many hours later, tired, hungry and pretty frustrated with her efforts, she heard voices coming from the great room. She realized the rest of Jack's family had arrived, and she was in no shape to meet any of them yet.

She darted up the stairs, grabbed a shower, blow-dried her hair and got herself into a simple white-and-silver tunic dress that shimmered as she moved. High heels gave her confidence, and she matched a pair of dangling black earrings to a dramatic necklace that highlighted the V neckline.

She heard the bedroom door open and turned to see Jack approach the en-suite.

"Ready?" he asked through the doorway.

The second she heard his voice, the night before came flooding back in all its reckless, sensual glory. She instantly realized she wasn't ready to face Jack or anybody else.

"Kristy?"

She swallowed. Should she acknowledge it? Pretend she'd forgotten? Hope he'd forgotten that she selfishly went to heaven and back in his arms?

"Kristy?" he repeated, taking a couple of steps into the room. Then he stopped behind her, gazing for a long second at her reflection in the vanity mirror.

"Please don't be embarrassed," he finally said.

What else could she possibly be?

"You were beautiful," he said softly, bringing his hands down to rest on her shoulders.

"I'm sorry," she muttered, covering her face with one hand.

A smile came into his voice. "Well, I'm sure not."

She dared to meet his eyes.

"Never," he assured her. "Not even for a second."

There was something comforting about his tone and his touch. She found herself relaxing.

"Besides," he said, giving her a squeeze, "I don't know if you noticed, but we've got bigger problems downstairs."

So much for relaxing. "I noticed," she said on a sigh.

"Then buck up," he advised. "Because your in-laws are waiting."

She nodded, finishing her lip gloss and chasing down a surge of butterflies that collected in her stomach. She reminded herself they weren't really her in-laws. She didn't have to win them over for life. All she had to do was smile, nod and try not to spill anything.

Jack gestured for her to go first. "My mother's name is Liza. My sister is Elaine. Then there's my aunt Gwen and my cousin Melanie, Hunter's sister."

Kristy repeated the names to herself as they made their way along the hall and down the main staircase. Garlands of fresh cedar adorned the railing and banisters. The charming scent filled the air.

A small group of people stood chatting in the great room. Hunter asked Jack a question as they walked through the door. Kristy could see Cleveland in a conversation in the middle of the room, a crystal tumbler in one hand, and Dee Dee parked by his feet. He was sporting a Santa hat, perched jauntily atop his head. Leaving Jack behind, she moved closer to Cleveland, then she crouched down slightly.

"Dee Dee," she sang softly to get her dog's attention.

Dee Dee raised her head, but didn't come to her feet.

"He's spoiled her," came a female voice next to Kristy.

Kristy straightened and smiled at the young woman. "I may have to leave her here when I go."

She was a brunette, twentysomething, and she arched a finely sculpted eyebrow. "You're going somewhere?"

"London," said Kristy easily. Then she held out her hand. "I'm Kristy Mahoney."

The woman gave a gentle handshake. "Not Osland?"

Kristy shook her head.

"Well, I'm Elaine Osland. We appear to be sisters-in-law."

"It's good to meet you."

"You, too." Elaine took a sip of her martini, watching Kristy closely. "I hear it was a small wedding?"

"About as small as you can get."

"In Vegas?"

"Uh-huh."

"Out of the blue I take it?"

"It was a whirlwind courtship."

"That's not like Jack."

"It's not like me, either."

"More like his grandfather."

Kristy laughed, but it sounded nervous even to her ears. "Really."

"I hear you're into fashion design."

"I am. And what do you do?"

Elaine waved a dismissive hand. "Let's talk about you."

Kristy paused. "I take it you're the interrogation committee?"

Elaine had the good grace to grin sheepishly. "That's because you haven't met my mother yet."

Kristy glanced around the room.

"In the green sequin jacket," said Elaine.

The woman's shrewd eyes met Kristy's gaze, and Kristy quickly looked away.

"Any tips?" she asked Elaine.

Elaine chuckled. "Stand up straight, don't let her intimidate you and always tell the truth."

"Are there any electrodes or heart-rate monitors involved?"

"Only if you make her suspicious."

"Suspicious of what?"

"Your motivations for marrying my brother, silly."

"I had no motivations."

"See, she's going to wonder."

"It was a crazy weekend romance in Vegas," Kristy told Elaine honestly. "He took me on a balloon ride, and I was a goner." She wasn't even lying about that part.

She felt a hand on the small of her back and knew immediately it was Jack.

"Everything okay here?" he asked.

"The electrodes haven't come out yet," said Kristy.

"We're just having a chat," Elaine put in, giving her brother a quick hug.

"You be nice," Jack warned his sister.

"I'm always nice. I hear you fell in love on a balloon ride." She cocked her head to watch his expression.

"You heard right," said Jack. "It was over the Grand Canyon, and I was charming as hell."

"Hmm," said Elaine.

"Don't 'hmm' me," Jack retorted.

Elaine glanced back and forth between the two. "Only two days?"

Jack sighed. "Back off. And tell Mom to back off, too."

Elaine snorted indelicately. "Yeah, right." She turned

her attention to Kristy again. "So, tell me all about your design business."

"I mean it," said Jack.

"I'm simply making conversation," Elaine retorted.

Jack took Kristy's arm. "I'd like to introduce you to my mother." He guided her away.

"Will I do any better with her?" she whispered as they crossed the room, feeling as if she was being put in front of a firing squad.

"You're doing fine."

"I'm going with the truth. It was a whirlwind courtship in Vegas, and you were charming."

He nodded. "That works." Then he put a broad smile on his face as they approached the slender woman in the emerald-green jacket.

"Mom," he said. "I'd like you to meet Kristy."

The woman turned to face them. She was somewhere between fifty and sixty, and her hair, makeup and jewelry were obviously the products of considerable wealth. Kristy recognized the jacket as a Delilah Domtar, and the slacks as William Ping.

She was tall and beautiful, but the warmth in her eyes when she greeted Jack dimmed somewhat when she looked at Kristy.

"Kristy, this is my mother, Liza."

"It's a pleasure to meet you," said Kristy, bravely holding out a hand.

Liza looked her up and down. "The pleasure is mine, I'm sure."

The words were correct, but the tone left Kristy wanting to apologize for something.

"There you are, Kristy!" Cleveland's voice boomed. "Meeting my youngest daughter, I see."

Kristy smiled in relief, and she bent down to pick up Dee Dee, a welcome distraction. "Hello, Cleveland. Nice hat."

"Thanks. Kristy here is a genius," Cleveland said to Liza.

"I'm sure she's quite the little scholar," said Liza.

Hugging Dee Dee close, Kristy caught an apology in Jack's eyes.

"Don't get yourself in a snit," Cleveland admonished Liza.

Liza glanced at Kristy and then Jack. "An invitation to the wedding was too much to ask?"

"It wasn't really a wedding," Kristy blurted, experiencing a pang of sympathy for the woman. Her own mother would be—

Her mother.

Good Lord, her *mother.*

She turned to Jack, feeling the blood drain from her face. "I have to make a phone call."

He looked confused. "Now?"

"I'm sorry." She handed Dee Dee to Cleveland and started to move away.

Jack caught her arm to stop her.

She mouthed the words *my parents.*

He drew back, comprehension dawning in his eyes.

"Will you excuse us for a moment?" he asked the group of guests.

"Dinner is in fifteen minutes," warned Liza.

With Jack at her side, Kristy left the great room and paced to the rotunda foyer.

"This is a disaster," she hissed.

"Just tell them what we're telling everyone else."

She stopped and turned around in front of the settee. "They're my *parents.*" Joe and Amy Mahoney were hard-working, generous and hopelessly romantic. Amy's wedding dress had been preserved in blue tissue paper for thirty years, waiting for either Kristy or Sinclair to find the right man. And when they sold their house in Brooklyn, instead of buying beachfront in Florida, they bought something modest, a block away, to make sure they could afford fashionable weddings for their two daughters.

He gestured back to the great room. "Who do you think we were just talking to?"

"That's different."

His lips compressed. But then his eyes unexpectedly softened. "You're right. It is. Tell me how I can help."

She looked at the floor. There was nothing he could do.

Her mother would be thrilled, *thrilled* to hear that Kristy had fallen in love. Her father would hold off until he met Jack—which would be as soon as humanly possible. Then there'd be talk of grandchildren. Her parents would emotionally engage in some big, complicated fantasy of the future. Then their hopes would be dashed when the divorce was announced.

Kristy groaned.

Jack slipped an arm around her. "It's going to be okay," he muttered. "We'll make it okay."

She shook her head in denial. It wasn't going to be okay. It was going to be horrible. "They'll want to get on a plane. They'll want to meet you in person."

"I'll send the jet."

"They can't come *here*."

Jack nodded. "Oh, right. That would be way too complicated." He gripped the back of his neck. "What about London?"

"London?"

"Ask them to meet us in London."

"You're not coming to London."

He paused. "Good point. Okay. How about this. Tell them you've *met* a nice man. And you're spending Christmas with him, and you'll keep them posted. That way, if they find out about the marriage, you can say we were planning to surprise them together in person. And if they don't find out, we divorce, life goes on and everybody's happy."

Kristy considered the idea.

It was a long shot. But it might work. At least it gave them a fighting chance.

Jack handed her his cell phone.

CHAPTER NINE

A WEEK LATER, Kristy's double fashion collection mirrored double life.

On the one hand, she was plain old single, struggling Kristy Mahoney. On the other, she was Mrs. Jack Osland. Her husband was flying in fabrics and accessories from Paris and Milan, while wedding gifts arrived almost hourly from pricey boutiques around the globe. She was careful not to let herself get attached to any of the expensive silver and china, and she was leaving Jack to worry about returning it when all was said and done.

Out in the workshop, she was working on two sets of sketches and two clothing collections. One was the revamped collection developed with the help of Irene and the Sierra Sanchez team. The other was the wild fantasy clothing she'd created around her Vegas trip with Jack.

Two assistants had arrived the first morning after she'd shown up at the mansion. Local women, Isabella and Megan were both competent seamstresses and cheerful companions. Kristy was making steady progress on the real collection during the day. In the evening though, she couldn't resist using the expensive laces and fabrics to mock up some of the fantasy pieces.

"More lace," Isabella called above the hum from Megan's sewing machine. She balanced a huge white box in her arms as she closed the door behind another delivery man.

"Look at that," Megan whistled as they opened the box.

Kristy crossed the room. The box held beaded, corded, Chantilly, metallic and colored laces.

Isabella tsk-tsked. "I sure wish we were making something with lace."

What Kristy wished was that they were *showing* something with lace. The Irene collection—as she'd begun calling it in her head—was sleek and sophisticated, where the fantasy collection was flirty and fun. Kristy would be able to use all kinds of different lace on the fantasy collection. It was just too bad nobody but her would ever see it.

She was halfway through sewing the sexy, short desert dress. For that one, the lace would be key. It had to be stiff to fill out the skirt, and the edging needed to be dramatic to draw the eye, but the detail had to mimic the frothing waterfall. Kristy smiled at the memory.

"What?" asked Isabella.

Kristy immediately erased the smile. "We'd better get back to work."

They closed the box, but Kristy didn't take her own advice. Instead of settling on a fabric for the Irene collection slacks, she gazed out the window at the delicate snowflakes catching the bare branches of maple trees.

She saw the hot-air balloon again. It morphed into striped pants made of thin nylon in the same primary colors. She'd pair that with a cropped top of blue or red or…the lace! That was it. Thin out the stripes, make the top out of lace—flat cotton eyelet perhaps. She could even use a color, or maybe colored buttons down the front of the top.

Kristy surreptitiously flipped to a blank page in her sketch book. Multicolored buttons would match the colors in the pants. The lace would tie in with the frothy skirt. She put a few bold strokes across the pages, and she was off and running.

"Kristy?" Megan's voice seemed a long way off, and Kristy realized a couple of hours had gone by. Her shoulders and hand were starting to cramp.

She looked up. "Yes?"

"We're heading out now."

Kristy nodded. "Of course. Thanks."

"We can probably do a first fitting on the blue dress tomorrow. The Harold Agency said they'd send a couple of models."

Kristy nodded again. "That's great. And the green one?"

"We can cut the silk tomorrow," said Isabella.

"Thanks, guys," said Kristy.

"See you in the morning." They waved and opened the door, nearly bumping into Hunter on their way out.

They greeted him, and he bade them goodbye, then closed the shop door after them.

"How are you holding up?" he asked, strolling over to Kristy.

She closed the sketch book of fantasy designer drawings like a guilty little secret and stood to stretch her shoulders. "Not bad."

He nodded, glancing around. "Looks like you're doing a lot of work."

"That's because I am." In fact, it was double the work it should have been. But that was Kristy's own fault. Her own, self-indulgent fault.

"You working late again tonight."

"For a while. Did you need something?"

"Gramps asked if you'd—"

The shop door burst open, cutting off Hunter's words.

Kristy blinked in astonishment at the image of her sister in a bright-green woolen coat with a matching beret.

She stood. "Sinclair? What on earth?"

Sinclair marched into the room, gesturing to Hunter with her thumb. "Is this the guy?"

"What are you *doing* here?"

Sinclair whipped off the beret, revealing her wild auburn hair. "Am I not your best friend? Your confidante? Your partner in crime?"

"Hold on," said Hunter, drawing Sinclair's attention, and her ire.

"And *you*," she said to Hunter, marching forward. "You *married* my sister?"

The word *married* clanged in Kristy's ears. "Wait a minute. How did you—"

"The old man in the house." Sinclair kept her focus on Hunter. "Where did you meet her?"

"On my jet," said Hunter.

"Hunter, don't—"

"Money doesn't give you carte blanche," said Sinclair, pacing around him. "She has a family, people who love her. People who *deserved* to meet you, before—"

"*Sinclair.*"

"Before I kidnapped her and dragged her off to my lair?" asked Hunter.

"There's no need to be sarcastic," said Sinclair.

"And there's no need to blitz in here like the Tasmanian Devil."

"I want some answers."

"Then shut up for a minute and listen."

To Kristy's surprise, Sinclair actually did.

"He's not my husband," said Kristy.

"Somebody looking for me?" drawled Jack from the doorway.

Sinclair spun to face him. She blinked from one man to the other.

"Jack, Hunter. This is my sister, Sinclair. Sinclair, this is my husband, Jack, and his cousin Hunter."

"Mom told me you'd met a man." Sinclair unbuttoned her long coat.

"I did."

Sinclair eyed Jack up and down. "She didn't tell me you'd married him." She pulled a cell phone from the pocket and hit a speed-dial button.

Kristy jerked forward, visions of her mother on the other end of the line. "Who are you calling?"

"The airline," said Sinclair. "I had a four-hour stopover. But clearly, I'll be staying the night."

"Is she always this bossy?" asked Hunter.

"Is he always this rude?" asked Sinclair.

"Pleasure to meet you," said Jack, advancing with his hand out.

Sinclair shook, cradling the phone against her neck. "I have a few questions."

"Me, too," said Jack. "You know how to skate?"

Before Sinclair could answer him, her phone call connected, distracting her. She listened for a few seconds, then pushed a button.

"We're skating on the pond tonight," Jack explained to Kristy. "It's a traditional thing. Mom would love to have you join us."

"I should talk to Sinclair first."

"She can talk to both of us," said Jack.

Sinclair covered the mouthpiece. "I don't really care who I talk to. As long as somebody starts talking."

"Jack and I met in Vegas," said Kristy. "It was a whirl-wind courtship."

"You…*you* got married in Vegas?"

"I did."

"And this doesn't warrant a phone call?"

"We were waiting—"

"For what?"

"To tell Mom and Dad in person."

"I'm not Mom and Dad."

Kristy blew out a breath. "I know."

Jack put an arm around her. If he'd tried that when she'd first arrived at the mansion, she would have shrugged it off. Now, she reveled in the strength and comfort of his simple gesture. "I think Kristy was somewhat embarrassed. She's not normally impulsive."

"And you know what she's normally like, do you?"

"She's my wife."

Sinclair shook her head. "Hello?" she said into the phone, turning away. "Yes. I'd like to change my ticket."

"You okay?" Jack asked.

"Not really," replied Kristy.

Hunter moved closer. "You want me to get rid of her?"

Kristy couldn't help but smile. "You offering to harm my sister?"

"I meant get her out of the room," clarified Hunter.

"She'll calm down in a minute."

Sinclair finished her call.

"I'll skate if I have to," she informed Jack. "As long as somebody does some talking while I'm skating. And as long as there is some kind of alcoholic beverage at the end."

Then she moved forward and drew Kristy into a one-armed hug. "I wanted to be a bridesmaid," she muttered. "How could you do this to me?"

"Jack is persuasive," Kristy answered.

Sinclair drew back, smoothing the front of Kristy's hair. "Obviously. And I want to hear all about it."

THE MOON WAS full, the stars snapping bright, and strings of white Christmas bulbs illuminated the periphery of the glassy pond. Jack's gloved hand was tucked into Kristy's as they made lazy circles around the edge of the ice.

He could see Hunter in the distance, annoying Sinclair by skating around her as she struggled to stay on her feet. Further back was his family. Cleveland carried Dee Dee, while Elaine and Melanie laughed their way through fumbled spins and jumps.

Beside him, Kristy looked beautiful. Her cheeks were rosy beneath her fur-trimmed hat. Her lips were full and dark, and her eyes glowed indigo beneath her thick lashes.

"I seriously thought about telling her the truth," she admitted, referring to her private conversation with Sinclair at the beginning of the excursion.

"But you didn't?" Jack asked, enjoying the feel of her small hand in his. He turned and snagged the other, skating backward so they were facing each other.

She sighed. "I stuck with our story."

The urge to lean forward and kiss her was so strong. "Will she tell your parents?" he asked instead.

Kristy shook her head. "She promised me she'd wait and let me tell them in person."

"That's good."

"There's nothing at all good about this."

"I disagree."

"How can you disagree? The whole damn world thinks we're married."

He shrugged, not really caring what anybody in the

world thought. It was getting harder and harder to regret spending time with Kristy. In fact, he was getting greedy for more of it. She was working such long hours on the collection. He was proud of her.

"You know what they say," he offered, fighting the urge to draw her closer.

"There's something about our circumstances people 'say'?"

He smiled softly, the idea gelling in his mind. "There is— If you can't beat them…"

"What are you talking about?"

"Join them," he offered. "Haven't you ever heard that saying?"

"Join them in what?"

"Thinking we're married."

Her eyes narrowed. "That's ridiculous."

"No, it's not. Think about it for a second. What if we were to buy into it along with the rest of them and be married for a while?"

"You're suggesting we pretend we really *are* married?"

"We don't have to pretend," he reminded her.

"You know what I mean."

"We had fun in Vegas. Didn't we have fun in Vegas? You liked me there, right?"

"Vegas was a fantasy."

"But you married me. That means I'm not such a bad guy." He gave in and drew her toward him, letting them glide to a stop on the far side of the pond.

She gazed up at him, and there was a hint of something encouraging in her blue eyes. "You're a liar, a cheat and a con man."

He tipped his head, hoping he was right about the message in her eyes. "But you want to kiss me anyway."

"No, I don't."

"Liar," he whispered, moving closer.

"This better be for show," she said.

"This isn't for show."

"Jack."

"I really am going to kiss you."

"I can't pretend we're married."

"Sure you can." His lips touched hers.

They were cool and soft and erotically delicious. In a split second, she was kissing him back.

He twined their fingers together, deepening the kiss, bending her backward, fighting the instinct to pull her fully into his arms. He kissed her as long as he dared. Then he slowly broke away.

"This is a bad idea," she said.

"This is the best idea I've ever had. We are *great* together."

He could see her skepticism.

He could tell she was about to say no, so he kept on talking. "Plus, we both know it's a fantasy. How can there be anything wrong with a good fantasy?"

"Jack."

"There's some serious chemistry between us, Kristy. I know it, and you sure know it." He could still feel her slick body responding under his hands. "We're both adults," he continued huskily. "We have a fantastic time. And we both walk away at the end."

He kissed her again, this time he kept going until she was breathless.

"Where's the harm?" he asked against her mouth.

She inhaled deeply, hesitated, then spoke. "Can I think about it?"

No! he wanted to shout.

"Sure," he said instead.

"No. Oh, *no!*" Sinclair's shriek echoed in the distance.

Jack and Kristy turned to the sound.

Hunter was behind her, hands on her hips, pushing her faster and faster and faster across the pond.

Jack couldn't help but chuckle.

"She's going to kill him," Kristy muttered.

"I'd say he's got the upper hand."

"Sooner or later, he'll have to stop. And then she'll kill him."

Jack doubted that.

He put an arm around Kristy. He wasn't going to waste valuable time worrying about his cousin. He drew her against his side. It felt good, too good. He wished he dared put forward another argument. He couldn't bear the thought of another celibate night sleeping next to her in his bed. There were moments when he honestly thought it might kill him.

But he knew he had to wait. Married or not, he was asking her for a holiday fling, and she had every right to say no.

KRISTY WAS going to say yes.

She'd known it before breakfast.

Heck, she'd known it half the night.

She'd forced herself to sleep on the idea. But deep down inside, she'd known all along she was going to make love with Jack again. He and Vegas had been constantly on her mind. It showed in the way her body hummed around him, and it showed in the fantasy clothes she'd created.

She was staring at them now. Megan and Isabella weren't due for another half hour. Every morning, they dropped their kids off at school before making their way to the mansion.

Kristy ran her fingers over the waterfall dress and the hot-air-balloon pants, holding the kicky crop top up against her chest.

She'd added a bikini for the swim she and Jack hadn't taken at the waterfall. She'd also mocked-up a cocktail dress out of a gorgeous piece of hand-dyed Mikado silk. It was black at the bottom, rising to midnight blue and orange then yellow like the desert sunset they'd shared.

She'd also created a sexy wisp of a dress, dark green from the casino, with diamonds of lace inset in the sides. But the crowning finale, the one she couldn't wait to finish, was a dramatic red charmeuse silk evening gown. It was strapless, with a tight bodice and a straight full-length skirt. She'd sewn tiny triangles of lace into the hemline, flouncing it out with crinoline to mimic the roulette wheel.

She sighed.

Maybe someday she'd see one of these on a runway.

"Hey, Kristy?"

Before Kristy could react, Sinclair was through the door and into the workshop.

"There you are," said Sinclair.

Kristy shifted in front of the collection, hoping her sister wouldn't notice it. "I knocked on your door this morning," she told her sister.

"I guess I slept in."

"What happened? Did you two stay up late fighting?"

Kristy and Jack had left Sinclair and Hunter in the great room with mugs of liquor-laced hot chocolate and in the midst of a ridiculous debate about dating etiquette.

"I won pretty quick," Sinclair told her, her gaze sliding to the clothes. "What are those?"

Kristy blocked her view even further. "Just…uh…something I'm fooling around with."

Sinclair went around her.

"They're great," she said with genuine enthusiasm, lifting the green dress on its hanger and holding it against her body. "Very sexy."

"These, over here, are the ones for the show." Kristy tried to direct Sinclair's attention to the Irene collection.

But Sinclair wouldn't be distracted. "You made all of them?" She put the green dress back and switched to the waterfall dress.

"I did," said Kristy. "But, these ones—"

"Are boring," said Sinclair, with a dismissive wave of her hand. "Why not take the good ones to London?"

Kristy raised her eyebrows at the ludicrous suggestion. "I can't."

"Why not?"

"Because I've had expert help with *this* collection. And it's the one Cleveland and I made the deal on."

"So, tell him you've changed your mind."

"I can't change my mind."

Sinclair traded the waterfall dress for the crop top. "Then tell Jack you've changed your mind."

"I can't do that, either."

Jack didn't respect her skills or her talent. He was only going along with having her in the contest because Cleveland had forced him.

"You're sleeping with him, right?"

Kristy didn't know what to say to that.

Sinclair watched her closely, then her voice took on an unnatural calm. "Right, Kristy. Because he *is* your *husband*."

Kristy blinked like a deer in the headlights.

Sinclair plunked the crop top back on the rack. "Damn it," she swore. "I hoped he was lying."

"Huh?"

"Hunter, dear sister." Sinclair paced in a semicircle around Kristy. "Your cousin-in-law told me your marriage was a sham."

Kristy opened her mouth, but nothing came out.

"He said Jack only married you to save his grandfather from a fortune hunter."

Kristy recognized the angry crackle in Sinclair's familiar blue eyes. She'd hated deceiving her sister.

"Am I not your partner in crime?" asked Sinclair.

Kristy struggled to frame a response.

Then a note of real hurt crept into Sinclair's voice. "Why would you lie to me?"

"Because I didn't want *you* to have to lie for *me*."

"To Mom and Dad?"

"Yes!" It was a choice between bad and worse.

"I've been lying to Mom and Dad for you since we were born."

"Not like this."

"What the hell happened?"

"I thought Hunter told you."

"Not all of it." Sinclair took a step forward. "He didn't know why you said yes. Why'd you go and marry Jack?"

Kristy didn't know.

She honestly didn't know.

"There were helicopters," she tried. "And dinner and dancing. Oh, Sinclair, you should see him in a suit."

"You were hot for him? That's it?"

"Totally," Kristy admitted.

Sinclair laughed softly. "I can respect that. But you couldn't have settled for a fling?"

"He proposed."

"The rat bastard," said Sinclair, but there was a wry grin along with the insult.

"As it turned out," said Kristy on a sigh.

"So, now what?"

"Now, I put these away, finish the *real* collection and go to London and try to win that darn contest." Kristy scooped two of the fantasy dresses from the rack and headed for the closet.

"Mistake," said Sinclair, nodding to Kristy's armload. "Those dresses are better. And he owes you."

"Do you have any idea how much they've spent on me already? I'm coming away just fine from this deal."

"Did you sign a prenup?"

"We are *not* going after his money." Kristy transferred the evening gown to the closet.

Sinclair leaned to peer out the window. "That's a whole lot of money, babe."

"And it's his, not mine."

"Depends on the state."

"I signed a prenup."

Sinclair gave a sigh of disgust. "Did I teach you nothing?"

"This is not a scenario even *you* could have contemplated." Kristy all but sprinted to the closet with the remaining items.

"What about future planning?" Sinclair called. "Self-preservation? Keeping your sister in the style to which she's planning to become accustomed?"

Kristy latched the closet. "Don't you have a plane to catch?"

"I could stay through the holidays, eat caviar, sip champagne."

"I thought you said they needed you at work."

"They do."

"And we can't both miss Christmas dinner."

"So you get to stay here with the hunky husband and eat caviar and drink champagne?"

Kristy crossed her arms over her chest in mock censure. "You got your sights set on my hunky husband?"

"Not exactly. But did you get a good look at his cousin?"

"You fought with Hunter all night long."

"Not the entire night."

Kristy stared at her sister's telltale expression. "You didn't," she whispered.

"Got a plane to catch," sang Sinclair, turning for the door.

Kristy hustled after her. "What *happened?*"

"The hot chocolate was great. He was cute. And there was all that leftover adrenaline from skating."

"So you jumped his bones?"

"It was more the other way around."

"I don't believe this." Then a memory kicked in. "Oh, wow. You have red hair."

"Yeah? It's how most people tell us apart."

"Plus, I'm taller."

"A single inch. Get over it."

"You slept with Hunter."

Sinclair responded with a secretive smile.

"Is this in some way going to screw up my life?" asked Kristy.

"Relax," said Sinclair. "We're both grown-ups, and it was a one-time, impetuous thing."

"You're not going to call him?"

"Not in a million years. It wasn't that good."

"It was so."

"Okay, it was. But I'm not going to call him. Quit worrying. Phone me from London. And take the cool clothes!"

* * *

"Fallen for your wife yet?" asked Hunter, sauntering into Jack's study in the early afternoon.

For a split second Jack wondered if Hunter had found out about his phone call this morning to Zenia Topaz, and the huge favor he'd just called in. But then he realized his cousin was only fishing.

He pointedly opened a financial report on a beauty products company acquisition that Cleveland was considering. "Don't you have work to do?"

Hunter shrugged, stopping in front of the desk. "I'm on holiday."

"Then how come I'm not?"

"Because you're a workaholic?" Hunter picked up a round, crystal paper weight and tossed it from hand to hand. "Or maybe it's because you're trying to keep your mind off a certain knockout blonde who's making you crazy."

Jack scoffed away the notion. "In case you haven't noticed, that knockout blonde is married to me…and sleeping with me." The last part was only technically true, of course. But Hunter didn't need to know that.

"Back to my original question," said Hunter, "have you fallen for your wife yet?"

Jack glanced back down at the spreadsheet, pushing aside images of Kristy asleep in his bed. "Absolutely not."

Only a fool would fall for his bride of convenience. Naturally, he wanted to make love with her. Who wouldn't? And he wanted her to succeed—as much for Sierra Sanchez as anything. But he was a long way from feeling more than lust, admiration and respect.

"If you're sure," said Hunter.

"I'm sure," said Jack.

Hunter set down the paperweight. "The moms wanted

me to remind you about the sleigh ride tonight. Seven sharp."

"I'll remember," Jack assured him.

Hunter moved to the doorway and stood there for a moment. "Mind if Kristy rides with me?"

Jack felt as if he'd been punched in the solar plexus. He glance sharply at his cousin. "Yes." *Hell, yes.* He bit back an order for Hunter to keep away.

A knowing grin grew on Hunter's face. "Gotcha," he exclaimed, backing out before Jack could form a response.

Not that there was any response Jack could reasonably form. Because Hunter was right to laugh at him. He was feeling entirely too possessive of Kristy. He was beginning to act as if she was his real wife. In fact, he was beginning to *wish* she was his real wife.

He turned back to the financial report, forcing the unsettling thought from his mind.

KRISTY SHOVED Sinclair and Hunter, and Sinclair's cavalier advice from her mind for the day. She had more pressing issues, like struggling to perfect the Irene collection and watching the clock until it was time for Isabella and Megan to head home. She couldn't wait to talk to Jack.

Jack.

She smiled just thinking about being held in his arms again. Then she got a hollow feeling in the pit of her stomach when she thought about the holidays ending.

Christmas Day was rushing up on them. And she was leaving the day after that. She'd already filled out a dozen forms for London, and her trunks were being shipped at the end of the week. The collection would be sent on a transport plane to meet up with her at the event. Cleveland had insisted on buying her a first-class ticket, accommodations at the luxury Claymore Diamond Hotel and limo service to and from the airport.

As she closed the last of the cupboards and drawers, she heard bells jingling outside. Then footsteps bounded up the stairs and Jack stuck his head in through the doorway. "You ready?"

"For what?"

"A one-horse open sleigh."

"Really?"

"Well, two horses. We're going along the river trail."

The harness bells jingled louder.

Kristy smiled to herself, forgetting about the end of their relationship, forgetting everything but the night stretching out in front of her. A romantic sleigh ride. What a perfect place to tell Jack she was on board, she wanted to pretend their marriage was real for a while.

"Let me grab my coat," she said.

"I've got gloves and a hat waiting for you downstairs."

Zipping up, she all but bounced down to the driveway where, to her disappointment, she noticed each sleigh held four people.

Cleveland, Aunt Gwen and Melanie were in the front sleigh with Hunter, while Jack and Kristy were riding with his mother and Elaine.

"You're in for a treat," said Elaine as Jack helped her up and over the lip of the sleigh. "The neighbors have a decorating competition every year."

"I can't wait," said Kristy, swallowing her disappointment and pasting a smile on her face. "Hello, Liza."

"I see you've been working hard," Liza responded with formality.

"I have a lot to do," said Kristy.

"I notice the jet's been busy—"

"Mother," said Jack, taking his own seat.

"I'm simply pointing out that Kristy has a fine selection of materials to work with."

"That I do," agreed Kristy, deciding to ignore Liza's jabs. "Thanks to Jack." She patted his thigh as he spread a plaid wool blanket over their laps.

He shot her a look of surprise. She kept her expression neutral as the horses stepped forward and the sleigh jerked to a glide.

Elaine and Liza were facing rear with an identical blanket covering their legs. A top-hatted driver sat up front on a raised seat, while two tawny-colored, golden-maned Clydesdales shook their heads and jingled the bells on their harnesses.

Settled against Jack's warmth, Kristy accepted the delay in her seduction plans and sat back to enjoy the view of the Oslands' gardens as they made their way toward the river trail.

Tiny white lights trimmed the branches of bare oak trees, while swooping ropes of color lined the hedges. Snow-covered spotlights gave the frozen fountains an incandescent glow. And, in the middle of it all, one huge pine tree sparkled color and shine all the way up to a golden star on top.

Kristy rested her head on Jack's shoulder. In response, he stretched his arm across the bench seat behind her.

"I've been thinking about a party," said Liza.

Jack looked at his mother. "I thought we were doing the big Christmas dinner this year."

"I don't mean a Christmas party," she responded. "I mean a wedding party."

Kristy straightened.

"People will expect something," Liza continued. "Perhaps at the Club, after the holidays."

"Mom, I'm not sure that's a good—"

"Nonsense." Liza interrupted. "You cheated Kristy out of a wedding."

"It wasn't him," Kristy put in.

"You told me he talked you into the hotel chapel," said Elaine.

Kristy glanced guiltily at Jack. She had decided to stick to the truth as much as possible. "But I wasn't holding out for a big wedding."

Liza and Elaine waited for her to elaborate.

"It was, uh, more the length of…"

Jack gave her shoulder a squeeze. "She couldn't decide whether to settle for me."

Kristy shot a glance skyward. "Nice, Jack."

"What?"

"You just told your mother I thought you weren't good enough."

Liza's lips pursed.

Elaine started to chuckle. "He's not."

"Yeah, right," said Kristy, with an exaggerated sigh. "Handsome, rich, intelligent and funny. I guess I was holding out for somebody who could also—I don't know—sing opera."

Elaine laughed again, and even Liza smiled.

"I can sing," insisted Jack.

"And that's what clinched it, darling," Kristy purred.

"Back to the party," said Liza. But she seemed more relaxed now.

"Look," Jack called, pointing across the river to a resplendent Santa display. The lighted reindeer swooped through the air. Santa's sleigh was festooned with red and green and white lights. The jolly old man himself glowed with tiny red lights that outlined his suit and his sack full of toys. In the background was a lighted Christmas forest— each tree glowing its very own color.

"Nice," said Kristy. "Times Square has nothing on you guys."

"It's most definitely a competition," said Jack. "As far back as I can remember, the Smythes tried to outdo the Comptons who tried to outdo the Baileys and so on."

"Has your family always spent Christmas here?" Kristy asked everyone in general, hoping to keep talk away from anything wedding-related.

"Since we were kids," answered Elaine.

"Hunter's family, too," Jack said.

The horses made their way past discrete pot lights lining the pathway, moving toward the faint glow of the next property.

"How does your family celebrate, Kristy?" asked Liza.

"Our Christmases were nothing like this," Kristy answered. "We had a house in Brooklyn. Nice neighborhood, plenty of decorations, even carolers—"

Jack took her hand in his beneath the blanket. His gaze caught hers, his eyes darker than usual, the muffled sound of the horses' hooves and the muted snatches of voices from the other sleigh filled the sharp, sweet air.

A rich, steady burn started in the center of her body. It radiated out, fingers of heat licking at her skin. She wanted to tell him she was in. She wanted to tell him so, for now and for later, for as many days as they had left. They could laugh, kiss, make love and sleep in each others' arms.

Another resplendent estate came into view.

Liza and Elaine craned their necks.

Unable to wait any longer, Kristy stretched up to whisper in Jack's ear. "Yes."

He jerked back, staring down at her with wide eyes.

She gave him a nod and a secretive smile.

He squeezed her hand. Then he pulled her close, the warmth of his body seeping deeply into hers.

CHAPTER TEN

KRISTY barely remembered the rest of the sleigh ride, and dinner had taken forever. Their gazes had practically melted each other over crème brûlée and cognac. But if anybody noticed, they were too polite to say.

They were also too polite to make a comment when Jack declared bedtime at nine-twenty-seven.

Kristy forced herself to say a measured good-night, happy that Liza seemed to be starting to like her, and that she'd agreed to postpone talk of a wedding party until after the New Year. Elaine's eyes twinkled when they met Kristy's, but Kristy couldn't bring herself to care. She was too busy struggling to keep from sprinting up the stairs.

The second the bedroom door was shut behind them, Jack pulled her into his arms. His openmouthed kiss was instantaneous. She answered in kind as his fingers fumbled with the buttons of her blouse.

She pushed his suit jacket off his shoulders, frantically working on his shirt as they gasped and kissed then kissed again. She yanked her arms out of the blouse, letting it drop to the floor. He snapped off her bra, then cradled her face with his palms, kissing her over and over and over.

When he finally drew back, it was to rip off his shirt.

Then he shucked his pants and fisted his hands in the fabric of her skirt, pulling it higher and higher, revealing her white silk panties, then slipping his thumbs beneath the delicate elastic.

She spread her palms across his broad chest, reveling in the texture of his muscles, stroking up to his shoulders, then down again, further and further, until he gasped and his hands gripped her buttocks.

"Don't," he pleaded.

"Why not?" She wanted him, wanted him right here, right now, right this instant.

In answer, he scooped her into his arms and deposited her on the bed. Then he pushed her skirt up to her waist and stripped off her panties in one swift motion.

"Too fast for you?" he rasped.

"Not fast enough." While he watched, gaze burning hot, she let her thighs drift apart, her feet dangle off the edge of the high mattress. She slowly, sensually raked spread fingers through her hair, loosening the ponytail, then dropped her hands to rest beside her head.

Jack squeezed his eyes shut and groaned.

He joined her on the bed, his palm covering her mound, his fingers sliding slickly and surely inside.

She arched her hips. "Yes."

He kissed her shoulder, her neck, her breast, increasing his rhythm as he drew a beaded nipple into his mouth.

"Now," she begged. "Please, now."

"Not yet," he rumbled, slowing down, feathering more kisses along her sensitive skin, whispering erotic promises in her ear.

She writhed against him, her hands grasping sections of the downy quilt.

His mouth moved to hers. He shifted across her, one

thigh replacing the hand that was driving her insane. She welcomed his weight, wrapped her arm around him, stroked her palms down his back, lower to his buttocks, pulling him to her, urging him inside.

He paused to gaze into her eyes. They hovered there, frozen for a heartbeat.

"Kristy," he breathed.

Then he pressed surely and swiftly into her, and her world turned to a kaleidoscope of sensations.

She brought her legs around his waist, and her arms around his neck, plastering her body against his, smelling his musk, tasting the salt of his skin, hearing the rasp of his labored breathing and feeling, oh, yes, feeling the slick heat of his body as he moved endlessly with hers on a plane above paradise.

He held her there. Held her, held her, held her until her body wanted to scream for mercy. Every nerve ending tingled. Every pore opened wide. Every ounce of hormone and passion her body possessed gathered and crested and hung suspended in space and time.

Then he cried her name again, and the dam burst free. Convulsions of color galloped through her mind over and over again.

Moments later, her muscles gave out. She all but melted into the mattress, Jack's body a delicious weight pressing her into the soft oblivion.

"You okay?" came his hoarse voice.

"Yes." She tried to nod, but something got lost in the message from her brain. She couldn't move an inch.

"Seriously," he said.

"Seriously," she assured him.

He took a couple more deep, shuddering breaths. "I didn't remember *that*," he rumbled.

"I remember something," she said, her strength slowly returning. "But I didn't remember a super nova and angels singing. Do you suppose we're dead?"

He chuckled, his entire body shaking in reaction. "If this is dead, I can handle it."

"Yeah. Me, too," she sighed.

He shifted his weight from her, holding her securely in his arms. "But I hope it's not."

"I'd hate to miss London."

They were both silent for a moment, and his fingertips toyed with a lock of her hair.

"How's that going?" he asked.

Kristy felt a twinge of unease. "I really appreciate everything you've bought me. Really I do."

"But…"

"It's hard."

They were both silent again, and she turned her head so that she could look at him. "It's really hard."

"Can I help?"

She shook her head. "You've done so much already."

"I want to help," he said.

"It's nothing you can find or buy. It's the clothes, the designs." How could she explain?

"You don't think they're good enough?"

"I don't know what to think."

Jack wrapped her in a big hug. "It's going to be okay."

She could feel a tear at the corner of her eye. "What if it's not? I've spent all your money—"

"You haven't spent all my money. You couldn't begin to spend all my money."

He kissed her forehead. "It'll be better in the morning."

"How?" She'd still have two collections. She'd still be confused and pulled in opposite directions.

"I'm not sure." He sounded a bit sad. "But it will be. It always is."

Kristy wanted to argue, but there was no point. Despite Sinclair's optimism, Kristy feared the clothes that made her happy would never sell. And the clothes that would sell would never make her happy.

AT THE END OF another long sewing day, Kristy made her way from the workshop to the house. Lights lined the curving driveway, delineated the porch and the roof line, and dotted every tree and shrub within a hundred yards of the main staircase.

Snowflakes floated down from the dark sky, settling on the naked oak tree branches, blurring the points of colored light and adding to the magic of the front garden.

Suddenly, she saw Jack.

He'd been waiting for her, sitting on the steps in his beautiful black wool coat and black leather gloves.

"Hey," she said, mustering some enthusiasm into her voice. She shouldn't have confessed her fears last night. The last thing she wanted was for Jack to think she couldn't pull off a collection for the contest.

"Hey, yourself," he stood and trotted down the stairs to meet her.

His dark hair was perfectly combed, face freshly shaven. It wasn't an unusual look for him, but she didn't remember there being a Christmas event tonight.

"I have a surprise for you," he said, taking her arm to guide her up the stairs.

Kristy resisted. "What kind of a surprise?"

"I need you to go upstairs and get dressed."

"Are we going somewhere?"

"We're staying in."

"Just you and me?" If so, why did she need to dress up? They'd be naked pretty soon if the look in his eyes was anything to go by.

"And a few others," he said. "It's a dinner party." He held her hand. "Come on."

This time, she followed him up the stairs, through the door, into the foyer that was festooned with pine garland, holly wreaths and white tapered candles.

"Why all the secrecy?" she asked as they headed up the main staircase.

"Because that's how you do a surprise."

"I feel silly."

"Well, you're about to feel great. Because that's what all the best surprises do for you." He paused at his bedroom door. "And *I* do really good surprises."

She couldn't help but smile at his self-confidence.

"To start," he said, pushing open the door. "A dress."

Kristy stopped to admire the lovely black silk dress with red spaghetti straps and piping, and a chiffon overskirt.

"It's a Zenia Topaz," he said.

"I know," said Kristy, moving forward. "I love her work."

"Good. Now, put it on."

Kristy took a quick shower, refreshed her makeup, brushed her hair, and slipped into the silky-soft creation. It fitted perfectly.

"How did you do this?" she whispered to Jack, turning so he could fasten the buttons.

"It was easy." His hands were warm against her skin, and he kissed the tip of her shoulder when he was done.

Then he reached around her, holding a long aqua box in front of her eyes.

"This goes with it," he said softly.

"I can't," she shook her head, recognizing the big, white bow that was Tiffany's signature.

"Ahh, but you must." He pulled the end of the bow.

She watched, mesmerized, as the ribbon fell away and he reached around with his other hand to open the box.

"It goes with the dress," he said, revealing a delicate choker of large, square-cut rubies.

"Jack," she breathed in astonishment. He made it so hard for her to remember reality.

"You'll be glad you did," he said, removing the necklace from the box. "Trust me on this." He fastened it around her neck.

She knew she should refuse, but she had a feeling it would be futile. Then, she turned to look in the mirror, and she no longer wanted to refuse. The necklace was stunning against her throat.

"Shall we go to dinner?" he gently asked.

She took a very deep breath, sliding into the fantasy. She was Mrs. Osland for tonight, and for tomorrow night and for three more nights after that.

"It's beautiful," she said to Jack.

"You're what's beautiful," he replied, taking her hand and twining her fingers with his.

SHE ENTERED the dining room on Jack's arm.

It was set with white linen and sterling silver, with three holly-and-white-candle centerpieces flickering in a line down the middle of the long table.

Cleveland sat at one end, with Liza presiding at the other. Elaine, Hunter, Melanie and Aunt Gwen were also present, along with a diminutive woman whom Kristy vaguely recognized. In her mid-forties, the woman had short, dark hair and a narrow face. Her eyes were a beautiful, deep brown. She was also wearing a—

Kristy nearly staggered to a stop.

Zenia Topaz.

Zenia Topaz was sitting at Jack's dining-room table.

Hunter rose from his chair next to her.

"Zenia," said Jack. "I'd like you to meet Kristy Mahoney. My wife."

Kristy found her voice. "Ms. Topaz, it's an honor—"

"Zenia, please," the woman's laughter tinkled. "The dress looks wonderful on you."

Kristy glanced down. "Did you bring the dress?"

Zenia nodded. "I hope Jack wasn't lying when he said you'd like it."

"No." Kristy shook her head. "I love it. And I'm so happy to meet you."

She couldn't believe she was talking to Zenia Topaz.

Hunter moved to one side and gestured to the chair he'd been occupying. "Please, Kristy. Sit."

She glanced at Jack.

"You're the guest of honor," he said.

"Zenia's the guest of honor." Kristy accepted Hunter's offer and smiling a greeting at the others around the table, she sat.

"Red or white, ma'am?" asked one of the stewards.

"Red, thank you," said Kristy as Jack and Hunter took their own seats.

"Jack tells me you're entering Matte Fashion," Zenia said to Kristy.

Other conversations started around the table and blended into the background as the staff served a crab salad appetizer.

"I've been working on a collection," Kristy answered.

"Would you mind if I took a look at it?"

Kristy hesitated, but quickly caught herself. "Of course not."

Zenia's dark eyes turned kind. "I understand you're experiencing some frustrations."

Kristy's stomach bottomed out. "Jack told you that?"

"It's why he asked me to come."

Kristy glanced at her husband, not sure whether to be grateful or offended. "He wants you to help me?"

"He thought a professional eye couldn't hurt."

Kristy nodded. It was true, of course. Kind of hard on the ego, but then she was the one who'd expressed her doubts to him.

Then, an idea took root in Kristy's mind. She could show Zenia the fantasy collection. If Zenia liked it, Kristy would have an ally. And there was a chance, a good chance, that Zenia could sway Jack.

Kristy felt a surge of hope.

She couldn't wait to finish dinner and get out to the workshop.

KRISTY STARTED with Irene's collection.

"Very nice," said Zenia with a nod, closely examining the last piece.

Dinner over, she and Kristy were alone in the workshop.

"It has extremely strong technical merit," Zenia continued, motioning to the pieces set up on mannequins. "I like the lines. You were wise to stick to the classics. I particularly like the tailoring on the blouse, and the sleeve detail definitely lifts it from the ordinary."

Kristy tried to pay attention to the analysis, but her mind was galloping ahead to Zenia's reaction to the fantasy collection.

"You might want to rework the bathing suit," said Zenia,

moving to look at it. "It's fun, but it's out of step with the other pieces. Have you thought about a single color instead of a print?"

Kristy nodded. But her gaze strayed to the furthest closet.

"You could go with two contrasting colors." Zenia pointed to a blue square on the geometric pattern. Then she pointed to a red line. Red on top, blue on the bottom?"

"Sure."

Zenia peered at her. "Is everything okay?"

Kristy nodded.

"You seem distracted."

Kristy swallowed, and her heart rate increased. She told herself it was now or never. "There's something—" Her voice rasped over her dry throat. "Would you mind looking at something else?"

"Not at all."

Kristy walked to the closet, forcing herself to measure her steps, her heartbeat deep and thick inside her chest. Sweat was breaking out on her palms. She opened the door and retrieved the waterfall dress.

"They're something…" she said to Zenia as she carried it across the room "…something I've been, you know," she laughed nervously, "just playing around with." She hung the dress on a rack then went back for the next piece.

Zenia cocked her head as the collection grew.

Once Kristy had all the pieces out, Zenia walked around the rack with a piercing stare.

After a full minute's silence, Zenia finally spoke. "I think," she said, and then she paused.

Kristy held her breath.

"It's a risk," said Zenia. "For a new designer."

"Can I take a risk?" asked Kristy.

What was the difference between risk and imagination?

How did you get the sparkle without taking a risk? Why were all these people telling her to get creative and then advising her to stick with the standard?

Zenia paused again, clearly searching for words. "Later in your career, perhaps. Especially if you establish yourself in Europe and you're looking for a high-end niche. But you're probably not going to find really broad appeal in the domestic market with this."

Kristy nodded, biting her tongue against the arguments that formed in her heart.

"Have I disappointed you?"

Kristy shook her head, then she stopped. "Maybe just a little."

"It's a tough business."

"I'm definitely learning that."

"You have to be flexible starting out. And it helps to have the hide of a rhino."

Kristy tried to smile at the joke. But she was tired of being flexible, tired of taking other people's advice. She knew how Jack felt about experts but, honestly, she wished somebody would give her a smidgen of credit occasionally.

"You have a solid start here," said Zenia, turning back to the Irene collection. "Win or lose, take advantage of the Breakout Designer Contest to start establishing yourself. I'll be there cheering for you. And I know you have a huge supporter in Jack."

"Jack's been amazing," Kristy agreed.

She knew now it was Zenia who'd chosen the fabric and accessories that had arrived in a steady stream from Europe. She knew now that Zenia and Jack were friends, and that Jack had enlisted Zenia's aid.

She should be more grateful.

She owed it to Jack to be a lot more grateful.

CHAPTER ELEVEN

JACK stroked his fingertip along the curve of Kristy's shoulder, simply because he liked touching her skin.

"You're quiet tonight," he said softly, inhaling the scent of her hair, enjoying the feel of her naked body against his in the afterglow of their lovemaking.

"I guess I've been working hard," she responded.

There were only two days left before they said their final goodbyes and she flew to London for the contest. They'd have Christmas Eve and Christmas Day together—that was all. She was flying out on the twenty-sixth, and he was purposely ignoring the meaning of that moment.

"Jack?" She turned onto her back, staring up at him, her cheeks flushed. She looked very serious. "Can I ask you something?"

Did he dare hope? Would she broach the future? Because he'd been thinking about their future a whole lot lately. He hoped they had one.

"It's about the contest."

Not quite what he'd been expecting. But, okay.

He nodded.

She sat up, wrapping the sheet around her naked breasts. "I have these ideas."

He waited.

She laughed nervously. "Well, really, they're…" She stopped talking.

"Yes?"

She bit her bottom lip. "I made some clothes."

"I know," he said slowly.

She frowned. "I made some other clothes."

He struggled to understand her point.

She reached out and touched his forearm. "I had some ideas that were different than Irene's. So I made them. And I like them. And I want to show them in London."

"Where in London?" He could probably help.

"At the contest."

"At Matte Fashion?"

She gave a rapid nod.

"But you already have a collection for Matte Fashion."

"I want to show a different one."

Jack didn't know what to say. It was only forty-eight hours before she'd be in London. "Irene helped you with this one. Zenia helped you, too."

"Hear me out."

He cocked his head sideways, biting back the obvious arguments.

"I think mine—the other outfits—are better. I really do. Everybody keeps asking me for sparkle. I think these have sparkle."

This was crazy. "Has anyone seen them besides you? Has Cleveland?"

"Zenia saw them."

"And, did she like them?"

"She wasn't really clear. She said they were a risk."

Jack sighed. "Kristy, I think *risk* is a euphemism for 'weak'."

"Not necessarily."

"Kristy—"

"Not necessarily, Jack. What if they're a good risk? I feel…" She pressed her palm against her chest. "In here, Jack. I can't explain it, but I fell like I *know*. You know?"

Jack had to nip this in the bud. He couldn't let Kristy go out there and embarrass herself. And he sure wouldn't let her compromise Sierra Sanchez.

"I was paying her to be here," he said. "She knew you were my wife. So of course she's going to be polite."

Kristy squared her bare shoulders. "So, you don't believe in me."

"Of *course* I believe in you."

"No. You believe in yourself. If you truly believed in me, you'd take a chance. You can't always do the safe thing, Jack."

The safe thing? Jack came into a sitting position. "When have I ever done the safe thing around you?"

"Marrying me wasn't mitigating risk?"

"You know what I thought back then."

"Yes, I do know what you thought," she said. "And you were mitigating the risk to your family."

Okay, he'd agree with that. Not that it was a crime.

"And you've been mitigating it ever since."

Now *that* he could not agree with. "I haven't been doing anything ever since."

She held out one arm expansively. "You bought me the finest materials, the finest equipment, the finest advice and assistance."

"And this is a problem, why?"

"Because you practically hired a babysitter in Zenia. You built me a safety net ten miles wide."

"That's what you do when the stakes are high. You play

it safe." He was making good business decisions, simple as that.

"No, that's not what you do when the stakes are high."

"And this is based on your years of experience dealing in high stakes?"

She sat back, compressing her lips. "There's no need to get insulting."

"I'm not—"

"You hired me to do a job," she tersely reminded him. "It would be nice if you'd let me do it."

"We *did* let you do it." The woman had been sewing for three weeks straight.

"No, you didn't. You were so busy circling the wagons—"

"That's ridiculous."

"No…" Her voice trailed away, and a faraway look came into her eyes. "In fact, it's all been pretty insulting."

His spine stiffened. "So sorry to have *insulted* you."

She gave a chopped laugh. "You know, now that I think about it, I was so busy convincing myself to be grateful, that I didn't even see you were smothering me."

Oh, so now he was smothering her? "Did you happen to *see* that I was spending a fortune? Or did you happen to *see* that you were consuming a fortune?"

She clamped her mouth shut.

He figured he'd made his point. But then her eyes turned to green fire, and he realized how harsh their words had become. They were practically yelling at each other.

He didn't want that.

He didn't want to fight with her, and he didn't want to hurt her. All he wanted was for her to be happy.

"Can we please stop?" he asked.

The fight seemed to go out of her, and her voice dropped to a whisper. "No. I don't think we can."

"I don't want to fight with you, Kristy."

"You simply want to do things your way?"

Well, yeah. That was basically what he had in mind.

His expression must have said as much because she shrank back.

"Kristy." He reached for her, but she was too fast.

She was off the bed, dragging the sheet with her. "I need to go," she choked out.

"We can talk about this."

"Talk about what? We can't talk about my career. Shall we talk about how you want to sleep with me, but it's only temporary?"

He opened his mouth to protest, but she kept talking.

"I thought it wouldn't matter, Jack. I thought I could take your money and your great sex, and whatever crumbs of respect you threw my way."

Crumbs? *Crumbs?* He'd given her everything that was in his power to give.

"But, I can't," she said. "I just—"

"Fine," he cut her off, his instincts turning to self-protection. "If you want it to end, by all means, pick a guest room. You've done your duty and then some."

He looked away, clenching his fists, ordering himself not to beg her to stay.

IT WAS FOUR in the morning on Christmas Day when Kristy finished packing the shipping trunks. She needed some kind of closure, and the simple work also kept her from trudging back to the lonely guest room.

She took one last, long look at her waterfall dress, the hot-air-balloon pants, the sunset and casino dresses, the bikini and the roulette evening gown. With a lump in her throat, she closed the trunk, leaving it with the boxes Isabella had agreed to ship to her in New York after the holidays. The other collection would come with her.

She told herself the Irene collection would be fine. It was a strong entry and a really great step for a young designer like her. She could make some connections at the show, build on the technical merit Zenia had seen in the collection, maybe get a chance to do something more creative in the future. Maybe she could even show the desert collection.

She'd see Zenia in London at the show, and Cleveland would fly over to represent Sierra Sanchez. But, after today, Kristy would likely never see Jack again.

She told herself it was for the best. What they'd had together wasn't real. It had never been real. It had started on a lie and gone downhill from there.

She latched the last trunk, shrugged into her coat, then wandered down the stairs and outside to the spectacular, twinkling gardens and the softly sprinkling snow. It was turning into a picture-perfect Christmas Day.

Her boots crunched on the driveway as she passed lighted trees, sweeping arches and the meticulously decorated porch and pillars that flanked the double doors. A wreath of boughs and pine cones hung on each one, encircling the polished brass knockers.

Kristy carefully pressed on the left-hand door. The hinges glided open, revealing the festooned, marble entryway. All was still and silent. It was as if the entire house held its breath waiting for Christmas Day to burst upon it.

Even though she was feeling tired and melancholy, Kristy couldn't resist a peek into the great room. A fifteen-foot tree overwhelmed one corner. A huge array of brightly decorated presents stretched halfway into the room, all but burying the stone fireplace. The tree lights were still on, and Kristy smelled fragrant smoke.

Her attention moved to a wisp of white curling into the air from a leather wing chair. It was Hunter.

"Hey," he greeted quietly.

"Hey," she responded, moving to the opposite chair. She had to pick her way around a couple of gifts to get there.

"You're still up?" he asked, swirling a measure of deep amber cognac in a blown crystal snifter. The cognac bottle and a tray with three other glasses sat on the low table between the chairs.

"I was in the workshop." She plunked down.

He held up the cigar. "You mind?"

Kristy shook her head.

Hunter leaned forward and poured a measure of the cognac into a new glass, handing it to Kristy. The fire crackled, and sparks flew off the wood, pinging against the glass front.

"Your last full day," he said.

"It is," Kristy agreed.

He raised his glass in a silent toast, watching her expression carefully.

"Merry Christmas, Kristy Mahoney."

She followed suit. "Merry Christmas to you, Hunter Osland." She took a sip of the expensive cognac.

He considered her over the rim of his glass. "You moved out of his room."

"It was time for me to go."

"But you moved out early."

She shrugged.

"Why?"

She shrugged again.

"Are you in love with him?"

Kristy nearly dropped the glass. "No."

She wasn't in love with Jack. He had simply shown his true colors—absolute allegiance to his corporation, his family and his precious experts.

"You married him," said Hunter.

"That was infatuation. Nobody falls in love in a weekend." She knew that. She'd always known that. She'd just forgotten it for a little while.

"I guess not. I am sorry you got hurt."

"I'm not hurt," she lied.

They both stared silently at the fire.

"What about you?" Kristy finally asked.

"Nothing hurts me."

"You ever been in love?"

He shook his head.

Kristy couldn't help but smile to herself. "Not even with the redheaded girl?"

"Not even with her."

"You know, Sinclair is a redhead."

He turned to Kristy. "Sinclair has a big mouth. And it's auburn."

"So you've noticed."

"I also noticed she's bossy and judgmental."

"Well, if you're going to get picky about it." A slow smile grew on Kristy's face. It felt like the first time she'd smiled in days.

Hunter frowned in return and polished off the cognac.

"We have twin uncles," Kristy noted.

"Kristy."

"I'm just saying, from a gypsy perspective…"

"Go to bed."

She rose and set down her snifter. "And, of course, there's Sinclair and me."

Hunter did a double take. "What?"

"Sinclair and I are twins."

"No, you're not."

"I'm pretty sure we are."

"You're taller."

"We're not identical."

He stared at her for a moment. "Really?"

Kristy leaned into him, stretching her smile from ear to ear. After the past couple of days, it felt good to goof around with somebody. "So, you see, Hunter, it's fate."

A wolfish grin grew on Hunter's face. "Maybe the gypsy didn't mean a redhead with twins. Maybe I get twin redheads. You could dye your hair."

"No, she couldn't," came Jack's deep, censorious voice.

Kristy reflexively jumped back.

"We're just messing around," said Hunter.

"So, I see," Jack growled, glaring at his cousin.

"Don't do this." Kristy scoffed.

He paced into the room. "Don't do what? Interrupt your late-night chat?"

"You know it's nothing."

"I do?"

Hunter came to his feet. "It's nothing, Jack. Trust her, don't trust her. But trust me. It's nothing."

Jack stared at Hunter as the silence thickened.

"Guess I'll head upstairs," Hunter finally offered.

"Good idea," said Jack, shifting his gaze to Kristy.

"I'll come with you," said Kristy.

"I'd like to talk to you," said Jack.

"It's late."

"No kidding."

She heaved a sigh. "I'm tired, and I really don't want to fight with you."

"Who said anything about fighting?"

"Maybe it's that frown on your face."

Jack spared another glance for his cousin. "Good night, Hunter."

"Right," Hunter muttered, heading for the door.

Kristy crossed her arms protectively over her chest, steeling herself against the familiar pulse of desire, promising to end the conversation quickly so she could climb into bed and bury her head under the covers.

Hunter's footfalls disappeared, and the silence seemed to boom off the walls. Firelight flickered on Jack's hard profile, shimmering in his hair, sparking the depths of his slate gray eyes.

He reached for the cognac bottle and poured himself a drink.

"You said you wanted to talk?" she prompted.

He straightened and drew a deep breath. "I really need you to understand."

"Oh, I do understand," she said.

It wasn't so tough to figure out. She was a distant second to Osland International. Understandable, even logical, but hurtful all the same.

He swirled the cognac in the depths of his glass, watching the amber liquid. "It should have been so simple," he sighed.

"Simple?"

He looked up. "I thought we'd be divorced by now. I thought you'd... I expected..."

She put an edge to her voice. "I'm sorry I disappointed you."

He took a step closer. "That's not my point."

"What is your point?"

"My point…" He gazed into her eyes, searching. "Do you have any idea how much I want you right now?"

Kristy's stomach hollowed, while her chest tightened with undeniable desire. "That's an interesting point," she managed.

"You know what I mean."

"It's over, Jack."

"Really? Because it doesn't feel over."

It had to be over. She'd found the strength to walk away last night, and she had to stay away, no matter what.

"Sleep with me tonight," he rasped. "We don't have to make love—"

"I can't." Her voice caught, emotions raw in her chest. It would kill her to sleep with him one more time. And, if it didn't, it would kill her to walk away again.

His voice went thick with emotion. "We had something, Kristy."

No they didn't, they couldn't.

"This week," he continued. "Last week. Back there in Vegas, we seriously had something."

"What we had, Jack, started with a lie, and then we lived another lie. You wanted to save your grandfather, and I wanted to win a contest. We used each other. I'm not very proud of that, are you?"

"I'm not proud," he said. "I'm a lot of things at the moment, but proud isn't one of them." The defeat in his voice leeched the fight right out of her.

"I'm just tired," she confessed.

Compassion turned his eyes to pewter.

He nodded and polished off the drink.

Then he set the glass down on the table. "And you need to go to bed. So, let me just say…" He drew a deep breath. "Goodbye, Kristy."

She gave him a shaky nod, fighting an instinct that urged her to throw herself into his arms, hang on tight and to never let go. Her throat clogged. She could barely get the words out. "Goodbye, Jack."

They stared at each other for a frozen moment. But then he glanced away, focusing on the fire behind her, and it was well and truly over.

CHAPTER TWELVE

THREE DAYS into the London trip, and Kristy could still see the haunted expression on Jack's face.

"Twelve pounds, ma'am," said the cabdriver, rousing her from her daydream. She realized they'd arrived at the Claymore Diamond Hotel.

She handed the man the fare and what she hoped was an appropriate tip and hopped out of the traditional black car.

Then she stared at the stone facade of the hotel, its lights already burning bright under the gloomy afternoon sky. She'd wandered aimlessly through a couple of museums, burning up time. This afternoon was the dress rehearsal in the convention center connected to the hotel. Tomorrow night was the big event.

She knew she should be feeling some sense of anticipation, certainly the other contestants she'd met were getting more nervous by the hour. But, she still hadn't emotionally engaged in the Irene collection. And, besides, she couldn't seem to get her thoughts off Jack.

Was he still in Vermont? At the mansion with Cleveland and Dee Dee? Had he flown back to L.A., or to New York?

Did he miss her? Did he think about her? Had he figured out what was between them?

Because she hadn't. And, worst of all, would she regret not sharing her last night with him in his bed after all?

JACK WAS GETTING into the limo to head for the airport, when Hunter's bellow stopped him in his tracks.

"You'd better get your butt up here," Hunter called from one of the workshop windows.

"I'll only be a minute," Jack told the uniformed driver.

"Take your time, sir."

"Can you call Simon and give him an update?"

"Yes, sir." The limo driver reached for his cell phone.

Jack slammed the car door then took the workshop stairs two at a time.

"What the hell?" he asked as he walked through the workshop door. "I'm going to miss my meeting in New York."

Hunter gestured to an open trunk of colorful clothes. "Take a look."

Jack stopped short. "Dresses? You called me up here to see dresses?"

"*Kristy's* dresses."

"So, send them to her." Jack was trying desperately not to think about Kristy.

"Not to wear," sneered Hunter. "Do you know what these are?"

Jack knew full well what they were. "Zenia didn't like them," he said.

"And?"

"And nothing. Cleveland made a deal on one set of designs. Irene helped her fix them. Zenia said they were technically strong. While these, these—"

"Are her heart and soul," said Hunter.

Jack flinched.

"She asked you," said Hunter. "She *asked* you."

"Is that what you were cozying up to her about on Christmas Eve?"

Hunter glared daggers. "That's what *her sister* told me."

"Oh."

"Yeah. Oh."

Jack squared his shoulders. "Fine. Is this conversation over?"

"Take the clothes to London," said Hunter.

Jack snorted his disbelief. Like he could drop everything and do that. Like he could compromise Sierra Sanchez's reputation.

"That's something Gramps would do," he said to Hunter.

Hunter took a step forward. "So what?"

"So, I'm not Gramps."

"Maybe not. But, cousin, you need to ask yourself some very serious questions."

Jack turned and started to walk away. He was done here.

"Do you want respect for your business?" called Hunter. "Or do you want Kristy?"

Jack kept walking.

"Do you want more fashion sales? Or do you want Kristy?"

Jack paused at the door, bracing a hand on the jamb.

"Do you want the family fortune? Or do you want Kristy?"

Kristy. There wasn't a doubt in Jack's mind. But how could he give in on every front just to make her happy?

"What if they're good?" Hunter asked softly. "What if *she's* good? What if she's *great* and you took that chance away from her?"

Jack scrambled to weigh the facts. Irene said she was competent. Zenia said the dresses were risky. Everything inside Jack screamed at him to listen to the experts. He always listened to experts. They had the facts, knew the odds, were always right.

"Stop it!" shouted Hunter.

"What?"

"Stop talking yourself out of it."

"I can't."

"Well then here's one for you. What if she loves you?" Jack faced his cousin.

"She married you," said Hunter. "Somehow Kristy doesn't strike me as the kind of woman who does that lightly. What if she fell in love with you that weekend in Vegas? What if, against all odds, with all the crap you've pulled, she's still in love with you? What do your experts say about that?"

"Who are the experts in love?" Jack all but yelled. "The gypsies?"

"I'd like to think," came Cleveland's level voice from the doorway. "That *I'm* the expert in matters of love."

Jack turned.

With Dee Dee tucked predictably under his arm, Gramps advanced into the room. "You boys both know I've been married a number of times."

"Yeah, Gramps," said Hunter, calmly. "We know."

"And I bet you're wondering how I feel when the young lady and I part ways."

Jack had never once wondered that.

"I feel great," said Cleveland. "There are never any hard feelings. No tears. Everyone has a good time. I never give her another thought."

He walked past Jack and peered into the open trunk. "They're fancy. I'll give her that."

Then he straightened and stood toe-to-toe with Jack,

looking his square in the eye. "How 'bout you, boy. You given Kristy another thought since she left?"

Jack didn't answer. He'd done nothing *but* think about Kristy since the moment she'd left the mansion.

"If not," said Cleveland. "Then you both got what you wanted." He glanced at the trunk again. "Sort of. But if you're thinking about her. If missing her is gnawing at your guts, and if you'd give anything to hear her voice or hold her in your arms again. Well, then you've got a problem. Because you're in love, and you've just screwed yourself out of the woman of your dreams."

Cleveland looked down at Dee Dee, ruffling the little dog's head. "Isn't that right, Pookie? Uncle Jack blew it with your mama."

Something that felt like an iceberg slid into Jack's chest and parked itself next to his heart. He stared at Hunter, and Hunter stared back.

"It's noon," said Hunter. "Do the math. You can make it if Simon fuels up now."

Not giving himself another moment to hesitate, Jack grabbed his cell phone, hitting the speed dial for Simon.

"Yes, sir?" came Simon's voice.

"Refile the flight plan. We're going to London."

"Will do. Do you have an ETA for the airport?"

"Twenty minutes."

"Roger that."

Jack flipped his phone shut.

Hunter snapped the catches on the trunk. "Grab an end."

WITH KRISTY'S trunk safely on a delivery truck at Heathrow, Hunter taking care of business back in New York and Zenia on deck for the switch off at tonight's fashion event, Jack climbed into the back of the waiting Rolls.

"The Claymore Diamond Hotel, please."

The driver nodded his acknowledgment and closed the door behind Jack.

Jack knew he should try to rest to combat the jet lag, but he was too excited at the possibility of seeing Kristy again.

Could Hunter be right? Was there a chance she was in love with him? If she was, she could make any damn fashion collection she wanted. He'd pay for it. Hell, he'd pay people to wear it if that's what it took to make her happy.

But first, he had to convince her to give him a chance. And that meant starting from scratch, doing it right this time.

He called out to the driver. "Excuse me?"

The man glanced in the rearview mirror. "Yes, sir?"

"Can we make a stop at Tiffany's?"

"Very good, sir."

"Thanks." Jack nodded. Hopefully, a two-carat, flawless solitaire engagement ring would start things off on a new, positive note.

"DON'T WORRY about the necklace," said Zenia. "They need you out front right away."

Kristy glanced around at the frantic buzz of the dressing rooms ten minutes before the Breakout Designer Contest. Elbow to elbow, makeup artists and hairdressers put the final touches on the models, seamstresses took care of last-minute repairs, and the technical staff shouted instructions or talked into their headsets. Photographers made their way between the rows of onlookers, searching for that potential cover shot. The lighting technicians were ready, music had been cued and the announcer was flipping through his notes, confirming last-minute changes to the program.

The show's stage manager negotiated a path through the chaos. "Contestants in their seats, please. The news networks will want footage."

Zenia gave Kristy a quick hug. Then she stood back and squeezed her cool hands. "You look fantastic."

"Thanks," Kristy whispered.

She'd designed the dress herself. It was the one thing she'd brought to London with her from the desert collection, short and basic black, with small triangles of lace sewn into the hem and neck, and sleeves capped with lace that matched her waterfall dress.

Early this morning, she'd come to terms with her Irene collection. It was technically sound. Zenia had said so herself. And Kristy could build on that. She could take the creativity part slowly, learn to add the sparkle and imagination as she went along. Zenia had suggested the hide of a rhino. Kristy could be a rhino. A rhino brimming with imagination and passion, but stubborn and driven and willing to take on the world. However hard she had to work, whatever it took, she was going after her dream.

The Breakout Designer Contest was televised because viewers liked to see the expressions on the contestant's faces when their fashions were paraded across the catwalk. They particularly liked to see the delight on the winner's face at the end of the evening.

So, along with her eleven fellow contestants, Kristy left the backstage area, took the small, side staircase down to the floor, and slid into her seat in the front row.

A program was handed to her. She flipped through the pages, the buzz of chatter wafting around her as she waited for the opening music.

A calm settled over her as the announcer's voice came through the speakers. The spotlight hit the stage. Kristy had seen the other designers' collections, both in the dressing rooms and at rehearsal. But nothing compared to seeing the creations strutted down the catwalk with the music blaring and a real audience applauding from the seats.

Kristy reached out to congratulate those closest to her as their models went by.

And then it was her turn.

She heard her name, felt the spotlight shift. And right then she didn't care that it was her second choice of a collection. She was part of this fabulous show, and it felt wonderful.

The spotlight hit the model, and Kristy jolted back in her seat, blinking in confusion. Lucinda was wearing the flirty waterfall dress. Kristy's swooping desert stripes glittered under the strong stage lights. The lacy crinoline bounced, showing off the sleek legs of the model.

Lucinda winked at Kristy as she passed by, but Kristy was too astounded to react. How had Zenia done it?

Next came the hot-air-balloon pants, with a pair of strappy black sandals, then the bikini and the sunset dress. By the time her roulette evening gown crossed the stage, Kristy recognized that the applause was strong and steady.

They liked her work.

They respected her talent.

She wanted to run backstage and wrap Zenia in her arms.

The contestant next to Kristy nudged her, and like the others before her, she rose and took a brief bow as the roulette-dress model headed back toward the curtain.

FROM HIS hard folding seat tucked away in a back corner, Jack watched the red evening gown disappear and shook his head in complete amazement.

She was great. She was better than great. And the collection, the collection was *them*. From the hot air balloon in the Grand Canyon to their night at the casino. Kristy had immortalized their whirlwind relationship in fashion.

He'd watched her face all through her part of the show. Her gaze had stayed on the models, and she'd smiled in response to comments from those around her, but he could tell she was still in shock.

God, she was gorgeous. And she was right—he hadn't given her nearly enough credit.

He patted the inside pocket of his suit, trying to figure out what he could possibly say that would convince her to take another chance on him. Things had started off badly between them, and he'd definitely let her down since. But if there was a speech on earth that would win her back, he was going to find it, and he was going to repeat it to her as many times as it took.

AT THE END of the show, the contest director took the stage. She gave a brief speech, congratulating the contestants and thanking the sponsors. She talked about the difficult choices of the judges and the enormous level of talent in the room.

Kristy only half listened.

Even when the drumroll sounded to signify the opening of the judges' decision envelope, her attention was elsewhere. How had Zenia done it? *Why* had she done it? She had to find her and thank her.

"And now," the director's voice boomed, "the winner of this year's Matte Fashion Breakout Designer Contest is—"

She thought she saw Zenia at the side of the stage, and the rest of the words blurred in Kristy's ears.

"Kristy!" hissed the contestant next to her.

"Huh?"

"It's you!"

"What?" She glanced around and realized everyone was applauding madly and staring at her.

"Kristy Mahoney," the contest director repeated.

Kristy's entire body turned numb.

Her neighbor gave her a shove. "Get *up* there!"

Kristy forced herself to stand up on her shaky legs. She found the staircase and made her way to the stage, staring past the smiling director, past the curtain, even past Zenia.

And then she was at the microphone, and the director was shaking her hand. It was overwhelming, and she had no idea what to say.

And the applause was dwindling.

And she was supposed to start talking now.

Luckily, she couldn't see any of the audience members past the bright floodlights, or she probably would have passed out.

"Thank you," she managed, her voice quavering. "Thanks to the judges, to the sponsors, especially to Sierra Sanchez. To Cleveland Osland for believing in me. To Jack and Hunter Osland for their incredible support. And to Zenia Topaz." Kristy paused, gathering her emotions. "Zenia. I can't thank you enough for everything."

Kristy paused long enough that the applause began again. The models gathered around her, looking wonderful in her creations, congratulating her as the audience came to its feet. In her memory, she saw the waterfall, the hot air balloon, the casino and Jack. Jack was everywhere, in everything, and she desperately wanted to see him.

She needed to hear his voice, to feel his arms around her. She needed to taste him, to smell him, to hold him tight against her body long into the night. But mostly, she just needed him to be here, to breathe the same air as her, to tell her what he thought about the show, to tell her what he thought about the world.

Suddenly, she couldn't get off the stage fast enough.

She was going to call him.

No. She was going to fly back to L.A., or to New York, or to wherever he was at the moment. She'd beg him for another chance. The clothes didn't matter. The award didn't matter. All she wanted was Jack.

She made her way off the stage, smiling, automatically responding to people with what she hoped was logic.

She found Zenia and hugged her tight. "How did you do it?"

Zenia drew back from her. "I didn't. It was—"

"Do you have a cell phone?" Kristy interrupted.

"Sure." Zenia produced a phone.

Kristy flipped it open. "I need a plane ticket. I want to go back to New York. Now. Tonight."

Zenia glanced to a spot past Kristy's ear. "Why?"

Kristy looked down at the phone. "It's Jack. I need the number for the airline."

"What about Jack?"

"I love him. I'm in love with him. Oh, Zenia, I never thought I'd say this, but I don't care about the collection. I mean, I'm thrilled." She hugged Zenia again. "And I'm so grateful you brought it. But it doesn't matter. What's the damn phone number of the airline?"

"It wasn't me," said Zenia.

Kristy blinked at her.

"It was Jack."

"What was Jack?"

"Jack sent the collection from Vermont."

Kristy's heart stilled.

"About time I started to get a little credit," said Jack from behind her.

Kristy whirled around in astonishment.

He grinned at her, looking gorgeous and sexy and *here*. So here. He opened his arms, and she threw herself into them.

"How much did you hear?" she demanded.

"That you love me."

Kristy was embarrassed, but she wasn't about to take back the words now. "Eavesdropper," she accused.

"Hell, yeah. It's the only way I learn anything." He winked at Zenia. "Come on," he said to Kristy, taking her hand to lead her through the crowd.

"Where are we going?" Not that she cared. She glanced back to share a smile with Zenia.

"I want to show you something." Jack led her from the backstage area, down a small hallway and past a man in a security blazer.

"Where are you taking me?" she asked.

"Just wait," he answered, as they came out into a round, glassed-in room overlooking a rainswept garden and a group of lighted fountains.

"Hey," said Kristy. "This reminds me of Vegas."

"I know." Jack cracked a self-satisfied smile.

Then he led her to a painted, wrought-iron chair that sat next to the window. With the raindrops splattering on the glass and concrete, he motioned for her to sit down.

She perched on the edge of the chair and crossed her legs, staring into his dark eyes. She loved him so much.

He took a breath. "It occurs to me—" he said, reaching into his jacket pocket and coming down on one knee.

Before the significance of the position could register with Kristy, he revealed a turquoise jewelry box and opened it to expose a huge solitaire diamond ring. "—that I may not have done this right the first time."

Kristy's eyes went wide, first staring at the ring, and then staring at Jack.

"Will you marry me, Kristy? Or at least be kind enough not to divorce me?" He quirked an unexpected grin, leaning closer. "Because I think I figured out what's between us."

She felt her own mouth stretch into a smile. "Yeah? Well it's about time."

"As I recall, you were having the same problem."

"*I* already said it."

He cocked his head. "That was only ten minutes ago. I bought a ring and flew all the way from Manchester."

"Big whoop."

"Is that a yes?"

"Yeah," she told him. "That's a yes." She wrapped her arms around his neck and squeezed him tight. "Yours better be an 'I love you.'"

He rose to his feet, drawing her with him. "Mine's an 'I love you,'" he rumbled. "Mine's an 'I love you so much.'"

He tightened his arms around her waist, and she leaned her cheek against his chest, reveling in the feel of his strong, solid body. She had to blink away a tear.

"I loved your clothes," he rasped against her hair, cradling the back of her head with his palm. "I was so damn proud of you up there."

"You brought me my clothes." Part of her still couldn't believe it had happened.

"Damn straight," he said.

She pulled back to look at him. "But what changed your mind?"

"You changed my mind. Because you were right. I needed to stop playing it safe."

"Damn straight," she said back.

He grinned and placed a quick kiss on her lips. "Once I trusted your instincts, I started trusting my own."

"And?"

"And my instincts brought me right here, to you."

Then he kissed her again, while thunder rumbled in the distance. Raindrops clattered furiously against the glass.

He broke the kiss. "Can we please get this ring on your finger?"

She nodded and held out her hand.

He slipped the ring over her knuckle, anchoring the band in place. "I do love you, Kristy Mahoney."

She held her hand to the light, gazing at the twinkling diamond, joy filling her heart. "I think it's Kristy Osland now."

"Now." He kissed her knuckle above the stone. "And forever."

What She Really Wants for Christmas

DEBBI RAWLINS

Dear Reader,

I loved writing this story. Liza is one of my favourite heroines ever. I admit that when I first realised that Liza was supposed to sue her friends, I was turned off, and didn't know how I could write such a character. How could I bond with a woman like that? Or make her sympathetic to readers?

The hero, Evan, came to the rescue. He's perfect in every way, and I really wanted Liza to deserve him. I wanted him to be perfect for her, too. She needed someone stable and patient, with a good sense of humour. She deserved someone who would accept her unconditionally. Evan has his own baggage to lose, as well. He needed Liza as much as she did him. And when they finally let go, magic happened.

I hope you enjoy their story.

Debbi Rawlins

CHAPTER ONE

Rumor has it that Atlanta's own *Just Between Us,* the three-year-old, sex-themed, hot-topic afternoon television show hosted by Eve Best, is soon going into national syndication. Geared toward women's perspectives and concerns, the local show has garnered a widely growing audience and advertisers have taken notice. While taking on contemporary, cutting-edge topics, Ms. Best's energy and spontaneity has captured the attention of teens and mothers alike.

Recently, however, the local show has drawn a maelstrom of not-so-flattering publicity. Most of you already know about the state lottery win, shared by six employees of the show, including Ms. Best. But what this reporter has just learned is that despite attempts to keep the unpleasantness quiet, a lawsuit filed by a former segment producer, Liza Skinner, has halted the disbursement of the winnings.

According to my source, Ms. Skinner was an original member of the lottery pool before leaving the show nearly a year ago. There is some confusion as to whether she still had money in the pot, but the number 13, which she'd chosen, was among the six winning numbers, and apparently she seems to think she deserves a share.

LIZA QUIT READING the article and threw the copy of last week's *Atlanta Daily News* onto the passenger seat of her compact car. When she got home, she was throwing the tattered paper away. No use continuing to torture herself. The wheels were already in motion. Soon it would all be over. She hoped.

She pushed a shaky hand through her tangled hair and tried to get comfortable—not easy with her long legs. She had no business being here. Her attorney had told her to stay away from the *Just Between Us* studio. At least until her lawsuit was settled. Of course then there'd be no reason to be here, in the parking lot, waiting, like a smitten schoolgirl, for a glimpse of Eve and Jane. No matter which way the suit went, her friends would never speak to her again.

She didn't blame them. All she'd done in the past year was cause them pain. Hadn't they warned her about Rick? From the start, they knew he'd be trouble. They'd been her best friends since the sixth grade, closer to her than anyone in the whole world. Why hadn't she listened to them?

Liza let her head fall back against the worn cloth upholstery and forced herself to breathe. He'd been just her type, wild and sexy and a little dangerous, and she'd thought he was the one. He turned out to be way more dangerous than she'd ever imagined.

Movement caught her eye and she turned her head just in time to see a woman step outside, the sunlight glimmering off her pale-blond hair. She looked like Nicole, the *Just Between Us* segment producer who'd replaced Liza. The woman who was going to get Liza's share of the lottery money. Unless the lawsuit was successful.

God, why didn't they just pay up? It wasn't as if each of them wasn't going to still be filthy rich after coughing up her share. She closed her eyes, blocking out the image of the woman walking toward a red convertible. A reminder of how much Liza had lost. Just another month and it would all be over.

Although, if she had the guts, she could go to Eve and Jane now. Confess everything. The idea took hold and her breathing quickened. Slowly, she opened her eyes. Could it be that simple? After nearly a year of selling her soul? Ha. Sure, confessing would ease her conscience, but that wouldn't solve anything. Eve would still be vulnerable to public humiliation. And it would still be Liza's fault.

She hung her head and stared at her pitiful cuticles. Nowadays she couldn't even afford a manicure. The small inheritance she'd received after her father's death last year was nearly gone and there was rent to pay, attorney's fees and a myriad of other things. But what she resented the most was the money Rick spent on cigarettes, booze and drugs. Money she could've used to buy a better car, live in a better neighborhood.

Maybe when this was over she'd be able to find a decent job. Never one like she had with *Just Between Us*. That had been a dream job. The once-in-a-lifetime kind. She knew because she'd been a part of it from the beginning. Those crazy, fifteen-hour days when none of them knew what they were doing, but they pushed forward, tackling any task they were given, their passion making up for what they'd lacked in experience.

Their hard work had paid off. The show was a huge success. This should have been the best time in Liza's life. But she was no longer a part of her friends' lives or a part of the show. All because of her stupidity. Even if Eve and Jane eventually forgave her, she seriously doubted she could forgive herself.

Eve walked out of the redbrick building, and Liza bit down on her lower lip. The radiance in her friend's face made Liza's stomach knot. Behind her was the reason for Eve's glow. Tall and good-looking, with dark hair, the man put a familiar hand at the small of Eve's back.

Liza had heard Eve had found someone, Mitch Hayes, the guy who had once represented the television network wanting to sign *Just Between Us*. She looked happy. Happier than Liza had ever seen her.

Damn. No way was Liza getting her friends involved now. She'd push for the settlement, pay off Rick and then she'd disappear. Start a new life where no one knew her, where she wouldn't be considered scum of the earth.

And never see her friends again.

Liza squeezed her eyes shut, willing the threatening tears away. At least Eve would be spared any humiliation. A tear escaped and, angry, Liza swiped at it. Crying wouldn't solve a damn thing. Never had. Never would. She scrubbed at her eyes, disgusted at the display of weakness.

And then she heard something. Knocking. At the car window.

Opening her eyes, she swung her face toward the sound. A man with short dark hair and concerned brown eyes stared back at her. It took a moment to recognize him…the doctor who consulted for the medical drama shot in the studio next to *Just Between Us*. Dr. Evan something. He'd asked her to lunch once. She'd blown him off. Sedate and conservative. Definitely not her type.

She took another furtive swipe at her eyes, annoyed that he might have seen her crying. When he motioned for her to let down her window, she was tempted to ignore him. But that was bound to make matters worse, and the last thing she needed was a scene in front of the station.

Lucky she could afford a car at all, she didn't have the luxury of automatic windows and manually rolled it down. He ducked through, gripping the top of the door, and smiled. She didn't.

"Liza, hi." He paused. "Remember me?"

She deliberately frowned and gave a small shake of her head. If the slight embarrassed him, maybe he'd leave her alone.

"Evan Gann." He inclined his head toward the building. "From the studio beside *Just Between Us*."

"Oh, right. You're the consultant."

He nodded, his eyes probing. "I haven't seen you for a while."

"I'm persona non grata around here. Surely, you've heard."

"Ah, the lawsuit." His eyebrows drew together. "I don't know the details—"

"You wanted something?"

His mouth curved in an annoyingly tolerant smile. "I was surprised to see you. Look, you want to have a drink sometime?"

"Why?"

He chuckled. "Because you're attractive and I like you?"

It took Liza a moment to collect herself. Was this guy nuts? He'd probably be banned from the station just for talking to her. She frowned. Except he really wasn't nuts. He was this straightlaced, normal kind of guy. "I've got too much going on right now." She reached for the knob to roll up the window, and when he didn't move, she said, "Do you mind?"

"Why don't you take my number for when you have some time? I'll buy you dinner."

"Look, Evan, you're a nice guy but—"

"Thought you didn't remember me?" His slow, teasing grin did something to the inside of her chest.

She almost smiled. "See you around," she said, and this time when she attempted to roll up the window, he let go and stepped back. She started the engine, reversed out of the parking spot and drove off without looking back.

EVAN REACHED INTO his slacks' pocket for his car keys and used the remote to unlock the doors. His silver Camry was parked right next to the spot Liza had vacated. That was the only reason he'd noticed her, sitting behind the wheel of the small white compact, crying. Wisely, he hadn't mentioned it. From what he knew of her, she wasn't the type of woman who indulged herself with tears. In fact, from what he'd heard around the station, she'd been more prone to express her anger or pain with a few choice words.

Still, the lawsuit she'd launched didn't add up. Until a year ago, Liza, Eve and Jane had been inseparable. He'd admired their loyalty and friendship. The show was really taking off, thanks to Eve Best's charismatic personality and Liza's creative genius. And then suddenly Liza disappeared. No one seemed to know why she left or where she went, and he had to admit, he was a bit curious.

Mostly because he'd liked Liza from the first time he'd met her. He'd been on his way to the set of *Heartbeat* when he'd bumped into her. Literally. She'd been talking to someone over her shoulder and hadn't seen him come around the corner. Abruptly she'd turned and plowed right into him. Unfortunately for him, she'd been holding a cup of coffee.

He smiled when he thought about how she'd tried to right the wrong, using her napkin to blot his suit, regardless of where the coffee had landed. When she'd finally realized that pressing the napkin to his crotch might not have been the wisest move, she'd looked him in the eye, apologized and asked to be given the cleaning bill.

No nervous twittering or inane remarks. She wasn't like so many of the women he met, either on the set or at dinner parties hosted by his well-intentioned friends, who were determined to find him a wife. Liza was straightforward, to the point, and he liked that. Normally he preferred petite blondes, which made his attraction to her all the more curious, since she was tall with long, unruly brown hair.

Not that it mattered. He'd asked Liza out to lunch once, and in her no-nonsense fashion, she'd turned him down flat. No excuses, no little white lies to let him down easy. Just a frank refusal that told him not to ask again. After that there was the occasional exchange of greetings when they passed each other in the lobby or parking lot.

Realizing he was still staring after her long-gone car, he opened the door of his Camry and slid behind the wheel. Eve had walked out of the building ahead of him, but obviously she wasn't the reason Liza had been here. So why was she here? More importantly, why did he care? She'd just shot him down again.

IT WAS SO LATE by the time Liza got home that there wasn't a single parking spot left in the complex and she had to park a block away from her apartment. Sighing, she cut the car's engine and then grabbed the bag of burgers she'd picked up from a drive-through. She really hated parking on the street, especially in this crappy neighborhood. Hopefully, any thieves would go for the nice new black sedan parked in front of her.

Not that she loved her secondhand lemon of a car. But if something happened to it, she couldn't afford to buy another one. Rick had naturally insisted on buying a brand-new Harley-Davidson for himself. With her money. Amazing he hadn't cracked it up yet. Not that it would hurt her feelings if he had. In fact, in her more stressed-out moments, she'd actually wished he would. He didn't have to die or anything, just end up in a coma for a good five years.

Her steps slowed as she thought about how he lived in the apartment right next to hers, and that if he happened to look out of the window he'd see her walk up the stairs. Inevitably he'd come outside and grill her about where she'd been. His language would be foul and he wouldn't give a damn about who overheard. But if she was lucky, he'd be passed out and she wouldn't have to deal with him until tomorrow.

Sighing, she took the first few stairs, her daze darting toward Rick's door, praying, hoping she'd have an evening of peace and quiet. So far, so good...

"Hey, Liza, what you got in the bag?"

The sound of her new neighbor's high-pitched voice made Liza cringe. She waved for Mary Ellen to keep it down and then, with one eye on Rick's door, she hurried the rest of the way to the third floor.

Leaning over the railing, which was decorated with a string of large colored Christmas lights, Mary Ellen waited, dutifully keeping her mouth shut until Liza joined her. "I think he's passed out," the younger woman said in that strange drawl of hers.

She claimed that she and her kid were from Mississippi

but Liza had her doubts. The apartment complex's residents weren't exactly members of mainstream society. At least once a week Liza heard a shot fired nearby, or watched the police drag away an abusive husband or boyfriend. But the rent was cheap and since she had to fork out money for both her place and Rick's, this was the best she could afford.

Rick thought it was stupid to have separate apartments, mostly because he wanted complete control over her. But that was the one thing she wouldn't negotiate with him. She didn't care that she'd end up broke, but as threadbare as it was, her sanity wasn't something she was ready to give up. Bad enough that he tried to keep track of her every move, she sure didn't need him in her face.

She reached the third-floor landing and furtively peeked into Rick's open window. Sure enough, he lay flat on his back on the tattered brown corduroy couch that they'd picked up at a thrift store. An empty bottle of vodka sat on the end table, but she knew he'd consumed more than booze. Good. Maybe she could have a quiet meal with Mary Ellen and her daughter.

"Told ya." Mary Ellen inclined her dirty-blond head toward Rick's apartment, but her gaze stayed on the fast-food bag.

"Hungry?"

"Starving."

"I bought extra burgers for you and Freedom."

Mary Ellen broke into a wide grin that displayed a missing back tooth, which wasn't usually noticeable since she didn't smile much. "Oh, goody. I thought we were gonna have to eat macaroni and cheese again." She turned around, put two fingers into her mouth and let out an ear-piercing whistle.

Liza cringed. With dread, she took a step back and

squinted into Rick's apartment. He was still out cold. However, Freedom heard her mom's whistle and came bounding up the stairs.

"Hi, Liza." The eight-year-old tomboy was covered with dirt. She pulled off her red ball cap and dust flew everywhere.

"Time for dinner?" she asked her mom, her hopeful blue eyes going to the bag.

"Liza bought us burgers."

"Yahoo. Fries, too?"

Liza unlocked her apartment door. "They would've gotten cold."

"The hamburgers are cold, too," Freedom said, with perfect logic.

"That's true," Mary Ellen said, her slight frown accentuating the scar paralleling her lower lip.

Sighing, Liza led them inside and went straight to the microwave. Eating cold French fries wasn't the same thing, but Liza didn't want to get into it with them. She wanted them to eat and leave. In fact, she should've given them the food to take back to their own apartment, but she had a soft spot for Mary Ellen and her daughter.

As pitiful as Liza's place was with its chipped paint and stained, olive-green carpet, the other two managed to live in a cheaper, cramped studio apartment. Mary Ellen still ended up two months behind on the rent since her welfare checks didn't quite cover all their expenses. With her pronounced limp, she'd had trouble finding a job that would support the two of them. Liza had never asked her about the bum leg, but she had a bad feeling about it.

She finished nuking the burgers and Mary Ellen had already put napkins on the small table. It was only big enough for two, so Freedom sat on her mother's good knee. She quickly wolfed down her burger, and eyed a second one.

Liza pushed it across to her, wishing she'd bought more than five sandwiches. When Mary Ellen finished hers, Liza offered her the last one.

"What about Rick?"

Amazing how just the mention of him could knot her stomach and send the hair straight up off the back of her neck. "What about him?"

"Isn't he eating?"

"Don't know. Don't care."

Mary Ellen regarded her quizzically. "Why do you stay with him?"

"I'm not *with* him." Liza grabbed the used wrappers and crumpled them as she got to her feet. She'd seen the curious looks Mary Ellen had given her on the unfortunate occasions when Rick was drunk and he'd yelled from the door of his apartment as Liza was trying to slip quietly down the stairs. But she didn't intend to discuss her problems with Mary Ellen. Or anyone else.

"Why do you live next door to him, then?" the other woman asked.

Liza disposed of the wrappers, using the time to compose herself. Anyone else and she would have told them it was none of their damn business, but having to look into Mary Ellen's perpetually sad eyes, Liza just couldn't do it.

"It's complicated," she said finally.

"That means you don't want to talk about it, huh?" the little girl mumbled, her mouth full.

"Freedom," Mary Ellen admonished her. "This is grown-up talk. You be quiet."

Liza hid a smile. Poor kid was going to grow up to be like her. Smart-mouthed and always in trouble.

"You went to college, didn't you?" Mary Ellen asked.

Liza slowly nodded, not liking the conversation.

"You're so pretty and smart and I don't understand why you'd be living in a dump like this."

Right. Real smart. So smart that she'd put herself in a position to be blackmailed. "Look," Liza said in a tight voice, casting a brief glance at Freedom, who'd turned to licking her fingers instead of listening to the conversation. "I don't think you want to start a question-and-answer session."

Mary Ellen looked grimly down at her weather-roughened hands. "No," she said quietly, and then cleared her throat and rose from the table. "Freedom, come on. We need to be going. Thanks for dinner, Liza." She pulled her daughter along with her, keeping her face toward the door.

"See you later." Liza stayed in the small open kitchen and watched them go. She probably should've made nice. Mary Ellen hadn't meant anything bad by what she'd said. The woman seemed to have such a lonely life, likely she only wanted to talk.

But Liza didn't have it in her. Not today. Everything had gone wrong. After being decisive all of her life, she'd become as stable as a palm tree in a hurricane. She should never have allowed the blackmail to get this far, but she'd panicked and everything had spiraled out of control before she knew what had happened. Winning the lawsuit would save her ass, if she could only keep her act together.

She walked to the love seat and sank down, careful to avoid the bad spring in the center. God, was this headache ever going away? She leaned forward, rested her elbows on her knees and cradled her head in her hands. She needed a couple of aspirin. But that meant leaving to get them. No way. She was staying right where she was to enjoy the peace and quiet while Rick was passed out.

Going to the station had been a bad idea. She'd known

it before she'd gotten in the car. But that was the sort of stupid irrational behavior she couldn't seem to control anymore. Even though she'd never made it out of her car. Thanks to Evan Gann. People didn't know how to mind their own damn business.

If she'd gotten into the studio, she might have learned whether another settlement was being considered. The last offer they'd made, Rick had flatly refused. Although since she'd pumped Zach Hass, the new guy, for information, everyone named in the lawsuit had probably been warned not to talk to her. For all she knew, security wouldn't even have let her inside. Unless...

She abruptly brought her head up.

Evan Gann. He could get her inside. No one could stop her if she was going to see him. Damn it. Why hadn't she taken his phone number? Grudgingly she pushed to her feet, and got her cell phone. She hoped like hell his number was listed.

CHAPTER TWO

AT THREE FORTY-FIVE Evan took a few minutes away from the set and called his office and then his answering service. Because of the consulting job, he only saw patients three days a week, but inevitably, on the rare occasion that he wanted some personal time, there'd be an emergency that would consume the rest of his day. Fortunately, this afternoon he was free to see Liza.

What a shock it had been when she'd called last night. As a result he'd been on edge all day. It seemed as if every shot had gone wrong and there'd been so many retakes that he was afraid he wouldn't be done when she arrived at four fifteen. He'd finally had to pull the assistant director aside and tell her that he was going to be out of here by four, no matter what.

The truth was, his concentration wasn't what it should be anyway. He didn't get why Liza had decided to see him. No sign she'd been interested yesterday. So why the sudden change of heart? And why did she want to meet him at the studio? Strange that she'd want to show her face here at all.

Even stranger that he was still interested in her. Especially this time of the year. Ever since medical school and the Angela debacle, he had no use for the holidays. So what was it about Liza? He couldn't quite grasp the attraction. Had to be something chemical. Pheromones, maybe. Or maybe that he was a sucker for a crying woman. He had an annoying urge to rescue them.

He checked his watch and saw that the AD had noticed. She gave him a small nod and he didn't think twice before grabbing his jacket and heading off the set. He was early but he kept an electric razor in his car's glove box. He could barely make it through the day without dark stubble covering his chin.

He'd made it halfway through the lobby when he heard the receptionist call out his name. Melinda wasn't at her usual station but was decorating a Christmas tree in the corner. She was blond, petite and pretty, and she wasn't shy about making her interest in him known. But she was too young and a little too brazen for his taste. Besides, she reminded him of his ex-fiancée.

"You're right on time, Evan," she said brightly, holding a glittering star and standing on a short ladder. "I can't reach the top." She demonstrated by stretching so high that pretty much everyone in the lobby noticed that she wore pink lacy underwear.

Evan kept his eyes on her face as he stayed en route to the double doors. "Where's Leroy?" The ex-basketball-player-turned-security-guard wouldn't even need the ladder.

"I don't know," she said petulantly. "Can't you help me?"

"I'm running late." He hesitated and glanced out the glass doors. "All right."

She smiled and handed him the star before slowly descending the ladder, with a seductive sway to her curvy hips.

The tree had to be eight feet tall and since he was only six-two he didn't dare try securing the star without using the ladder. He got up a couple of rungs and felt Melinda's hand near his right thigh. He frowned down at her.

"I'm holding the ladder for you," she said with a wink.

He ignored her, placed the star on the top of the tree and then quickly got down.

"You're leaving early." The woman had no concept of personal space.

He backed away from her, at the same time glancing out the glass doors. He spotted Liza pulling into a parking space. "I've got to go."

"You have a date or something?" she asked in a teasing tone.

"Yeah," he said, and headed out of the building without giving her a second look.

The sky was darker and the air chillier than when he'd come to work midmorning. He buttoned his jacket as he walked, watching for Liza, his gaze staying on the large black SUV she'd parked behind. A second later he saw her, dressed in jeans and a bulky red sweater that unfortunately hid her curves. He waved to get her attention.

"What are you doing out here?" she asked as soon as she got close enough.

Evan checked his watch. "Weren't we supposed to meet at four fifteen?"

Resentment flashed in her eyes. "Too embarrassed to be seen with me inside?"

"Never even crossed my mind. I was done, and I walked out here to meet you. Is that a problem?"

Her gaze flickered toward the station doors. "No."

"Shall we take my car?"

"I guess."

He didn't appreciate her indifferent tone. "Look, if you've changed your mind, no problem."

Liza shook her head. "No, I'm sorry. I'd like to have a drink with you. Anyplace. You choose."

Evan tried not to smile. Originally she'd asked him just to go for coffee, which was okay because he'd considered it a nice start. A drink was better. Maybe it would even lead to dinner. "How about we go to Sardis?"

"That's a couple blocks away, isn't it?"

He nodded.

"Let's walk."

"You're not cold?"

Liza laughed. Nice husky sound. "It's only the beginning of December. Ask me next month."

Would she still be around then? Naturally he said nothing. He simply walked alongside her, and when they got to the sidewalk, promptly swung around to take the outside position closer to the street.

Her lips lifted in amusement. "A perfect Southern gentleman, I see."

He shrugged sheepishly. "My grandfather once made me promise to never let a woman walk on the street side. Do you know how the custom came about?"

"Ah, no."

Evan smiled. He could tell she didn't care but she was going to hear it anyway. "It started back in the old west. Unpaved roads, puddles of water...you starting to get the picture?"

She shook her head in mock disgust, but he saw the smile dancing at the corners of her mouth.

"A gentleman always walked on the outside to protect the women from getting their long skirts splashed."

She laughed, making her eyes sparkle. She wasn't classically pretty but she had an interesting face. Her eyes were small and almond-shaped, and her nose looked as if it had been sculpted by a skilled surgeon. Although she didn't strike him as a woman who'd go in for that kind of thing.

He smiled. "And now you know."

"Is that true?"

"I have no idea."

Her eyebrows arched. "You made it up?"

"No, I heard it from my grandfather. I imagine he did read it somewhere, though. I remember him always reading a book or newspaper."

She looked away. "I don't remember my grandparents. I was a baby when they died."

"All four of them?"

"Yeah," she said, showing undue interest in the Santa window display they were passing.

He got that it might be a sore subject and dropped it. "You look nice."

She gave him an annoyed look. "This is a drink, okay? You're not getting lucky."

"No problem. I'm celibate." As much as he wanted to see Liza's expression, he had to look away because he had a lousy poker face.

Fortunately, at that moment they arrived at the bar, both of them going for the door, but he got it first. He held it open for her.

"Celibate and a gentleman. This is going to be interesting," she murmured as she proceeded him.

Evan followed her, disturbed by the new view he was getting. The sweater wasn't hiding any curves. She'd lost a lot of weight. About twenty pounds that she hadn't needed to lose. Was she sick? Was that the reason for her sudden disappearance? Is that why she needed the lottery money?

The light vanilla fragrance of her hair distracted him, and drew him closer than was polite. When she stopped suddenly, he nearly rammed into her. She turned to say something and their eyes met. She didn't look pleased.

"There's a table over there," he said, discreetly backing up a foot.

She hesitated, her gaze turning toward the dimly lit room, the walls covered with racing memorabilia and autographed pictures. Artificial garlands interwoven with Christmas lights were draped along the heavy wooden bar. A Christmas tree stood in the corner but it hadn't been decorated yet. There were a lot of customers for the time of day, talking and laughing or thoughtfully sipping their cocktails.

Evan only recognized one person who worked at the station—a cameraman from another show that was filmed down the hall. Luckily, he had nothing to do with *Just Between Us* and he was probably new enough that Liza wouldn't recognize him.

"This okay?" he asked close to her ear.

"This is fine. I could do without all the damn decorations. but I don't think we can get away from that."

"Don't like Christmas, huh?"

"Not particularly."

"Me, neither."

She looked at him with surprise but a couple came in behind them and since there were only two available tables, he and Liza headed toward the one he'd spotted in the corner. It hadn't been cleaned off yet from the previous customers and a waitress promptly removed the empty glasses, wiped off the tabletop with a towel and then said she'd be back to take their drink orders.

After a brief but awkward silence, Evan spoke first.

"You can tell me to go to hell, but I'm going to ask the burning question. Where have you been for the last year?"

Liza leaned back in her chair and stared at him. "Does it matter?"

That, he hadn't expected. "I guess not."

"Good." A hint of a smile played at the corners of her mouth. "Now I don't have to tell you to go to hell."

"Go ahead. I can take it. I've got broad shoulders."

"Do you now?" She gave him an obvious once-over. "I see that you do."

"Careful or I'll think you're flirting with me."

She laughed. "I wouldn't do that to a man in your condition."

Now that he thought about it, he was painfully close to celibacy. His nurse thought he was too picky. "How thoughtful."

Liza opened her mouth to say something and then closed it again when their waitress appeared. The woman waited patiently while Liza changed her mind twice about what she wanted to drink. Finally, she settled on a tequila sunrise with an extra cherry. Surprising, because he'd expected her to drink something like scotch or beer.

After he'd given his order and the waitress left, he waited for Liza to pick up the conversation again, but when she didn't, he asked, "What have you been doing with yourself?"

She looked uncomfortable, shifting in her seat and feigning interest in the picture of a Grand Prix racing crew on the wall. "Nothing much."

"You have a job?"

"I'm looking."

"In the same field?"

"Why so many questions?" she snapped.

"Well, let's see, I suppose we could talk about the weather."

Liza sighed. "I really don't know what I'm going to do yet."

"Waiting for the lawsuit to play out, I imagine."

She flinched. "It's not about the money."

"Oh?" Jeez, he really was just making conversation.

She moistened her lips. "Have you heard anything?"

"You mean, around the station?"

She slowly nodded, her anxious hazel eyes staying fastened on his.

He chuckled. "Your name has popped up from time to time."

"I know they all think I'm a bitch."

"I wouldn't say that."

Her chin went up in defiance. "You don't have to protect my tender feelings. I really don't give a damn."

"I know. I was talking about the janitor. He doesn't speak English, so I doubt he has an opinion of you."

Liza grinned. "Very good, Dr. Gann."

"Why, thank you." Silly how good it felt to have impressed Liza. But mostly it was about how her face relaxed when she smiled. How pretty she looked.

"Here we go." The waitress set the tequila sunrise in front of Liza along with a small white bowl of maraschino cherries. She put a bottle of imported beer in front of Evan, and then another bowl of pretzels in the center of the table.

"Thank you." Liza looked at the waitress, an odd expression on her face, almost as if she was surprised by the kindness.

"I'll check back with you later," the older woman said as she took out the pencil she'd stuck behind her ear and then moved to the next table.

Liza reached for her second cherry, while eyeing the pretzels. "I wonder if the gang still goes to Latitude Thirty-Three," she said with an unexpected wistfulness.

"I think they do. If you want we can go there after—"

"God, no." She took a quick sip of her drink. "No one from *Just Between Us* wants to see me."

"Why were you in the parking lot yesterday?"

She frowned. "Can we talk about something else?"

"Name it. I can't seem to get it right."

She tilted her head to the side, her eyebrows drawing together. "I don't get you."

"Me? I'm an open book."

"Are you married?"

That annoyed him. "I wouldn't be sitting here if I were."

Liza shrugged. "Why? This is merely a friendly drink, yes? Plus, you're celibate."

He smiled. "I was ten minutes ago."

She shook her head in mock exasperation. "Okay, were you ever married?"

"No."

"Hmm."

"What does that mean?"

"You seem like the marrying kind. Kids. The white picket fence. Steady. Stable. You know the type."

Evan knew exactly what she meant. Liza was on the wild side, which meant she'd find someone like that boring. The thing was, he pretty much was that guy. He would have had it all by now if Angela hadn't screwed him. And, literally, two of his friends. "I have the white picket fence. Came with the house."

Liza chuckled. "Ah, so you do have the whole house-and-mortgage thing."

"Gotta live somewhere."

Her expression fell and her shoulders sagged. "I think I'd like a house someday," she said softly. "With a small yard and garden. Apartment living is getting old."

"Where are you now?"

She looked warily at him. "You wouldn't know the place. Anyway, I'm not even sure I'm staying in Atlanta. Probably won't. Too hot and humid."

"Great for growing gardens."

She gave a shrug of indifference and in just those few seconds she became the old Liza. "I'm not really the hearth-and-home type. I was only making conversation."

"Ah, I see." He didn't really. Better to let it go, though. "You must have something in mind, assuming you win the lawsuit."

She'd just picked up her drink and it slid from her hand. Half the liquid sloshed onto her lap before she could right the glass. "Damn."

He rose. "I'll get a towel from the waitress."

"No, that's okay. I've got it." She used both their cocktail napkins but he knew that couldn't have done much good.

"I can get a towel."

"No," she said curtly, and then took a furtive look around before staring back down at her lap.

Only the couple at the next table had noticed, and they'd already restarted their conversation.

Evan just watched her swipe at her jeans with an angry frustration that went well beyond a spilled drink. She bit her lower lip so hard he wouldn't be surprised if she drew blood. He wanted to help, to at least say something comforting or funny to distract her, but he knew better. He had this really strong and unexpected feeling that Liza needed to battle her own demons.

* * *

THIS WAS SO STUPID. She wasn't about to dry her jeans this way, but she didn't want to meet Evan's eyes. Bet he was sorry that he'd asked her out. Served him right. What had he expected?

"Excuse me," she said finally. "I need to go to the restroom and take care of this."

She only briefly looked at him as she slid out of her seat. There was no pity in his eyes, not even curiosity. In fact, she didn't know what to make of his bland expression.

"Shall I order you another drink?" he asked calmly.

"No, thanks," she murmured, and gave him her back as she blindly searched for the ladies' room.

It had to be in one of the corners, and it was the second place she looked. She didn't give a damn about her jeans and went straight to the sink. She turned on the faucet and splashed her face with cold water. At the last moment she remembered that she'd actually applied a little makeup before coming out. Too late now.

Didn't matter, though. Unlikely she'd see Evan again. He probably couldn't wait to finish his drink and get rid of her. She wouldn't be surprised if he'd already paid the bill. Ironically, she'd enjoyed being with him. He wasn't as stuffy as she'd expected him to be. Still not her type, but he'd been pleasant company. Didn't take her crap, either. Always a refreshing discovery.

The problem was, she hadn't found out anything about the lawsuit. She knew damn well people gossiped around there, especially in the coffee room. Evan wasn't the type to participate, but he still might've heard something useful.

Staring at her reflection in the mirror, she cringed at the dark circles under her eyes. A couple of years away from the big 3-0 and she already had pronounced crow's-feet at the corners of her eyes. Her skin was too pale, and now that she'd washed off the tinted moisturizer, she really looked like hell.

She pushed the hair away from her face and, as she'd seen her mother do a hundred times, a zillion years ago, Liza pinched her cheeks to give them some color. She didn't do a very good job because the right side looked more like a bad mosquito bite. Great.

She grabbed a couple of paper towels and blotted her jeans, and then washed the stickiness off her hands. If Evan hadn't already bolted, she'd come right out and ask him what he'd heard about the lawsuit. All he could do was tell her to get lost. But she doubted he'd do that. He was too much of a gentleman. And damn it, she liked that.

CHAPTER THREE

LIZA'S HEART DID A funny little hop as she approached the table, and he smiled. His hair was too short for her taste, but he had great eyes, the perfect shade of whiskey-brown, and a square jaw with a dimple in the center of his chin that she found terribly appealing. That he had some stubble and wasn't clean-shaven, as usual, was right up her alley.

The table had been cleaned off and her empty glass had been replaced with another tequila sunrise. She reclaimed her seat and noticed that he was also on his second beer. Guess he wasn't going to run screaming from the room.

"Trust me with another drink, I see." She decided not to point out that she'd said she didn't want another.

"I asked for a lid but they didn't have one."

She smiled in spite of herself. Either she was really starved for male company or Evan was truly turning out to be less stodgy than she'd perceived him.

"What kind of doctor are you?" she asked, genuinely interested.

"An internist."

"How did you get the consulting gig for *Heartbeat?*"

"The producer is an old frat brother of mine."

"From med school?"

He chuckled. "Undergraduate. You don't have time for a fraternity in med school. Between working and studying I was lucky to get four hours of sleep a night."

"Here I thought you were one of those rich kids who had a trust fund."

"Yeah, right."

"Seriously, I did. You seem the preppy type."

"Bad assumption. I just finally paid off my student loans, thanks to the consulting job."

"I still have ten thousand outstanding myself." Liza had no idea why she'd offered the information. It galled her to know that part of her inheritance had been used to buy Rick's bike instead of making her debt-free.

"That's not bad."

"I guess not. Though I don't like to owe any money."

"Me, too. My parents scraped together every penny to pay down their mortgage. The day they made their last payment they had a huge barbecue in the backyard and invited all the relatives and neighbors."

Liza smiled at the fondness in his voice. "You have a big family?"

"Two brothers. Lots of cousins, most of whom live here in Atlanta. How about you?"

"No siblings. Except Eve and Jane. They're like—" She cut herself off, horrified at what she'd revealed. It was Evan's fault. He was just too damn easy to talk to.

He looked clearly curious, but graciously filled the conversation gap. "My father is retiring in three months. He and Mom are thinking about buying a small condo in Florida but they're not sure where. You're from Jacksonville, aren't you?"

"I was a kid when I lived there, and then I left after college." She quickly picked up her drink and took a cooling sip. She didn't like this warm squishy feeling of gratitude. Evan didn't need information on Florida. He could've asked her all kinds of awkward questions. Not that she'd have answered, but still.

"Are your parents living there—in Jacksonville?"

"My dad died last year. My mom is there."

She didn't know where exactly, but that wasn't something she'd share. Besides, with his background, he wouldn't understand what it was like growing up with an alcoholic and a pill-popper.

"I'm sorry about your father."

"Yeah. Guess it was his time." She looked away so she wouldn't see the revulsion on Evan's face. She hadn't meant to sound so callous, but a life of hard drinking never ended well. When she finally looked at Evan again, he smiled kindly. It annoyed her. Why was he so nice? What the hell did he want from her? She didn't deserve his kindness. Or anyone else's. Didn't he understand that?

"You getting hungry?"

"Why?"

"Well," he said slowly, the corners of his mouth twitching, "it's approaching the dinner hour and traditionally people eat a meal at that time."

"I'm not traditional."

"True." He loosened the knot on his tie. "That's what I like about you."

"Hmm." She couldn't come up with anything witty to say. She was too busy watching his long fingers work, and noticing the smattering of hair across the back of his hands. His skin was tan and more rugged-looking than she'd expect of a doctor. Probably belonged to a golf or tennis club.

"Liza?"

"What?"

He frowned at her. "I asked if you'd like to go to dinner."

"Dinner?"

"Uh-huh, you know, eating."

She glanced at her watch, shocked at how much time had passed. Yet she hadn't gotten a word out of him about the scuttlebutt around the station. Rick had been sleeping when she left, and she wanted him to stay that way until she was safely in her apartment. "I can't. I'm leaving after this drink."

"All right." He looked disappointed as he leaned back in his chair. His shoulders really were quite broad. She wondered what he'd be like without the jacket. "Another time, maybe?"

She nodded absently. He kind of looked like a jock. Not her favorite. But he definitely seemed as if he were in shape. The most exercise she got these days was climbing the stairs to her apartment.

"Your enthusiasm is heartening."

"What?"

He smiled sadly. "One of the other things I like about you is your directness. If you don't want a repeat, go ahead and say so. You're not going to hurt my feelings."

"That's not it." She cleared her throat. What a great opening he'd handed her. "It's this whole lawsuit thing making me crazy. I'm not myself."

"Ah. I understand."

She fingered her straw, keeping her gaze lowered, hoping she sounded casual. "Have you heard anything?"

"About what?"

"The lawsuit. My attorney thinks they're about to make another offer."

"Good." He slowly set down his beer, clearly avoiding

her gaze. "I'm sure everyone wants to put this behind them."

"But you haven't heard anything?"

This time he looked her straight in the eye. "Is that why you called? So you could pump me for information?"

"Yes."

He didn't even blink at her bluntness. "Sorry you wasted your time." His expression grim, he reached into his pocket. "And mine."

"Wait. Initially I did want to meet with you so that I could find out what was going on."

He pulled out some bills from his silver-and-turquoise money clip and picked up the check the waitress had left.

Liza plucked the slip of paper out of his hand. "I called you. I'm paying."

"Will that assuage your guilt?"

"Had you been listening, you'd realize that I qualified my answer. This evening turned out to be a pleasant surprise."

His mouth curved in a patronizing smile.

"Look, I'm glad I came, okay?" She dug through her purse, searching for her wallet. Mostly, she didn't want to face Evan. Screw him. At least she'd told him the truth. She could've gone all dewy-eyed and saccharine-sweet to get what she wanted. But she hadn't. Not that she'd ever use that tactic in a million years.

"Liza?"

Grudgingly, she looked up at him.

His gentle smile disarmed her. "I'm glad you came, too."

"Yeah, well, now that the mutual admiration society has met, time to get out of here." She found a twenty and looked at the bill. God. Even the beer was expensive in this place. She started fishing in her wallet again, but Evan reached over and touched her hand.

"I'm getting this," he said and before she knew it, he grabbed the check out of her fingers.

"Give me that."

"Nope." He already had the money ready and handed the bills to the waitress as she passed by on her way to another table.

"This is the twenty-first century, in case you've just woken up."

"A gentleman supersedes any period in time."

"Oh, brother."

"You ready?"

"You can stay."

He snorted. "Right."

"So now you're insisting on walking me to my car?"

"You bet."

She shook her head as they both got to their feet. "You're something else."

Winking at her, he took her arm with a flourish, the way his grandfather might have escorted his wife.

Liza laughed. "What am I going to do with you?"

His smile was far from patronizing when he asked, "Open to suggestions?"

AS THEY LEFT THE BAR, Evan placed his hand at the small of her back. She was pretty thin, which revived his earlier suspicion regarding her health. Yet her coloring was good and her energy level didn't seem to be lacking.

"You've lost some weight," he said once they got on the sidewalk and he'd positioned himself on the outside. Rush-hour traffic hadn't subsided, and it wouldn't for another couple of hours.

She frowned slightly. "Have I?"

"Must be the stress of the lawsuit."

She moved away, self-consciously wrapping her arms around herself. "I guess."

"You want my jacket?"

"Huh? Oh, no. Thanks."

"By the way, I haven't heard anything about the lawsuit."

She turned back to him, lowering her arms, suddenly interested again. "Nothing?"

"Nada." He shook his head. "But I'm not in the loop around the station. When I'm done for the day, I'm out of there."

She turned away again, clearly disappointed.

"Sorry."

"It's okay."

Was it? Now that she knew he couldn't be of use to her, would she still go out with him again? "I wish you luck, though."

She slowed. "Do you? Why?"

"Because you apparently believe you have a claim. I don't know the particulars, but—"

"Don't give me that. The story's been splashed across the damn newspaper."

"Do you believe everything you read?" he shot back and enjoyed the bewilderment on her face.

She stared at him for a long moment and then picked up the pace again, her eyebrows pinched together in a fierce frown. "I don't understand you," she muttered.

"I believe you've already pointed that out." He tried not to smile and show just how much he enjoyed puzzling her. She was a bit of a wild one, and he absolutely wasn't. But that didn't mean he didn't like a taste of the exotic once in a while.

"Yes, well, things haven't changed."

Evan finally smiled. "How about tomorrow night?"

"What about it?"

"Dinner, and a chance to figure me out."

Her lips started to turn up, and then she sighed and shook her head. "I can't."

"Okay, how about Thursday night?"

"I can't."

"In other words, I should quit asking." He watched her closely, hoping he was wrong. Hoping that she hadn't merely been using him tonight.

She looked down at her hands and pressed her lips together. "I surprisingly had fun tonight…."

"Thanks," he said dryly.

"I'm awful. I know. But that's the truth. I expected you to be different," she said, reminding him how much he found her frankness refreshing.

"Somehow I sense a 'but' coming."

"I can't see you again."

"Okay," he said slowly, realizing he deserved the mental slap. "Seeing someone else?"

"No," she said quickly.

Annoyed with himself, he kept walking beside her, facing straight ahead. He shouldn't have asked if there was another guy in the picture. The lady said no. That was enough. He was raised better than that.

They continued in silence to the station's parking lot. Along the street, Christmas decorations were everywhere. Lights were strung around telephone poles and animated Santas and reindeers blinked from merchants' windows. It was enough to sour his sudden precarious mood.

Damn, but he wished his parents would go to Florida for the holidays. But, no, they insisted on staying so the family could have a festive dinner together. They probably only maintained the tradition to keep Evan's spirits up.

Ironically, getting together or even acknowledging the holidays was the last thing he wanted to do. Better to hide out at home, play some tunes, read a good book. And try not to think about Angela. About how this Christmas Eve would've been their seventh anniversary.

"Well, we're here."

He snapped out of his reverie. They'd already gotten to his brand-new Camry, and Liza was staring at him with open wonder.

"Thank you, Evan. I had a great time. Really."

He motioned for her to keep walking. She started to protest and then closed her lush, pink mouth when she must have realized that he was going to walk her to her car whether she liked it or not.

Most of the lot was unusually empty for this time of day. Then he remembered hearing that one of the departments was having a Christmas party tonight. Otherwise, no one left until the director had his or her perfect shot. He saw Liza's compact about a half dozen stalls away. The car was an older model and didn't come with the convenience of a remote so he waited until she manually unlocked her door.

She got it open and then stood back. "I wish you would've let me pay the check."

He smiled. "You're welcome."

She made a face. "I'm getting in now so you can leave knowing you've done your gentlemanly duty."

He held the door for her until she was sitting behind the wheel. It took a good deal of willpower not to lean over and kiss her. Just a brief touching of lips. Nothing threatening. But she probably wouldn't welcome the overture and he wasn't one to push. "Drive safely," he said, and closed the door.

Before he could walk away, she promptly rolled down the window. A floodlight from the building shined on her face, making her hazel eyes glitter. "I really did have a nice time, Evan."

"Who are you trying to convince?"

She smiled. "Okay, I deserved that."

"For the record, me, too," he said and headed for his car before he gave in to his impulse and did something foolish. The woman wasn't interested. He was a mature adult. He could accept that he wasn't her type. Didn't have to like it, but he could certainly accept the fact.

He got out his keys and used the remote to unlock the car doors. He was too busy to be dating, anyway. As it was, his receptionist constantly begged him to expand his office hours. She was tired of turning away patients. In about three years he figured he could quit consulting on the television show and start looking toward the future. Build a nice solid practice, work hard, retire early if he chose. Although he doubted it, because he really did like practicing medicine. The consulting job was a necessity for now.

He took off his jacket and laid it across the backseat before slipping in behind the wheel. It was cool for a moment, but then he turned the key in the ignition and both the promise of warmth and soft rock filled the air. The radio was too loud, but the volume always was deafening when he first started the car. Funny how it never seemed loud when he parked. Maybe that's why he never remembered to adjust it.

The sun had recently set, leaving a pink tinge along the horizon, but it was dark enough that he glanced in his rearview mirror to make sure Liza had safely left the parking lot. Her car was still there. He squinted but he couldn't see her behind the wheel. What the hell...

He grabbed the handle and jerked open the car door. He got out, and she was right there, so close, he nearly knocked her over.

"Liza, what's wrong?" He gripped her upper arms.

"I'm okay," she said with a nervous laugh. "Really, I'm okay."

He didn't let go of her. It felt good being this close. Close enough to feel her warm breath brush his chin. Close enough to smell the vanilla scent that clung to her hair.

"Evan? You're kind of hurting my arm."

"Oh, jeez." He quickly lowered his hands. "I'm sorry." He gave her some room. "What happened? Is something wrong with your car?"

"No, no. My car is fine." She briefly glanced over her shoulder. "Well, other than it looks as if it's been through a war zone. Can I change my mind about tomorrow night?"

That took him aback. "Sure."

"Ever been to Simone's?"

He smiled. No problem. She could choose the restaurant. "No, but I know of it."

"How about seven?"

"That works for me."

"Good." She hesitated, and then took a small step back. "Thanks again for tonight."

"My pleasure." Was it his imagination or was she reluctant to leave? "I'll wait until you start your car."

She sighed. "Good night, then."

"Good night."

She made a sound of exasperation and came toward him. He was only about five inches taller, but she grabbed a fistful of his shirt and pulled him down to her mouth.

She hesitated, as if she'd changed her mind. He smelled her fear, and gently coaxed her lips to soften. Then they parted slightly and he readily accepted the invitation, slipping his tongue inside and exploring the tempting fleshy part of the inside of her cheek. She responded briefly. When she pulled back, he didn't push. That was enough. For now.

CHAPTER FOUR

"DON'T WALK AWAY FROM ME, you stupid bitch."

Liza foolishly hesitated before continuing toward the apartment door. The next second, she felt Rick's vile hand grip her shoulder. He jerked her so hard she spun around. That was the second time he'd actually touched her in anger.

She took a deep breath and in a low voice said, "Don't ever do that again."

"Or what?" His blue eyes were bloodshot, and the long blond hair she used to find so hot was tangled and matted after not seeing a comb for a week.

"Or I'll withdraw the lawsuit and you can find another meal ticket."

He laughed uproariously. "Bullshit. We both know you won't do that."

"Don't be so damn sure." She was so tired of him—the lifestyle, the lies—and she had a feeling he saw it in her face because for the first time, she saw fear in his.

"Come on, Liza." He went to put his arm around her but she ducked away.

"I mean it, Rick. I don't want you touching me." She looked at the dirty clothes piling up on the floor in the corner of the living room. Empty booze bottles and beer cans vied for space with crumpled fast-food wrappers on all available tabletops. She didn't even want to know what had created the brown stains in the beige carpet.

Careful not to make contact, he stuck a finger in her face. "Better watch your friggin' mouth. Looks like you're forgetting who has the diaries."

She stepped back. Not because she was afraid, but because he smelled so bad. He'd been wearing the same ripped blue T-shirt two days ago and she seriously doubted it had been washed since then. Or whether he'd had a shower in the past week.

Most disgusting of all was the fact that she'd ever found him attractive. A little over a year ago she'd been so damn in love with him that she would've done anything to keep him. How pathetically certain she'd been that he was the one. The one man who could make her whole. Heal all the scars from childhood. Show her the love her parents had been incapable of giving. Sure, he'd been attentive and charming at first. Sexy and somewhat dangerous. Turned out he was just another boozing addict like them. How could she have been so blind and stupid?

"Look," she said finally, "we're taking the next offer they present."

"Is that what that jackass attorney is telling you?" Rick threw the beer he'd had in his hand across the room. "You think I can live on half a million?"

With all that stuff he was shooting in his arm, he probably couldn't. His problem, not hers. "I haven't even talked to the attorney. This is my decision. I can't live like this anymore."

"What do you mean you haven't talked to the attorney?"

Too late. She remembered that's where she'd told him

she was going when she met Evan yesterday. "I got the date of our appointment mixed up."

His gaze narrowed in suspicion. "You banging him?" The telltale tic started at the side of his throat. He was going to start losing it. "You better not be banging him."

"Grow up. I want him to get the money so I can get you off my back." Again, she headed for the door. He wouldn't stop her this time. He needed a fix. "And you damn well better have the diaries for me before I hand over a dime."

A few seconds after she closed the door behind her, she heard something hit it. She hurried toward her apartment, comforted by the knowledge that he'd pass out soon. Truth be told, she was becoming afraid of him. He was getting more agitated and his appetite for heroine more voracious. She just hoped his brain didn't get too fried before he turned over Eve's diaries.

Next time she had to give him money she was slipping it under the door. No more stepping a single foot in his apartment. And if he made a scene outside of hers, she'd threaten to call the police. She was pretty certain that would keep him away without jeopardizing exposure of the diaries.

As soon as she locked her own door, she went straight to the bedroom and sprawled out on the unmade bed. She would have to start getting ready for dinner in an hour. But a quick nap would really help. By the time she had to go, Rick would be out of it and she wouldn't have to worry about him chasing her to the parking lot like he'd done last week when she'd simply planned on going to the market.

She pulled the covers over her body and closed her eyes. Ten minutes later sleep hadn't come. Not unusual. Sleep was a luxury these days. Something else Rick had stolen from her. When she'd worked as a producer for *Just*

Between Us there had been many long stressful days. But none of them compared to what she'd experienced in the past year.

If she wasn't lying awake worrying that Eve's diaries would somehow make it to the tabloids, Liza would be stressing over how she was going to make the rest of the money stretch out until the lawsuit was settled. If she didn't get awarded anything, that would bring on a whole new set of problems. Rick would blame her, of course.

She had no idea what she'd do then. Other than going to Eve and Jane and explain why she needed the money from the lawsuit. It was also the very last thing she wanted to do. Admitting that she'd deliberately gone against Eve's wishes and taken Rick to help pack up Grammie's house after she'd died was the least of it. The diaries Rick has stolen had spanned some troubled years for Eve.

Her parents had tragically died in a car accident and Eve's charmed life had ended at age eleven, although she'd been taken in by her wonderful, loving grandmother, and in a way Grammie had taken Liza in, too. Home had been such a horrific place for Liza, and Grammie's house had been a refuge. She even cooked. Real meals. Not mushy frozen stuff. And the stories she would tell. Wonderful, colorful stories that were so real Liza would dream about them at night.

Even after she and Eve and Jane had gone off to college, it was Grammie's house where they congregated for holidays. The news of her sudden death had been like a dagger to Liza's heart. Her own father's death hadn't hit her nearly as hard. Not even close. That was her only excuse for taking Rick that weekend to Grammie's. Eve had been so devastated that she was incapable of packing up the old house. She'd asked Liza, who, devastated herself by the woman's passing, felt she needed Rick's support to complete the task.

God, how incredibly dumb she'd been.

She dragged the covers over her head. Eve had always been the best of friends, and Liza betrayed her. Life had been hell since then. Justice was definitely being served.

No, if justice was truly being doled out, she wouldn't have run across Evan again. She smiled, thinking about how he'd insisted on walking on the outside of the sidewalk. Such a goof. And that kiss. Holy crap. Who knew the guy could kiss like that?

Plus, she'd had a really nice evening. At times she'd even forgotten her mission to find out about the lawsuit. But then, it was a long shot that he'd be privy to any information.

Damn, she was anxious to see him again. Disturbing thought, really. He totally wasn't her type. The timing was definitely wrong. Nothing to fret over. It was the nonthreatening adult conversation that appealed to her, especially when that aspect of her life was woefully lacking.

During the past few minutes, she'd gotten drowsy. Thinking about Evan. Smiling, she rolled over and buried her face in the pillow. He'd be real happy when she pointed out to him that he'd put her to sleep.

EVAN DIDN'T HAVE TO check his watch again to know he'd been stood up. Damn her. She could've found a way to get a hold of him instead of letting him sit here for forty-five minutes drinking by himself. Ironically, he'd thought about giving her his cell phone number in case she had to cancel, but he hadn't wanted to make it that easy for her to back out.

Apparently he was wrong about her. She was an assertive woman and sometimes others felt threatened by that quality. Clearly, she really could be that self-absorbed. That's okay. Now he knew. He was done with her.

He downed the rest of his wine and looked around for the waitress. The place was small, holding only ten tables, but he didn't see her. He supposed he could go ahead and eat. The menu was okay. Traditional items, mostly. Certainly reasonable. The décor was nothing to speak of, with mass-produced photos of different kinds of flowers on the light-green walls. The tables were covered with white tablecloths, and each one had a fresh flower in a vase.

If the place had been busy, he would've been out of here by now. But besides him, only three other tables were occupied. Obviously not a popular restaurant. And definitely not one he would have expected Liza to have chosen.

He heard the front door open. He would've had a clear view of anyone who entered if not for the coatrack. Not that he thought she'd finally decided to grace him with her presence. He knew at least half a dozen women who'd accept his offer of a date before he got the last word out. Not because he was good-looking or well-built or anything other than he had a degree from Harvard medical school.

That didn't impress Liza. In fact, he had a feeling that for her it was a deterrent. Maybe her indifference was what he found appealing. Or maybe because she was the exact opposite of Angela.

Liza came into view and everything else faded.

Her long hair had that slightly wild look he liked so much. Not on most women, but Liza pulled it off. The short denim skirt showed off her long shapely legs, but another bulky sweater, this one black, hid everything else. Again, she wasn't wearing a coat.

He should be angry but he was too glad to see her. After she sat down across from him he said, "I'd just given up on you. I was ready to leave."

"I'm so, so sorry. I took a nap and overslept."

"You could have called. I'm listed and my service would have gotten the message to me."

"I know." She fidgeted with her napkin. "But if I called, I might have chickened out and canceled."

"Now why would you do that?"

She wore only the barest hint of makeup, but enough to bring out the green flecks in her hazel eyes. "There's a limit even to my bluntness," she said, glancing around at the people at the other tables. She seemed a little edgy.

"You look great."

Her tongue darted out to moisten her peach-colored lips. "Thank you," she said softly, shifting as if uncomfortable with the compliment and picking up the menu the waitress had left for her. "Have you looked at this?"

"About seven times."

She glanced up at him. "I was rude, I apologized, if you can't get past that, then—"

"Take it easy. I'm only teasing."

"Sorry. I don't wake up well."

A crash came from the kitchen and Liza just about flew out of her seat. She put a hand to her throat. "Scared the hell out of me."

"I noticed." He sensed there was something more than the loud noise making her jumpy. "This place a favorite of yours?"

She glanced around with a slight frown. "Actually, this is my first time here."

"I didn't think this seemed like your style."

"No?"

"Is it?"

"Tell me how you arrived at your diagnosis, Dr. Gann."

"A premed student would've come to the same conclusion. This place is too tame. Too ordinary."

"Really." She tossed her hair back over her shoulder and leaned forward. "Describe the kind of place you think I'd like."

He put his elbows on the table and met her halfway. "How about I show you instead?"

Her gaze slowly moved down to his mouth, then went to his chin and lingered. "I'm listening."

"No more talking. I lead, you follow. You have to trust me."

"And if I don't?"

Shrugging, he leaned back. "Your loss."

The waitress showed up to take her order, and Liza looked hesitantly at him.

"Your call," he said.

"Thanks, but I won't be having a drink."

The waitress readied her pad. "Ready to order dinner then?"

"We won't be having dinner after all. I'll take the check when you have a moment," Evan said, aware of the flash of dismay on the woman's face.

Still, she smiled pleasantly as she dug into the pocket of her white apron, produced the check for his glass of chardonnay and laid it down on the table.

He got out his silver money clip. The one Angela had given him for his twenty-sixth birthday and the only memento of her he kept. The perfect reminder to keep him from being stupid about a woman again.

"No rush on that," the waitress said. "You folks have a nice evening."

"You, too." He'd missed Atlanta while he was away at school. The city had grown dramatically since he was a kid but there was still a basic niceness that hadn't disappeared. The woman had to be disappointed that she wasn't going to rack up a hefty tip, but she remained gracious.

Evan included an extra twenty and laid the money and check facedown. He pushed back his chair. "Ready?"

Liza got up and walked alongside him to the door. He stopped to get his coat and noticed her peering intently out of the window into the darkness.

"Anything wrong?"

She turned to him abruptly. "No. Why?"

He shrugged into the camel-colored cashmere coat he'd found at an end-of-season sale last year. Still, it seemed like a big splurge when he'd had so many student loans. "I don't know. I thought maybe someone was stealing your car."

She adjusted his collar with a familiarity that startled him. "Then they'd be doing me a huge favor." Their eyes met and she quickly lowered her hands.

"I don't suppose you have a coat with you," he said and continued buttoning.

"What do you think?"

"Right." He opened the door and she preceded him into the dark parking lot. "My car okay?"

"I could follow you."

"Promise to have you back anytime you say."

She looked tentative at first, but then nodded and followed him to the Camry. She smiled when he opened the passenger door for her. He did it out of habit, but was rewarded when she swung her long legs into the car and her skirt rode up to an indecent height. She saw him watching and he immediately closed the door.

The air was cool and damp, which could easily ruin his plans. Although he did have a blanket in his trunk that would help. He got behind the wheel and immediately turned on the engine. Fortunately, the heater did its job. Liza had to be chilled, no matter what she said.

He heard the passenger window go down and turned to

her in astonishment. She slid her finger over the control and it went back up.

She looked over at him. "Wow. A grown-up car. Real automatic windows and everything."

"I even have an automatic hood. Want to play with it?"

"May I?"

Evan smiled as he pulled into traffic. "You win that lawsuit and you can have any kind of car you want."

Her grin disappeared and she turned to stare out of the window.

"I say something wrong?"

"I'm not doing it for the money," she said quietly.

"Your business." He hadn't been prying. He hadn't even given thought to his words. They'd just come out.

After a long silence she asked, "Where are we going, anyway?"

"You like Chinese?"

"I like the noodles and sweet-and-sour chicken."

"Good."

"So where—"

"You're not allowed any more questions."

She snorted. "Says who?"

It was a moot question since they'd reached their destination. He pulled into a spot in front of the small mom-and-pop take-out place and turned off the engine. There was a short counter where customers occasionally ate, but primarily it was a to-go business with three different entrée choices each day. Fortunately, vegetable chow mein and sweet-and-sour chicken were a staple.

"You coming?" he asked after he'd opened his door and she was still sitting there.

"I have to make a phone call. It's kind of important." She averted her eyes. "And private."

Evan stared back. Hell, yeah, he minded. He wouldn't if she hadn't looked so guilty. What the devil was going on? Was this Angela all over again?

LIZA COULD TELL he was angry. He had every right. Through the glass window she watched him order their food while she listened to the fifth ring. Next it would go to voice mail. And then she could relax.

Just as she'd hoped, she heard the switch-over to the computer voice that gave instructions to leave a message. Liza flipped the phone closed, and breathed a sigh of relief. It meant Rick wouldn't be bothering her tonight.

All she needed was for him to be lurking in the shadows and have followed her to Evan's, assuming that's what he had in mind. She couldn't imagine where else they'd be going to eat takeout. It was probably her imagination but she could've sworn someone had been on her tail ever since she left the apartment complex. More than likely it was her strained nerves after the fight she'd had with Rick that had made her late.

That he was actually on his feet and semicoherent had caught her totally off guard. With the amount of booze and heroin that she assumed he had in his system, he should have been flat on his face. Instead, he was staggering around, although he probably wouldn't remember a thing tomorrow.

Still, she couldn't help looking over her shoulder. For the first time today she'd stood up to him. Actually threatened him, and possibly made the grave mistake of driving him to desperation. Best thing she could do from now until the settlement was to stay away. Give him money when he asked. Whether it was for drugs or booze or food, she didn't give a damn.

She laid her head back against the leather seat and continued to watch Evan. He really was a nice guy. Even though he wasn't her type, spending time with him had reminded her of what it had been like to have a real life. To simply enjoy a stress-free dinner out with a friend, and not have to constantly check the time as if she were a sixteen-year-old with a curfew.

It didn't take him long to come out carrying a large white bag. He opened the door and handed it to her without saying a word. If she wanted to salvage the evening, she had to apologize. She just wasn't sure how, without doling out too much information or start crying on his shoulder. Yeah, like that would happen.

"Smells good," she finally said after they'd gotten back on the road.

He nodded. Didn't even spare her a glance.

She took a deep breath. It didn't help. "Look, if you wanted cookies and milk, you should've called your mother for a date."

He looked over at her then, as if she'd totally gone out of her mind. "You are really something. You know that?"

"'Something' not being good, I take it."

"To tell you the truth…" He pushed a frustrated hand through his short hair. "I don't know."

Liza grinned. "Okay, so I have a fifty-fifty chance. I'll take it."

He shook his head, pretending disgust, but she saw the corners of his mouth twitch.

Satisfied, she sat back in the comfy leather seat, and thought about that kiss.

CHAPTER FIVE

THEY WEREN'T ON THE ROAD long when Evan turned off. Or maybe it was because he'd been quiet and she'd been day-dreaming that the time seemed to go by so fast, but they definitely weren't in a residential area. "Where are we?"

"A park."

"I can see that."

He took the bag from her. "You want to eat in here or outside?"

She looked around, not that she could see much, except for a picnic bench not too far away from the car. Half of the trees were bare, the other half were huge pines that kept the place from looking too stark. The lighting was poor except in the parking lot. Normal people didn't wander around in forty-degree weather.

"I have a blanket in the trunk, but it's your call."

She grinned at him. "You devil."

"The blanket is part of an emergency kit," he said dryly. "I keep it in the car at all times."

"Of course," she said just as dryly. How could she have thought otherwise? In fact, he hadn't even tried to take her to his house, like she'd expected.

After last night's kiss, she thought perhaps Dudley Do-

Right might have a wild streak in him. Might even ignore the gentleman's dating rule book he probably kept on his nightstand. A kiss on the cheek after the second date. The lips came after the third date, but only briefly. By the eighth date he might even get bold and try to cop a feel.

Not that they would have that many dates, so if she wanted to get laid she'd have to make the first move.

The thought of seducing and shocking him cheered her immeasurably. "Outside," she said finally. "We can share the blanket."

"You got it."

He left the bag and got out of the car to go around to the trunk. She waited until she could see him from the side mirror, the blanket draped over his arm, then grabbed the bag of food and got out to meet him.

They walked toward the picnic bench together, and she had to admit, she was pretty cold. Her legs, mostly, because of the short skirt. She'd be damned if she'd admit it, though, after all that bluster over not needing a coat. She shivered. Maybe they should've stayed in the car.

He didn't say a word, just placed the folded blanket over her shoulders and adjusted it so that it protected her bare neck. She didn't object. She kind of liked the way he fussed over her. It was different. Nice. Sort of sweet.

The uneven sidewalk, combined with the darkness and the odd pinecone underfoot, made it difficult to walk, but he kept his hand cupped over her elbow and she had no doubt that he wouldn't let her fall.

They got to the table, and between the trees she got a glimpse of a stream of gold and red city lights angled below them. "Wow!"

"Nice, huh?"

"Who knew?" The area he'd chosen was slightly elevated and if they were fool enough to venture farther there would undoubtedly be a great view. "I'm not sure where we are."

"A secret place."

Grinning, she set down the plastic bag. Two more minutes and the food was going to be cold. She didn't care. She watched him wipe off the bench for her, making sure it was dry and free of leaves and pebbles before he gestured for her to sit.

"If it gets too cold at anytime, we'll go back to the car, okay?"

She nodded. "I thought you were taking me to your house."

He smiled. "I thought about it."

"But?"

"I didn't want you to misunderstand."

"Misunderstand what?"

His low chuckle made her want to see his expression. But the light was behind him, which meant he could see her but she couldn't see him. No fair.

"After all, you are a guy," she said, and felt a surge of heat when he slid in next to her, his thigh warming hers, his elbow brushing the side of her breast.

"Last time I looked." He pulled out a white carton and a pair of chopsticks. "Here."

"I don't know how to use those things. I've tried, but it isn't pretty."

"Then you'll need these," he said and set a stack of white paper napkins in front of her. "Don't let them blow away. I don't want to be running around in the dark trying to pick them up."

She didn't doubt he'd do just that. Every last napkin would be accounted for before he'd leave. She hated litter herself, but she wasn't anal about it.

She looked in the bag in case he was kidding. No plastic utensils. "You're implying I should use my fingers."

"If you're hungry enough."

"I guess I can spear with the best of them."

"Look, it's easy to use chopsticks. I'll show you." He slid an arm around her and pulled her against his chest, close enough to run his arms along hers until his hand covered her hand. "Pick up the chopsticks."

Silly the way her heart slammed inside her chest. Made getting a grip on the stupid bamboo sticks really, really hard. Her fingers shook and she dropped the utensils once before securing them firmly in her hand.

"Okay?"

"Ready," she said.

"Rest one stick against the length of your middle finger like this." He maneuvered her fingers so that she had it aligned with the chopstick. "The other one you hold between your thumb and forefinger."

She tried to do as he said, and the sticks flew into the air. One landed on the table and stayed, the other one rolled off the side onto the ground.

"I'll get it." He withdrew his arm from around her to look under the table.

In the next second, she felt his warm breath on her bare thigh. His roughened chin scraped the skin at the side of her left knee. Instinctively she wanted to squeeze her legs together, but she resisted and tried to breathe in deeply. It wasn't as if he was going to do anything down there. Not that she'd mind if he did do a little exploring.

He came up too quickly. Clearing his throat, he tossed the recovered chopstick into the empty bag. "Good thing I picked up a spare pair."

"Of course you did." She noticed he hadn't looked at her. Was he embarrassed?

"What does that mean?"

"You're like a Boy Scout. Always prepared."

The light caught his wicked smile. "And that's a problem how…?"

A light, chilly breeze had her pulling the blanket tighter around her shoulders. "Now that I think about it—"

Evan's mouth came down hard on hers. She hadn't expected it and the blanket slipped from her fingers. She didn't need it anymore. Heat traveled all the way down to her toes. She could hardly breathe.

She didn't care. His practiced tongue dove deep and probed every recess of her mouth, using just the right amount of pressure and speed to taunt her, to make her crave more. He framed her face with his hands, and she gripped his shoulders. It wasn't easy twisting around like that to face him and her skirt hem rose nearly to her panties.

She really wanted him to slide his hand along her bare skin. Usually she wasn't shy about making known what she wanted, but she wasn't sure with Evan. This would be a hell of a time to scare him off. But then again, he did start it all.

He eased up and pulled back a little, but she wasn't ready to quit. She didn't want to upset the rhythm. She leaned in to him and he lowered one hand, his palm skimming the outside of her arm, dipping at her waist and then molding against her hip. He finally rested his hand on her thigh. He traced a finger to her panties and then stopped, pulling all the way back so that he could look at her.

"You have to be freezing."

"Not so much."

"What happened to the blanket?" He reached behind her and apparently saw that half of it had fallen to the ground.

"Don't worry about it."

"But I—"

She grabbed hold of his shirt, pulled him close and whispered, "For once, don't be a gentleman."

A flash of white teeth and then he claimed her mouth again. No sweet start. No gentle brush of the lips. He plunged his tongue inside, and his hands found the spot where her bikini panties rode high up on her hip. He hooked his finger around the elastic and she shivered with surprised pleasure when he started to drag it down her thigh.

She released his shirt and smoothed her hands down his chest until she got to his belt. Lingering there for a few moments, she toyed with the buckle, and smiled when she felt his reaction in the deepening of the kiss.

"Keep that up and we will end up at my house," he murmured against her mouth.

"You won't hear me complain."

Moaning, he lightly bit her lower lip.

"Hey." She cupped his bulging fly. "How's that for—"

Behind them, someone cleared their throat, at the same time a circle of light bounced on the table and then streamed up to Evan's face. "Mighty cold out here for a picnic, isn't it, folks?"

Evan turned red. As discreetly as possible, he lowered his hand from under Liza's skirt. "Good evening, officer," he said evenly. "Anything wrong?"

The police officer shone the light in Liza's face. She raised an angry hand to block the glare. "That isn't necessary."

He wouldn't move the light away from her face. "What are you two doing out here?"

"Having a damn picnic," she said. "As you've already pointed out."

"Liza, it's okay." Evan tried to take her hand, but she jerked it out of reach.

"No, it's not. He's harassing us for no reason." She stared at the older man. He was about the same age that her father would've been, and he had that kind of cocky grin that made her nuts. "Now that you've determined we aren't stealing any trees, you can leave."

He glared at her, one eyebrow going up in challenge. "ID, please, ma'am." He glanced over at Evan, who looked annoyed. "You, too, sir."

"No problem." Liza got up and had to tug her skirt down before swinging her legs over the bench to the other side. "My purse is in the car. And then I'd like your badge number."

"Liza, wait." Evan tried to catch her arm. "Come on."

She didn't look at him or the cop as she stumbled in the dark toward the car, grateful that she hadn't fallen flat on her ass. God, but she hated cops, especially older smug ones, who still drove cruisers because they couldn't manage to pass the lieutenant's exam so they took it out on everyone else.

The law was supposed to protect people. But the fine folks in blue protected each other first. No matter what the cost. Even if it meant sacrificing their spouses and children.

She opened the car door and found her purse on the floorboard. First she got out a pen. A recent gas receipt was the only piece of paper she could find. Then she retrieved her wallet and slid out her driver's license.

"Ma'am, have you been drinking?" The cop was right behind her, his flashlight in hand, and he shined a light in her face as soon as she turned around.

She battled the urge to slap the damn thing out of his hand. "I wish. Here," she said, shoving the driver's license at him and then moving out of the light.

He studied it for a long time, which no doubt was to make her squirm. Screw him. She'd get his badge number, and tomorrow she'd write a letter to his commanding officer. One thing she could still do was write a mean letter. Just the thought of it soothed her.

Evan joined them, carrying the bag of cold food and the blanket. He stared at her with a mixture of annoyance and curiosity, which only fueled her anger. He didn't understand. She didn't expect him to. She didn't *want* him to.

She got the pen ready, ticked off that her hands were shaking. God forbid anyone get the idea that she was scared. She was angry and she wanted them to damn well know it.

The cop looked up. "Ma'am, I'm sure you're aware this license expires today."

"What are you talking about?" She grabbed it out of his hand. "It doesn't expire until my birthday."

Frowning, the cop slid a brief look at Evan. "That's today."

Liza stared at the two men. "It is?"

THEY'D DRIVEN A COUPLE of miles out of the park and still neither of them had said a word. Evan rarely got angry. But given the last five minutes he was ready to take her back to her car and say adios. For good.

The way she'd reacted to the police officer had been so over-the-top, Evan had been both irritated and embarrassed. If she'd just cooled it, the officer would've been gone in a minute, and they could've resumed making out like a couple of silly teenagers.

The stunned look on her face when she'd realized it was her birthday leveled the playing field again. His anger had evaporated as quickly as it had sparked. How could she not remember it was her birthday? As much as he wasn't one to celebrate holidays, he at least knew when his birthday was. He also knew his parents' birthdays and each of his brother's. And if by chance he was busy the morning of the event and temporarily forgot, his mother would be quick to remind him. Didn't Liza have anyone to remind her?

"So," he said finally. "I gotta ask. How could you not know today was your birthday?"

She sighed loudly. "Half the time I don't even know what date it is."

"Well, happy birthday."

"Thanks," she muttered and continued to stare out of the passenger window.

"Why the long face? Is this the big three-o?"

That got her attention. She turned to give him a dirty look. "No."

He smiled. "It's no big deal. I'm halfway to forty myself."

"You're thirty-five?"

"Yep."

"Wow, I've never been out with a guy as old as you before."

"Very funny." He pulled over to the curb and threw the car into Park.

"What are you doing?"

He stretched his arm across the top of her seat, ignoring the cars that steadily whizzed by them. "What was that about with the police officer?"

Her expression turned into a petulant frown. "I don't like cops."

"You made a big thing out of nothing. He was just doing his job."

"He was unduly harassing us."

"He was reacting to you."

"You know what, it's none of your business." She folded her arms across her chest and angled herself toward the window.

"The hell it isn't. I was there, too, remember?"

At his raised voice, she turned back to him. "My dad was a cop."

"So you didn't get along with him, and now all cops are bad."

"My father wasn't just a cop, he was a drunk, okay?"

"I see."

Even in the semidarkness he saw anger flash in her eyes. "Nice, you probably did a rotation with a shrink during your residency and now you know everything about me."

"There you go again."

"What?"

"Treating me like the enemy."

"It's that superior attitude of yours."

His temper started to climb. "Explain that to me. How have I come off superior?"

She opened her mouth to say something, and then shut it again and looked away.

"You can't explain because it isn't true, but you can apologize."

She kept her face averted for a moment, and then pressed her lips together and slowly met his eyes. "You're right. I'm sorry."

He'd been ready to drive her back to her car, and then she'd caught him with an unexpected apology. This woman was going to make him insane. She was one contradiction after another. To keep seeing her would inevitably be asking for trouble. Ironically, that pretty much made her perfect. This was not a woman who elicited emotional involvement.

"This isn't an excuse," she continued, sounding defensive, "but the man who referred to himself as my father wasn't what you'd call a pleasant drunk."

"He hit you?"

"Came close a few times, but no."

"Your mother?"

Liza abruptly looked the other way and murmured, "She wasn't so lucky, and nobody seemed to give a shit."

Evan didn't ask anything more. He got the picture.

He knew more than he wanted to about adult children of alcoholics. For many, their early experiences lingered and governed their future decisions. Control was often a big issue for them. Liza had some baggage, all right. But hell, so did he.

"Just so you know, I'm not looking for pity," she said. "A lot of kids had it worse than I did."

"Good. I'm not offering any." He put the car back in Drive, and then pulled out into traffic.

Liza laid her head back and laughed softly. "You constantly surprise me."

"Is that good or bad?"

"I'm not sure yet."

He slid her a glance in time to see her smile. "Still hungry?"

"The food is cold."

After they'd gone three blocks, he turned onto Peachtree.

Straightening, she looked around. "Where are we going now?"

"My place."

CHAPTER SIX

RICK SHAKILY PUSHED himself up to a sitting position. He could see the digital clock if he squinted, but the red numbers were one big blur. The table lamp had burned out three days ago but he didn't have a replacement bulb.

Liza. Where the hell was she? The stupid bitch was supposed to take care of things like that.

A beer bottle sat at the edge of the coffee table. His mouth was so friggin' dry he couldn't even swallow. He grabbed the bottle and tipped it to his lips. Empty. He threw it against the wall between his and Liza's apartments. The *thud* echoed in the blackness, followed by the sound of glass flying everywhere.

He hoped it woke the bitch up. She had no damn business paying for a second apartment. He needed that money. She was getting stingier and stingier, not even picking up packs of cigarettes for him anymore.

"Hey!" he yelled at the wall.

Stumbling to his feet, he cursed when a shard of glass poked through one of his socks and cut him. He made it to the wall and banged at it with the flat of his hand.

No sound from the other side.

"Hey!"

He banged again, hurting the hell out of his palm and nearly tumbling face-first onto the floor. Screw her. A carton of cigarettes sat on the kitchen counter. He needed a smoke. His heel caught on a jagged piece of the broken bottle and he yelped in pain.

"Son of a bitch."

Tomorrow he was going to talk to that damn lawyer himself. No more waiting for Liza's measly handouts. He knew she was lying to him. She had money. Her daddy had left her a nice insurance policy. Nice enough to keep Rick in smack until the real money came.

He made it to the kitchen, flipped on the light and opened a beer before fumbling for the cigarettes. The lighter slipped and bounced on the floor and he cursed. He didn't like the way Liza was acting lately. She was getting too mouthy for someone he was supposed to have by the balls.

He gulped down half the beer and then opened the nearly empty bottle of vodka. With one pull he finished it off, then wiped his mouth with the back of his hand. Shit. Something was different about her. She didn't jump anymore when he talked. Normally, he didn't have to ask for cigarettes or booze.

She always kept him supplied. Not now.

Maybe she planned on taking off with the settlement money. Screw him. Screw Eve. Shit.

The thought tore through him like a tornado. The stupid bitch. If she bolted…

He ran to the front door and jerked it open. The lights were off in her apartment. It had to be after midnight. Tough shit if she was asleep. They needed to talk. Now. He pounded on her front door.

"Liza!"

No answer.

He tried to peer into the window but the drapes were drawn too tight to see anything. He pounded at the door again. "Open up, bitch!"

Nothing.

A light came on from the apartment on the other side of hers. The door opened and a burly guy stood there naked, his face an angry red. "Shut the hell up, or I'll come out there and do it for you."

Rick backed away. He glanced down at the parking lot, scanning the cars for as far as he could see. No sign of her old compact. Didn't mean anything. She could've parked anywhere. But if she was gone, that cow with the kid might know where Liza was.

He hung on to the rail for support and stumbled to the end of the corridor. He wasn't sure if the end unit was the right one but he saw the kid playing there a lot. The apartment was dark, just like most of the others in the complex.

Pressing his ear to the door, he knocked lightly so he wouldn't piss off the naked guy. A light immediately came on. A second later, the door cracked open. Bingo. He had the right apartment.

With one fearful eye, the woman peered out at him through the crack. "What do you want?"

"Where is she?"

"Who?"

"God damn it. You know who I'm talking about."

The woman shrunk back.

"Who is it, mama?" Yawning, the kid tried to squeeze between her mother and the door frame. Her eyes widened when she saw Rick.

"Go back to bed." The woman cut her off. "Now." She

turned to Rick. "I don't know where Liza is. It's late. Maybe she's sleeping."

She wasn't bad-looking up close. Except for the scar. Didn't matter. It had been a helluva long time since he'd gotten laid. Rick slid his hand in and hooked a finger under her chin. "You wouldn't lie to me, would you?"

Fear flashed in her eyes. She jerked away. "Go to hell!" she said, and slammed the door on his wrist.

"Fuck." He broke free and cradled his wrist with his other hand. "You stupid cow. You're going to pay for that. You and Liza."

Several more lights went on in other apartments, and he hurried back to his own. Friggin' Liza. No more sneaking off. From now on he'd follow her. She wasn't going to make a move without him knowing about it.

EVAN TOOK THEM to a part of town Liza didn't recognize. She'd only lived in Atlanta for about four years in a Midtown apartment that was only a few blocks from the studio. She'd worked long hours and rarely ventured past the local bar where they all congregated. But she was familiar with the posh suburb of Buckhead, a place where a practicing doctor who also consulted on a popular television series could afford to live, but this wasn't it.

The subdivision was nice enough, just not what she expected. Nor was the modest ranch-style house that Evan slowed down in front of. He turned the car into the driveway and used the remote control to lift the door to the two-car garage, which was neater and cleaner than her apartment, with a row of gardening tools hanging from a rack on the wall. Very middle American. *So* not her style.

But neither was biting the head off a police officer she didn't even know. God, what was wrong with her? She snapped in a second and she couldn't seem to control it. And what the hell was wrong with Evan? If he had a brain in his head, he would've dropped her off at her car. Why was he sticking around? Probably because deep down he was a loser. Just like all the other guys she attracted.

He inched the car forward and stopped when a red beam suddenly appeared on the wall in front of them.

"Pretty fancy," she said.

"Ingenious, actually. You don't want to know how many walls I've dented."

"You?"

"I have other good qualities," he said blandly and pressed the remote to lower the garage door before getting out of the car.

She got out, too, and followed him past two recently used dirt bikes stashed in the corner. "Are these yours?"

"One belongs to my brother." He opened the door to the house, reached in to flip on a light and then let her go first. "The housekeeper was here today so I'm safe."

At the sight of the clean, glossy tile floor, she sighed. "I want a housekeeper."

Evan smiled. "After living in dorms and shared apartments, I'd gladly spend my last dollar on a housekeeper."

Liza walked farther down the hall. The kitchen was on the left, the floor covered with more of the creamy-colored veined tile. Not just any tile, but the really cool twenty-inch kind. The cabinets looked like custom-made cherry and the appliances were all stainless steel.

"You cook much?" she asked, noticing the well-equipped island under hanging brass pots.

"Hardly ever." He came from behind her and threw his keys on the granite countertop. "Although I make a damn good tuna sandwich."

"Why do you have all this?" She wandered over to the bay window area where there was a glass table with four contemporary chairs.

"The appliances came with the house." He opened the refrigerator. "Gladys, my housekeeper, makes me meals about three times a week. What would you like to drink?"

"Surprise me."

"I hate that."

She turned to him, smiling. "What?"

He held the refrigerator door open and motioned for her. "Get your cute little butt over here and choose something."

With an exaggerated sway of her hips, she approached, smiling seductively. When she got to him, she leaned over to look into the refrigerator, knowing full well that in this position, her short skirt hid very little.

He didn't hesitate to mold his hand to her backside. "See anything you want in there?"

She did a wiggle under his touch, not sure who she was teasing more. "Hmm, let me see…"

He dipped his hand so that it was partially wedged between her thighs. Her panties grew damp as his hand moved. He slipped a finger under the elastic. She gasped and had to grab the door to steady herself.

"I found something I want," he whispered, his finger probing deeper.

She closed her eyes. It had been so long since she'd been touched like this….

The door started to move, threatening her balance, and she quickly opened her eyes.

Evan removed his finger and urged her to back up. She didn't want to—his exploration felt so good—but it happened fast, and then he closed the refrigerator door. He took her by the shoulders and forced her to face him. Then he slanted his head and kissed her gently on the mouth.

Her hands were free to explore and she found his bulging fly. He moved against her touch, but when she started to unzip him he stopped her.

"Come," was all he said, and took her hand.

They passed the living room, which was sparsely decorated, but centered on a state-of-the-art large-screen television. The short hall led to his bedroom…very masculine in shades of brown and rust. He had a TV in there, too, a small older model sitting on a very plain cherry dresser.

The bed was huge. Probably a California king, although she hadn't actually seen one before. Just knew it was big. The nightstands matched the dresser, each one holding a heavy brass lamp. On the right one was an elaborate-looking phone system.

He started taking off his jacket. "Good thing Gladys changed the sheets today."

"Why? Did you have another guest last night?" She watched him toss the camel jacket onto the dark wood-and-brass valet in the corner.

"What kind of remark was that?" He didn't look at all amused as he turned to face her.

"Oh, come on." She walked over and pulled his tie loose. "I guess that was my clumsy way of saying I know this is just about sex and that's okay with me."

He shook his head, his eyes staying fastened on hers as she pulled the tie free and threw it in the direction of the valet. "You are a handful."

She smiled. "It hasn't stopped you yet."

His mouth curved in an unexpected predatory smile, and he grabbed her wrist when she went for his belt buckle. "It's not going to stop me now."

Liza sucked in a breath when he reached under her skirt and pulled down one side of her panties. She froze, totally caught off guard. "Why, Dr. Gann," she whispered breathlessly.

"Don't move," he said.

She couldn't if she wanted to. He let go of her wrist and she stood there perfectly still while he crouched and pulled the other side of her panties down until they were around her ankles. He didn't have to tell her to step out of them. Clutching his shoulders, she did it automatically.

"What about you?" she asked in a voice she didn't recognize.

He only smiled and ran his palms over her calves and then up past her thighs, pausing for a second before filling his hands with her fleshy buttocks. While squeezing gently, he took the hem of her skirt between his teeth.

She nearly fell backward. Luckily, she was close enough to the bed so that she wouldn't have ended up on her ass. Didn't he understand that there was a certain order to the way things went?

Not that she wasn't adventurous…far from it. But this wasn't a move she'd expected from him. Man, had she ever had a misconception about doctors. Obviously, they weren't all stodgy brainiacs.

He got the skirt up high enough and pressed a kiss right in a very sensitive spot. She felt the tip of his tongue and goose bumps chased up her spine. Her fingers dug into his shoulders.

"I see you're not a breast man," she said to ease some of the tension.

"I'm getting there." His hands moved up from her backside and he yanked her sweater out from her waistband.

"Hey." She shoved at his shoulders but he wouldn't back off. "I want your shirt off first."

"Too bad." He ran his hands up her back.

"Don't I get a say?"

"Nope."

She laughed. "That's not how it works."

"Relax, Liza," he said, carefully laying her back onto the bed. "You don't always have to be in control."

She blinked. "What are you imply—"

He cut her off with an all-consuming kiss. She hadn't even realized that he'd pushed her sweater up past her bra. That he'd unfastened the front hook and cupped her bare breast. Using his thumb and forefinger, he lightly pinched her nipple before putting his mouth on it.

Her whole body thrummed with excitement. She could hardly breathe. This man literally stole her breath away. He knew exactly what to do, and when to do it to drive her insane. It had to be because she was so starved for physical touch. More than a year had passed since she'd been with a man. Rick. The thought was like an ice-cold shower. Made her want to gag.

She pushed Evan hard, catching him by surprise, then he rolled over onto the bed. His mouth wet, his eyes wary, he stared at her. "What's wrong?"

She wasn't going to let Rick ruin this. No way. "Take your shirt off," she ordered and when he didn't move, added, "I mean it."

One side of Evan's mouth slowly went up. "You want it off, go for it." He laid back with his hands clasped behind his head.

He looked way too smug. She'd fix that. She got up on her knees, letting her sweater fall back down and cover all the goodies. She paused, enjoying the disappointment on his face, and then she lifted the hem and pulled the sweater off. The unfastened bra was easy. A little shimmy and it fell down her back, leaving her naked from the waist up.

His lips parted, the struggle for control etched in lines at the corners of his glassy eyes, and he reached up to touch her extended nipple. She slapped his hand away. He met her gaze, a cocky smile starting to form.

That's okay. She wasn't through with him yet. She swung a leg over his waist and straddled him. The skirt hid nothing. His gaze shot to the prize. She reached behind and found his erection, still hardening under her touch.

Liza quickly figured that stretched back like this was exposing more than she'd planned. She thought to leave the position, but it was too late. He entered her with his finger, going deep in the slick wetness, and rubbing the nub that felt way too good this early in the game. She didn't want to come right away....

"Don't," she whispered. "Please."

He had her nether lips spread, his gaze fastened there, his fingers working skillfully. "Liza, you really want me to stop?"

She moaned. "I—I...don't want—" Oh, it was too late. She fisted the comforter and bit down on her lower lip as the sensations started to mount. As the spasms came faster, harder, without mercy, her entire body felt as if it were on fire. Her mind became so fuzzy she couldn't see.

Wave after wave of heat sluiced over her skin until she thought there'd be no reprieve. That she'd burn forever, and never be the same again. She opened her eyes. Evan's face slowly came into focus.

He withdrew his hand and started unbuttoning his shirt. She didn't move. Lethargy seized total control. She wanted to help him, but she could only watch him fumble with each button. When she realized he was wearing a T-shirt beneath his dress shirt, she had to suppress a giggle. Of course he would be properly dressed. This was Evan.

"You could help," he said.

"I don't know. You wore me out."

He groaned. "I better not have."

She freed the last button and then, noticing he was distracted by her exposed crotch, she promptly got off of him. He sat up and got rid of both shirts while she worked on his belt and fly. He hadn't cooled down any, making the zipper difficult to maneuver, and she felt the earlier excitement returning.

No more power play. They both got totally naked. The sight of his toned belly and impressive hard-on got her juices flowing again. He wasn't overly muscled, but it was obvious he didn't sit on his ass all the time, either. His chest was nice, too. Just a little bit of hair and lots of definition.

She ran her palm over his pecs and one small brown nipple, and then down over the slight ridges on his belly. He didn't move until she went lower and traced his shaft. He tensed then and cupped her breast.

"A shame to be wasting this nice big bed," he whispered and did a flicking thing with her nipple that would totally let him have his way.

To her surprise, she was the one who insisted on pulling the comforter down and getting in between the sheets. He seemed to be ready to get down and dirty, screw the comforter.

She crawled in first, while he used the opportunity to rub his palms over her backside. She wasn't usually ticklish but he got her just so and, laughing, she hurried to the other side of the bed and flipped onto her back.

He slid in next to her. As if by magic, his hand ended up

between her thighs. He got two fingers inside her before she could say anything.

"Hey." She wiggled away. "I have some exploring of my own to do."

"Be my guest," he said, lying back and kicking the sheets away.

Liza smiled. Such a guy. She took his thickness in her hand and watched his eyes close. She traced a finger around the smooth, silky tip and then under the rim. He looked as if he was having enough trouble keeping still, and when she touched the tip with her tongue, he nearly came off the bed. He murmured something she couldn't understand.

It didn't matter. She was getting carried away, too. She used the moisture from her tongue to pump him, slowly at first, but gaining momentum with her own arousal.

He reached up, curled his hand around her neck and pulled her down for a brief but blistering kiss. "Just a minute," he whispered against her mouth.

In an instant he'd gotten something out of the nightstand and was back, savagely taking her mouth while he took care of business. In another moment, he had her on her back, and slowly entered her. The strain of control was on his face, in the way his neck corded, how his biceps bunched.

She moved her hips upward, wanting to snap that control. Wanting him to plunge hard and deep inside her. But he stayed slow and steady, filling her nearly to completion, and then withdrawing again until she almost begged.

"Relax," he said softly. "Just relax."

"Are you crazy?" she murmured.

As he sunk into her again, he whispered, "Happy birthday, baby."

CHAPTER SEVEN

LIZA PULLED THE thick down blanket up to her chin and snuggled farther into the covers. Evan had his arm thrown around her waist but he was so sound asleep he wasn't bothered by her moving around. He stayed on his stomach, his stubbly chin close to her face as they shared the same pillow. A really great pillow. The dense kind that still managed to stay soft. She used to have one of those. Before she'd been forced to stay in a cheap fleabag apartment.

She opened her eyes and stared at his lashes resting on his cheek. She hadn't noticed how thick or long they were, or the tiny mole just at the corner of his eye. His hair was too short and, even now, after a night of rolling around in the sheets, wasn't very messed up. Across his shoulders was a scattering of freckles, which seemed odd because he really wasn't that fair-skinned. Ten to one he really hated them.

God, how different he looked right now. Nothing like the geeky man she used to see at the station over a year ago. He'd changed, or maybe she had.

As much as she wanted to just keep staring at him, she had more pressing business. A soft glow came from the master bathroom from the night-light Evan kept in there.

Earlier, she'd teased him about being afraid of the dark. Now she was glad for the beacon showing her the way in the unfamiliar room.

She slowly moved Evan's arm from around her waist, and then inched her way toward the other end of the bed. Parts of her that she'd nearly forgotten how to use ached like crazy. Evan had reminded her. Boy, had he. The guy sure had paid attention in anatomy class.

There wasn't an ounce of inhibition or modesty in the man's genes. He'd surprised her over and over again. For hours. Stamina was another one of his attributes. She had him totally wrong. Well, not totally. He was a little obsessive about keeping things in tidy rows. She smiled. Must have driven his college roommates nuts.

Quietly she closed the bathroom door behind her. She flipped on the light and faced herself in the mirror. Ugly red marks marred the skin just above her right breast and on the side of her neck. Another beard burn claimed a spot under her ear. Damn, damn, damn. Just what she needed. Hopefully makeup would cover up the mark.

She turned on the water, waited until it was warm and then splashed her face. The air was chilly without Evan's body heat. She hadn't even done her business yet, and she couldn't wait to get back into bed with him. Who would've guessed he could be so energetic?

The trouble was, it wasn't just because he was a warm body. Last night, Evan had made her feel safe. Ridiculous, of course. She meant nothing to him. They were consenting adults who enjoyed sex. Period. No big deal. She doubted there'd be a repeat performance. In fact, if she were smart, she'd tell him this was it. He was too much of a distraction.

Although, one more night wouldn't hurt.

She hurriedly used the john and then turned off the light. She was about to open the door when she realized the night-light wasn't on. Yet light came from behind her. She turned around. Sunlight seeped through the frosted glass window.

Shit.

It was morning.

She quickly collected her clothes and purse, and then called a cab before she got dressed.

LIZA GOT TO HER attorney's office, her legs still shaking from the scene with Rick. Half an hour after she'd gotten home from Evan's, Rick had shown up at her door, yelling and screaming and demanding to know where she'd been all night. Good thing one of the neighbors had threatened to call the cops. That had shut him up fast. But he wasn't done with her yet. She knew that all too well from past experience.

No more sneaking out. No more seeing Evan. He was a nice guy, and he had amazing hands that made her forget. But Rick was becoming more volatile and she couldn't afford him finding out about Evan. He didn't deserve being Rick's target. And sadly, she didn't deserve someone as nice as Evan.

She shut off the engine and noticed that the gas was close to the empty mark. Great. Just great. She'd used nearly all her cash on the cab from Evan's house to her car. Sighing, she climbed out and smoothed her sensible wool slacks. It hadn't been easy to get Kevin Wade to take her case. She knew he'd thought she was some kind of crackpot at first. The least she could do was look like a normal person. Maybe he'd even have good news for her today.

The offices of Kregel, Fitch & Devine were on the twelfth floor. Liza swore the damn elevator had stopped at every floor before she finally got to theirs. Topping things off was the big Christmas tree sitting in the middle of the foyer. God, she couldn't wait for all the holiday crap to be over.

Recognizing her immediately, the receptionist picked up the phone and called for Kevin's secretary. Liza had made a total pest out of herself for the past two months, and pretty much everyone on the floor knew her.

Too bad.

"Just go on back, Ms. Skinner," the receptionist said, and then went on with her typing.

Liza followed the corridor toward Kevin's office. Along the way were numerous other offices belonging to junior associates. She got two doors down from Kevin's office and heard a familiar voice. Talking to an older woman was Jenna Hamilton, CATL-TV's attorney. She was the same attorney being used by Eve and Jane and the rest of the lottery winners.

Did this mean good news? Was there another offer on the table? Liza's heart pounded as she entered Kevin's office. He looked up from his computer screen and smiled. Unfortunately, not a good-news kind of smile. She took a deep breath.

He motioned to the brown club chair opposite him. "I have news."

"Yeah?" Hope soared again.

"We have a court date."

"Oh. I thought— I just saw Jenna Hamilton."

Kevin shook his head. "That was nothing to do with your case."

"They aren't countering?"

He narrowed his dark brown eyes on her. "What counter? You flatly refused their offer."

"I know that." She put two fingers to her throbbing temple. Too little sleep. Too much stress. "I just thought maybe they'd come up with another amount."

He leaned back in his chair and looked sternly at her. "You can't have it both ways. You told me you were firm on the seven-way split."

"Right." She cleared her throat. How could she possibly be offended that Eve and Jane weren't willing to settle, or that they were willing to drag her to court? What irony. To them she was no longer a friend. She cleared her throat again. "When's the court date?"

"On the twenty-second."

"Of this month?"

He nodded.

Her pulse raced. "Is it good to go before a judge so close to Christmas?"

"It could go either way. But you told me you wanted this over with as soon as possible." He paused. "Your friend Rick called."

"He what?" Oh, no. She'd been careful not to leave a business card around, hoping he'd forgotten the law firm's name. But she'd underestimated him. This was bad. He was getting desperate. She had to watch herself, not give him a reason to be suspicious or feel insecure. "When?"

"Yesterday."

"What did you tell him?"

"Nothing, of course. He's not my client. You are." Over his long brown steepled fingers, Kevin regarded her with a kindness he hadn't shown before. He didn't have to tell her that Rick had been angry and vile. "The man is a liability to you, Liza. I recommend he not be in court with you."

Anger, sarcasm, hatefulness—all of that she could take.

But not kindness. She lifted her chin. "I hope you didn't call me all the way over here to tell me that."

He smiled. "Actually, I wanted to see for myself how you're holding up."

"Yeah?" What nerve. She got to her feet.

"You're a wreck."

"Thank you."

"I'm serious, Liza. You don't want to go into court looking like some desperate druggie who dropped off the face of the earth for nearly a year, and then pops up and sues her friends."

She winced. "I don't do drugs."

"Appearance is everything. Dress smart, look alert. Take care of yourself."

She swallowed. Okay, so she'd been up all night. Lost a few pounds. None of his business. Self-consciously she raked a hand through her hair. There were so many tangles she couldn't get all the way through. "I'll be fine," she said. "You just worry about winning the case."

BAD ENOUGH SHE HADN'T left a note yesterday morning when she snuck out of his house, Evan still hadn't heard from Liza.

If she'd wanted, she could've easily contacted him yesterday at the studio, or even been waiting in the parking lot. But she'd chosen to leave him hanging, and he was getting more than a bit irritated over her rudeness.

Hurt, really. The sex had been great. He really felt as if they'd connected on some level. He'd been moved that she'd even confided in him about her father. And then, poof. The disappearing act.

"Dr. Gann?"

He looked up from the chart he'd been reading in his office. Normally his desk was organized and nearly spotless. Today it was a total mess of folders and journals. He hadn't even hung up his jacket. It lay across one of the black leather-and-chrome chairs sitting opposite him that were used for patient consultations.

"Is something wrong?" Betty asked with concerned blue eyes. She'd been his nurse from day one. He'd played tennis with her husband numerous times, and he'd even been to her kids' birthday parties. Other than his brothers, she was as close to a friend as he had.

But he couldn't tell her about Liza. Betty would get excited and want to meet her. That wouldn't happen. "Just a little tired. What's up?"

Her frown told him she wasn't convinced but all she said was, "The lab work came back for Mrs. Gardner. You might want to have a look at it before lunch. Her appointment is in two hours."

"Lunch?" He looked at his watch. It was already after two.

"I can order something for you."

"No, I'm not hungry." Damn, he'd planned on sneaking out for an hour. Try and catch Eve. See if she had Liza's cell number. "What have you got?"

She handed him the lab results and went to the door. "Oh, I almost forgot," she said, turning around. "A woman called earlier, she's not a patient…"

His entire body reacted. His pulse raced, his palms started getting clammy. *Liza.* Finally.

"She was hoping to get squeezed in today. Carolyn Sager recommended her."

"Anything serious?"

She smiled. "No. And I told her you had a tight schedule. She's coming in next week."

"Thanks. I'd like to get out of here by five." He went back to scanning the lab results, effectively avoiding Betty's inquiring look. She knew he didn't have a life. Normally he'd stay until seven, if necessary.

Not tonight. He had to figure out this thing with Liza. He seriously had no clue why she'd ditched him like this. If something had happened, or if she just wasn't interested, he wanted to know. Eve might be able to enlighten him. In fact, he had quite a few questions for her.

"I'M GLAD YOU CALLED," Eve said, gesturing for him to sit. "Or you would've missed me. As it is, I'm sorry but I only have ten minutes." She was pretty and charismatic, with a dynamite smile, and he could see why her show had become such a huge success.

Yet Liza was the one who'd caught his eye from the beginning. No explaining it. His lab partner in medical school would have explained the attraction as pure chemistry. Evan didn't buy that stuff.

"As I told you on the phone, I wanted to talk to you about Liza," he said, accepting the seat she offered.

She gave a small nod of her head, her face perfectly masked, except for the sadness in her green eyes she failed to disguise. "I'm not sure I can tell you much. I haven't seen her for some time."

"I know. She told me."

One of her eyebrows went up. "You've talked to her."

"We've met for dinner or drinks a couple of times this week," he said.

She blinked, surprise written all over her face. "How did that happen?"

"I saw her out in the parking lot one afternoon, and we got together."

Eve pressed her lips together and looked away, but not before he saw the hurt in her eyes.

"I think she was waiting to see you," he offered. "That day in the parking lot."

"I doubt it. We have nothing to say to each other."

"You were friends for a long time."

"Since we were eleven. Apparently that means nothing to her." Eve turned back to him, anger replacing the hurt. "Did she send you here?"

"No." He wanted to laugh. "Actually, I'm trying to find her."

"She pulled a disappearing act on you, too?" She shook her head and sighed. "Don't expect much. She has a habit of doing that."

"I guess that means you don't have her phone number."

She looked at him as if he'd asked her to moon her audience tomorrow. "Since I have nothing to say to her, no, I do not."

"I think she's in some kind of trouble," he said, watching her closely. Despite her attitude, Eve wasn't nearly as angry as she was sad and disappointed.

She blinked and opened her mouth to say something, but quickly shut it again. She looked down at her hands, absently shaking her head. "I have to go."

"Tell me what happened to split you guys up."

She warily raised her gaze to his. "Didn't you ask her?"

"You know Liza."

She started to smile and then sighed. "Honestly, I don't know. The show was going great, largely because of her creativity. Then one day we disagreed on a segment, like we'd done many times before, and she blew up. Stormed out of here like we'd personally attacked her. I didn't call her, or anything. That was a Friday. I figured she'd cool off and everything would be okay by Monday morning."

"You never saw her after that?"

With a bitter laugh, she said, "Not until after the lottery win." Then she turned pensive. "If she's in trouble it's because of Rick."

"Rick?"

"Her boyfriend. He was trouble from day one but Liza couldn't see it. Toward the end we thought he was maybe using some kind of drugs, even drinking a lot."

"She said she isn't seeing him."

"I sincerely hope you're right." She got to her feet. "I'm sorry. I really do have to go."

He stood, too. "Thanks."

"You might try her attorney, Kevin Wade." She walked him to her office door. "He'd know how to get ahold of Liza."

"Right. Thank you."

"I don't know his number but he's with Kregel, Fitch and Devine," she called after him.

He was already headed down the hall, fishing his cell phone out of his pocket.

LIZA FOUND A PARKING SPOT right near the stairs to her apartment and pulled out her bag of groceries. If Rick saw her car there and thought she'd stayed home all night maybe he'd back off. The ordeal was almost over. Two more weeks and a judge would decide her fate. She was so damn tired that no matter what the outcome, she was getting to the point that she'd just be glad when it was over.

"Hey," Mary Ellen called out when Liza was halfway up the stairs. The woman was leaning over the railing, her voice lower than usual. She pointed to her apartment and then motioned for Liza to follow.

Liza's gaze automatically went to Rick's window. It was too cold to be open. He was probably listening for her. Waiting to finish what he'd started earlier. She wasn't in the mood. Even though he'd be pleased with news of the court date, and it might even shut him up for a while, she just didn't want to deal with him right now.

She quietly ascended the stairs and went straight for Mary Ellen's apartment. She stood in the doorway, looking fearfully toward Rick's room.

"What's wrong?" Liza asked, her head starting to pound.

Mary Ellen put a finger to her lips and quickly went inside. Even though the place was so tiny, it was immaculate. No toys laying around or dirty dishes sitting on the counter. The bed had been returned to being a sofa and the pillows were stacked neatly in the corner.

As soon as she shut the door behind Liza, Mary Ellen said, "He was looking for you night before last."

"I know." A sick feeling gnawed at her gut. "Did he come here?"

Mary Ellen nodded. "He thought I knew where you were."

Liza muttered a curse and then took the other woman's hands in hers. "I'm so sorry, Mary Ellen."

"It's not your fault." She shrugged her slim shoulders. "He didn't hurt us or nothing. Billy Ray over in twenty-one threatened to kick his ass and he took off real fast." A small smile lifted the corners of her lips before she frowned. "But he's really getting worse, Liza, and I'm afraid he's gonna hurt you."

"He won't." She gave her hands a final squeeze. "I promise."

"You can't make that promise," Mary Ellen said, solemnly shaking her head.

"I won't give him a reason to be mad, okay? Anyway, it's almost over."

"What is?"

"Look, in about two weeks he'll be moving out." Either way, no matter how the lawsuit's outcome was determined, she'd be done with him. She didn't want any of the money. She just wanted him gone.

Mary Ellen's sad eyes widened. "And you?"

"Me, too."

She shook her head. "But you're the best friend I've ever had."

Liza's heart broke a little. They were hardly friends. "We'll keep in touch, silly."

The door opened and both women jumped.

"Is it time for dinner yet?" Freedom's face was red from the cold, yet all she had on was a sweatshirt. "Hi, Liza."

"Close the door, honey," Mary Ellen said, already on her way to lock it.

"It's okay." The girl took off her red ball cap. "He's still passed out."

Liza exchanged glances with Mary Ellen. This kid was only eight. She shouldn't even know those two words. Although at that age, Liza had known the term all too well. God forbid Freedom grew up to be a mess like her. "Look," Liza said softly. "Next time you call the police."

"I don't have a phone," Mary Ellen reminded her.

"Here." Liza dug in her purse for her cell. She found her wallet and her sunglasses. Breath mints and a nail file. A hard candy had come unwrapped. She sifted through everything a second time. No cell phone.

It had to be here. She checked again. She'd had it just this morning before going to the store....

Oh, God. The last time she remembered having it was in Rick's apartment.

CHAPTER EIGHT

EVAN SAW HER CAR parked in the lot as soon as he left the station the next day. She hadn't returned his call, but that didn't matter now. He should be angry. And he still was a fraction. But he wanted so badly to talk to her. Find out what had gone so wrong that she'd sneaked out of his house.

He got halfway to her car when she opened the door and got out. After glancing over her shoulder, she turned to glare at him, her face flushed. As he got closer, she met him partway between a late-model black BMW and a midsize SUV.

"What the hell do you think you're doing?" she asked, her voice low but furious.

"Liza…"

"You had no right contacting my attorney," she said, her hand shaking as she pushed the hair away from her face.

"Calm down, Liza."

"Don't tell me to calm down."

He reached for her hand, but she jerked away. "All I did was leave a message with him."

"What made you think I wanted to hear from you? The sex was great. Is that what you wanted to hear?"

"Jeez, Liza…" He looked around to see if anyone was within earshot. A couple of cameramen were walking toward them, but he didn't think they'd heard her. He couldn't see past the SUV. "Can we go someplace else to talk," he asked, angry now himself.

"There's nothing to talk about," she said in a lower voice, and then glanced over her shoulder. "It was a one-night stand. Get it?"

"Actually, I don't." At this point, he wasn't sure it mattered. She was a friggin' whack job. What had he seen in her in the first place?

"Please, Evan," she whispered, her lower lip trembling. "I can't do this."

He thought he saw her eyes well up, but she blinked and anything that might have been there was gone. That vulnerability was what kept him on the hook. She seemed tough one minute, and the next she looked as if she was going to shatter into a million pieces. "Liza, please tell me what's wrong."

She shook her head and backed up. "Nothing. I just have a lot going on right now."

He followed her to her compact. Something was wrong. The way she kept looking over her shoulder… She was afraid of something. Or someone. "Give me ten minutes," he said. "Just ten minutes."

"I can't do this, Evan. I cannot do this."

He put up his hands in supplication. "Okay."

Their eyes met, and he didn't mistake the regret in hers. "You're a good guy. I wish—" Shaking her head, she abruptly turned to the car door. And dropped her keys.

Evan moved quickly, snatching up the keys and then handing them to her. "If you ever need someone to talk to—"

Liza touched his hand. "You make this so hard."

"Good."

She almost smiled. "You're crazy."

"I thought I was boring."

Her lips parted, her brows lowered in indecision and then she briefly closed her eyes and shook her head. "I'm the crazy one," she muttered more to herself, and then said, "Let's go."

"Where?"

"I don't know. Anywhere." She glanced around. "Let's take your car."

"Sure."

"Come on." She spotted his car and hurried ahead of him.

He didn't know what the hell to think, but he'd figure it out later. He had to really move to catch up with her. "My house?"

"No."

He opened the car doors. "I have several other rooms besides the bedroom."

She gave him a small smile before slipping inside the car. "Take me someplace I've never been."

Evan laughed. "Am I allowed any hints?"

She laid her head back and closed her eyes. "No."

"Okay, then. I know just the place."

LIZA HAD TO BE OUT of her damn mind. If Rick woke up before she got home, he was going to go absolutely berserk. Mary Ellen and Freedom were safe. That was the main thing. Billy Ray had promised to keep an eye on them. The biker had to be three hundred pounds of muscle, with arms that were bigger than Liza's thighs.

Fortunately, Kevin had left her a message to call him instead of giving Evan her number. Rick had intercepted the voice mail before she could retrieve her phone from him and he'd blasted her with questions regarding what Kevin wanted. But none she hadn't been able to get around.

But the truth was, the smart thing for her to do was stay low for the next two weeks. Not give Rick any reasons to get suspicious or panic. That made him dangerous, and meant she should stay away from Evan.

What was it about him that made her get stupid? Or maybe it wasn't Evan. Maybe it was anyone with a dick. No, that wasn't true. She had no problem being alone, and definitely didn't have trouble telling a guy to kiss off. But Evan was different. He made her laugh. He made her feel safe. That in itself didn't make sense. Because there was no safe place. Not for someone like her.

"This time we're eating dinner," Evan said. "You like ribs?"

"Without the sauce."

He gave her a mock glare. "What kind of Southerner are you?"

"Technically, I'm a Yankee."

"Say it ain't so."

Liza smiled. "I was born in New York."

They came to an intersection and he stopped at the red light and looked at her. "I thought you were from Florida."

"We moved there when I was eleven. Before that we lived in Connecticut, New Jersey and Pennsylvania."

"All before you were eleven?"

She frowned at him. "Don't give me that look."

"What look? I was waiting for the light to turn green." Which it did at that moment and he made a left.

She let the conversation lag while she stared out the window. It was her own fault that he pitied her. She'd told him too much about her past, about her father. Evan wasn't stupid. He'd put two and two together. So many moves in such a short period of time all related to her father's drinking. And her mother's lack of backbone. Weren't mothers supposed to protect their children? Apparently Beverly Skinner had skipped that chapter from the parenting guide.

Liza laid her head back and sighed. She wasn't going to go there. All that would do was make her angry, or worse, horribly sad. She couldn't afford any negative emotions. She had to focus. Kevin Wade was right. She had to pull herself together before she went before the judge.

"You're quiet," Evan said, five minutes later.

"Enjoy it."

"I'd rather talk."

She heard the seriousness in his voice and wished she'd never gotten into his car. "I really don't have anything to say. I'm just trying to de-stress."

This time he lapsed into silence. After a few minutes, he asked, "I talked to Eve."

"When?"

"Yesterday afternoon. I thought she might have a phone number for you."

Just hearing Eve's name was like a knife in the heart. She and Jane's friendship had been the only truly good thing that had happened to Liza. And she'd allowed a man to destroy that. She wasn't even worthy of their friendship.

She swallowed around the lump in her throat. "Why in the hell would you think that?"

"Because you were friends."

"*Were* being the operative word." She couldn't take it anymore. Next time he stopped she was going to get out. Run as fast as she could.

"I think she misses you."

"Drop it."

Neither Eve nor Jane missed her. How could they? They thought she was the scum of the earth, and she didn't blame them even the tiniest bit. She was the one who missed them. Terribly. The irony was that she'd always depended on herself, handled her own problems, but if she'd ever really been up against the wall, it was Eve or Jane that she'd go to for help. This was the biggest mess of her life, and she didn't have a soul to turn to.

Evan pulled the car up to a curb behind a long line of cars and trucks. They were in a neighborhood she didn't recognize and not a particularly great one. Mostly there were houses one after another, a convenience store on one corner and a gas station on the other. Was he taking her to a party? That would be absurd.

"I think this is as close as we're going to get. Good thing it's unseasonably warm tonight." He shut off the engine, and then glanced down at her feet. "Tennis shoes. Good."

"Where are we?"

"You're going to like it. Trust me."

"Trust you?" Was he kidding? She didn't trust anybody. Not anymore.

"Can you do that?"

She looked into earnest brown eyes, remembered how good she'd felt in his arms. She couldn't let her guard down again. "Let's go."

"Wait."

Her hand on the door handle, she warily looked at him. She didn't want to talk anymore. It was way too easy to talk to Evan, and she didn't want anything slipping out that she might regret.

Cupping a hand around the nape of her neck, he leaned in and pressed his lips coaxingly against hers. She didn't want to give in. Still, this was better than talking. Better than just about anything. His mouth was warm and minty and his skillful tongue made it difficult not to participate.

She leaned closer and placed a hand on his thigh for balance. He shifted and her finger grazed the bulge straining his fly. He slackened his hold at the back of her neck and drew his hand over her shoulder and down the side of her arm. When he got to her hand, he covered it with his and, interestingly, was the one who broke the kiss.

"I've been waiting two days for that," he whispered and then briefly kissed her again before retreating.

"Glad you got it off your chest." Her glibness was undermined by the shakiness in her voice.

He smiled, and she turned away and exited the car.

"I hope you're not taking me to a party," she said after he came around the car and they started down the sidewalk. None of the houses looked as if they were especially rocking, but she couldn't see where else they'd be heading to.

"You're supposed to trust me, remember?"

"Those were your words, not mine. I don't trust anybody." She looked away from the disappointment that flickered in his face. She wasn't responsible for how he felt. Not her job.

They walked for a full block in silence, and then crossed the street and kept walking. She'd be lying if she said that she wasn't intrigued. Although knowing Evan, they were probably going to a book club discussion or a poetry reading. Nothing wrong with either one. But definitely not her style.

Liza's thoughts went back to Eve, and whether she'd mentioned Rick to Evan. She'd give just about anything to find out how that conversation went. To know how much dirt Eve had given up about Rick, and about what a damn fool Liza had been to put up with his arrogance. Well, she'd give almost anything. Not her pride.

By the time they reached the middle of the next block she saw a house at the far corner, sitting by itself, that was ablaze with lights. Even the trees flanking the driveway had small white lights spiraling up their trunks. Several groups of people milled around the front yard. Behind the house, smoke filled the air. As they got closer, she caught a whiff of grilled meat.

She looked over at Evan.

He was watching her, a smile playing at the corners of his mouth. "It's not a party. It's part rib joint, part bar. Very public."

"Afraid I'm going to attack you?"

"Yep."

"You wish."

"Yep."

Liza grinned. "Seriously, a restaurant out here in the middle of a neighborhood?"

"Not exactly. We had to park back there because I knew we wouldn't get a closer space. But the house sits on the main drag," he said, pointing at all the cars going by on the other side.

"I bet the neighbors are happy."

He shrugged. "Poor zoning. I know I would've moved."

Liza smiled at his blasé attitude. "Here I thought you were a Republican."

"Maybe I am."

"Hey, Evan." A man holding a bottle of beer saw them approach the driveway. "Eric's been looking for you."

Evan lifted his chin in greeting. "Out back?"

The guy nodded and then returned to his conversation with two blond women who apparently weren't bothered by the chilly air, either, judging by their cute skimpy dresses.

Liza dismally glanced down at her old faded jeans and ratty black sweater. She hadn't planned on going anywhere, much less someplace with Evan. Hell, what did she care? She wasn't trying to impress Evan or anyone else. Tossing her hair over her shoulder, she lifted her chin as she walked alongside Evan into the house.

What apparently once had been the living room was a mass of tables and chairs, not necessarily matching. At some point there had to be a wall separating the kitchen from the living room, but it had been knocked down and the two-person manned kitchen was now divided only by a counter, crowded with plates of potato salad, coleslaw and French fries. Sticking out from under each plate was an order ticket.

The noise level was high and annoying, and nothing like she thought Evan would appreciate. But he apparently came here often enough that five people had greeted him by the time they made it to the back door.

He'd introduced her each time, and each time the person looked surprised. The way she was dressed had nothing to do with it because as dumpy as she looked, mostly everyone else was in jeans, too. Made her wonder how often he brought a date with him.

He opened the back door, and they walked into a large enclosed patio. In the corner was a three-man band playing eighties rock. Not too loud, just enough so that you could actually enjoy the music. The rest of the floor was taken up with picnic tables. Beyond the enclosure were more wooden tables where groups of people sat, drinking beer, laughing and talking. Around the side of the house, two men stood over split barrels, turning slabs of ribs over an open fire.

The place was crowded but Evan steered her to an available table to the right of the stage. They received several interested looks as they weaved their way across the patio, and then she realized it was because everyone seemed to know Evan.

They'd only sat down for a few minutes when a dark-haired waitress wearing jeans and a tight, lime-green T-shirt brought them two light beers. "Hey, Doc," she said, setting the bottles on the table and then wiping her hands on her jeans. "You eating?"

"Later." He turned to Liza. "Okay with you?"

"Fine."

The woman sized her up. "Been here before, honey?"

"Nope. I'm a virgin."

The younger woman's throaty laugh sounded like a two-pack-a-day habit. "I'll bring a menu then check back with you later, Doc."

Liza watched the waitress go to an old refrigerator in the corner and take out five beers that she loaded on a tray. "How did you find this place?"

"I've been coming here for years. By the way, they have wine and soda if you prefer."

"No, beer is good." She tipped the cold bottle to her lips.

"If you want a glass you have to ask for it. The glass will be clean, the look will be dirty. They're big on low maintenance."

"Amen to that."

He reached across the table and touched his fingertips to hers. "Why don't you come around and sit on this side with me?"

She gave him a teasing grin. "Then how can I gaze into your eyes?"

"I'll give you something else to gaze at."

"Ooh, I like it when you're naughty."

"You want to see naughty? Get your sweet little back-side over here."

"I dare you."

"You won't know until you get over here."

Liza laughed. She wasn't so sure he wasn't serious. The more she saw of Evan, the more she believed she truly didn't know this man. That wasn't totally true. She knew the important stuff. That he was kind and patient and understanding, and that he had a great sense of humor. But there was this other side to him, a side that contradicted the doctor image.

Maybe it was her own biased opinion of the type of person she thought would become a doctor. The kind of student in college who practically lived in labs and librar-ies, while she'd been hitting every party and club that would overlook her lousy fake ID. If a guy rode in on a bike, Harleys being her favorite, the odds were three-to-one she'd be riding home with him. She'd liked them rough and tough, screw the guys that cultivated their sen-sitive sides and wanted to explore their feelings.

"What do you think of the music?" Evan asked, break-ing into her thoughts.

"They're good. Just my kind of music." She smiled at him, got up and went around to his side. "Move."

"Yes, ma'am." He slid over but didn't leave her all that much room.

She reached across the table for her forgotten beer and then slid in beside him, pressing her thigh to his. She gave him a nudge with her hip, and he surprised her by picking up her hand and kissing the back of it.

"It's okay that I sit on the outside then?" she asked, lik-ing that he held on to her hand.

He frowned slightly. "Now that you mention it…"

"I'm not moving."

"Good," he whispered, his gaze on her lips.

She thought he was going to kiss her, but then the band stopped playing and he looked toward the stage. She turned, too, but all she saw was the band members putting down their instruments.

The long-haired drummer left the stage and headed toward them. He slid onto the bench she'd vacated, glanced at her and then said to Evan, "About time you got here, bro."

"Liza, this is Eric."

"I've heard about you," Eric said before she had a chance to say anything. "Glad you could make it. Sorry I'm gonna have to steal your date." He turned back to Evan. "I need you for about an hour."

"Forget it."

Liza finally remembered who Eric was—he was Evan's brother. Even if she didn't know, the melting brown eyes gave it away. But there, any similarity ended. Eric was taller and lankier and hadn't picked up a razor in at least a week. His jeans were torn and his Grateful Dead T-shirt was a size too small, although it showed off surprisingly hunky biceps. Back in the day, if Liza had met him at a party she'd have been all over him.

"Come on," Eric said, and then took a sip of Evan's beer. "Just until Tony gets here. You know I'm not so hot on the drums."

A blonde wearing black leather came up behind him and slid her arms around his neck, her fake platinum-blond hair spilling over his shoulders. She lowered her red lips close to his ear. "You sounded good to me."

Eric didn't look thrilled. "I'm talking to someone here."

"Can't I sit with you during the break?" she asked and snuggled up beside him before he could answer.

"Later, Stephanie."

She sighed. "It's Melanie." Then she got up and wandered over to the bass guitarist.

The scene made Liza's stomach turn. God, had she ever been that bad? No, she had more pride than that. Except when it had come to Rick.

"Liza," Eric said, "mind loaning him out for an hour?"

Evan exhaled sharply. "What part of no don't you get?"

Liza looked from Evan to his brother. "What's this about, anyway?"

Eric grinned at his brother. "Don't you wanna see the best drummer in Atlanta bring down the house?"

CHAPTER NINE

LIZA TURNED and stared at Evan. "You play the drums?"

He actually looked embarrassed. "Not really. A little bit."

Eric had just gotten a beer from the waitress. Chuckling, he uncapped it. "Damn near put himself through medical school playing the drums."

She blinked at him. "You did?"

"I was in a band." He shrugged. "We mostly played on weekends. I still worked a research job a couple of times a week."

"Would I know the name of the band?"

"I doubt it."

"Tell me."

He grimaced, clearly uncomfortable with the subject. "Messed Up."

She laughed. "Interesting."

"I was twenty."

"He could've stayed in the biz if he wanted and made some real dough," Eric said before taking another long pull.

"Yeah, unlike practicing medicine," Evan said dryly.

"I'm just saying. Everybody wanted you."

"Go play," Liza said suddenly.

He shook his head. "I want to have some dinner, then—"

"Come on," she said, putting a hand on his thigh and squeezing gently. "I really want to hear you play."

Evan's brows went up in warning.

Eric grinned. "Better go practice a few minutes. We're back on in fifteen."

Evan rose and shrugged out of his jacket. Liza took it from him and carefully laid it across her lap. "Even if Tony doesn't show up, I'm done after the set," he said, rolling back his sleeves two turns. "Got it?"

"Got it." Eric winked at Liza and then they watched him head to the stage. "I knew he wouldn't let me down."

Liza smiled at the fondness in Eric's voice. Must be nice to have a brother to depend on. "Where do you fall in the Gann pecking order?"

"In the middle. We have a younger brother. Elton's in his second year of law school."

"Wow. Talented trio."

He smiled, and she saw that was something else he shared with Evan. "I have a degree in English lit myself, but I never got around to using it."

"You Gann boys sure do surprise me."

"Yeah, wait until you hear my boy up there play. He's gonna blow your skirt up."

Again, the fondness in his voice and gaze tugged at Liza's heart. Envy wormed its way in there. She couldn't lose the petty feeling, even knowing that it was just as well her parents hadn't had any more kids to suffer their cruel indifference.

One of the other guys from the band motioned for Eric and he excused himself. She didn't mind sitting alone. She liked being able to watch Evan undisturbed. He was the only one of the group wearing short hair and a shirt that hadn't gone through one too many washings. Even though he looked out of place it didn't seem to bother him. She admired his confidence.

Eric produced another guitar, while a shorter, stockier guy tuned his bass. The singer, his sandy-blond hair nearly down to his waist, practiced his cocky smile on a bevy of big-busted groupies before joining the rest of the band.

A few minutes later when the set started with Miami Sound Machine's "Conga" she understood the reason for Evan's self-assurance. The guy was totally awesome. He was like a different person up there. The way he moved with incredible rhythm, the way he really got into the song, his expression a reflection of the lyrics.

She'd always loved music, mostly classic rock, but she wasn't a connoisseur by any stretch of the imagination. She just knew what she liked. And what Evan was doing up there…well, that certainly tipped the like scale.

If this whole evening had been orchestrated to turn her on, the attempt was a rousing success. By the fourth song, she had a good mind to yank him off that stage and drag him back to his house. When he did a solo, she just about melted into the bench. In fact, the hour seemed to go by exceedingly fast and when the last song for the set was announced, she wasn't sure if that made her happy or disappointed.

"You were fantastic," she said as soon as he joined her again. "How did you learn to play like that?"

"I got my first set of drums for my ninth birthday."

"And your parents didn't go crazy?"

"The rule was that I played only in the garage. I don't think my parents liked the neighbors on our left."

She smiled. "Tell the truth, were they sorry they bought them for you?"

"Not in the least. Come on, let's get some ribs." He signaled the waitress. "I worked up one hell of an appetite."

A few people stopped by the table to tell him how much they enjoyed his performance, and although he thanked them politely, he subtly let them know that he didn't want to chat. That all he wanted was to be with Liza. The warmth that spread throughout her chest and down through her belly ended quite predictably. But she doubted he'd want to skip dinner a third time.

The waitress came for their order and Evan explained that there were only two items—ribs or chicken, and each came with a choice of potato salad, baked beans or fries. Coleslaw, corn bread and pickles came whether you wanted them or not. With a snort, the waitress reminded him that a few people tried to talk her out of a couple of extra dill pickles from time to time. He gave her a smile that could melt butter, and she giggled like a schoolgirl.

After she left, Liza elbowed him in the ribs.

Evan jerked. "What's that for?"

"You charmer."

"You mean Colleen?" He glanced at the waitress who'd stopped at the next table. "She's a good kid."

"Kid?"

"She's still in college. To me that's a kid."

"You are old."

"Okay, I admit it."

"But not where it counts," she said, rubbing her hand against his thigh, her fingers close enough to the mother lode to make him smile.

"Is that an invitation?"

"I've always been a sucker for a drummer."

"Wish you'd told me earlier." He placed a restraining hand over hers when she got too bold.

Laughing, Liza withdrew. "I'm glad I met your brother."

"He's a good guy. So is the youngest one. Very smart. He has a bright future."

"Elton."

He looked at her. "You and Eric talked, I see."

"Some."

"What else did he tell you?"

She shrugged, curious at his intense reaction. Did he think Eric gave away family secrets? "Nothing, really. Only that Elton was in law school. Is anything wrong?"

"No, of course not."

"Oh, Eric did tell me he was an English lit major, which, I gotta tell you, surprised the hell out of me."

Evan smiled. "He surprised all of us. I think he'll end up teaching. But he's still young, single, no kids. Might as well do what he wants now."

"What about you?"

He didn't look at her. Just kept staring straight ahead at the stage, even though the band hadn't returned from their break. "What about me?"

"Ever get close to walking down the aisle?"

He didn't answer at first and she was beginning to think he wouldn't when he said, "Once."

"When was that?"

"Right after med school." He got distracted by something and craned his neck toward the patio door. "Good. There's Tony. He's their regular drummer."

A nicer person would drop the subject. "Were you actually engaged?"

"Yep."

"Are you going to tell me what happened, or do you want me to shut up?"

He stayed silent for a moment, and by the way his mouth and jaw tightened she could tell it wasn't an easy thing to talk about.

"Don't say a word. Forget I asked."

"It's okay. It was a long time ago, and it's certainly not as if I'm still in love with her. Any feelings I had for Angela died the moment I walked in on her and one of our friends in my bed."

"Ouch."

"Yeah, at the time."

Liza didn't know what to say. She kind of wished she hadn't asked. Although Evan didn't seem torn up about it. The original tension she'd detected was gone. His attention went to his brother, who'd just returned to the stage, along with the other guitarist.

"The funny thing was she still wanted to go on with the wedding," he said without a trace of bitterness. "She claimed it was just sex, that it didn't mean anything."

"Sometimes it is just about sex," Liza blurted, and then wanted to kick herself all the way back to Midtown.

Evan turned to look her in the eye. "But then, you don't talk marriage."

"True." Liza needed to just keep her big mouth shut. Everything was coming out wrong. Whoever that woman was had to be a complete moron. Evan would make a perfect husband. Not that Liza was in the market. "I didn't mean—"

He touched her arm, and then rubbed it with a familiarity that warmed her. Yeah, Angela was totally insane. "It's okay, Liza. That's what I admire about you most. You're up front about what you want. We know exactly where we stand. It is just about sex."

She forced a smile. He was right. Absolutely. So why did she suddenly feel so bad?

EVAN THREW HIS CAR KEYS on the counter, next to the mail his housekeeper had left for him. "Want something to drink?" he asked Liza.

Before he could turn around, he felt her hands on him. Her breasts pressed against his back, she slid her arms around his waist, and then went for the buckle.

"Hey, slow down." He turned to face her, and then intercepted her questing hands.

"Why?"

He lifted her chin so that he could look into her eyes. Something was wrong. He just didn't know what. The ride home had been quiet and he'd half expected her to tell him she'd changed her mind and wanted to be dropped off.

He smiled. "Dare I say we have all night?"

She blinked. "Damn." She walked away, looking restless suddenly.

"What's wrong?"

"I should have picked up my car."

"I'll take you back to get it anytime you say."

She paced the small kitchen. "Maybe I should go get it now."

"It's safe in the station's parking lot, not as if it's going to get towed."

She waved a dismissive hand. "I don't like being stranded."

"I'll try not to take that personally." He took off his sports jacket and laid it over his arm. "I'm going to go get a fire started in the bedroom. Come talk to me."

"Talk, huh?"

"Do anything you want to me."

Liza grinned, looking more like herself again. "Can I tie you up?"

"That one I have to think about."

"Can you see the headlines now?" She skipped a couple of steps ahead and turned to face him, backing her way down the hall. "Famous Atlanta doctor—"

"You blew it already."

"What?"

"Famous?"

"Your name is on the credits for *Heartbeat*. That makes you famous."

"Only according to my mother's bridge group."

"Still, it— Ouch." She backed into the linen closet door where the hall dead-ended. "You could've warned me."

"And ruin your story?" He motioned for her to precede him into his room on the left.

She did, but kept an eye on him over her shoulder. "Now, I forgot what I was going to say."

"What a shame." He went into the closet to hang up his jacket.

"It had something to do with the famous doctor being bound and taken advantage of for hours and hours by some insatiable nymphomaniac."

"Isn't that redundant?"

"I can change the story."

"No, no, I like that part." He unbuttoned his shirt and threw it in the wicker hamper.

She stood, leaning a hip against the door frame, watching him. "Today was the first time I've seen you without a tie."

"That hurts. That really hurts."

Her eyes widened. "What?"

He grinned. "For the past three years I have rarely worn

a tie to the station. A sports jacket, yes. Guess who obviously never gave me a second look?"

"Guilty."

"Make it up to me."

The slow curve of her lips said she knew exactly what was on his mind. She pulled off her sweater. Her bra was red and transparent, her nipples already firm. "What about the fire?"

He kicked off his loafers. They landed somewhere in the back of the closet. "I'll get to it."

One fast flick of the clasp and her bra was gone. She unsnapped her jeans but didn't unzip them. "If you're not going to let me tie you up, I should at least get to be the boss."

He had a difficult time dragging his gaze away from her perfect breasts. They were small but the way they seemed to tip up really got his attention. "I think you called the shots last time."

"You're complaining?"

"No, ma'am."

"Come here." She moved toward him, unzipping her jeans.

He did the same with his slacks and toed off his socks until all he had on were navy-blue boxers.

Liza got down to a red thong. At least that's what he thought the tiny triangle was. He'd never actually seen a woman wearing one before. As she reached for the top of the comforter, she gave him a backside view. Oh, yeah, definitely a thong.

She pulled the comforter halfway down and then stopped to look at him with mock displeasure. "Don't just stand there. Start the fire while I get the bed ready."

"Anything you say," he murmured and went to do her

bidding. Although it was difficult to walk away from the view. He was already getting ridiculously hard, his defense being that men were visual creatures.

"Wait. Get rid of the boxers." Her gaze went purposefully down to his crotch.

"Yes, ma'am," he said, and slowly lowered the waistband, his cock immediately springing to attention. He kicked the boxers out of the way and then touched himself, cupping the weight of his arousal.

Liza moistened her lips. They were the same shade of pale pink as her nipples. "You play dirty and I'll have to punish you."

"That's supposed to discourage me?" He started toward her but she put up a restraining hand. "Oh, right. The fire." He found the switch on the side of the wall that turned on the gas and flipped it on. On cue, the flames sprung up.

She scoffed. "That's cheating. I thought we were going to have a real fire."

"Stick your hand in there and tell me it's not real." He pulled down the other side of the comforter, trying not to stare at her breasts.

"In the interest of time," she said, her gaze skimming his erection, "I'll let it slide."

He laughed. "Baby, I gotta tell you. I plan on doing a lot of sliding."

She tried not to smile, and abruptly turned away, which was perfect because he came up behind her and pressed his cock against her firm, smooth backside. She bent slightly, and rubbed against him, making him shudder. Even without saying a word she was still in control.

He closed his eyes and reached around to cup her breasts. As a doctor he saw a lot of naked bodies, but he'd never seen nipples quite like hers. When they blossomed they grew more than twice the normal size, as if begging to be touched and suckled. He loved the feel of them between his thumb and forefinger, and apparently she did, too, because she reacted with calculated hip movements that brought him too close to the edge.

He pulled her around to face him, and then kissed her deeply before she could protest. She wound her arms around his neck, her taut nipples teasing him as she pressed closer. He squeezed her buttocks, pulling her against his rock-hard cock.

A few movements of his own made her moan softly against his mouth.

"Stay the night," he whispered, and recognized the mistake when she tensed.

She slackened her arms around his neck. "Let's not get ahead of ourselves."

"No pressure. I just want to wake up with you beside me."

"Why?"

"Couldn't say." And that was the damn truth. Crazy as it was. Usually he felt the opposite. Small talk led up to the event, and after that it was "have a nice day." He wasn't a pig about it, but that's how it went.

She'd pulled back to look at him, her hazel eyes a stormy gray he hadn't seen before. "This is still just about sex, right?"

He nodded, although without his earlier conviction. Not that he'd changed his mind. Single life suited him. No expectations, no promises, no dreary routine. And he knew for sure Liza felt the same way. But saying it out loud again didn't feel right somehow.

She lifted herself on tiptoes and kissed him gently. "I promise I won't walk out without waking you."

"I promise to hold you to that promise."

"Don't worry. A taxi ride back to my place costs a fortune."

"Thanks." He pinched her bottom.

Liza laughed, and then pinched him right back.

"Enough horseplay." He scooped her up and dropped her on top of the bed.

She wiggled over toward the middle and he crawled in beside her. He took a nipple into his mouth, and she arched her back. Then he slipped a hand between her thighs. Good. She was as wet as he was hard.

CHAPTER TEN

LIZA RAN HER PALMS up Evan's chest, over his shoulders and as far as she could reach down his back. She loved the way his taut skin molded over each bone and muscle, how it dipped and curved and how his firm derriere filled her palms. His waist and hips were narrow, his shoulders broad even without his padded suit jackets.

Because she'd lost some weight—probably too much, judging by the way her old jeans had hung way down on her hips—she was self-conscious about how she felt to him. Her chest had gotten a little bony and her hip bones stuck way out even when she wasn't lying on her back. The loss hadn't been voluntary. Too much stress had seemed to change her metabolism. She hadn't given it too much thought until now.

"You look so serious." Evan lifted her chin. "What's the matter?"

"I was thinking how weird this is. You and me. You know?"

He moaned dramatically, putting a hand to his heart.

She took a nip at his lip. "You know what I mean. We've seen each other around the studio for over three years and nothing happened."

"I asked. You turned me down." He tweaked her sensitive nipple. "Remember that?"

"Hey." She got him back with a hard grip at the base of his cock. "Really?"

He looked grimly at her. "You don't remember?"

She shook her head. She wasn't going to lie. "It was a bad time in my life."

"Rick?"

She withdrew her hand. "Why would you bring him up now?" She moved toward the edge of the bed. "You just ruined everything."

"I'm sorry. I didn't know he was a touchy subject. I thought he was out of your life."

"He is." She looked back over her shoulder at him. "He is."

"Okay."

Liza took a deep breath. "I don't see him anymore. But he's still around."

"Don't run away, Liza."

She felt the bed dip behind her. And then his hand was on her thigh, rubbing, soothing. "I can't believe you remembered him."

"I didn't. Eve brought him up yesterday."

She jerked away from him and got to her feet; so they had discussed him. "This keeps getting better."

"I was only trying to find your phone number."

She reached for her bra and sweater. What the hell did she do with her jeans?

Evan came around the bed. He didn't have a stitch on and he was still semihard. Taking her by the shoulders, he said, "I think I deserve an honest conversation here."

"A reward for talking behind my back?"

"It wasn't like that."

"How the hell did Rick come up?"

"Eve said that if you were in any kind of trouble, it would be because of him."

"She never liked him." Her voice cracked. Damn it. "And she was right. Both her and Jane. They can gloat all they want. Who cares?"

"I doubt very much that's what they want."

She moved away. He didn't know crap about her life. About the hell she'd been through with Rick. "Where are my jeans?"

"Stop it, Liza."

She spun around to glare at him. "You stop it. I don't owe you anything."

The hurt mirrored in his eyes got to her.

"You're right. I thought maybe—" Looking resigned, he shook his head. "Absolutely right." He found her jeans and his slacks at the same time. "Here."

Liza took them, but she just stared down at her hands. What was wrong with her? Evan had been nothing but nice. He was a really good guy. Too good for her. "Evan, I'm sorry."

"No apology necessary." He scooped his boxers off the floor and stepped into them.

"Ah, dammit."

He frowned at her.

"Now, I just have to take those off again." She smiled seductively, but he wasn't having it.

"Sex isn't going to make this go away." He shook out his slacks.

She groaned in exasperation. "What is the matter with you? That is so not a guy thing to say."

That did get a slight smile. "Look, there's no reason not to at least have honesty between us. No strings to me doesn't mean I mess with a woman who's already taken."

"I swear to God, there is nothing happening between Rick and me. In fact, I despise the man." Was it her tone of voice? Her expression? Because she saw it in his face that he knew she was hiding something. "Rick is an asshole. He can't let go and sometimes he stalks me. That's why it may have seemed that I was acting oddly."

With heartwarming concern in his face he came to her. He put his hands on her waist. "What have the police done about it?"

She shook her head, feeling only slightly bad about the lie. Obviously she couldn't tell him everything, but he had to know there was nothing between her and Rick. "There's no proof. He's very sly."

"I know this detective—"

"No. Absolutely not. Getting anyone involved will only make matters worse."

Evan sighed, pulled her against his chest and hugged her close. "Is that why you need the lottery money? To get away from him?"

Being held like this by Evan felt too nice. He wasn't the solution to her problem. In fact, him knowing too much about Rick and the diaries could hurt her. "In a way."

"How can I help?"

"You're already doing that." She tipped her head back and waited only a second for his kiss. It lasted only another second.

"Liza, I want to help."

She put a finger to his lips. "Let's not ruin tonight."

He clearly didn't want to back off and the struggle in his eyes made her weak. Made her want to tell him everything. She tossed aside her jeans and slipped her hands under his waistband. He didn't argue when she slid the boxers down and then got rid of them.

She led him back to the bed, and then got in first, holding up the sheet and blanket for him to join her. He was already getting hard again and he'd barely stretched out when she reached for his cock.

She liked the hard, silky feel of him against her palm and cupped her hand around him. She pumped him slowly, just enough to get a low groan out of him. He briefly suckled each nipple, and just as she slackened her grip, he moved lower, and forced her thighs apart.

"Tell me what you like," he whispered.

"I think you've already figured that out."

He smiled, taking a long leisurely look, his gaze touching each breast, wet from his mouth, and then lingering on the triangle of hair at the juncture of her thighs.

First his fingers explored and taunted. She shifted, but he stayed with her. Finding it hard not to move erratically, she stretched her arms over her head, searching for the headboard and then grabbing hold of it.

He spread her legs even farther apart so that her ankles nearly reached the sides of the large bed. After he'd looked his fill, he used his thumbs to spread her even farther. His tongue scouted for the perfect spot, and each time she squirmed even the slightest, he put two fingers inside her. Not that the feeling wasn't heavenly, but it was as if he knew she was waiting for his tongue to make that connection. To tease the little nub that would bring so much pleasure.

He flicked his tongue over the spot and her bottom came off the bed. He slid his hands beneath her, squeezing the fleshy cheeks just the right amount to make her thrust upward. His tongue worked its magic until she didn't think she could take any more.

She didn't want to come yet. She wanted to play a while, so she used her grip of the headboard and pulled herself back out of reach. He looked up, confused, and she made her final escape.

"What's wrong?" he asked, sitting back on his haunches.

She saw that his arousal hadn't suffered from the setback. "Not a thing. As long as you remember who's in charge."

"Is that right?"

"I had a moment's lapse." She fluffed one of the pillows and put it back down. After scooting over to make room for him, she pointed to the pillow. "Here."

"Ah."

He crawled over, stopping to lave her right nipple. She should have stopped him. She was supposed to be in charge, but it felt too damn good. Finally, she shoved him away.

"Right," he muttered and flopped onto his back.

Liza smiled. "Poor you," she said, running her palm ever so lightly over his chest and down to his belly. "Is this so difficult?" she asked, using her wrist to brush the tip of his cock.

"No," he said in a forced falsetto.

She laughed. "I wonder just how sensitive these are." She rubbed the pad of her finger over one dark-brown nub, and then the other. They were already hard and responsive and his hands fisted at his sides. "Good boy. You keep your hands right there."

"Don't push it."

"Or else what?" She curled her fingers around his penis and squeezed gently.

His eyes briefly closing, he muttered an oath.

She moved down to where she could taste him. Her tongue replaced her hands, coursing up his shaft and then back down. She flicked the skin around the base. By the time she worked her way back up and drew him into her mouth, he could hardly keep still. She sucked him hard. He tried to reach for her but she held her ground.

She got between his thighs and, as he'd done to her earlier, she reached under his firm cheeks and held him right where she wanted him. Exploring him with her tongue only got her worked up. She really wanted him inside her. Filling her. Taking her to that safe place where she was untouchable. It was crazy. She didn't know him that well. But she couldn't deny how he'd made her feel in this very bed three nights ago.

Slowly, reluctantly, she released him. She slid her hands back around to use as leverage. Again he reached for her. But she was quick, and when he realized her intention, he laid back, his eyes mere slits as he gazed at her, his chest heaving. She saw the silver packet he'd left out on the nightstand just as she swung a leg over him.

She smiled. The good doctor was being responsible. She reached for the packet, tore it open and slowly unrolled the condom down his cock, making him shudder. For good measure, she pumped him a couple of times.

He moaned.

"Just making sure it fit," she said, laughing softly when he gave her a frustrated look.

"Now let's see how I fit." She lifted herself over him, holding his cock so that the tip just barely touched her. She wanted to sink down, ride him 'til he screamed, but then it would be over and she definitely didn't want that. Not yet.

She would take him to his limits and, in the process, the rest of the universe would vanish.

Evan moved his hips up, trying to enter her.

She smiled, closed her eyes and moved herself an inch away from him.

Ignoring his moan, she braced her legs more firmly on the bed, and braced his cock more firmly in her hand. He wasn't going anywhere she didn't want him to go. Right now, that meant skimming along her lips. Teasing, nothing more. He would feel her heat, the hint of moisture. He would be patient, but only for so long.

She reached behind her with her left hand. It was an awkward pose, since she wasn't letting go with her right hand. Bending back as far as she could, she tickled the inside of his thigh.

Obediently, Evan parted his legs, giving her access to her real objective.

He was a natural kind of man, not one of those poster boys who shaved every damn thing. Her fingertips played with his soft hair, then the softer skin of his balls.

He hissed, arching once more.

Retaliation was swift. Her hands left both holds, her thighs, feeling the burn now, lifted her away from any contact.

His curse was quite vivid, but she figured he was catching on. When he'd relaxed once more, she lowered herself, then with her right hand, she gripped him under the glans. With her left, she massaged him—quick flicks with each finger, fluttering, her nails brushing the tender skin in a soft legato.

"Liza, Liza," he repeated, but his teeth were clenched and it took her a few seconds to understand him.

"Hold on tight," she whispered.

She slid the crown of his cock inside her. She knew she was wet and hot, and that it had to feel amazing as she moved him back and forth.

His thighs, pressed against her own, started to tremble. She knew he wanted to thrust up into her. He'd get his wish…eventually.

Right now, though, she guided him to her clit. Increasing the pace of the rubbing, she started breathing harder, losing her rhythm as the sensations spread from between her legs to the rest of her body.

Sadly, she had to abandon her teasing. She needed her left hand to steady herself, to guide him away from her sensitized clit to a deeper victory.

Moving her hand down, she placed him a few inches inside, to where she could grip him not with her hand but with her vaginal muscles.

He arched again, but just his back this time. That, and he pulled the sheets so hard with his fists that they came off the mattress.

"Good boy," she said, her voice low and guttural.

"You're killing me."

"I would never do that," she said, but in truth, she wasn't sure she was strong enough to tough this out. Her body screamed for him to plunge, deep and hard, but all she did was squeeze and release.

Her hands were free again, and she wasn't sure what to do with them. When she saw his gaze sweep over her body, the answer seemed obvious.

As she milked him, she took her nipples in her fingers. Not only did it feel delicious, she knew the view would make him crazy.

She squeezed her own flesh in counterpoint to squeezing him, although that only lasted for a moment. She had to synchronize—she simply didn't have the coordination anymore. Not as molten heat swirled inside her, bringing her to that sharp edge, that precipice, so close to coming she had to be careful.

Now, deeper. And a whole different kind of ride.

Tightening all her muscles, she lowered herself as slowly

as she could until he was all the way inside. And then she stopped.

For a long moment, all she felt was the trembling of their bodies. All she heard was the deep, almost gasping breaths that filled the sex-scented air. A trickle of sweat snaked down her neck and she had to stop playing with her nipples because they were too sensitive.

He groaned and it turned into a growl. When he said her name, she realized time was running out. He was going to lose it. Or was that her?

She squeezed him once, then she rose up until she held him by just an inch.

"Please."

It was said so sweetly, she granted him his wish.

She lowered herself down, and with no hesitation, rose up again. The sensation of his upper thighs on the back of her ass, the way she shivered as he hit bottom…it felt beyond incredible.

Faster now, both of them panting, both of them thrusting. She moved only enough that each thrust rubbed her a new way, rubbed against her swollen—

It hit her like a giant wave, crashing her off balance. She gritted her teeth as she came explosively, as she heard him groan his own climax. She wanted to see him, to watch his face, but she couldn't open her eyes. Not until the quaking stopped.

Not until she found her breath. Until her heartbeat slowed to a hundred beats a second.

When she finally opened her eyes she couldn't see through her tears.

LIZA STARED AT THE FIRE, completely mesmerized. Shadows danced on the ceiling and walls. Amazingly, the gas fire made the room so warm they'd cast off the sheets and blankets. She looked over at Evan, sound asleep, lying facedown, the most perfect male butt in the whole world hers for the gawking.

He really did have a great body, but who would know it with him hiding under suits and sport coats. She'd really like to see him in jeans, she decided. Tight, worn jeans that couldn't hide a thing.

A flame shifted, its shadow licking the ceiling and drawing her attention back to the stone fireplace. When she was younger and hopeful, and life hadn't gotten in the way yet, she'd decided that her dream house would have a Jacuzzi in the master bathroom. She'd only been in one once. That first night she and her parents had moved to Jacksonville. The motel had screwed up their reservation, and after her father's drunken rants, the manager had put them in the honeymoon suite.

Looking back it was really a hokey motel, and the suite was hardly that, but at the time, Liza had thought she'd landed in paradise. The towels were thick…at least thicker than the threadbare offerings of the other motels they'd stayed in along the eastern coast. And there were two bars of soap, one for your hands, and one for the bath. Next to the sink there'd even been a free bottle of moisturizing lotion and shampoo. A big deal to an eleven-year-old who still wore last year's outgrown shoes.

But it was the Jacuzzi that had stolen her heart. Right off the bedroom, it sat in the middle of the tiled bathroom. You even had to walk up two steps to get inside the monstrous tub. It had been pure heaven, sitting in there, alone, with all those bubbles, the jetted water hitting her tired fanny after sitting on a suitcase in the backseat of her parents' sedan for ten hours.

Heaven fell apart when her father had walked into the bathroom and yanked her out of the tub. His handprint on her bare fanny lasted for days. She never did find out what had set him off that time. Her mother had taken her pills and was sound asleep. That they were prescribed, in her mind, sanctioned her addiction.

Liza changed her mind. Screw the Jacuzzi. A fireplace in the bedroom was totally the way to go.

"Hey." His voice was groggy with sleep and he barely had one eye open. "What time is it?"

She leaned over him to look at the digital alarm clock, and then sank back into the soft down pillow so that they faced each other at eye level. "One-thirty."

He threw an arm across her waist. "Tell me you don't have to go now."

She should. If Rick were awake... No. She wouldn't think about him. Not tonight. He'd already ruined enough of her life. "No, I don't."

He pulled her closer, and she gladly pressed herself against his side. His skin was so warm and smooth, but the possessive way he hooked his arm around her made her feel safer and more wanted than she ever had in her life.

"It's earlier than I thought," he said with a crooked smile, and attempted to raise himself.

She gripped his forearm, keeping him right where he was. "Go back to sleep," she said softly. "I'm not going anywhere." She kissed his shoulder. She knew he was tired, and he had to get up early to go to work tomorrow, but she didn't. "Let's both go back to sleep."

"Will you?"

She nodded. Even though in a few hours, she'd have hell to pay.

CHAPTER ELEVEN

"NEXT TIME, HOW ABOUT you let me pick you up at your apartment?" Evan said after he got them on the road. As usual, he expected traffic to be brutal once he left the neighborhood and the extra ten minutes it would take to get her to her car was going to make him late for his first appointment.

When she didn't answer he looked over at her. She stared absently out of the window at the lineup of kids waiting for the school bus. At least now he understood why she was sometimes jumpy. He figured she was worried about Rick seeing them. Evan hoped like hell the guy did follow them one day. It would be the perfect excuse to get in the guy's face. Let him know what it felt like to be the victim.

Evan took one hand off the steering wheel to touch her arm. "Did you hear me?"

Slowly she turned to look at him. "This is really a nice neighborhood."

Evan sighed to himself. If she didn't want to talk about something, she was awfully good at changing the subject. Maybe he should leave it alone. Let her meet him anywhere she chose, and not bring up Rick. That was her business.

"No, seriously, the first time I came here I thought a doctor could do better than this. But I like it." She wrapped her arms around herself and shifted to watch a flock of sparrows perched on a bird feeder. "It feels homey. Happy. Even with all the leaves gone."

"I don't plan on staying here forever. But the price was right, and it suits me for now." Although he did like the older neighborhood with even older trees shading the houses.

"Come on, Doc, you make oodles of money. You could be living in Buckhead."

He smiled at the way she baited him. "Eric told you, huh?"

"Told me what?"

He shook his head. Her tone alone told him his brother had opened his big mouth. The tuition arrangement between Evan and his youngest brother was supposed to have been private, but somehow the whole damn family knew about it. "Elton's going to pay me back later by handling my malpractice cases."

"Malpractice? You?"

"You'd be surprised how many nuts are out there looking for a free ride."

Her silence spoke volumes.

"Liza?"

She dug into her purse and pulled out a pair of sunglasses. "Did I tell you I have a court date?"

"When?"

"The twenty-second."

"Of this month?"

She cleaned off the lenses and then slipped on the glasses. "Yep."

"Well, good." He nodded without enthusiasm. "Good for you."

Even with the glasses on he saw her disappointed frown. "Why do I suddenly feel like I'm sitting on the wrong side of the bleachers?"

"It's not that." If she won, she'd be gone before Christmas. No strings and all that, but he wasn't ready to watch her walk away.

"Right."

He'd never been so glad to see a traffic light turn red. With the string of cars in front of him, they'd inevitably sit through two lights. Taking advantage of the stop, he slid an arm along the back of her seat. "Haven't we been honest with each other?"

"I think so."

"Well, I have," he said, and waited for her to make the same claim. She didn't, so he added, "I told you that the lawsuit was your business. If I didn't sound like the cheering committee it's because I wanted to spend Christmas with you."

"Christmas?"

"Yeah, Christmas."

"I thought you hated Christmas."

"I'm not crazy about the holiday but my family always has this big dinner...."

She stared at him, as if waiting for him to finish. It was gonna be a long wait. She could figure this one out. Finally, with a look of disbelief, she asked, "You want me to go with you?"

"Would that be so terrible? You've already met Eric."

She wrinkled her nose. "But I'd have to meet your parents."

"They won't bite. They're actually pretty nice people. You might like them."

She looked away. "I don't do parents very well. And

Christmas…well, you know how I feel about that whole thing."

"Fine." He turned back to watch for the green light. It was dinner. No big deal. But if she had other plans, that wasn't any big deal, either.

"I didn't say I wouldn't go."

It was so ridiculous how this woman had him feeling like an adolescent. Hopeful one moment, annoyed as hell the next. He'd obviously missed the light change because someone behind them honked. So much for sitting through two lights. "We have two weeks. Just let me know."

"Listen, if you're going to be mad—"

"I'm not mad," he said calmly. "In fact, I have tickets for a concert Monday night if you'd like to go."

"Weird night for a concert." The wariness was back.

"It's not a ruse. I already showed you my etchings."

She didn't ask about the type of music or the group. Just smiled. "What time?"

"I can't remember. I'll have to give you a call. Don't forget to give me your cell number." He glanced over to see her reaction. Reluctance was written all over her face.

"Do you have a pen?"

He reached inside his jacket for one and handed it to her. "Or you can program your number into my cell."

She tried to hide a smile. "What if I don't like the concert? I might not go out with you again."

"Is that right?"

She nodded smugly, and wrote the number on a piece of torn paper.

"Here I thought you liked my fireplace."

"Oh, baby, I love your fireplace," she said, giving him the once-over.

"You're pretty hot yourself."

Liza laid her head back on the headrest and laughed softly. "It's easy being with you."

"I'm not sure how to take that."

She turned her head to face him, her cheek still pressed to the headrest. "This is touchy ground."

"Ah." Evan's gut tightened. Liza was one of those kind of unpredictable, free-spirited girls he'd known in high school. He'd always been attracted to them but never once dared asked one out. They would've laughed him back to the chemistry lab. "This is where you tell me I'm a nice guy and I'll make some woman a great husband one day."

"No, this is where I tell you that I think you're a terrific guy and I love being with you and hope you don't run the other way."

Traffic was heavy and he had no business taking his eyes off the road, but he had to look over at her to see if she was teasing him. The earnestness in her eyes said otherwise. "Next time we'll have to get up early enough so I can make you breakfast."

She looked sad suddenly. "You cook?"

"A little."

"That's more than me."

"Good to know." He almost missed their exit. He had to do some fancy maneuvering to get over, and then waited until he cleared the off-ramp and said, "I know this Italian place with awesome baked ziti. We can go before the concert."

"What?" she asked, blinking at him, looking as if her thoughts were already miles away.

"Nothing," he said, and went back to concentrating on his driving with the feeling that she had no intention of joining him Monday evening.

* * *

LIZA PARKED AROUND the corner from the apartment complex. She'd stopped at a discount store and bought a new
cream-colored sweater. Coming home in the same clothes
she'd left wearing yesterday would be plain stupid. Overly
paranoid maybe, but she wasn't taking any chances.

Her apartment key already in hand, she quietly made it
up the stairs without incident. On the third-floor landing
near Rick's apartment, a string of Christmas lights had
been crushed and left on the concrete. It gave her a sick
feeling and she made it the rest of the way with heavy
steps.

Once inside, she dumped the package with her black
sweater, along with her purse, on a kitchen chair. Just
slightly bigger than a checkbook, the poor little brown
leather purse was embarrassingly worn. Just like her shoes,
her clothes and everything else she owned. Not totally true.
She still had some nice things that she hadn't donated to
charity, but were safely locked away in a small storage unit
on the west side of town.

Mostly, though, she'd had to travel light. The more un-
stable Rick had grown, the more they'd had to move. God,
how could it have been a year ago that she'd first walked
off the set of *Just Between Us*. She was only supposed to
have disappeared for a long weekend. Teach them all a lesson for taking her for granted. For shunning Rick.

She'd been bone-tired between partying too much with
Rick and the demands of the show. It had really killed her
that Eve and Jane hadn't liked him. They hadn't even been
subtle about excluding him from social events. In retro-
spect, of course, they were right about him. But that they
hadn't supported her decision had hurt. All she'd wanted
was for them to be happy for her.

After she went to the bathroom and stared into the mirror—she was horrified at her gaunt appearance—she headed into the bedroom and flopped onto the bed. What did Evan see in her? She looked like hell. She didn't even have a job. He was probably one of those guys who liked rescuing women. Not that she needed his help. She could take care of herself. Because she'd done such a super bang-up job so far.

She closed her eyes. That one weekend a year ago had changed everything. She and Rick were supposed to have gone to Atlantic City for four days. Show Eve and Jane that she didn't need them, but they needed her. Atlantic City had been Rick's idea. He had this grand idea, he'd told her, and he had a surprise for her. Foolishly, she'd thought he was going to ask her to marry him.

What a joke. Poker and blackjack had proven to be his true loves. But he sucked at it. By the second day he'd drained her substantial checking account. When she'd refused to give up her savings, that's when he'd told her he had Eve's diaries.

Liza rolled over to bury her face in the pillow. She could see that scene in her head as if it happened an hour ago. They'd been sitting in the posh hotel suite he'd blithely paid for with her credit card. Him, so damn cocky, she wanted to tear his eyes out.

She'd totally panicked. She'd yelled and screamed and threatened to call the cops. He'd given her that evil smile she'd remember until the day she died, and told her that he was calling the shots from now on. If he couldn't get the money from her, he'd get it from the tabloids.

Eve's show had really taken off. She'd become the sweetheart of the local cable station with promises of bigger things to come. The truth was, her career could've weathered anything revealed in the diaries. The publicity might even have helped the show, which garnered its popularity partly from the frank, open discussions. But Eve, the woman, would have been deeply wounded by her private thoughts being splashed across the headlines. And Eve was Liza's friend, even more, the sister she never had.

The stupid bastard didn't care. Rick had been using smack right under Liza's nose, and she'd been too caught up in a maelstrom of lust and resentment to see what was happening. She'd totally underestimated him every step of the way. He'd even known about her inheritance before she had by intercepting the attorney's letter. When her savings was gone and she figured she finally had nothing more he wanted, he played his trump card.

The true irony was that now Liza saw that she hadn't loved Rick. Had she married him that weekend it would have been to defy Eve and Jane. Force them to accept him.

What a complete and utter moron she'd been. She was even crazier for replaying all this in her mind, which she did whenever she was exhausted. She doubted she'd had more than four hours sleep last night. Poor Evan. He didn't have the luxury of taking a nap, something in which she had every intention of indulging.

As her eyes drifted closed, just thinking of him made her smile. But only for a moment.

Because if she really wanted to be a stand-up person, she'd cut the cord with him. She didn't deserve a good man like Evan, and he didn't deserve her baggage.

RAIN POURED DOWN IN SHEETS. Visibility was almost nil. The road was so slick that cars skidded everywhere—through stop signs, into the middle of intersections. Sirens blared in the distance.

Damn stupid night to be riding a Harley. Rick used the

back of his arm to wipe the rain from his face. He couldn't see shit. Couldn't even tell how close he was to the curb. Familiar with the intersection he was approaching, he knew there'd be a stop. He lightly applied the brakes. The bike wouldn't slow down. Panicked, he slammed down harder and went into a skid.

Light flashed off the side of the semi barreling toward him. The big white truck didn't stop. Rick veered to the left. He didn't see the massive oak tree. Until he wrapped his mangled body around it…

There were so many beautiful flowers. Oranges and yellows and stunning purples. Who the hell had sent them? How could anyone possibly have cared enough about his life or death? Liza watched them lower the casket into the ground and breathed a sigh of relief. She was finally rid of him. Finally. Thankfully…

Liza's eyes flew open. The dream hadn't woken her. Someone was knocking at the door. She closed her eyes again. If she ignored them, maybe they'd go away. Except if it were Rick. Her chest and gut tightened and she opened her eyes again. No, he'd be pounding. Screaming for her. But if she didn't stop the person who was out there now, they were likely to get his attention, too.

"I'll be right there," she called on her way to the bathroom. She stopped to splash her face with cold water. This was the second time she'd had the same dream. Both times it seemed so incredibly real. And both times she'd felt overwhelming relief. If that made her a horrible person, too bad.

That indifference didn't stop her hand from shaking as she peeked through the blind. Luckily, it was only Mary Ellen.

Liza opened the door, and covered an unexpected yawn.

"I wasn't sure you were home." Mary Ellen frowned. "I'm sorry. You were sleeping."

"Only a short nap." She pushed a hand through her messy hair. This afternoon she would splurge and get a trim and a manicure. She'd just paid the rent last week and had a few bucks left over. "Come in."

Mary Ellen hesitated. "Am I bothering you?"

Liza waved her inside. "Come on before Rick knows I'm home."

The woman quickly stepped inside. "I haven't seen him today."

Liza closed the door. "How about last night?"

"He was carrying on a bit. But someone from the second floor threw a bottle at him and he disappeared."

"Have a seat." Liza went to the refrigerator, her entire body tensing. One of these days someone would call the police on him, and who knew how that would set him off. "I've got cola or orange juice."

"Juice, please."

"Where's Freedom?"

"Outside playing."

"No school today?" Liza asked casually, already knowing the answer. She really hated that Mary Ellen kept her out of school. The child was too gifted, for one thing, and in all of the craziness of Liza's childhood, education had been her saving grace. She'd been a good student in spite of herself, mostly because she'd loved books of any kind. They'd been her escape. And eventually, her fondness for reading helped get her into college.

"No," Mary Ellen said quietly, and took the glass Liza handed her.

Liza sat across from her with her own glass of juice. She didn't like the stuff but she'd taken her attorney's advice to heart. Showing up in court looking like crap wouldn't help the case. "She's a bright girl. I bet she does well in school."

Mary Ellen stared down at her lap. "I'm holding her out for a year."

"Is that wise?"

The woman's head came up. "Don't call social services. I teach her the best that I can at home."

"I know it's none of my business but—"

"You're leaving. What do you care?" The slight belligerence in Mary Ellen's voice was a total surprise. To her, too, apparently. She looked away sheepishly. "I'm sorry."

Liza didn't say anything at first. She had her own problems to deal with. "Look, in a couple of weeks I might be able to help you out. Get you a better apartment. Find a good school for Freedom."

Mary Ellen frowned. "Why would you want to do that?"

Good question. The old Liza wouldn't even have made friends with this woman in the first place. She sighed. "I might be coming into a little money."

Mary Ellen said nothing, but looked at her expectantly.

"And I want to be nice. That's all."

"Oh," she said, blinking several times, as if the concept was entirely foreign to her.

Liza got it. This was new for her, too. How self-absorbed she'd been these past few years. Hadn't she learned anything from her parents? Hadn't she sworn she'd never be like them? "Hey, when was the last time you got your hair cut?"

She fingered the ragged ends. "I cut mine and Freedom's hair last week."

"No, I mean going to an honest-to-goodness stylist who even washes and dries your hair for you."

Mary Ellen's eyebrows shot up. "That costs a lot of money."

"It's okay. We're going today. My treat."

"Really?"

"Yep. I know a place near the discount store around the corner that takes walk-ins."

"I'll have to take Freedom with us, but she can sit in a chair and wait."

"Good." Liza mentally calculated how much money she had in her purse and how much gas in her car. "We'll have burgers and shakes after that."

Mary Ellen beamed. "Cool. I'll go call Freedom."

"Not too loud, all right?"

Mary Ellen nodded, her solemn eyes acknowledging that if they woke up Rick, their afternoon would be ruined.

After the woman left, Liza went to brush her hair, and then got her purse and keys. Paying for two haircuts meant no manicure, but she didn't care. The look on Mary Ellen's face was worth it.

Liza made sure the door was locked and then went to meet the other two at Mary Ellen's end apartment. Freedom came running out the door.

"Mama's putting on lipstick," she said, all excited. "I never saw her do that before."

"Did she tell you why?"

"We're going out." She grinned, displaying a missing front tooth.

"Okay if I come?" Liza teased.

"If Rick will let you."

She stared in disbelief at the child. "I don't need Rick's permission."

She nodded, her expression somber. "Yes, you do. You're an abused woman just like Mama."

CHAPTER TWELVE

"MEET ME FOR LUNCH," Evan said the moment after Liza answered her cell phone.

She smiled. "Who is this?"

"The guy with the fireplace."

"Oh, that guy. In that case, I'm interested." She took the phone into the bedroom with her, and stretched out on the lumpy mattress. Just hearing his voice and her resolve to keep her distance went right out the window. "Are you at your office?"

"Yep. Someone canceled, so I have an extra half hour. Hold on a second."

She waited, listening to him talk to the nurse about referring a patient to an endocrinologist. She heard the rattle of paper near the phone, and then heard him murmuring some numbers as if reading from a chart. Finally, he gave the name of a couple of prescriptions for the nurse to call in to a pharmacy.

"Sorry about that," he said. "So what do you say? Want to save me from all this?"

Liza briefly closed her eyes. The moment she stepped foot out of the apartment Rick would be all over her. Like two days ago. What a nightmare. As soon as she'd gotten back with Mary Ellen and Freedom, he'd been in her face, demanding to know where she'd been and wanting money for cigarettes and booze. Of course, he was stoned out of his mind. And that Freedom had to witness any of it had made Liza so angry she'd nearly hauled off and knocked him down the stairs.

The worst of it had been the calm acceptance in Freedom's eyes. Liza had felt as low as an ant. She hadn't left the apartment since, and Freedom's words kept bouncing off the walls. The wise little girl knew what Liza had refused to face for the past year. The difficult thing was, what was she willing to do about it?

"What time?" she asked slowly.

"Give me another moment," he said, and she heard a woman's voice in the background.

"No problem," Liza said, but he was gone before she even got the words out.

She sat up briefly to rearrange the pillow behind her back and then settled in. She wasn't ready to leave right away, although at least her hair still looked decent. Amazing since all she'd done was lie around all day and feel sorry for herself.

She knew she had to have a serious talk with Evan, about the diaries, about Rick, and she dreaded it with every fiber of her being. It wasn't something she could comfortably explain over the phone, and she'd planned on doing it after the concert this evening. But maybe it was better to talk to him at lunch. Not only to get it over with, but a finite period of time would preempt questions she didn't want to answer.

The thing was, she wasn't quite sure what she wanted to say to him. Or at least how she wanted to say it. In less than two weeks her entire life would change, whether the judge ruled in her favor, or not. If she lost the suit…

She didn't want to think about that possibility. But her persistent avoidance was a huge problem, too. She had to be prepared for an adverse outcome. And getting seriously involved with Evan was exactly what she didn't need right now, for her own sanity, but mostly because it wasn't fair to him.

"Liza?"

"I'm here."

"Well, I'll have to rescind the lunch offer. One of my patients had the audacity to have an emergency."

"That's pretty rude of them."

"I thought so." Lowering his voice, he said, "But I plan on making it up to you tonight."

She smiled. "What's tonight?"

"The concert."

"Oh, I forgot."

"You are coming, aren't you?"

"Yes, I was teasing. What time?"

"I'll pick you up at your place at six-thirty. You'll have to give me the address."

Yeah, right. That would happen. "I'll meet you at the station parking lot."

"Come on, Liza. That's ridiculous."

Tonight she'd explain everything. Not now. "I thought you had a patient to attend to."

"She's on her way in. I have another ten minutes."

"Then grab something to eat."

"I'd rather talk to you," he said quietly. "I miss you."

A catch in her throat stopped her for a moment. "I saw you a day and a half ago."

"I know. It feels like a year."

"Stop it."

"Am I embarrassing you, or making you uncomfort-

able?" he asked, and she could hear the smile in his voice.
"Too bad. I've gotten used to your mug across from me."

That couldn't possibly be true. Although why not? She
missed him. As soon as she'd seen it was him calling, like
a stupid twit, her pulse had quickened. "We haven't even
gone out for two weeks yet."

"So?"

"That was eloquent."

He chuckled. "Deal with it."

Liza laughed. Even though lunch wasn't going to work
out, she liked that he'd asked her. The afternoon wouldn't
have finished in his bed. He apparently just wanted to talk.
Share a meal. Because he missed her. Damn. This was not
good. This was only supposed to be about sex.

"I'll have to be going," he said, "so about tonight…"

She squeezed her eyes shut and took a deep breath, before staring at the cracked ceiling. "This will be the last
time we meet at the station. I promise, Evan."

After a brief pause, he asked, "Is everything all right?"

At the quiet concern in his voice, her resolve to come
clean with him seemed to strengthen. It felt so right that a
year of tension seemed to evaporate from her body. She was
going to tell him everything. No holding back. He'd be the
only other person on this earth who knew about Rick and
the diaries. She wouldn't ask for Evan's help. Wouldn't accept it if he offered. But no more lies. "The best it's been
in a long time."

"Liza…"

"It's okay, really." She sat up. "Tonight. What shall I wear?"

"Something sexy."

"Right."

"Anything. You always look gorgeous. I'll see you at
six-thirty."

"Hey, wait. I've been meaning to ask…" She wished she could see his face at that moment. She hoped she wasn't being totally nuts for hoping too much. "What do your folks usually have for Christmas dinner?"

LIZA HAD NEVER BEEN into clothes or fashion trends. When she'd worked for *Just Between Us* she'd actually owned a couple of dresses that she needed to wear on occasion. But even then, since her job was behind the scenes and had little to do with airtime, she mostly wore jeans. But tonight, she wanted to be different. She wanted to feel pretty. She really wanted to wow Evan.

How many times had she passed him in the hall at the station? How many times had she heard the assistant producers and wardrobe women making remarks about him? Every single one of them would've drooled all over themselves had he asked them out. In fact, she was pretty sure that Sally in wardrobe had taken the step herself. Although Liza didn't think anything came of it or she would've heard about it. The whole studio would've heard. Oh, boy, Evan would've loved that.

Liza smiled. Just because she'd thought of him. Man, when did she get so goofy? When had she started thinking beyond how great the sex was? She'd even told him she'd go to his parents with him for Christmas. The thought was sobering. She hadn't given her own mother a phone call for the past two Christmases. Nor had she received any calls from her.

It had been like that since Liza's father had died. Ironic since Liza had always thought he was the one who disrupted the cohesion of their family. But his body had barely gotten cold when resentment started to build, like a hurricane, gaining momentum each day and methodically destroying the fragile bond between Liza and her mother, until Liza couldn't stand the sight of the woman who was supposed to have protected her.

Restless suddenly, she paced the small apartment, trying to get mentally organized. If she wanted something nice to wear that meant shopping. Not her favorite thing but she could handle it. At least the outing would distract her from her decision to come clean. Since she'd hung up the phone she'd changed her mind twice. In less than two weeks everything would be decided. If she wanted to wait, she could explain everything to Evan then.

No, she was done being a coward. She liked Evan, and she wanted him to know the truth about Rick and about the lawsuit. He'd respect her more, right? Knowing that the lawsuit wasn't about personal gain. A huge plus, but most of all she didn't want to remain under Rick's thumb. She didn't want to be another Mary Ellen.

After Liza balanced her checkbook, trying not to get depressed, she wrote down a figure that she needed to sustain her and Rick for the month, and then another sum she'd be forced to give him for booze, drugs and cigarettes. The amount left was pitiful. No matter what the outcome of the lawsuit, she had to get a job after the first of the year. She looked forward to it. She never thought she'd actually long to be normal. Good grief, what had Evan done to her?

Shaking her head, she grabbed her car keys and purse. She had three hours to get to the bank, go shopping and deal with Rick. This afternoon she'd give him an extra forty bucks. That ought to get him good and stoned. And out of her hair for the evening. Yeah, that was mean and ugly, and she didn't care. As long as he stayed out of her face.

HER COAT WAS OLD and ratty and should've been retired a year ago but Liza slipped it on anyway and quietly left the apartment. She didn't want anyone to see her dressed in the new off-the-shoulder royal-blue sweater and sleek black pants, not even Mary Ellen, and least of all Rick. Although she was pretty sure she didn't have to worry about him. He was already so damn wasted before she gave him the vodka he'd asked her to pick up earlier.

She knew, too, that he had two extra grams of smack stashed under the couch. In the old days she would've confiscated it in the hope he'd forget about it. That maybe if a day without the stuff stretched into a week his craving would diminish and the old Rick would be back. She'd been incredibly naive to think she could stop him from getting high by throwing out his drugs and booze. He always found more. Always. As if by magic. Even when it seemed impossible.

Just like her father had seemed to always have money for his beer and gin, when only canned tomato soup stocked the pantry for his wife and child, or that for a week at a time she'd been sent to school without lunch money, or even a lousy piece of fruit to quiet her empty belly.

Now she knew better. She couldn't change someone who didn't want to change themselves. All she could do was maintain her physical and emotional distance to keep herself as sane as possible.

Once she made it to her car, she removed the coat and threw it on the backseat before she got in. For a second she thought she heard the revving of a motorcycle engine and she quickly looked around. A few cars were parked behind her, and two kids were playing with a large orange ball. No motorcycles in sight.

Chalking it up to nerves, she started the car. Traffic was fine on this neighborhood side street, but she knew it would be heavy on the way to Midtown so she allowed herself an extra ten minutes. She'd been lucky to find the sweater on sale. It was truly gorgeous, and it fit her perfectly. So did the satiny slacks, and it felt as if she were in high school again, so anxious to see Evan that she wanted to burst.

She wasn't the most patient driver, especially during rush hour, and a dozen expletives later she pulled into the station's parking lot. A whole lot more cars than normal were still there and she wondered what was going on. Did the unusual crowd have anything to do with *Just Between Us*? Sometimes they had a special show or a special guest. And as senior producer, had she still been working there, that show would have been her baby.

A pang of nostalgia got her right where it smarted the most, and she had to block it as fiercely as a mother bear protecting her cub. She had to stay sharp. Unemotional. Tonight was important.

She found a spot at the far end of the parking lot. No way would Evan be able to see her, which meant she had to get out and wait closer to the station door. The idea certainly didn't thrill her. She didn't need to bump into Eve or Jane or any of the other lottery winners. But she had little choice, short of parking illegally, which in itself was nearly impossible in the crowded lot.

After checking her makeup in the rearview mirror, she climbed out of the car. Out of habit, she glanced around, although she'd bet her car that Rick wouldn't wake up until tomorrow. Another check of her watch and then she started in the direction of the station door.

Evan was already standing outside. Instead of a sports coat, he wore a gray suit and red tie, which made her glad she'd gotten more dressed up than usual. He smiled as soon as he saw her, and her heart all but burst in her chest. A large pickup truck blocked their views for a moment and then she stepped around it just as he came off the curb.

He pointed toward his car, which was parked in the middle of the third row. She nodded and veered off in that direction. He caught up with her partway there and surprised her with a kiss on the lips and a hug that stole her breath.

"Hi to you, too," she said, taking a step back.

"You look fantastic."

She scoffed, plucking at the top of her sweater, and with a pronounced Southern accent, said, "This old thing."

They both laughed, and he slipped an arm around her shoulders, steering them on course. "Of course, you look pretty damn good in jeans, too."

"Someone's looking to get lucky tonight."

Smiling, he hugged her closer. "I already am lucky."

"Corny, Gann, very corny."

He laughed, and she felt the vibration in his chest. A combination of muskiness and confidence, his familiar scent filled her with a deep contentment that was both foreign and scary, yet she wouldn't trade it for anything. Having his arm around her, pressing against the strength of his chest...well, that made her feel invincible. Foolish, yes. She didn't care. Not even the tiniest bit.

The air was a little chilly and she slid her arm around his waist. He glanced down at her and kissed her temple. She heard laughter behind them and turned to see where it was coming from. A group of people were exiting the building.

"A Christmas party, I think," Evan said.

"For *Just Between Us?*"

He shook his head. "The studio next door. I overheard a cameraman talking about it when I was getting coffee."

"That's one point for not working. No Christmas parties and baby showers you have to go to."

"Scrooge."

"Guilty and without apology." Until she spotted Eve's car, Liza hadn't even thought about looking to see if Eve or Jane's cars were still there. She took another look over her shoulder. She still hadn't quite shaken the feeling that someone was watching her, but paranoia was nothing new.

"What's wrong?" Evan stopped and turned around, too.

"Nothing. I saw Eve's car. I thought maybe— Come on. I'm hungry. I hope you're feeding me before the concert." She tugged him along with her toward his Camry. "I never asked you what kind of concert it is."

"My nephew's third-grade class is putting on a Christmas pageant."

She looked at him. "I hope you're kidding."

"I don't have a nephew."

She pinched his arm.

"Ouch." Evan chuckled. "I wish I did have one, then maybe Mom would back off on the 'I should be a grand-mother already' thing."

"That's right. You're the oldest."

"You're an only child. You must get it worse."

"Hardly."

"Really?"

"My mother could barely cope the first time around. Grandmother material she isn't."

"But your dad was—" Evan frowned at her, and she truly wished she'd kept her mouth shut. "Who took care of you?"

"Me. Didn't do too bad a job, huh?" She nudged him with her shoulder. "Come on. Lighten up."

But it was too late. The pensive frown that caused lines

between his dark eyebrows had grown deeper, but thankfully there was no pity in his face or she wouldn't have been able to stand it. She didn't dwell on what her parents should or shouldn't have done. She'd made peace with the past. Made peace with the fact that she and her mother could never have a relationship.

They reached his car and in true Evan fashion, he walked her all the way around to the passenger side and opened her door. She didn't argue. In fact, in a tiny, tiny way, she was beginning to like it. Not that she'd admit it in a thousand years.

She smiled and was about to get in when he stopped her. He tilted her chin up and kissed her. Not a brief friendly kiss, but one that told anyone who happened to be watching that this was no casual relationship. His tongue teased the seam of her lips and she opened up to him more out of shock than anything. When he finally withdrew, she had the urge to look around and make sure no one saw the display.

Instead, she slid onto the seat and let him close the door. While she waited for him to join her inside the car, she noticed a couple staring at Evan as he went around the hood. The rumors would start flying around the station tomorrow. Glad she wasn't…

The passenger door flew open. Startled, she swung around and met Rick's furious bloodshot blue eyes. Oh, no.

"Get out, you stupid lying bitch."

"What are you doing here?" She looked back toward Evan. He'd just climbed behind the wheel. She glared at Rick, fear clogging her throat. "Get away from me. Get the hell away," she spat out.

"Liza, what's happening?"

She couldn't look at Evan now. She kept her gaze on Rick, struggling not to let him see her fear. "Leave right now, or I swear you won't see another penny."

"We've come too far, baby." He reached for her, and she slapped his face. Momentarily he moved back.

Cursing, Evan got out of the car.

"Evan, no. Please." She couldn't stop him, so she pushed Rick out of the way and got out, too.

Evan was coming around the hood. People walking to their cars stopped to watch the commotion. She couldn't let this play out, not in front of all these people, especially not in front of Evan.

She put up a restraining hand. "Evan, please. It's okay. I can handle this."

His face was dark with fury. Focused on Rick, he wouldn't even look at her. "Step away from the lady."

"Lady?" Rick laughed.

"Stop it!" Liza grabbed Rick's arm. "Let's go." He wouldn't budge. He wouldn't break eye contact with Evan. Desperate, she whispered in his ear, "Let's leave right now, and tonight will be like old times."

He blinked, and then his gaze darted to her. "Okay, baby, whatever you say." And then, shooting a triumphant look at Evan, he snaked an arm around her waist and put his filthy mouth on hers.

She wanted to jerk away. Her stomach rolled at his touch, at the foulness of his breath. But she couldn't without making matters worse. She knew Rick too well, and to make this all stop, she could only give in, pretend she wanted the kiss.

Finally, she tugged Rick away, and tried not to look at Evan, but she couldn't help herself. At the last moment, she slid him a glance. The shocked hurt on his face cut her to the bone.

CHAPTER THIRTEEN

EVAN STOOD PERFECTLY STILL, watching her weave through the cars, holding hands with that filthy sleaze, until she was out of sight. He couldn't move if he tried. He could barely breathe.

She'd sworn that Rick was out of the picture, and Evan had believed her. It wasn't just that she'd lied, but the sight of Rick himself was hard to take. The long, shaggy, dirty hair and filthy jeans. He couldn't bear to imagine what was under the black leather jacket. Evan hadn't even gotten that close and he could smell the guy from fifteen feet away.

And Liza had kissed him. The unbidden image sent a shiver down Evan's spine. How could she have done that? And in front of him? What hold did this guy have on her? Or hadn't she thought Evan could've handled that poor excuse for a man? Is that why she'd gone off with him? She hadn't wanted to leave with him, Evan could tell that much. But why not call the police? None of this made sense. Liza was too strong a woman to allow herself to be treated like that.

He drew in an unsteady breath. What a chump he'd been. He'd actually broken his own damn rule and started to have feelings for her. Although he couldn't complain. They'd openly agreed their relationship was just about sex. So that was on him.

"Evan?"

It took a moment to register that someone was talking to him. He turned around. Decked out in cocktail dresses, Eve Best and another woman he'd seen around the station stood a few feet away. The shaken looks on their faces told him they'd seen everything.

Damn.

"Yeah?" he said, realizing he still stood in front of his car. He patted his pocket for the keys and then remembered they were already in the ignition.

"Evan, can we talk for a moment?" Eve followed him to the driver's door.

"We did that the other day."

"I know." She got in the way when he reached for the door handle. "I wasn't helpful. I've felt badly ever since."

"Well, I'm not feeling so hot myself right now, so if you'll excuse me…"

"Please, Evan." Eve wouldn't back off, and there was no way he could open the door without ramming her. "Do you know Jane?" she asked, indicating the blond woman with serious blue eyes beside her. "She's with *Just Between Us.*"

Evan nodded to her, and she gave him a small smile.

"I suppose you figured out that was Rick," Eve said.

Evan's laugh was bitter. "Uh-huh, I kind of figured that out."

"I was excited to hear that you were seeing Liza." Jane glanced at Eve. "We both were. We thought that meant Rick wasn't around."

"We hoped that Liza had come to her senses, and would come back to the show," Eve said.

"Come back to us," Jane added softly.

"Hmm, it doesn't appear that's the case. Look, ladies, I have a concert to—"

"Do you care about her?" Jane asked with a sad earnestness that was difficult to blow off.

"I did. Or at least I thought I did."

"It's Rick. It's not her."

"You know Liza better than I do," he said, aware that people lingered within earshot. "Does she strike you as a woman who'd put up with a man she didn't want?"

"But Rick is—" they both said at the same time, and then stopped and looked at each other.

Eve spoke next. "The three of us have been friends since we were eleven. I had just lost both of my parents in a car accident when I met Liza. My life had been turned upside down. I was horribly unhappy." She glanced at Jane. "She was going through her own preteen angst. And then Liza came into our lives. And she was fun and mischievous and got us into all kinds of trouble. But she always pulled us back out."

"Always," Jane said, nodding. "We were like the Three Musketeers, you know? Always together. Always backing each other up. In high school I was really self-conscious about wearing braces, and if a kid even looked at me wrong Liza was in their face."

Evan frowned. Nice trip down memory lane. What did it have to do with him?

"We went to college together. We started this damn show together," Eve continued, motioning toward the station, the frustration evident in her stormy eyes. "Nothing ever came between us."

"Except Rick," Jane finished.

"We didn't help matters by telling her what a bum he was. But she should've known better. Running off with him like that was—" Eve gave an impatient shake of her head. "He's behind this lawsuit. I just know it."

Evan put up a hand. "That's none of my business. At this

point, I really don't give a damn what she's doing, or why she's doing it."

"I don't care about the lawsuit or the money," Eve said with a sincerity that gave him pause. "She's a really good person, but you already know that or else you wouldn't have gone out with her. We're simply asking that you not judge her too harshly."

"Don't give up on her." Jane laid a hand on his arm. "Please."

He stared at the two women, not knowing what to think. How could they defend her? How could they possibly give a damn about her? At one point she obviously had been very special to them, which made her betrayal all the more devastating and incomprehensible.

But yet here they were, pleading her case. What the devil did they expect him to do about it, anyway? She went willingly with Rick, disgusting sort that he was. Granted, Liza probably hadn't wanted to cause a scene, but to kiss the guy like that? Evan got queasy at the thought. Inexcusable. He'd already endured one cheating, lying woman. That was one too many in a lifetime.

"I really do have a concert to attend," he said, and waited for Eve to step away from the door.

She nodded and moved back with a tight slant to her lips. He didn't even want to look at Jane. That one wore her heart in full view. Not that either of them could sway him. He'd had more than enough of Liza Skinner.

"WHO THE FUCK was that guy?" Rick's words had started to slur a block away from the station. Whatever he'd taken earlier obviously started to kick in.

Good thing she'd insisted on driving despite his ranting about leaving his bike behind. "Nobody."

"Nobody." He snorted and reached over, fisting a handful of her sweater. "You dressed like this for nobody."

"Get your goddamn hands off me."

He made a grab for the steering wheel. She shoved him away but momentarily lost control and the car swerved erratically over the center line. Horns blared, a jogger yelled, but luckily the oncoming traffic was far enough away that everyone escaped damage.

"Do that again and I'll drive you straight to the police station." Her hands shook so hard that she gripped the wheel until her knuckles turned white.

When he didn't answer, she slid a look at him. His head drooped, his chin nearly touching his chest, and he appeared to be struggling to keep his eyes open.

She took a deep breath and said nothing more for the rest of the ride home. He stayed quiet, too, his breathing deep and even, and after she parked the car she slowly opened her door, hoping he'd stay asleep. She had no qualms about leaving him out here. Maybe she'd get lucky and he'd freeze to death. The stupid bastard.

Using the back of her arm, she wiped her mouth. It didn't help. Rick's revolting taste had crawled down her throat, permeated her belly so that she wanted to puke. She could feel him in her hair, smell him in the fabric of her new sweater. She couldn't wait to take it off. Throw it into one of the giant garbage bins behind the complex. No, burn it. Even better.

She closed her eyes and prayed Rick would stay asleep. If he did, she could call Evan and explain…she choked back a sob. Explain what? What could she possibly tell him that would erase the past half hour?

God, she would never, ever, not in a million years forget the wounded look on Evan's face as she walked away. Rick's disgusting arm around her. The bleakness in Evan's eyes was enough to want to make her want to weep. How could she have been so foolish? She'd underestimated Rick before, and swore she never would again. Now she wasn't the only one paying for her stupidity.

Liza got out of the car and was just about to close the door when he stirred. She froze, hoping it would turn out to be nothing. He muttered an oath and brought his head up. He looked straight at her, the streetlight shining in his haggard face.

Sadness swept over her. He'd been good-looking and charming once, but smack and booze had dragged him through the gutter a couple of times. He looked fifty, yet he wouldn't be thirty until next month. Another wasted life.

His head came up. "What are you looking at?" Spit flew everywhere. Some of it had dried at the corners of his mouth. Some of it caked to his white T-shirt where the leather jacket didn't cover.

She shuddered. "We're home."

He squinted, looking around as if he thought she was trying to trick him.

For an instant, she'd actually experienced a pang of sympathy. Amazing. She slammed the door and started toward their building. Screw him. She didn't care that the car would be unlocked overnight. Right now she didn't care about anything. Tomorrow her attorney could tell her she'd been awarded a hundred million dollars and it would mean nothing. After what she'd just done to Evan, she didn't deserve the clothes on her back.

She heard Rick get out of the car, and she mentally

braced herself for what was inevitably ahead for the evening. When he yelled for her to stop, she kept walking. It was the dinner hour and the complex was quiet, but it didn't matter if he made a scene here. Not like it had mattered back at the station parking lot. In front of Evan. Eve and Jane had been there, too. She'd caught sight of them out of the corner of her eye as she was leaving.

Sniffling, she picked up her pace when she sensed him behind her. Any vile thing he had to say to her could wait until they got inside. She got to the stairs and ran up to the second landing before she turned around to check his progress.

He staggered quite far behind, using parked cars for support, taking two steps and falling back one. If he couldn't make it up the stairs, that was his tough luck. She'd leave him where he was and hide out until he slept off whatever crap he'd stuffed into his system.

She headed up the next flight of stairs, making it halfway up when she heard a car alarm go off. Several apartment doors opened and people stuck their heads out. She didn't turn around. She knew what had set off the alarm. Rick had gotten too close to one of those new cars with a touchy system. The blaring lasted just long enough to be annoying. Maybe he'd get his butt kicked by one of the bikers who lived on the second floor. Wouldn't hurt her feelings.

Finally, she got to her floor and couldn't help sneaking another look. Rick stumbled to the bottom of the stairs. He plopped down on the first step. She continued to her apartment, barely getting the door unlocked when she heard him yell something about not being finished with her.

She went inside, closed the door and leaned back against it. What a nightmare. What a friggn' nightmare. Less than two weeks and it would've been over. What had she done so wrong in her life that she deserved this kind of karma? She heard him yell again, and slowly garnered her mistake.

She was prolonging the nightmare. If she got him to his apartment, he'd pass out soon and she'd be in peace for the rest of the night. Yeah, that's what she'd thought before she'd left to meet Evan. Shit. She couldn't think about him right now, she told herself as she hurried from the apartment. She had to gather her strength. Get Rick inside. He couldn't possibly stay awake much longer. Tomorrow he'd have questions, and she'd have lies.

He was so out of it by the time she got downstairs she was afraid she wouldn't be able to get him to the third floor. But as soon as he saw her, the point was moot. He seemed to rally. Mumbling curses, he grabbed the railing and pulled himself upright.

"You trying to sneak away from me again," he spat out, his anger sending him backward. He hooked his arm around the railing in time to keep himself from falling.

"I'm trying to help you," she said tightly and started to reach for his arm. The thought of touching him gave her the willies and she immediately withdrew. "Can you make it up the stairs?"

"I made it down, didn't I?" He stared at her with so much hatred it shrouded her like a dark cloud.

For a moment she flashed on an image of her father, looming over her, his hand drawn back. Although he'd rarely hit her, the threat had been enough.

She blinked. Her father was gone. But with a shudder, she realized she'd replaced him with Rick.

He wobbled, leaning toward her. "Get out of my way."

She put her hands up. "Fine."

She stood back and watched him struggle to the next step. Even with all the crap he'd put her through, there were times—like back at the car—when she'd actually felt sorry for him. When she'd truly wished she knew how to help him fight the addiction. Right now, he could fall and break his neck and she wouldn't shed a single tear.

Unable to watch him another moment, she fled up the stairs but stayed on the second-floor landing. She waited until he got close, and then she went to the third floor. He crawled up to the last landing. Watching him, she was amazed how she could feel nothing. No pity. No anger. Nothing.

He'd left his apartment unlocked, surprising because he was usually worried about his drug stash. She pushed the door open and waited for him to approach before stepping aside. His foul breath reached her before he did. She turned her face before she gagged.

"What are you doing standing out here?" He fell against her, and she automatically grabbed his arm and shoved him away. "You didn't forget your promise, huh, Liza?"

She reared her head back. How could he remember that? Not that she had any intention of spending the night anywhere near him. "Get inside."

He could barely lift his lids. "You first."

"Come on, Rick."

"You want the diaries? Get your ass in there."

She stood her ground for a moment, and then realized how stupid she was being. The important thing was to get him inside. He wouldn't last long on his feet.

"Fine." She went first, stepping over empty bottles and the same fast-food wrappers that had been there for two weeks. The place smelled as bad as he did.

He slammed the door behind him and then kicked an empty tumbler out of his way. It hit the coffee table and shattered, pieces of glass flying across the carpet.

She stepped farther back, giving him a wide berth to the couch. But he headed for her instead. Panic gripped her. He was in too bad a condition to be a serious physical threat, but that didn't mean he couldn't do damage. Besides, just the thought of him touching her again...

"Where's the rest of my stash?" Rick asked.

"What are you talking about?"

"You have it."

She drew in a deep breath. They'd gone through this before, but that was when she'd thought she was helping by hiding his stuff. "I don't have anything of yours. You must have hidden it and forgot where you put it."

He grunted in disbelief, but then he blinked, looking confused. "You don't have it?"

"No."

He looked toward the kitchen, and then stumbled in that direction, muttering to himself.

She heard the oven door open and then the rattle of paper.

Rick reappeared with a bag in his hand. He went straight for the couch, without looking at her, and went to work preparing his injection as if he'd forgotten she was there.

Liza didn't move, in fact she barely breathed as she watched him prepare for his trip into oblivion. With what he'd already ingested, in the next few minutes, he'd be out and she'd be home free.

He took a rattling breath, and then slumped against the paisley upholstered pillows, his eyes closed. She turned slowly toward the door. Keeping her gaze on him, she moved as quietly as possible. She stepped on something that crackled, and she froze until she was certain he hadn't been disturbed. After transferring her attention to the floor in front of her, she continued toward the door.

She grabbed hold of the doorknob.

The next second his hand circled her wrist. She cried out, more surprised than hurt, and twisted free. He stumbled, too weak and wasted to maintain a grip. But still, he swiped at the air, trying to strike her. She shoved him hard, and watched him trip over a bottle.

He hit the floor, butt first, and then his head slammed the corner of the coffee table. He lay there, not moving, his legs askew, his eyes closed, his ravaged face a deadly pallor.

She covered her mouth, cutting off a frightened cry. Jesus, had she killed him? She lowered her hand from her mouth. "Rick?" No answer. No movement. Not even a twinge. She walked over to him and dropped to her knees. "Rick!"

Nothing.

Silence. Deafening silence.

Her hands shook so badly that when she checked his wrist she knew that she wouldn't find a pulse even if there was one. She stared hard at the side of his neck, looking for a pulse there. Her vision blurred. She tried to swallow but her mouth was too dry. She pulled back, sinking onto her heels, and wrapped arms around herself. Her upper arms were tender, bruised from his grip earlier.

How many times had she wished him dead? She'd even dreamed about it. What had she done? She tried to take a deep breath but it wouldn't come. She closed her eyes and forced herself to breathe. She tried a visualization technique she'd learned in college, but as soon as she summoned the image of Eve and Jane and herself playing on the beach in Fort Lauderdale the summer after they'd all met, panic overtook her.

She opened her eyes. The diaries. If he died, would she ever find them? Could they still hurt Eve?

She had to calm down. If he died, she'd have more than that to worry about. Everyone would think she'd killed him on purpose. No one would blame her, not here in the complex, anyway. They all thought Rick was an asshole. But that gave her motive.

"Oh, Rick, you stupid bastard." She hugged herself tighter, rocking back and forth. She freed her arms and shook out her hands. She had to find a pulse. If not, she'd have to call 911.

The thought terrified her. She picked up his cold, limp hand and pressed her thumb to his wrist. Was that a pulse? Did she feel something? Or did she want it so badly she imagined it?

She sat back again, staring at his lifeless body. There was no blood. That was good. She took her first really deep breath. Maybe this had nothing to do with the fall. The amount of drugs and booze in his system could be enough to take him down.

"Come on, Liza, think," she said out loud. She could call Mary Ellen to at least help her find a pulse…. No, the woman had enough trouble of her own. If the police ended up getting involved…

Evan.

He was a doctor. He would know what to do.

She scrambled to her feet, while looking for her purse. She saw it laying on the floor by the door. Quietly she got back down and crawled toward it, and then glanced over her shoulder, before getting out her cell phone. She pressed his speed dial number. "Evan? Please, Evan. I need your help."

CHAPTER FOURTEEN

HE ALMOST HADN'T answered the phone. He usually didn't when he was driving. The pager was a different matter. Only his nurse and answering service had that number, so a call usually meant a patient emergency.

"Evan?"

"Liza?" He wasn't sure. Her voice barely made it to a whisper.

"I need your help. I think I—" Her voice cracked and she sniffled. "Please come."

"Where?"

"My apartment."

He nearly missed a stop sign. He pulled over to the shoulder. "What's going on?"

"I can't explain over the phone. Please, Evan, please... I need you."

Pitifully, that's all it took. He got her address, listened as calmly as he could as she gave directions, because she was anything but calm, and then he turned the car around. He did hope he wasn't being a damn fool. She'd said she needed him, and he went running. Barely a question asked.

In his defense, she did sound panicked. Even though she hadn't explained the problem, it had to be about Rick. If he'd hurt her… Evan couldn't think about that. He couldn't think about the conversation with Eve and Jane that he'd kept replaying in his head. He needed to concentrate on his driving. Traffic was heavy and he wasn't that familiar with the area where she lived.

Half an hour and two wrong turns later, he saw the name of the apartment complex she'd given him. He had to look twice because several letters were missing from the sign. After he entered the parking lot, he understood how big the complex was, with no particular method to the layout. Reluctantly, he stopped to ask a man in a gray hoodie getting groceries out of the trunk of a car where to find building three. But the man didn't speak English.

The place was in disgraceful shape, with litter on the ground next to the trash cans, and damaging potholes throughout the parking lot. The buildings were no better, with improper outside lighting and chunks of missing railing going up the stairs. Broken bottles littered the ground. This couldn't be right.

He stopped the car and studied the directions he'd written down. How could Liza live in a dump like this? Aesthetics aside, the place wasn't safe, especially not for a single woman. But his directions were right on. All he needed was to find building three.

After taking the next turn, he saw a chipped number against the dirty brick that could either be three or eight. Then he saw Liza's car parked near the building. There were no empty spaces nearby but he managed to squeeze into an illegal spot near the stairs. If he got a ticket, so be it. He needed to get to Liza.

As soon as he got out of the car, she stepped out of the shadows near the stairs. No coat, even though it had gotten terribly cold since sunset, and still wearing the off-the-shoulder blue sweater she had on earlier. She didn't come to him, but stayed where she was, shivering, hugging herself.

"Liza, are you okay?" he asked, quickly looking her over as he hurried toward her.

She shook her head.

He got to her but carefully kept his hands to himself. "Are you injured?"

She shook her head again, her eyes frightened, her face pale.

"Okay, good." He wanted to reach for her, hold her against his chest but he kept his hands to himself.

"Come," she whispered, her voice catching.

She turned around and led him up the stairs, one hand clinging to the rail. She faltered once, and he bracketed her waist with his hands until she steadied herself, and then let go when she continued.

She got to the third floor and went only a few steps before stopping in front of an apartment to wait for him.

"Is this your apartment?" he asked. She said nothing but just stood there shivering.

"No. Rick's. That's mine," she said, glancing over her shoulder.

A bad feeling gripped Evan's gut and wouldn't let go. "Is Rick hurt?"

Her lips quivered. She opened her mouth but nothing came out. With a soft cry she launched herself against him and wrapped her arms around his waist, clinging to him as if she teetered on the edge of a precipice and letting go would mean certain death.

"I think I killed him," she whispered. "He's not breathing."

Christ Almighty. He gently pushed her back and looked

at her terrified face. What the hell had she done? "What happened?"

"I shoved him. He hit his head on the corner of the table."

"You have a key?"

"It's unlocked."

He turned the knob and the door opened. Among the litter, Rick laid on the dingy carpet, one leg twisted ominously, his face pasty white.

"Did you call 911?" Evan went to the man and crouched beside him.

"No. Just you."

He looked sharply at her. "Do it. Now."

She hesitated. "I didn't mean it. He lunged for me, and I shoved him…."

"Liza, please," Evan said calmly. "Make the call."

She didn't move. Just stood there staring at the shaggy-haired man on the floor, as if she were in a trance, her entire body shaking.

"Liza."

She nodded and, with trembling hands, pulled her cell phone out of her pocket.

He checked the pulse at Rick's neck. Faint but steady. Evan breathed in with relief. The pulse was weak enough he could see how she'd missed it, but it was there. The guy was definitely alive. Gingerly, Evan slid his hands under Rick's head. No blood or obvious wounds. His arms and legs seemed all right, too. He checked his eyes. Not good.

"It's my fault," Liza said, staring. "He was already high and I should've stopped him from shooting up. But I didn't. I wanted him to shut up. To go to sleep so I could call you and explain. I wanted him dead." She shot Evan a panicked look, as if realizing her admission.

Evan forced himself to stay focused on his patient. He had a lot of questions for her, but now wasn't the time. "Did you call 911?"

"Yes." Tears streamed down her face. She seemed to be having difficulty drawing a breath. "What have I done?"

"He's not dead."

She blinked. Disappointment flashed across her face. She quickly lost it. Relief took its place, but was it real?

The hair on the back of Evan's neck stood. He definitely hadn't mistaken the disappointment. The thought of it made him queasy. Was she using him to help mount her defense? Had she wanted to get rid of Rick that badly that she'd tried to kill him? He did not want to believe that. "Do you know if he might have used anything else besides the heroin?"

"He's been drinking a lot. Beer and vodka mostly."

"Did you give him the drugs?"

She visibly swallowed. "I gave him the money to buy them."

Evan looked away from her and stared down at Rick. "Why did you call me?"

"You're a doctor."

"The paramedics would've gotten here faster," he said, meeting her eyes.

"I was scared, Evan. I didn't know what to do. I thought I'd killed a man."

He looked back down at Rick. She might not be directly responsible, but the guy was in bad shape. Would he make it? Evan had no idea.

"You're angry." She dropped down beside him, putting a hand on his thigh for balance.

"I'm confused."

"I'll tell you everything." She looked around at the first sound of the sirens. "I was going to tell you tonight at dinner."

Of course she was. "Right now, let's concentrate on getting Rick to a hospital."

"I swear, Evan," she whispered, desperation making her voice thick. "I know you don't believe me but—"

He picked her hand up and set it aside, and then got to his feet. Had this been her plan all along? Get rid of her boyfriend and use Evan to justify a self-defense claim? He really didn't know what to think at this point. Maybe it was better that he didn't think. Go on autopilot. Be Dr. Gann and get Rick taken care of before engaging in any conversations with Liza.

"Where are you going?" she asked.

He was at the door already. "To flag down the paramedics. This building isn't easy to find."

"I'm sorry, Evan. I didn't know what to do. I really didn't mean to get you involved."

He stopped and looked at her, crumpled in a heap on the floor. In spite of himself, he softened. He had to at least give her the benefit of the doubt. But that didn't mean he'd let himself be her doormat. "I have no intention of getting involved."

LIZA HAD NEVER FELT so alone in her entire life. Ironic, since just yesterday she'd dared to be happy, to actually harbor hope in her heart that Evan would be someone with whom she could share a part of herself. But it wasn't his fault that everything had fallen apart. She screwed up. In a major way. Would he ever forgive her?

She looked over at Rick, his mouth partially open, disgusting spittle caked at the corners. She shouldn't hate him. He deserved her sympathy. But she did hate him. More than she'd hated anyone. Even her father.

The sound of the sirens got so loud that the ambulance had to be right outside. She struggled to her feet and went to the door but stayed inside. She didn't want to see any of her neighbors, and they'd all be out there, gawking, wondering if the ambulance had come for her or Rick.

Nearly everyone had heard Rick's vitriolic rantings at one time or another. They'd seen her trying to sneak off, and heard him yelling at the top of his lungs to get her ass back to the apartment. Stoned out of his mind, Rick had knocked on doors in the middle of the night looking for her. If he didn't make it, what would those people tell the police?

She hoped Mary Ellen and Freedom weren't out there, too. But then why wouldn't they be? The sirens were so damn loud....

Liza put a hand to her throbbing head and ducked for a quick look. The paramedics had just pulled their equipment from the back of the van. Evan said something to one of them. The man nodded and got inside the ambulance, a minute later climbing out and dragging the end of a gurney. The second paramedic grabbed the other end and they brought it up the stairs, swiftly and efficiently, followed by Evan.

She got out of the way, and they entered the apartment and immediately went to work on Rick. Liza stepped farther back, unable to stop shaking. Yes, she still felt horrible and responsible for Rick lying there, but watching Evan made her feel worse. He was such a good man. Always doing the right thing, and she totally didn't deserve him. Not that it mattered either way now.

She really wanted to talk to him, though. Even if she never saw him again, she wanted him to know the truth about Rick, the lawsuit, everything. It would kill her if Evan thought she'd betrayed him. But it wasn't going to be easy to talk to him when he wouldn't even meet her eyes.

Time seemed to inch by as she waited, expecting to see the police show up at the door. But the only people she saw were nosy neighbors ducking their heads in for a look. Evan made them move as the paramedics prepared Rick for transport. Once the path was clear, they picked Rick up and started down the stairs.

Neither paramedic said a word to her, and she knew she had Evan to thank for that. Not that she thought she'd get out of being questioned, but later she'd be more composed. She grabbed her purse, making sure her keys hadn't fallen out, and then followed them down, face straight ahead so that she didn't have to look at the crowd of people who'd gathered. Not trusting her weakened knees, she kept a firm hold on the railing, even when she heard Freedom call out to her.

But Liza did look up then, and motioned Freedom to stay back. Mary Ellen stared in horrified silence. Liza managed to give her a reassuring smile before joining Evan and the paramedics at the back of the ambulance.

"We're taking him to Grady Memorial," the taller, muscled paramedic said, with a glance in her direction.

"I guess I should follow," she said, not sure if the words had stayed in her head or passed her lips.

Evan looked at her, his gaze going to her trembling hands, which she still couldn't seem to control. "I'll take you."

"Thank you," she said softly.

"Go get in the car." He pointed the remote at the Camry and unlocked the doors. "I'll be right there."

She nodded, her gaze straying to the ambulance. The doors were open and she could see Rick lying on the gurney. One of the paramedics was hooking him up to something.

"Go, Liza."

She looked over at Evan, wanting reassurance. His expression was grim.

EVAN SPOKE TO the E.R. doctor for a few minutes, giving him a rundown on Rick's condition and the events leading up to his losing consciousness. He probably should've let Liza do the talking, but she was still a mess and since he was pretty sure she had nothing to do with what happened to Rick, Evan didn't see the point.

He went to the crowded waiting area where he told her he'd meet her. She sat forward in one of the hard brown chairs, hands clasped, her elbows resting on her thighs, her head hanging. She didn't seem to be shaking too much anymore. Good. He wouldn't have to give her a sedative.

She glanced up when he picked up her purse, which had been sitting on the chair next to her. "How's he doing?"

He handed her the purse, and then sat down. "He'll live."

This time she genuinely looked relieved. Straightening, she asked, "Was it the drugs?"

Evan nodded. "I'm pretty sure he has a concussion, too, but the drugs are what got him."

"Are the police coming?"

"You didn't do anything wrong, Liza."

She briefly closed her eyes and then stared down at the floor. "You have no idea."

"You said you shoved him in self-defense."

"I did." She looked warily at him. "That's not what I'm talking about."

He looked away, his attention landing on a little girl clutching a dirty rag doll with one hand, and the arm of an older woman with her other. Grady Memorial was a nightmare. On any given night, the trauma center was likely to have more shooting victims than they could handle and tonight was no exception.

"Evan?"

It was late. He was tired. More importantly, did he really want to hear what she had to say? He checked his watch and got to his feet. "It's after midnight. I'll drive you home."

"What about the hospital paperwork?" She got up, too, and put a hand on his arm. "Don't I have to sign something?"

"Are you two married?"

She blushed, and lowered her hand. "Of course not."

"Then you don't have to worry about it," he said, studying the way she tightly clasped her hands together. In spite of himself, he wondered what the hell this guy held over her.

"I guess not, but I am kind of responsible for—" She gave an angry shake of her head. "No, you're right. This isn't on me."

The place was so packed someone had already claimed their seats, and Evan motioned for her to precede him between the narrow rows of chairs. Besides, this was a hell of a place to be discussing anything so personal.

He watched her from behind, admiring how she'd dressed up in the off-the-shoulder sweater and silky pants. Had tonight gone as planned, they'd have had a nice dinner, gone to the concert and been in his bed by now. But that wasn't going to happen. Not tonight. Not ever again.

Neither spoke until they'd passed the sad-looking Christmas tree in the lobby near the exit doors. Then Liza said, "Thank you, Evan, for coming to my rescue tonight. For bringing me here. I don't know what I would've done without you."

"No problem." He couldn't look at her. Instead he busied himself with fishing his keys out of his pocket. Frankly, he would've preferred silence all the way back to her place. At this point, there wasn't anything she could say that would stop him from feeling like a chump. No matter which way he cut it, she'd used him.

"I know it's late—"

"Yep, and I have an early appointment tomorrow." Out of his peripheral vision he saw her turn sharply away.

"I need to talk to you," she said in a small voice he barely heard.

He paused, really tired all of a sudden. As if he'd been working a twenty-four-hour rotation. "I doubt there's anything to say."

Her laugh came out shaky. "I have so much to explain it could take the rest of the night."

Luckily, they got to his car quickly. He'd cheated and used the physician's parking area. Although he wasn't on staff here, tonight he figured he'd earned the spot. He unlocked the doors and, out of habit, he went around to open Liza's. Their eyes briefly meeting, a small regretful smile lifted the corners of her mouth before she got inside.

He went around the car, gulping in cold air. This would be a damn long ride to her place. If he'd been thinking straight, he would've called her a cab. Given her the money for the ride home. He'd done enough. Hell, who was he kidding? He could never have thrown her into a cab. Not tonight. Tomorrow was a different story.

He got behind the wheel, not knowing what to say. Nothing she could tell him would turn back time. The damage had been done. Maybe she'd figured that out for herself because she didn't say anything, either.

After they'd been on the road for about ten minutes, she

said, "I can't imagine what's going through your mind right now, and I don't expect us to pick up where we left off…."

Man, she got that right.

"I'm not sure I'm entitled to even hope for forgiveness, but I have to explain what's behind all this."

He shook his head. "No, you don't."

"Evan…"

"You know what first attracted me to you?" he asked, keeping his eyes straight ahead. "You were refreshingly straightforward. You told it like it was. No games or bull-shit."

"I am that person," she said softly. "This thing with Rick isn't just about me."

He shook his head as another thought occurred. With Rick out of the way, assuming she won the lawsuit, the money would be all hers. Evan exhaled sharply. Wow, he'd been such a damn fool.

"Please, Evan, I know an all-night coffee shop not far from here."

Right, so she could tell him more lies. Another block and they were at her apartment complex. He turned in and stopped in front of her building. "Good luck, Liza, I hope you get what you want."

He refused to look in her direction. He simply waited for her to get out, and then he sped away.

CHAPTER FIFTEEN

SHORTLY AFTER three-thirty that morning, sheer physical and mental exhaustion forced Liza to close her eyes. Sleep hadn't been soothing. Nightmares claimed her subconscious. Rick with his head bashed in and bleeding all over her. The police banging at her door. Handcuffs clamped around her wrists, while Eve and Jane stood off in the distance, laughing and pointing.

The most horrifying of all was the one where Evan sat on what appeared to be a throne, hovering several feet off the ground, watching her, shaking his head, tears brimming in his eyes. No matter how much she pleaded for him to listen, he said nothing and stared at her in abject disappointment.

Light had forced its way through the worn curtains before she opened her eyes again. She still lay on the couch where she'd collapsed after Evan had dropped her off. She still had on her clothes from last night and, fortunately, her watch. Feeling as if it weighed a ton, she lifted her wrist and squinted. It was already nine-forty.

The inside of her mouth was dry and nauseating, reminding her that she hadn't even brushed her teeth. She pushed to her feet. Someone pounded at the door. Probably one of the neighbors, maybe even Mary Ellen. Ignoring them, she padded to the bathroom. Looking into the mirror was painful, so she lowered her head and got to the business of brushing her teeth and washing her face.

Next she'd call the hospital and check on Rick. She hoped he was okay. Maybe the frightening episode would wake him up and he'd get the help he needed. Astonishingly, the animosity she'd felt toward him for the past year had vanished. A calmness had eerily settled over her at some point last night.

Maybe it was because she was too drained to feel anything, or maybe it was the fact that she'd already made her decision to end the lawsuit and tell Eve and Jane everything…to not allow Rick to hold the diaries over her head like a club.

Eve and Jane would think she was insane for waiting until a week before the judge was supposed to hear the case. She'd put them through so much, but sadly, it had taken this long for Liza to swallow her pride, tell them the truth and ask for their help. Nearly a year of her life wasted because of pride.

All her life she'd handled everything herself. "Never risk disappointment by asking someone for help" was her motto. Ironic that she'd decided to tell Evan everything at dinner last night. Expose herself as the fool she'd been, and then if he wasn't totally disgusted with her, ask for his forgiveness. Too late now. Evan would never…

A sob swelled in her throat.

Damn, she couldn't get all soft and mushy now. She had a lot to do today. None of it pleasant. In the end, she'd feel better. And Eve and Jane would still hate her. And Evan…she could not go there.

She finished toweling off her face, and decided on making a couple of calls before taking a shower. Whoever had been knocking at the door was at it again. Great background noise for her phone calls.

Annoyed with the person's persistence, she didn't check the window to see who it was and jerked open the door. It was Mary Ellen, without Freedom. Thank God.

"I have been worried sick about you," the other woman said and walked past her into the apartment. She turned to face Liza, her eyes wide with a mixture of fear and relief. "What happened last night?"

Liza closed the door but didn't encourage Mary Ellen to advance into the apartment. "Rick overdosed."

"Is he okay?"

"He was last night. I was about to call the hospital to check on him."

"You looked awful when the ambulance came," Mary Ellen said, her face pale, the scar near her lip pronounced. "I thought you killed him."

"I bet everyone did."

Mary Ellen nodded.

Oddly, Liza didn't care. What did bother her was that she wouldn't have any money from the lawsuit to help Mary Ellen and her daughter. "Is Freedom okay?"

"Yep, she's in the playground. She thought you killed the stupid bastard, too."

"She didn't say it like that, I hope."

Mary Ellen vigorously shook her head. "She's a good girl."

"Yes, she is." Liza sighed. Somehow she had to help them. She'd be getting a job soon, and there was still about twenty-two-hundred dollars left of her inheritance in a savings account she'd squirreled away for an emergency. "Look, Mary Ellen," Liza said, her hand on the doorknob.

"I have a lot to do today, but I'll see if I can pick up burgers for dinner."

"You don't have to do that."

"I know." She opened the door. "See you later, okay?"

"Good luck today," Mary Ellen said on her way out. After she stepped outside she turned back to Liza, and with a frown said, "You're different."

Liza smiled. "Actually, I feel like my old self for the first time in a year."

THE MIDTOWN ITALIAN restaurant, with its red-and-white checkered tablecloths and vases of fresh white daisies on each table, had once been a favorite of Eve, Jane and Liza's. Sitting as far back as she could, Liza waited for the other two to arrive, while mentally rehearsing what she was going to say to them.

It was simple, really. She'd tell them about Rick having the diaries—the reason for the lawsuit—and that as of three hours ago, his doctor expected him to make a full recovery. He'd probably still want money in exchange for the diaries. Yep, real simple.

Sighing, she pushed aside the second cocktail napkin she'd shredded. The fact that they'd agreed to meet her and hadn't told her to go to hell was a good sign. After what they'd witnessed last night, pity alone could be the reason. But she'd accept any crumb they were willing to throw her. She owed them an explanation.

She saw Jane first, her hair so much blonder and longer now. Eve was right behind her, turning heads as they walked across the restaurant. Liza waved and they headed for her. Feeling awkward suddenly, she wished she'd had a glass of wine or something to calm the butterflies fluttering around in her stomach.

"Hello, Liza," Eve said first, while pulling out a chair.

"Hi." Jane looked uncomfortable.

"Thanks for coming," Liza said, despising how formal she sounded. "I'm sure you'd rather have told me to kiss off."

"That's not true," Jane said, claiming her seat. "I've missed you. We both have," she added, glancing at Eve, who busied herself with spreading the white linen napkin across her lap and refused to look up.

Liza smiled. Jane looked different, but she was still the same sweet woman who'd always been the one to smooth over the rough spots among the three of them. Eve was another story. Not that she hadn't always been a great friend, but she could be a tough cookie.

"So, what's on your mind?" an unsmiling Eve finally asked, with caution in her eyes.

Liza cleared her throat. "First, I want to apologize. I know that sounds weak. You both have every right to be furious with me. But I—" Her voice cracked. She cleared her throat again and then took a quick sip of water.

Neither woman spoke, but the compassion and hope she saw in their eyes gave her courage. The waitress came and took their drink orders, giving Liza another moment to compose herself.

"Eve, I did something horrible," she said the second the woman left. "I'm going to explain, but please don't get angry, just listen. I need to tell you this. It's important. For you."

Eve frowned. "I'm listening."

Liza took a deep breath. "Remember after your grandmother died, I offered to pack up her house?"

Eve slowly nodded.

"You asked me not to take Rick. I did anyway." Liza had

loved Grammie as if she were her own grandmother. Not even Eve and Jane understood how devastating the woman's death had been for Liza. She'd been too good at playing tough. Letting everything roll off her back, including her parents' indifference toward her.

But when the time came to go to the old house belonging to the woman who'd made childhood bearable, Liza had crumbled like stale bread. She'd taken Rick with her for support. But that was no excuse, and she wouldn't use it now.

To her surprise, Eve's expression softened. "I should never have asked you to do that. It was selfish of me."

"No." Liza shook her head. "I was the selfish one. I failed you."

"You loved her, too, Liza," Eve said softly. "She was as much your grandmother as she was mine. You practically lived with us."

Liza had to blink back the emotion welling in her eyes. Eve understood about Grammie.

"Please tell me that's not what kept you away from us for the past year," Jane said, her expression horrified.

This was the hard part. Liza had to force herself to breathe. "There's more to it. Rick took something that belongs to you, Eve. I didn't know about it until…until a year ago."

The two women exchanged nervous glances, and then Eve asked, "What did he take?"

"Your diaries."

Eve slumped back and looking dazed. "The journals I started after my parents died," she said, more to herself. "How many did he take?"

"All of them."

"Oh, God." Jane covered her mouth.

Silence fell when the waitress returned with their drinks and set them down. They declined to order any food, and the woman left.

"There has to be a couple dozen notebooks," Eve said, her hand unsteady as she picked up her iced tea. "I stopped journaling right before we left for college."

"I didn't read anything," Liza assured her. "I didn't find out he took them until way after the fact." Seeing the fear in her friend's eyes, Liza wanted to cry, but that would do no good. "He wants money for them."

Eve's gaze narrowed before awareness dawned. "Is that what the lawsuit's about?"

Liza nodded.

"He's been blackmailing you?" Jane stared in disbelief. "This whole time?"

"Why didn't you come to us before now?" Eve asked, with so much hurt in her eyes that it left Liza cold.

"I was ashamed," Liza said quietly. "And I thought I could handle Rick, and that you would never need to know about any of it."

Eve stared down at her hand clutching the glass of iced tea. "So you just disappeared without a word."

"No, I was only supposed to be gone for a long weekend. To Atlantic City. Rick started losing money like crazy. After he drained my checking account and demanded more, I cut him off. I was going to leave him and catch the next flight back, and that's when he told me about the diaries."

"You should have at least called," Eve said, the fire back in her eyes. "It wasn't just about our friendship, you put the show in a bind."

"You're right. I have no excuse." She couldn't have called. Not without admitting what a fool she'd been and scare the hell out of Eve over the diaries, but she wasn't going to argue about that at this point. Pride had gotten her into enough trouble.

It didn't help that Eve seemed more concerned about Liza shunning them than she cared about the diaries. The thought made Liza sick to her stomach. How terribly foolish she'd been to not trust her friends.

Eve sighed. "Where's Rick now?"

"In the hospital."

"What happened?" Jane's eyes widened.

"I tried to kill him."

Both women gasped.

Liza gave them a wan smile. "He overdosed. Plus, he has a concussion from when I shoved him last night."

"You're not still with him, then," Jane said.

"God, no." Liza looked down, unable to meet their eyes. "Not really. But he's kept me on a short leash and I've allowed it. The show was really taking off, and when he threatened to sell the diaries to the tabloids I honestly didn't know what to do."

"You could've come to us. I thought that's what friends were for." The trace of bitterness in Eve's voice earned a sharp look from Jane.

"I know," Liza said quickly. "I was ashamed, and I honestly thought I could handle Rick. He needed money and I received a small inheritance from my father that I figured would—"

"I'm sorry. I didn't know. When did he pass away?" Eve asked, sincerity in her eyes.

"There was no love lost there."

"Still, I wish we'd known," Jane said softly.

Liza looked away. They'd been the best of friends, shared so many things, and she'd not only let them down, but had also held them at bay, making the occasional wisecrack about her parents but never letting them see how much she'd hurt. While they'd invited her into every aspect of their lives, she'd never totally let down her guard with them.

"My father was a lousy drunk," she said. "That's why there were never sleepovers at my house."

Eve smiled gently. "We knew that, Liza."

"No, I don't mean he got drunk once in a while, he was a drunken asshole six nights out of seven. Sometimes he'd hit my mother. Not me, not really, just the occasional slap, but that was probably because I wasn't around much."

Jane snorted. "We weren't stupid."

She looked closely into each of their faces. They did know. "You guys never said anything."

Eve shrugged. "What would that have changed?"

Liza's eyes burned. She did not want to cry now. She sniffed, cleared her throat. "Okay, here's the deal. I can withdraw the lawsuit and tell Rick to screw off but I have no idea how he'll react. I've looked everywhere I could think where he might hide the diaries and I've come up empty. Or we can see how the judgment plays out and if there's any money awarded, exchange it for the diaries."

Jane frowned. "Can't we go to the police?"

Liza shook her head. "We can't prove he stole them, or that he even has the diaries in his possession. Once he sells them to the tabloids, he's out of here."

They both looked at Eve, who'd remained silent. Finally, she said, "It's not fair to the others. They shouldn't have to pay blackmail money."

"I'm willing to give up half my share," Jane offered. "What about you, Eve?"

"Thanks, Jane, but I can't let you do that." Then, ignoring Jane's protest, Eve looked at Liza. "Would my share be enough? Would he take that?"

Liza looked at her friend, unable to stop the tears filling her eyes. What had she done? "I don't know. He should. That's all he would've gotten from the lawsuit."

"Liza, don't. It's okay." Eve left her chair to sit in the one next to Liza. She scooted it even closer, and then took Liza's hand. "It's only money. Not worth ruining our friendship. Do you hear me?"

The floodgates really opened then, and Liza grabbed a tissue out of her purse. "I've already done that. I've ruined everything."

"No, you haven't," Eve said, and Jane echoed her.

"You warned me Rick was scum, and I wouldn't listen."

"Like we ever thought you would have," Jane said.

Liza smiled, and dabbed at her cheeks. "You should've just hit me over the head."

"The thought crossed our minds." Eve squeezed her hand. "When is Rick getting out of the hospital?"

Liza hiccupped. "It'll be a while. He's going into detox first."

Eve nodded thoughtfully. "I think I should speak to my attorney about this before we do anything."

Jane nodded. "Eve, look at me."

At the firmness in Jane's voice, Eve and Liza both turned. She wasn't used to this new assertive Jane.

"I'm in this, too," Jane said. "I am giving half of my share, and it's not up for negotiation."

Eve rolled her eyes.

Liza sniffed. All she had to contribute was the problem itself. "I want you guys to know it really killed me to file the lawsuit," she whispered. "At the time, I didn't feel as if I had a choice. I'm so sorry."

"Forget it already." Eve smiled. "You know I'm not that famous. The tabloids might not even be interested in a bunch of teenage ramblings."

Jane and Liza exchanged looks. Yeah, right. First, she *had* become that famous, and second, what tabloid wouldn't love to take a shot at syndication's newest rising star?

"You remember writing anything too hot and heavy?" Liza asked.

Eve's smile vanished. "Right after my parents died I was pretty angry and bitter. Not very forgiving, either, as you well know." She exhaled slowly. "I doubt there would be anything in the diaries that would lastingly damage my career, but I won't lie, I don't look forward to the humiliation of having my private thoughts and crazy teenage angst publicized."

"We won't let that happen," Liza said, aware that she hadn't done such a great job so far. "When I leave here I'm going to Rick's apartment and tear it apart. Without him looking over my shoulder I may be able to find a clue as to where he's keeping the diaries."

"I'll go with you," Jane said.

"Unfortunately, I have an important meeting with the network bigwigs in less than an hour." Eve glanced at her watch. "I'll be free this evening."

"That's okay," Liza said quickly. "I can do this by myself." The thought of Jane or Eve seeing the degrading way she'd lived for the past several months made her want to crawl into a ball and weep.

"I want to help," Jane insisted.

"Have I told you how terrific you look?" Liza asked, not just to distract her, which was part of it, but because Liza really meant it. "Your hair, your clothes, everything about you is really amazing."

Jane blushed. "I've been seeing this guy…."

"Anyone I know?"

Jane shook her head. "But I can't wait for you to meet him. His name's Perry."

While they talked, Eve's interested gaze stayed on Liza, her brows slightly furrowed as if she was obsessing over something that puzzled her. In the old days, Liza would've made a teasing remark. But not now, and it hurt so badly to realize that their once solid relationship was now too fragile for even the slightest misstep. All her own fault.

"So, Liza," Eve finally said, "tell us about Evan."

Hearing his name was all Liza needed to burst out into tears again.

CHAPTER SIXTEEN

AFTER SEARCHING Rick's apartment, Liza showered twice and still she felt his filth coating her skin. She'd filled three huge garbage bags of empty booze bottles and rotting food that, with the help of two guys working on a car, she hoisted into the Dumpster. She swore he hadn't washed his clothes or linen in months, and with total disgust she rummaged through each and every pocket, hoping for a clue as to the diaries' location. But she found nothing.

She'd worked at it well into the night, and eventually collapsed in exhaustion on her couch, too tired to even check out the refrigerator for a cola or some juice. Earlier Mary Ellen had knocked on the door and offered to make macaroni and cheese for dinner since Liza had totally forgotten to pick up burgers, but she wasn't in the mood to be around anyone. She wasn't only physically tired, her brain had gone in circles all day and had started to fizzle out.

Tomorrow was going to be a big day. She had to talk to Kevin Wade about withdrawing the lawsuit. That wouldn't be pleasant. He'd inevitably have questions she wouldn't want to answer. At least he'd already been paid. A total waste of money, but she'd already let that go. Then she had to talk to Rick.

The mere thought made her stomach roll. She hated seeing him, even more than she hated offering him one cent of Eve and Jane's winnings. And she wouldn't yet. First, she'd try and bluff him. He couldn't spend the money from prison, and she found enough heroin hidden in his apartment to put him away for a while. He'd been so messed up most of the time that he probably had forgotten his hiding places.

She realized the case could get sticky since she'd given him the money for the drugs, but at this point she didn't care. What did she have to lose? Not a damn thing. She'd already lost everything that mattered. Eve and Jane were still her friends, but they had to harbor some ill feelings. They were, after all, human.

Evan hated her. He had to.

She shuddered, thinking of the disappointment on his face. He'd made it clear that there was nothing she could tell him that would make a difference. He was right, of course, so she hadn't even bothered trying to call him.

But there was still this huge part of her that wanted to tell him she wasn't as bad as he thought she was. That she'd made foolish mistakes but her intention had been honorable. Even if he never wanted to speak to her again, did he have to think she was such an awful person?

Her cell phone rang, and damned if it wasn't sitting clear across the room. She struggled to her feet and reached it right before it would've gone to voice mail. It was Eve.

"Hey," Eve said as soon as Liza answered.

The casual familiarity of her voice had an amazingly emotional effect on Liza and it took her a second to compose herself. "Hey. Wish I had good news."

"No?"

"I searched places where no man or woman should have

to go, especially without a tetanus shot. I found nothing. I'm sorry."

Eve paused. She had to be disappointed, but didn't let it show when she said, "You shouldn't have had to do that alone."

"Are you kidding? Do you remember who got us into this mess?"

"Knock that off. We're in this together, remember?"

"If you make me cry I'm gonna be so pissed off."

Eve laughed softly. "Have you been to the hospital yet?"

"No. That's tomorrow."

"Have you called Evan?"

Liza briefly closed her eyes. There were some things she didn't miss about having well-meaning but in-your-face friends. "That won't happen."

"Why not?"

"He doesn't want to talk to me, and I don't blame him."

"Okay, here's the problem…Nicole, the woman who took your place, she's leaving. Going home to California after the holidays. So if you're taking your old job back, you'll likely be bumping into—"

"Wait a minute."

"What?"

Liza's heart somersaulted. "Are you offering me my old job?"

"Yes, I am."

She heard the smile in Eve's voice, and dared to hope. Maybe there truly were no residual ill feelings. Well, that just made her feel worse. "I sued half the people associated with the show. I think that might be a little awkward."

"Maybe at first. But you are dropping the lawsuit and you're a damn good producer."

For one of the few times in her life, Liza didn't know

what to say. She didn't deserve to have her old job back. Yet she wanted it with all her heart. "Have you discussed this with Jane and Cole and the others?"

"Of course Jane is over-the-moon excited at the prospect. Cole is the only other person with whom I've discussed this. He wants you back."

Cole Crawford was the supervising producer with whom she'd always gotten along, but he was also one of the lottery winners named in the lawsuit. "Seriously?"

"You'll make his job easier. He's also the only other person I told about the diaries. He even offered to kick in some money if it comes to that, which, of course, I wouldn't allow, but still that's Cole."

Liza swallowed around the lump in her throat. "I don't deserve any of you guys."

"Stop it already. Just say you'll come back."

"I want to. I do, but—"

"Then it's settled."

"If it causes any problems at all—"

"We'll address them at the time." Eve paused. "In the meantime, you should call Evan."

"Why?" Liza asked, although she knew where Eve was coming from. Working at the station, she was bound to occasionally run into Evan. The thought made her pulse quicken. Foolish to get excited, though. He thought she was scum.

Eve scoffed. "Don't be obtuse."

"He'll ignore me and that'll be fine."

"Liza."

"Look, Eve, I know you're trying to help, but trust me, I'm the last person in the world he wants to hear from. Leave it alone."

"If you don't quit being so damn hard on yourself, you'll never know, will you?"

Liza bit back a remark. "I'll think about it."

"Right. You do that." Eve paused, and Liza could hear someone talking in the background. "Look, you're off the hook for now. I've got to go."

Liza smiled. "Go."

She disconnected the call and got comfortable on the couch again. It wasn't about to be easy trying to slide back into her old life. There was bound to be resentment. And seeing Evan was going to be beyond horrible. But she wasn't about to pass up the opportunity to return to the best job she'd ever had or would ever have again.

Evan wouldn't be a problem. He'd be the perfect gentleman, smiling appropriately and greeting her in the halls, albeit briefly. An unknowing spectator wouldn't have a clue that there was bad blood between them.

She was the one who'd suffer, watching him, knowing she'd screwed things up, knowing she'd never again be in the arms of the best man she'd ever been with. And she'd deserve every last excruciating minute.

"THANK YOU FOR meeting with me. I really appreciate it," Eve said as soon as Evan walked into her office. "If you don't mind, would you close the door?"

Evan did as she asked and then sat down on the chair opposite her, the same chair he'd sat in last week when he'd come asking for her help. That was the only reason he was here now—to return the favor, even though any conversation about Liza was pointless. Two nights ago her actions had said it all. Nothing more to talk about.

"Would you like a cola or a bottle of water?" she asked.

"No, thank you. I only have a few minutes."

"Right." She smiled knowingly. "I won't take up much of your time."

As if on cue, his cell phone rang. "Excuse me, I have to take this." He looked at the caller ID. It was someone from Grady Memorial. Had to be about Rick, but why call him? He hesitated. This may not be a conversation he wanted to have in front of Eve.

"Do you need some privacy?" she asked.

"No, I'll return the call." He slipped the phone back into his pocket, curious as all get-out. "If this is about Liza, our conversation won't take long."

Eve looked at him hard. "I can't begin to imagine what you're thinking right now...."

"To tell you the truth, I've stopped thinking. Nothing to say, nothing to think about." He meant it. He'd beaten himself up enough for being a chump.

"I was there night before last. I saw what happened."

"You and everyone else."

Eve gave him a long, measuring look. "I hope this isn't about ego."

He laughed humorlessly. "She lied to me, and then she used me. Is that clear enough?"

Jerking her head back, she frowned. "How did she use you? She did no such thing."

He stared back at her, confused. "So now you're suddenly on her side?"

"I know Liza, and obviously she's done some stupid things, but she's never used anyone."

"You know what?" He got to his feet. "This is a complete waste of time."

"Wait, please. Let me explain something to you, and then I swear I'll never say another word about Liza."

Between curiosity and the pleading in her green eyes, he stopped. How could she still defend the woman who'd betrayed her? "This better be good."

"Oh, it is." Eve gave him a weary smile. "Everything she's done in the past year, including filing the lawsuit, has been to protect me."

That got his attention. He sank back into the chair. "I'm listening."

EVAN THREW HIS CAR KEYS on the counter and went straight to the refrigerator. Usually he kept a six-pack in there in case Elton or Eric dropped by, but he couldn't remember what was left. Man, he sure could use a cold beer about now.

First, the meeting with Eve, and then the call from the E.R. nurse. His head hadn't stopped spinning since he left Grady Memorial an hour ago. He opened the refrigerator door and muttered a thanks. A lone green-tinted bottle sat on the top shelf. Perfect. He only needed one.

He uncapped the bottle and took it with him to the living room. Before he dropped onto the tan leather couch, he pulled the key the nurse had given him out of his pocket. It clearly belonged to a safe-deposit box. The nurse had found the key in Rick's sock the night he was admitted, and knew Evan had a keen interest in Rick's case. She'd taken a professional and ethical risk and called Evan. He'd promised her and her husband dinner, and against every grain of good sense and ethical bone in his body, he'd accepted the key.

The question was, what should he do with it? Give it to Eve? Or call Liza? He took a long cool sip of beer. After what Eve told him, he wanted to talk to Liza. He'd misjudged her. But she sure had helped feed his imagination. She could've explained about Rick, about the lawsuit. Yeah, he knew she'd tried, but only after the fact.

Hell, that was his ego talking. He'd wanted to rescue her. Be her knight in shining armor. He'd wanted to help solve her problems. But who the hell did he think he was? She hadn't turned to anyone for help, not even her best friends, women she'd grown up with. She'd wanted to handle her own mess. Call it pride or self-sufficiency. That's who Liza was. Take her or leave her.

She certainly didn't make it easy.

Shaking his head, he tipped the bottle to his lips. Less than two lousy weeks. That's all it had been since he'd really gotten to know her. How could he be in so emotionally deep? Was it because he'd finally caught the prize after admiring her from afar, or finally achieving success after having been shot down? He'd never been about the chase. Obviously, because even when he'd thought she'd used him, his feelings for her hadn't truly changed.

He'd been angry, mostly with himself, but that hadn't stopped him from wanting her, from lying awake thinking about how good it had been between them. That made him all the more an idiot. Angela had taught him a valuable lesson—don't get emotionally involved. Don't be gullible. Have fun, be up front, have great sex. That's all. How often had he reminded himself? Yet when it came to Liza, his common sense took off in the wind.

He was glad Eve had told him about the diaries. As misguided as Liza had been, she'd tried to do what she thought was the right thing. Eve and Jane had forgiven her. She'd get back some of her old life. But that didn't mean everything would go back to the way it was between him and Liza. He didn't even know if she'd stay in Atlanta.

He laid his head back and swung his feet onto the oak coffee table, sending an old issue of *Psychology Today* flying across the room. He had to call Liza. Tell her about the key. It would be juvenile to ignore her and give it to Eve.

He mentally laughed at himself. As if he would deprive

himself of the pleasure of delivering it to her. He still wanted to play the hero, wanted to see the look on Liza's face when he handed her the key and she realized he'd saved her ass.

He took a last gulp of beer and glanced at his watch. It wasn't too late. He'd go to her apartment. A block from there he'd call to tell her he was on his way. She'd wanted to explain about Rick, and Evan hadn't given her the chance. By now she might not even want to see him. Too bad.

He got up, jerked off his loosened tie and then dropped it on the couch. After leaving the empty bottle on the kitchen counter, he grabbed his keys and went out the back door. He hit the garage door button on the wall pad and as the door slid open, he got into his car. He put the car in Reverse and, waiting for the door to finish opening, his gaze went to the rearview mirror. A car pulled in behind him. It looked just like Liza's.

SHE SHOULD'VE CALLED. It was late, and what she had to say not only could've waited until tomorrow, but also until after Christmas, for that matter. But Liza wanted to see him. Had to see him. That is, if she ever wanted to get a good night's sleep again.

She squinted at the street sign on the right. Not that she'd ever paid much attention when she'd come to Evan's house before, but she was pretty sure that this was his street. She made the turn and saw the redbrick two-story house with the white gazebo that she'd noticed the morning he'd driven her to her car.

Nearly every house was decorated with colored lights strung along the eaves or woven through hedges and trees. The brick ranch-style house next to the two-story had a trio of animated reindeers sitting on the lawn, and the one after that had a large blow-up Santa swaying in the chilly breeze. Only two houses on the street were devoid of decorations. One of them belonged to Evan. She could see the starkness of it from half a block away.

She slowed the car down while her pulse sped up. He didn't want to see her. What if he refused to open the door? Just left her standing in the cold. No, Evan was too much the gentleman. He'd let her in, listen to what she had to say and then throw her out. He'd be polite about it, of course, but there would be no mistake that he didn't want to see her again.

She squared her shoulders, and turned into his driveway. Admittedly, she'd been through worse. And she did have a perfectly legitimate reason for coming to talk to him. If she was going to be working for *Just Between Us* again and be at the studio every day, it was only right she warn him. Make sure they could be civil toward each other and not cause tension around the station.

That's what she'd told herself, anyway, when she'd been sitting in her apartment stewing over being unable to explain herself to him. He could listen for five crummy minutes. However, now that she was here, sitting in his driveway with the garage door slowly lifting, she wanted to get away as fast as she could. Although she just sat there, suddenly unsure.

Evan got out of his car first. Liza followed suit. They walked toward each other but he had the advantage of the garage light shining in her face. His was totally in shadow.

"Hi," he said. "I didn't expect you."

"I should've called."

"No, it's okay." He had on a white dress shirt, no tie and no suit jacket. Odd, because it was cold.

"If you're on your way out I can..." She cleared her throat, and took a step back. "I'll call you tomorrow."

"Why did you come?"

She hesitated. The gentleness in his voice unnerved her.

"It's business. Sort of."

"Yes?"

"First, I want to thank you for the other night and what you did for me. After that scene at the station...well, you could've told me to go to hell."

"No problem. I was doing my job."

"Speaking of jobs..." She cleared her throat. "I've been offered my old one." Damn, she wished she could see his face.

"Really?"

She sighed. He wasn't going to make this easy for her. "I know you can't forgive me for the other night, but I hope we can be civil."

"You're staying in Atlanta, then?"

"Yes."

He took a step closer, the streetlight illuminating his face. At the tenderness in his eyes her chest tightened. "Only for the job?"

"I don't deserve you, Evan." She probably would've run if fear and shock hadn't rooted her to the ground. He couldn't still want her. Was this some kind of cruel payback?

The corners of his mouth lifted ever so slightly. "Why not?"

"What do you mean?"

"That's a pretty strong opinion. I'd like to know how you arrived at it."

She glared at him. Why was he putting her on the spot like this? "I never would've believed you had such a mean streak in you."

"Tell me why you don't think you deserve me."

"Damn you."

"Is it me? Or don't you think you deserve to be loved?" He must have realized she was about to take off. His hand darted out and he grabbed her wrist. "You want to keep running? How will that change anything? You'll only take the problem with you."

Liza tried to twist free but he wouldn't let her go. "Don't try and psychoanalyze me."

"No trying necessary. You lay it all out there." He pulled her closer. "Liza Skinner doesn't need anyone. She can take on the world. Translation—the further she keeps herself away from people, the less she'll get hurt." He hauled her up against him. "Guess what? I'm not going to let you get away with it anymore."

She had to tip her head back to look at him. She saw it then, the fierce determination in his eyes that told her he wasn't giving up on her. What a time to want to cry. She clung to him, blinking back the tears. She'd done too much crying in the past couple of days, more than in her entire adult life.

He brushed the back of his hand down her cheek. "Go ahead, let go," he whispered. "I've got you."

"And waste the moment?" Swallowing back the tears, Liza went up on tiptoes and touched his lips with hers. Softly, sweetly, letting him know how much he'd come to mean to her. How much she never wanted to let him down again. And then she kissed him like she never had before.

EPILOGUE

New Year's Day

THE PARTY TO CELEBRATE the recent distribution of the lottery money had already started by the time Evan and Liza entered the restaurant. The private back room where Eve and Jane and the rest of the staff had begun the festivities was buzzing with excitement. Liza looked forward to meeting some of the new members who had joined the show since she'd left. The initial sting of seeing everyone else was gone.

Between Eve and Jane and one too many Christmas parties, Liza was no longer persona non grata. Everyone who needed to know had been advised of the blackmail, but the details were kept to a minimum. Eve had welcomed her back with open arms and that seemed to be good enough for everyone else.

Christmas decorations were still up, and Liza whispered to Evan, "It'll be nice not to have all this stuff around, huh?"

He slid an arm around her shoulders. "Oh, I don't know. I have a new perspective on Christmas."

She smiled. "Yeah?"

"Yep."

"Any particular reason why?" Making sure no one saw them, she brushed against his fly.

"You will pay for that." Stepping sway, he smiled at Eve, who waved them over to where she and Mitch and Jane and Perry were sipping champagne.

Liza laughed and linked an arm through his as they walked toward the group. The truth was, she'd also changed her mind about the holidays. How could she not after spending Christmas morning in front of the fireplace in bed with Evan? They'd barely made it to his parents' house in time for dinner.

"About time you two showed up," Eve said, waving an impatient hand. "Here." She passed them each a flute of the bubbly. Liza had already met Mitch and Perry, but Evan hadn't, so introductions were made.

"Nicole just informed me that she really doesn't want a going-away party so we're having a farewell toast soon," Eve said.

Liza said a silent thanks to Nicole, who was standing near the dessert table smiling at her significant other, Devon, who'd be going to California with her. Liza really didn't know Nicole, the woman who'd replaced her, but because she was leaving, Liza would be back at her old job tomorrow.

Cole Crawford, the show's supervising producer, walked up with his girlfriend, Jessie, and shook Evan's hand, and then kissed Liza on the cheek. "Where's Liza and what have you done with her?"

"Knock it off. You've seen me in a dress before."

"Once."

Liza frowned down at the simple-cut black dress that probably made her look way too thin. "No."

"Yes," Eve, Jane and Cole said at the same time.

"Okay, already."

Carrying drinks, Zach Haas and his girlfriend Kelly, an actress whom he met when she was a guest on the show, joined the group. Liza didn't really know Zach. He'd started with *Just Between Us* as a cameraman after she'd left. But she sheepishly recalled talking to him once when she'd wanted to pump him for information about the lawsuit.

"So," Evan said, "now that you all are filthy rich, what are your plans for the money?"

Zach laughed. "I don't know about filthy rich. I've always wanted to make a small indie film. That'll about wipe me out."

"Really?" Jane looked from him to Kelly. "You're exaggerating, I hope."

Kelly smiled fondly at him. "It's a huge risk, but he's going to do such an incredible job, he'll get his money back ten times over."

Conservative Jane frowned. Liza understood. Blowing all that money on one thing was scary. But she loved how Kelly supported Zach and his dream.

"What about you, Cole?" Liza asked. "I hope you don't have plans of retiring soon."

Eve scoffed. "He'd better not."

Smiling, Cole slipped an arm around Jessie. "We're taking the girls on one of those Disney cruise vacations," he said, referring to his twins, for whom he had sole custody. "And then we'll leave them with Annie and George while we tour Europe for three weeks."

Jessie beamed at him. "He's such a good guy, he's buying Annie a new car, too. But it's a surprise."

Cole looked embarrassed. "The rest goes into college

funds. The little monkeys are growing so fast I can't keep up with them." He looked at Eve, clearly eager to redirect everyone's attention. "What about you?"

Eve glanced cryptically at Jane, whispered something to her date, Mitch, and then looked at Evan. "May we borrow her for a moment?"

Before Evan answered, Jane took one of Liza's arms and Eve took the other. They steered her to the far corner of the room away from everyone, and faced her.

"We have something to say and I'm warning you that this is not a negotiation." Eve had on her no-nonsense face. "Nor is it a request."

"Got it?" Jane added.

Startled, Liza nodded.

Eve reached into the small silver evening bag hanging over her shoulder. Jane's hand disappeared into a pocket of her blue silk dress. They exchanged pointed glances before each withdrew separate folded pieces of paper, and then at the same time, shoved each one into Liza's hands.

She looked down. It wasn't just paper. They each had given her a check. "What is this?" She unfolded one of them and nearly fell over at the sum.

"It's for you," Eve said. "Jane and I decided our shares should be split three ways."

Liza shook her head, and tried to give the checks back. "No way. I'm serious. No way."

Jane glared at her. "You wanna bet? Didn't Eve make it clear this is nonnegotiable?"

"You guys…" She couldn't accept this money. It wouldn't be fair. "If I cry and mess up my makeup, I'm gonna be really pissed."

"Tough." Jane wasn't having any of it.

Liza still hadn't gotten used to the change in her. "Seriously, this is such a nice gesture but—"

"Seriously...shut up," Eve insisted, "we have the diaries back and it didn't cost us a thing, thanks to Evan. Rick will not be seeing the outside of a jail cell for a while. Life is good. Enjoy."

Liza opened her mouth to protest further, but Jane cut her off. "Look, give some of the money to Mary Ellen, if it makes you feel better."

That got Liza's attention. She'd promised Mary Ellen that she'd help get her and Freedom out of that unsafe apartment complex. But that would have to wait until she got her first paycheck. The thing was, Liza was so broke that she could really use the money herself. Her pride told her to pass the checks back. It took every ounce of humility to keep them in her hand.

"Thank you," she whispered. "You guys are the best."

"Enough of that." Eve waved a hand. "Did you like Evan's parents? You went there for Christmas, yes?"

"Oh, here we go," Liza said, bracing herself to be interrogated. "Yes, they were very nice. Yes, Evan and I are talking about moving in together."

Jane let out a shriek that got everyone's attention. She briefly covered her mouth. "Sorry, but that is so cool."

Eve smiled, looking extraordinarily pleased. "He's a good man, Liza."

"You don't have to tell me that." Her gaze drifted toward him. He met her eyes and winked.

Neither of them looked away. How did she get so lucky? To have the best friends ever, and a guy she never dreamed could be so terrific. She hadn't told anyone yet, but she'd looked into trying a twelve-step meeting for adult children of alcoholics. If someone had suggested such a thing a year ago, she would've told them where to go. Not now. Evan meant too much to her. No way was she going to screw up this relationship.

She watched him say something to Mitch and Perry, and then head her way. As if they knew Liza needed a moment with him, Eve and Jane sort of drifted back to the guys.

Liza was standing alone when he reached her. He picked up her hand and kissed the back of it. "You are the most beautiful woman in this room, and I am the luckiest guy."

Readily, she stepped into his arms. "You couldn't be more mistaken, Evan," she whispered, tilting her head back for his kiss. "I'm the luckiest one by far."

Baby, It's Cold Outside

CATHY YARDLEY

For my agents, Annelise Robey and Christina Hogrebe, for being extraordinarily patient. Thank you!

Dear Reader,

Everyone loves the holiday season – the parties, the traditions, all the celebrating and fun with family and friends. But, on the other hand, this time of year can be very stressful. So I thought what happens when you take a woman who embodies small-town tradition and match her with a guy who thinks "home for the holidays" is a sure recipe for disaster. And just like that I got *Baby, It's Cold Outside*, a story I hope you'll really enjoy!

Best,

Cathy Yardley

PROLOGUE

Sixteen years ago…

"COLIN REESE, YOU disappoint me," Mrs. Norton, the principal of Tall Pines High School, said with an exaggerated sigh.

Colin shrugged. He'd developed shrugging into a highly complex sign language. This shrug said, *I'd love to care, but I really don't.*

"You're a senior, Colin. I would have thought you were old enough—and mature enough—to have moved beyond these juvenile pranks."

Colin sent her a slight grin and shrugged again. *You'd think, wouldn't you?*

"Defacing school property…" Mrs. Norton patted her hair, making sure her bangs were still lacquered in place, a sign that she was really upset. Colin had been in the principal's office enough in the past four years to read her like a comic book. "We could have you arrested, Colin."

"Oh, come on, Mrs. N.," he protested, the statement outrageous enough to prompt more than a shrug from him. "Putting a statue of Eamon Stanfield in a dress isn't defacing school property."

"You made him look like a hooker."

"No, I made him look like Sexy Mrs. Santa," Colin corrected, quoting the mail-order catalog. "It's Christmas. I thought it'd be festive."

"You put makeup on him," Mrs. Norton added. "The janitors are having a hard time getting the lipstick off."

Don't laugh, he warned himself. His latest prank may have gone a bit too far. "I'll wash off the old guy myself," he volunteered.

Mrs. Norton sighed heavily. "You continually pick our town's most honored and cherished traditions to poke fun at, Colin. Last summer, you put pickled herrings in the planters at the Ladies' Auxiliary Orchid Show—"

"That was never proved," Colin said.

"Then there was the incident with the Otter Lodge fountain being filled with Jell-O…"

Colin opened his hands in a gesture of innocence. "Again…"

Mrs. Norton frowned. "And the bronze plaque that had the names of all the town's founding fathers, including Eamon Stanfield, went mysteriously missing last semester."

"Hey," Colin protested, "I had nothing to do with that one. I don't steal."

"What I want to know is—when is all this nonsense going to stop, Colin?"

Colin felt a surge of anger. *"When I get the hell out of this town."*

Mrs. Norton looked surprised, then supremely saddened. Colin immediately felt like a jerk.

"I'm sorry," he said. "I don't mean to hurt anybody. I'm blowing off a little steam, that's all. They're stupid little jokes, meant to be funny, not destructive. I mean, I see the absurdity in a lot of our traditions, and nobody else seems to."

"What you see as absurd," Mrs. Norton said stiffly, standing up, "a lot of us see as sweet and comforting. And every little act of rebellion you commit doesn't make you look sophisticated. It makes you look mean-spirited and petty."

Colin grimaced, roiling in his own unhappiness. "I'm sorry," he apologized—and he meant it.

"I'm suspending you for a week, Colin."

He nodded. He'd been expecting that. "I'll head on home."

"No, you'll wait here," she said. "Your mother's on her way to pick you up."

"My mother?" He winced. "Why? I just live a few blocks away."

"I had to call her, Colin." Now Mrs. Norton seemed smug. "Besides, I wanted to talk about plans for the Spring Fling and then the grad-night party, since she's head of the committee."

Of course she is, Colin thought and wallowed in his misery.

"She was very, very upset to hear what you'd done to the statue," Mrs. Norton added. "I imagine she'll have some words for you when she gets here."

He nodded unhappily. *Some words.* A mild way to put what promised to be a very unpleasant episode.

He sat out in the lobby of the administrative office wearing his best trademark scowl.

"Oh, Colin," Ruthie, the front-office secretary, said with a small shake of her head. "How can such a sweet kid get into so much trouble?"

"Don't tell me you didn't giggle just a little seeing Eamon Stanfield all tarted up," he coaxed.

Ruthie glanced at the principal's office, making sure the

door was closed. Then she broke out into a wide grin. "It *was* funny," she admitted. "Especially since, from what I understand, Eamon Stanfield would keel over dead before wearing ladies' clothes."

Colin grinned back. "Exactly."

"Which is why we're in so much trouble." Ruthie sighed.

"What do you mean?" he asked.

Before he could get an answer, the door opened. A young girl, about sixteen years old, walked in. She was wearing a navy-blue plaid pleated skirt with a big safety pin in it and a moss-green sweater set. She was also wearing stylish boots—a nod to the weather. Her pale cheeks were rosy from the cold, and she wore her long auburn hair in a simple ponytail.

"Hi, Ruthie," she said. "Just wanted to drop off the money for the Spring Fling fund-raiser from the booster club. We raised even more this year than we did last year."

"Emily, you are a doll," Ruthie said with approval, taking the envelope. Then she looked pointedly at Colin. "Never in here for any trouble."

"I know," Emily replied. If Colin didn't know better, he'd think she sounded annoyed by the comment.

Ruthie's voice dropped. "Is your father still upset about the…statue incident?"

Colin sank lower in his seat. Emily Stanfield. Of course he knew her. She was only a living, breathing legacy of Tall Pines, Connecticut. Her family had been in the town since the beginning; it was her great-grandfather's statue that he'd dressed up in the red minidress. She was on almost every committee or volunteer organization imaginable. As a sophomore, she'd already been voted onto the homecoming court. She might as well have an entire wardrobe with *I Love Tall Pines* emblazoned on it in big sparkly letters.

Like all her forebears, she'd probably live in this little town till she died.

She was the complete opposite of Colin, the angel to his devil. She even looked angelic. Which might explain why he couldn't stop staring at her when he thought she wouldn't notice. He chalked it up to a perverse fascination—as if by studying her he could figure out how she avoided the frustration and rebelliousness that the town of Tall Pines seemed to invoke in him on a daily basis.

Emily nodded. "I told my father it was a senior prank." She shot a quick glance over at Colin, her blue eyes meeting his green ones. "I said it was a tradition. He's still sort of steamed, but he's calming down."

"So…no police?" Ruthie said.

"No police," Emily assured her, and Colin felt his muscles unknot with relief. Then she shot him another glance, only this time the smallest ghost of a smile haunted her lips.

He found himself smiling back with approval. She was awfully cute for a sophomore. Not to mention cute for a Tall Pines poster child.

"*Colin Reese,* are you insane?"

He blinked, wondering the same thing himself, although he was still staring at Emily as he thought it. He turned his attention to the woman yelling at him. "Mom?"

His mother stormed into the lobby, looking like the Angel of Vengeance in a lavender-blue pantsuit. "I have *had* it with you, mister," she said sharply. "I swear, if you weren't so close to graduation, I'd send you off to…to *military school!*"

He sighed. This was going to be a bad one, he could tell.

"You're coming with me." She held the door open. "And you wait till your father gets home!"

Colin sighed, rolling his eyes. Ruthie sent him a look of

sympathy. Emily, he noticed, had a mischievous smile. Then, to his shock, she winked at him.

Which was why he was smiling as his mother yanked on his arm and dragged him out the door. He barely heard her as she launched into yet another tirade on the problems with his behavior and why couldn't he be more like his sister and brother and why in the world he had a problem with the small town.

"For God's sake, Colin," she said, exasperated, "can't you think of one thing, just *one thing,* that represents Tall Pines that you don't feel like mocking and making fun of?"

He closed his eyes for a moment, thinking hard.

Emily Stanfield, his mind supplied. Given the chance, he got the feeling he'd take her very, very seriously. But he couldn't admit that, so he stayed silent and let his mother continue her litany. He'd be out of here by June, anyway, and then all of this, including Emily Stanfield, would be a thing of the past.

EMILY WATCHED AS Colin Reese stalked off, his mother lecturing him in a growing crescendo of chastisement.

"That kid." Ruthie let out a long breath. "It's hard to believe he's Ava Reese's son, you know?"

Emily didn't say anything, although she knew what Ruthie meant.

"So have you decided who you're going to the Spring Fling with, Emily?" Ruthie asked.

Emily cleared her throat. "Not yet," she said. "Too busy, and it's not for months yet."

"Still dating that Rothchild boy?"

It was funny, Emily thought. Ruthie knew about everybody in the school. Granted, it wasn't that big a school, but

Emily wondered halfheartedly if the kind woman didn't have better things to do with her time than track the little social dramas of teenagers.

"I wasn't really dating him," Emily demurred, her voice almost prim. "Anyway, I'd better get going. Don't want to be late for Biology."

She fled the office, heading up the hallway. She couldn't stop thinking about Colin.

She'd had a crush on him for years, since she'd been in elementary school. It wasn't just that he was good-looking, although he was—devastatingly so. It was that he was so…reckless. Daring. He'd been voted Most Likely to Do Anything two years in a row by the yearbook committee. He was in trouble a lot, but she also knew that he was very sweet—she'd seen a bunch of bullies picking on a younger girl because of her thick glasses and braces, and Colin had sent the bullies away with the mere threat of physical violence. He'd then made sure the girl was all right, saying a few quick words and sending her a lightning-fast smile. The girl had stared dreamily at Colin, and so had Emily, touched by his thoughtfulness.

It was silly. Everyone knew that Colin was practically building a tunnel to get out of Tall Pines, and Emily doubted she'd ever leave. But it didn't stop her from dreaming.

CHAPTER ONE

"SO IS HE HERE YET?"

Emily Stanfield smiled coyly at her best friend, Sue. "You're the desk manager. You tell me."

Sue made a face. "I knew I should've stayed at the inn. That way I could've called you when he checked in."

Emily shook her head. "Impossible. First of all, this is Ava Reese's annual Secret Santa party we're at. It's more than a tradition, it's an *institution*. We couldn't miss it." Much as she'd wanted to this year.

Sue sighed. "True, true."

"And secondly—" and Emily let her voice drop to a whisper "—there's no guarantee I'm going to sleep with this guy...this J. P. Webster."

Sue made a sound of protest. "But you said…"

Emily put a hand up, stopping Sue, then glanced around. No one was listening, thankfully—folks were too intent on their gift swapping and drinking from Ava's generous open bar.

"I said I was finally going to do something about my two-year celibacy. And I meant it," Emily declared, her body sending a pleasant zing dancing over her nerve endings at the thought. "But I've never even seen J.P. before. We've only exchanged emails."

"My sister got married to a guy she met on the Internet," Sue countered.

Emily rolled her eyes. "The last thing I need is to get married. I'm just… I just want…" She searched for a non-crude way to put it.

"You're just looking for someone to stuff your stocking." Sue winked.

So much for noncrude. Emily felt her cheeks redden. "Well, that's not how I would've put it. But…well, yes."

"So why shouldn't it be this J.P.?" Sue pressed. "You guys have been e-mailing for almost two years now."

"About business stuff only." J. P. Webster worked for a big hotel chain and taught a class on hotel management online. Emily had taken the class, then asked some questions after it was done. J.P. had been tremendously kind and helpful. They were exchanging e-mails once a month lately, and the correspondence had turned more friendly than academic. "Maybe he's ugly. Maybe he's old. Maybe he's *gay,* for all I know. We've never flirted or anything." Emily frowned, thinking about it. "We get along really well. Like we're old friends."

"Well, maybe he's young, cute and ready to be really, *really* friendly."

Emily smirked. Privately, that's exactly what she was hoping.

For the past few years Emily had lived for one thing and one thing only: the Stanfield Arms, the hotel she'd created from her family's mansion, one of the oldest buildings in Tall Pines, Connecticut. She'd buried herself in work and she hadn't even bothered with a relationship. Part of that was because she'd been far too busy, but part of it was also because of Tall Pines itself. A definite problem with living in such a small town was that with everyone weighing in on your dating decisions, if things didn't work out, not only would you face a postmortem from everyone on why the relationship ended, you were face-to-face with your ex almost every day. She'd experienced it in action. It was nightmarish.

So the hotel filled her days, but lately her nights were leaving her more and more restless. After Thanksgiving, she'd made the decision: she was going to have a physical relationship, something brief and discreet, preferably with an out-of-towner who would then leave. So far, the only prospect was J.P., who'd suggested staying at the hotel over the holidays.

Please, please let him be cute.

"Come on," Emily said. "Let's swap our gifts and get out of here. I want to head back to the inn."

Sue smiled knowingly. "Attagirl."

They walked over to the crystal bowl that held the names of everyone at the party on slips of paper. Sue drew a name first, grimacing as she read it.

"Damn. I got old Reverend Smith," she said. "I don't think he's going to like the Chocolate Orgasm hot chocolate I brought."

Emily laughed, drawing a slip of paper. She opened it, staring at the name and frowning. "Colin. Colin who?"

Sue's eyes widened. "Wait a minute. *Colin Reese?*"

Emily felt heat explode in her chest. "No. It couldn't be," she murmured. "He hasn't been back in town for the holidays since high school."

Sue shrugged. "I'm not surprised. He hated this town." She nudged Emily. "Didn't you have a crush on him? Way back when?"

Only for ten years, Emily thought, her heart rate picking up speed. She shook her head. "Okay, I'm going to give him the gift and get the heck out of here."

"I'm planning on grilling you the minute I get into work tomorrow," Sue said. "I want every detail about J. P. Webster!"

Emily chuckled. "If there's anything to tell." She was trying not to get her hopes up too high. She hugged Sue goodbye, then went in search of Colin.

She found him sitting in the living room, half-hidden by the enormous Christmas tree, drinking eggnog. She paused for a minute, trying to get her bearings.

For a woman who hadn't had sex in two years, the sight of Colin Reese was enough to blow out all her sensual circuits.

He was wearing a gray sweater that molded itself nicely to his broad shoulders, and his dark brown hair was still flecked with streaks of copper, even though it was cut shorter than she remembered…back when she used to stare at him, all those years ago. His eyes were still the same deep, deep green, she noticed, as he gazed absently across the crowded room.

Her palms started to sweat.

Just get it over with, she chided herself. No matter how much she'd fantasized about him, he was *not* a candidate to end her sexual drought. For one thing, he was the town's black sheep—if word leaked out, she'd never hear the end of it.

She gripped her gift bag, took a resolute breath and walked up to him. "Hi, Colin."

He looked at her, obviously distracted. Then he stood and focused on her, gracing her with a slow visual perusal and a lazy smile.

"Well, hi."

She smiled back, ignoring the tingle of excitement his drawled greeting sent shooting through her. "Merry Christmas. I'm your Santa this year."

"I'm in luck." His deep voice sounded sinfully smooth, rich and luscious as a dark chocolate truffle.

She handed him the bag, watching as he opened it. He raised a skeptical eyebrow. "Scented candles," he said with obviously fake enthusiasm. "Thanks."

She couldn't help it. She giggled. "Sorry," she said when he looked at her inquisitively. "Women usually out-number men two to one at this party. Scented candles are normally a slam dunk."

"Well, maybe I'll enjoy them with a cup of tea and a bub-ble bath," he joked. Unfortunately his comment caused her wayward mind to conjure up a picture of him naked and waist deep in hot water, the chiseled planes of his chest lit only by candlelight....

"So, um, what have you been up to?" she asked hastily, trying to dispel the image.

He shrugged. "I'm working on a new building. In Paris. I start after the new year."

"That sounds exciting," she said wistfully. "I've never been to Paris. Never took the time."

They stood there for a second in awkward silence.

Just tell him goodbye, she thought. *Then get back to the hotel and find out if J.P. is as cute as he is nice.*

"So, er, what about you?" Colin asked before she could open her mouth and make her escape.

"Same old, same old," she said noncommittally. "The inn's doing really well. In fact, I have to—"

"The inn?" He frowned. "What inn?"

He'd been gone for a while, she realized. "I turned the Stanfield mansion into a hotel, what, four years ago," she supplied. "It took two years to renovate, and then the past two I've been building up—"

"Stanfield," he said, then his eyes widened. "Wait a second. You're *Emily* Stanfield?"

That's when it hit her. He hadn't remembered her. He hadn't even known who she was until just now.

Glad I made an impression, she thought, her flush of infatuation chilling as though she'd been dropped in a snowbank. "Well, it's been great catching up, but I've got a hotel to run, so…"

"A hotel. Right here in town," he mused, and to her shock, he took her hand before she could turn and walk away. "Emily Stanfield, you're more than my Santa, you're my godsend."

She chuckled nervously, trying to ignore the sexual heat that his warm palm was sending up her arm. "That seems a little excessive for candles."

He smiled slowly, his eyes dark and persuasive, his voice going low. "Please, please tell me you've got room at the inn."

"What?" She blinked, confused by his sudden change of topic. "For who?"

He took a step closer to her, and she could feel the heat coming off his body as if she were standing in front of a fireplace.

"I was hoping," he said, "that you might have room… for me."

"I REALLY APPRECIATE this," Colin said, sitting in the passenger seat of Emily's Volvo, his bags in her trunk.

"Your mom may never forgive me," Emily answered with a rueful sigh, "which is going to make being on the Easter Festival committee with her next year a little unpleasant. Why couldn't you just stay at her house again?"

Colin grimaced. "My brother and sister and their spouses and kids are all staying there. I was sharing a room with my eight-year-old nephew, and with two more days till Christmas…"

"Been driving you crazy, huh?" There was a hint of a smile in her voice.

"You have no idea."

Colin closed his eyes, remembering the scene at the breakfast table that very morning. They'd taken turns subtly—and not-so-subtly—grilling him. Why was he moving so far away? What happened to his last girlfriend? Why was he traveling all over the place and changing jobs so often? When was he going to settle down? And the perennial *why couldn't he find a nice girl and move home to Tall Pines?*

He'd known it was a bad idea to stay at his parents' house for the week before Christmas, while his apartment in Paris was being readied. He just hadn't known how bad it was going to be until it was too late. The past three days had been hellish. He'd even suggested checking in to a hotel in a nearby town.

"And be so far from the house?" his mother had protested, scandalized. "With bad weather threatening the roads? You might miss Christmas with the kids!"

She'd had a point and he'd conceded. He did want to spend Christmas with his nieces and nephews, who were still small enough to make the whole thing fun.

Of course, his mother had neglected to mention the fact that there was a hotel right here in town.

He glanced over gratefully. Emily was staring intently at the road. Her auburn hair was swept up in a smooth French twist. Her high cheekbones and patrician nose, combined with her flawless skin, made her look cool and perfect, like a marble statue. Only the flash in her violet-blue eyes betrayed an inherent warmth.

No, he corrected himself, remembering. More than

warmth. *Heat.* He'd definitely felt heat from her gaze when he'd looked over to find her standing in front of him.

Which called to mind his first look at her—crisp white blouse with a discreetly low neckline, knee-length black skirt, black nylons, black boots. Combined with her tasteful jewelry and her wire-rimmed glasses, she'd looked sophisticated and proper, sort of like a professor.

He'd always had a thing for prim teacher types. They usually hid anything-but-proper desires, and he had a sneaking feeling that Miss Stanfield was no exception.

Who would have thought that Emily Stanfield, daughter of one of the founding families and walking infomercial for all things Tall Pines, would have grown up to such a hottie?

"You're lucky I had a cancelation," Emily said, still not looking at him. "It's one of my smaller rooms, but I think you'll find it quite comfortable."

Colin cleared his throat, feeling as if she could read his mind and realize the direction his thoughts were heading. "I'm surprised your family was okay with turning the mansion into a hotel," he said, fishing around for a safe topic.

She paused for a second. "My mother moved to Florida with her new husband. She doesn't really care one way or the other. My father probably would've minded, but he died five years ago, so…"

Colin felt guilt wash over him. "Oh, jeez. I'm sorry. I didn't know."

"You haven't been here. I didn't expect you to."

He sighed. "And the town? They were okay with it—you opening a hotel?"

"There are some people who are still getting used to it," she answered. "You know how Tall Pines is."

He clenched his jaw. Everything had to be preserved, as

if the smallest mailbox was some kind of historical monument. If there was a town more resistant to change, he never wanted to visit it. "Yeah," he muttered, "I know how Tall Pines is."

"It's been good for the local economy, so that's brought a lot of people around," she said. "And, honestly, being a Stanfield helped."

"I'll bet."

The name *Stanfield* was synonymous with *Tall Pines*. Still, Stanfield or not, he imagined Emily was both organized and driven enough to start her own business if she wanted to. Two years younger than he was, she'd always been visible in school: editor in chief of the school newspaper, on the yearbook committee, in student government. She had been everywhere, it seemed. Her uncle had been the mayor before he'd died, and Colin could even recall Emily handing out campaign flyers, looking like a crisp autumn morning in her plaid skirt and pink sweater.

By high school, his lone goal had been escaping the Norman Rockwell normalcy of Tall Pines, while Emily had seemed to represent everything that the small town stood for. He'd hated the town but had been reluctantly fascinated with the girl, even if she never knew it.

That fascination seemed to be alive and well, he noted with some amusement.

They drove past the town square and up the hill to where the fancier houses stood, legacies of days past, when several tycoons had had hunting lodges here. The Stanfield mansion was one of the most opulent and, decked out with Christmas lights, it looked downright regal. "Wow," he said, taking in the picture-perfect scene.

She parked the car, sending him a quicksilver smile that

caused his stomach to tighten unexpectedly. "Thanks. This hotel's my life."

"It shows." She'd obviously lavished a lot of love on the place.

For a brief, puzzling second, he envied the brick building. *Okay, you're losing it.*

That was why he hated the holidays, he thought as he hefted his bags and headed for the front door. They made a guy maudlin. He lived his life exactly the way he wanted it—full of adventure, with something new happening almost every day. He had no regrets. And right now the last thing he needed was to have some confusing, sentimental thoughts about a girl he hadn't seen in years.

The large foyer had a curving staircase to the second floor. "Evening, Phillip," she greeted a guy in a suit who stood behind an oak reception desk. "I'm going to need a key for Mr. Reese, here. For room twelve."

The guy—Phillip—looked ruffled. "That's going to be a problem," he said. "The Rivers party showed up after all. They decided to brave the weather and have the vacation."

"Oh?" Emily looked nonplussed for a second, then she turned to Colin, her expression apologetic. "I guess there's no room at the inn after all."

He winced. There was no way in hell he was going back to his parents' house. "Considering the season, I don't suppose you've got a manger or something," he joked, feeling a little desperate. "I don't take up much room."

She shook her head. "Even the garage is filled up with cars. Sorry, Colin. I'll drive you back."

"Wait a second," he said, pulling her aside, away from the inquisitive Phillip. "Seriously. Isn't there anyplace you could stick me? Maid's room? Good-size pantry? I'd even be happy with a broom closet."

She sighed. "I'd love to help you out, but…"

"You don't understand," he interrupted. "My six-year-old niece has been waking me up at five-thirty every morning to watch *Sesame Street*. My eight-year-old nephew, who's sharing my room, has been keeping me up until two because he's convinced that there are monsters. I've been crammed onto an army cot." He could see that it wasn't getting through to her…that no matter what his plea, she was the type who could withstand it.

He swallowed hard and played his trump card.

"My mother's been asking me why I haven't gotten married yet," he said. "At every. Single. Meal."

Emily's eyes widened. Then she laughed—a soft, rich sound that made him feel as though he'd just been brushed by mink.

"Knowing Ava, I can only imagine. I love her, but she is…" She grinned mischievously. "Shall we say, *persistent.*"

"As a Sherman tank."

She looked up at the ceiling as if mentally debating something. Then she sighed. "Okay, tell you what—I converted the attic to my own private apartment," she said. "You can crash on my couch for tonight. But just for tonight. Tomorrow we'll think of something else."

Gratitude washed over him. "I owe you for this. Big-time."

She nodded absently, then went back to the desk. "I'm going to have Mr. Reese here stay with me," she said, and Colin watched as a look of calculation and a slow smirk crossed the clerk's face.

"On her *couch,*" Colin emphasized.

"Of course," Phillip returned blandly.

"One other thing, Phillip?" Emily asked, her voice going soft. "Did a J. P. Webster check in?"

"At around six," Phillip said. "Room five."

"Perfect. Thank you."

There was an edge of excitement in her voice, Colin noticed. Unexpectedly he felt irritation. Who the hell was J. P. Webster? And why did she suddenly sound so thrilled?

"Colin, why don't you follow me and I'll get you settled in."

Colin followed her to a small private elevator, taking it up to her apartment. It was roomier than he'd expected. There was a small kitchen, a living room, a bathroom and the bedroom. There was even a small fireplace. It was well decorated and obviously expensive, but it still looked cozy and inviting. To his surprise, he felt tension start to ebb out of his body.

"This is it," she said artlessly. "If you'll excuse me, I'm going to change really quickly, then I need to go downstairs for a while. Business."

But that breathless quality in her voice suggested it had nothing to do with business. That irritation that Colin had felt before doubled.

"Mind if I light a fire?" he asked to give himself something to do besides ruminate on what exactly her *business* might be.

"Please do," she said before shutting the bedroom door behind her.

Within minutes he had a small fire going in the hearth. The room smelled like spiced apple cider. He'd probably be asleep in minutes, he realized. He hadn't felt this relaxed since he'd returned to Tall Pines.

He heard the bedroom door open and he turned. "I can't thank you enough…"

His words died on his lips.

She'd changed, all right.

Emily's hair tumbled in loose auburn waves, dancing slightly below her shoulders. She was wearing a rich red velvet robe with Stanfield Arms embroidered on the crest. He wondered absently if she was wearing anything under the robe.

Just like that, his body went hard as steel and all thoughts of sleep fled. He bit back a groan. "That must be some business."

Her ivory cheeks flooded with color, and she avoided his gaze. "It's nine o'clock at night. I just want to make sure that one of my…special guests…is comfortable."

Colin didn't say a word.

"Sheets, blankets and pillows are in the cupboard in the hallway there." She pointed, still not looking at him. "The fridge is stocked if you're hungry, and if you need anything, just dial eight for the front desk."

"When will you be back?" he asked.

Finally she met his gaze.

The heat in her eyes could have set the room on fire.

"I don't know when I'll be back," she said quietly. "So don't wait up."

IT WAS RISKY. Possibly even stupid, Emily thought as she belted her robe tighter around her waist. But she was going to do it anyway.

She was going to J. P. Webster's room wearing only a silk shortie nightgown and one of the hotel robes and—if everything went perfectly—she was going to have sex.

She could only imagine what Colin was thinking of her little announcement. She'd done everything but say, "Make yourself at home, I'm off to get laid." The look he'd given her as she'd shut the door was one of shock mixed with something else she couldn't quite identify. She hoped it wasn't shame on her behalf. Still, Colin was a world-fa-mous hotshot architect now, and if rumors were true, he had romanced women all over the continent. Several conti-nents, actually, if his mother's complaints were to be be-lieved. "Always with a different girl every month," she'd griped loudly at the last Otter Lodge pancake breakfast. "Last month, a lawyer from Hong Kong…the month be-fore, a model from Brazil…." So she'd be damned if she let herself be judged by Mr. Commitmentphobic, espe-cially since this was going to be her first fling ever.

Emily felt heat on her cheeks. She was blushing. She knew it.

Please, please let him be cute and let me go through with this. She couldn't face another restless night. She wanted to feel the delicious release that only a man could pro-vide—even if it was only temporary.

She got to room five and knocked on the door. "J.P.?"

The door opened slowly. She took a deep breath.

A beautiful blond woman, also in a robe, was standing there. "Can I help you?"

Emily goggled momentarily. This she hadn't antici-pated.

"I'm sorry." *Of course he would have brought his girl-friend! God, I'm an idiot!* "I was looking for J. P. Webster. I didn't mean for it to be so late…."

"That's quite all right," the woman said genially. "You've found her."

"Her?"

"J.P. stands for Joy Patricia. My friends call me Joy." She held out her hand, and, dumbstruck, Emily shook it. "I'm sorry…what's your name?"

"Oh. Right. I'm Emily Stanfield, the owner of the hotel."

And a moron. "I just wanted to stop by and make sure that you had everything you needed."

Unfortunately J.P. did not have anything *Emily* needed.

"Emily! It's so nice to finally meet you in person. And thank you again for suggesting I stay at your inn instead of spending the holiday alone while my family was in Bermuda. I got in and fell in love with this place," Joy enthused, seeming not to notice Emily's discomfort. "It's everything you said it was and more."

"Well, that is high praise," Emily said. "And I'm glad it's made such a good impression. I'm sure you're exhausted. I'll just say good night and let you sleep...."

"Are you sure you didn't want to hang out, talk shop?" Joy asked.

Emily shook her head. Considering the real reason she'd come down, she doubted she could spend the evening discussing linen-use rates and remodel tips. "Just wanted to make sure you're comfortable."

"I love these robes, by the way," Joy said, rubbing her hand over the sleeve. "I see you do, too."

Emily was blushing again. "Normally I don't meet business associates dressed this casually," she said, hugging her arms and making sure her robe was still tight around her. "But I was, er, about to go to bed."

"I see." Emily could have sworn she saw a glimmer of humor in the woman's eyes. "Well, good night, then."

"Good night," Emily echoed, then turned and made her escape.

She got in the elevator, turning the key for the top floor...and then froze.

Oh, great. Bad enough that she'd just had one of the most humiliating mistakes of her life. Now, she had Colin Reese to deal with.

When the door opened, he was making up a makeshift bed on the sofa in pajama bottoms and nothing else.

He looked good enough to eat.

All the frustration that had been building up and threatening to explode, especially in the past few months, seemed to bubble to the surface at the look of his half-naked body. Her hands itched to stroke over all that chiseled chest.

Thankfully she had the fiasco with Joy/J.P. still stinging her ego or she'd probably do something she'd regret. Like jump him.

He glanced at her, puzzled. "Forget something?"

"No," she responded coolly. "I got finished sooner than I thought. Now I'm tired and I'm going to bed."

Colin smirked at her. "How'd business go?"

"Fine." Damn him for bringing it up.

He studied her as she stepped in front of him. Then he put a hand out, surprising her by touching her shoulder gently.

"You look sort of upset."

"I'm fine," she repeated. She ran her fingers through her hair, a gesture of frustration. "That is, I *will be* fine."

"Listen, I've been really stressed this week," he said. "I noticed you had a bottle of wine, but I didn't want to open it, especially just for me. Care to join me?"

She hesitated. "I really shouldn't," she murmured as she breathed in some of his woodsy-smelling cologne.

"Just to unwind a bit," he coaxed. "It'll help you sleep."

Emily laughed at that. Sit next to this unbelievably sexy half-dressed man, drinking wine in front of a crackling fire…and he thought that was going to make her *drowsy?*

He had to be joking.

He stroked her arm, distracting her. "Come on. One glass."

"Just one," she heard herself say and then found herself sitting on the couch.

Oh, this is such a very stupid idea.

Colin went into the kitchen, opened the fridge and got out the light pinot grigio that she'd been chilling. He poured two glasses and handed her one, sitting next to her.

"Aren't you, uh, cold?" she said, nodding at his bare chest. If this kept up, she'd be blushing a permanent pink.

"Huh? Oh. I got sort of hot building the fire up." He glanced at her. "Does it make you uncomfortable?"

Uncomfortable *is one word for it,* she thought. "I wouldn't want you to get a chill."

He let loose one of those slow, sexy smiles. "Don't worry," he reassured her. "I did an eighteen-month build in Iceland once. I don't think I'll ever feel cold again."

She let her gaze dip down to his washboard stomach…and then lower still, to the dark blue flannel pajama pants.

No doubt about it. The man was definitely hot.

Emily took a sip of wine so hastily she choked on it. "So will the couch be comfortable enough?" she asked when her throat cleared. "You look pretty big." His eyes widened, and she realized he'd caught exactly where she'd been looking a moment ago. "I mean broad. That is, tall. Well-proportioned!"

He chuckled.

"Oh, hell," she said and drained the glass, barely noticing when he poured her some more. "I am not usually this stupid. I've just had a rough night."

"Do tell," he invited, taking a swallow of wine and then putting the glass down on the coffee table.

She surveyed him over the rim of her glass. "I barely even know you."

"And yet you're letting me sleep with you—in a manner of speaking," he said, causing her to laugh. "So what happened?"

She took a deep breath. What the hell. It wasn't as if he was *really* a citizen of Tall Pines, anyway. "Promise to keep it a secret?"

He made a gesture of crossing his heart, then held up his fingers in the Boy Scout salute.

"Okay. I was planning on having an affair tonight." She said it quickly, all in one breath.

He let out a low whistle. "That explains the robe." he said. She felt the heat of his gaze trace over its contours. It felt wonderful—and after the Joy incident, was a gratifying balm to her injured ego. "With whom, if I might ask?"

"An out-of-towner, someone I've been in correspondence with," she said, shaking her head. The wine was warming her, she thought, letting herself sink back into the plush cushions of her sofa. Or was it the company? "Anyway, it was a disaster."

"What, was he ugly or something?"

"Worse," she replied, finishing her wine and putting her empty glass down. "He was a woman."

Colin choked, then burst into laughter. Reluctantly Emily joined in.

"Serves me right for building up a fantasy around someone I haven't even met. It seemed like a good idea in theory. Unfortunately the theory got shot to hell."

"Why did you decide to sleep with someone you didn't even know?"

"Let's just say it's been a while." She sighed, feeling embarrassment start to swell up again. "And I thought an out-of-towner would be less, you know, complicated."

He nodded. "This town. A fling with a resident would

be like having a fling in the gazebo in the square, complete with the high school band playing accompaniment."

"Exactly," she agreed, grateful that he understood.

"So now what are you going to do?" He leaned back, as well, resting his chin on one arm. He looked devastatingly handsome with his hair falling rakishly over one eye. Like some kind of mischievous sex god.

She swallowed, trying to moisten her suddenly dry mouth. "I have no idea, honestly." Emily closed her eyes, smiling ruefully. "If some gorgeous out-of-town hunk decides to stay and seduce me, maybe I'll let him. We'll both have a great weekend or whatever and then he'll go on his merry way and I'll go on mine. But I think I'm done attempting to plan for it. If it happens, it happens."

"Very philosophical."

She stood up, noticing that her robe had come a little undone. She tightened the belt again. "Thanks, Colin," she said. "It's funny, but I really do feel a lot better. I appreciate that."

He stood, too. "No problem."

"Good night." Emily had started to turn and walk away when he stopped her again with a hand on her shoulder. She turned back.

Without warning, he leaned forward, kissing her with slow, deliberate, almost overwhelming intensity. His mouth was firm and hot and amazingly mobile. He didn't assault her. Rather, he coaxed her. And before she realized what was going on, she was kissing him back with equal desire.

Her passion leaped to life. She clutched his shoulders, reveling in the feel of the muscles bunching beneath her fingertips. His tongue swept through her mouth, tracing the outline of her lips before tangling with her tongue. She moaned softly.

He pulled away, almost as out of breath as she was.

"Just thought you should know," he rasped. "Technically *I'm* from out of town."

The sentence was like a slap, bringing her temporarily dormant conscience to life. *What are you doing? This is Ava Reese's son! This is the guy who couldn't even remember who you were a few hours ago!*

"Sorry," she breathed, taking a careful step back. "*Technically* isn't going to cut it. And I've made enough of a fool of myself for one night."

With that, Emily beat a hasty retreat to her bedroom, locking the door—not for her sexual safety but for his.

CHAPTER TWO

"MERRY CHRISTMAS, Uncle Colin!" his nieces and nephews chirped.

"Merry Christmas," he answered, taking a long swallow of his coffee and trying desperately to jump-start his sluggish system. It was nine o'clock Christmas morning, and he was dragging.

He'd spent the past two nights on Emily Stanfield's couch and had managed to get perhaps one hour's worth of sleep total, it seemed. While comfortable, it was still a couch—and worse, a couch that put him approximately seven feet away from Emily Stanfield.

Ever since his first night they'd been the picture of civility, and the only words they'd exchanged were pleasantries and logistics: "Good morning," "Do you need a key?" or "Please help yourself to breakfast in the dining room."

It was torture.

"What is *wrong* with you?" his mother asked as she put a plate of her famous Denver omelet and hash browns in front of him. "You're acting like a zombie. You're not sleeping well at that hotel, are you?"

"No, it's fine," he lied. "I've just been preoccupied."

"I knew she shouldn't have opened that inn," Ava fret-

CATHY YARDLEY 439

ted. "That lovely home, opened up to God-knows-who. Really a shame."

"She's done a great job with the place," Colin said. "I've stayed in a lot of hotels, and hers is top-of-the-line."

"Humph." His mother sounded unconvinced. "Well, her father's probably turning in his grave. You know how much Tall Pines and its traditions meant to him."

"Yeah." Then, without looking up from his French toast, Colin added, "Seems to me Emily is something of a traditionalist, too."

His mother didn't notice his sudden curiosity, thankfully. "Oh, she's still a Stanfield," she said, as if that explained everything. "She knows her duty. She's on the Garden Club Committee, the Easter Committee, she helps plan the Otter Lodge festivals and parties." She smirked, nudging his father. "She's dating the mayor, you know."

Colin's eyes widened. "Actually, no, I didn't know that." And it was something of an unpleasant surprise, he realized as he felt temper start to simmer in his bloodstream. Was she hiding it from him? And what about that whole sob story about not being intimate for a long time? "How long have they been together?"

"Well, now, I wouldn't exactly say they're *together*," his father corrected.

"Perhaps not technically. But they're perfect for each other," his mother continued, frowning at his father. "It's only a matter of time."

Colin instantly felt at ease. It was matchmaking, not an actual relationship.

Which meant Emily was still available.

And why exactly does that matter to you? She's already shot you down once, and you're only in town till tomorrow, anyway.

It was dumb. But for whatever reason, Emily's availability *did* matter to him.

"Enough about that," his mother said, sitting down next to him at the kitchen table. "So. You're single again."

He sighed, finishing a last forkful of the savory breakfast like a man enjoying his last meal. "Alas, yes."

"You're not thinking of marrying a French girl, are you? That's an awfully long way to travel for a wedding." She brightened. "Unless she'd like to live here."

His father chuckled. "In which case, you have our blessings, sight unseen."

Colin rolled his eyes. His father understood his mother's relentless nature and obviously sympathized with his son, but he also knew enough to stay out of it. After all, the man had to live here. "I'm still a bit young to worry about marriage, Mom."

"You're thirty-four," she corrected. "Before you blink, you'll be forty, and that's going to be hell on your system when you get to 2:00 a.m. feedings."

"Let me worry about the wife first," he grumbled, "before stressing about our kids."

"You need someone who can give you the stability and comfort of small-town living," she said. "I know that you haven't always enjoyed living in Tall Pines...."

Understatement of the year, he thought, taking another jolt of coffee.

"But I can't help but think you're not giving it a chance. Just like you're not giving marriage a chance." She crossed her arms.

This was more than her usual pestering, he noted. She was genuinely upset.

He sighed again. "Mom, we've had this conversation before," he said quietly. "I love you, and I'm glad you and the rest of the family want me to be settled and happy. But I need to travel. I need adventure. I can't explain it," he finished miserably. "It's not that I don't want to be happy. I seem to need…I don't know…something I can't find."

"Well, maybe you haven't been looking in the right places," she pointed out.

He rubbed his eyes with the heels of his palms. On top of very little sleep, this conversation was more than he could handle. "Let's watch the kids play with their toys, okay? I'm only in town till tomorrow morning—I'd like to enjoy it."

"Maybe," his mother continued with her trademark determination, "you could even look right here. Locally, I mean."

"Oh, I'm sure," he snapped. "I'll just go and marry Emily Stanfield tomorrow and give you a dozen more grandbabies, how about that?"

"Colin, don't be ridiculous," she chided. "There's no need to be snide."

"Sorry," he said. "I'm a little tired."

"Besides, Emily's not right for you," she said in a tactful tone.

Colin blinked. That wasn't the response he was expecting.

"She means Emily wouldn't have you in a million years." His brother Ted entered the conversation. "Mom, where are the batteries? Kasey's remote-control pony needs them."

"Well, that's insulting," Colin said. "What's wrong with me?"

"She's small-town right down to her marrow," his father pointed out. "And as is painfully evident to everyone including yourself, you're nothing of the sort. Beyond that, she's known for being somewhat discriminating when it comes to beaus."

Even his father thought Emily would have nothing to do with him?

Well, if their kiss was any indication, she might not want to marry him, but she certainly approved of some aspects of him.

Of course, she did *turn you down.*

He grimaced.

"She wouldn't be your type, anyway," his mother continued, her tone obviously meant to soothe the affront. "And like I said, she's dating the mayor."

"She isn't dating him," Colin growled.

His mother's eyebrow went up quizzically. He could just imagine her maternal-matrimonial radar beeping to life.

Damn it. "Listen, all this talk about marriage and stuff is giving me the heebie-jeebies," he said. "I don't mean to be cranky. I'll be on my best behavior. I just want to play with the kids and enjoy my family on the holiday, before I have to go. Okay?"

She sighed, finally relenting. "All right," she agreed, hugging his shoulders. "But I wouldn't pester you so much if you didn't worry me, kiddo."

"I know," he told her, hugging her back as they went over to the living room.

They watched the kids enjoy their presents all morning, and by lunch Colin was feeling more like himself. However, he had a new problem to deal with.

"It's been ages since I've been over to the hotel," his mother said. "You never mentioned—how's your room?"

"Great." Which was true. "Very comfortable."

"Queen-size bed or king?"

He had no idea. "Er…queen."

"She's a good manager, from what I've heard. A very hard worker. She's been obsessed with the place ever since…" His mother paused, frowning. "I'm sorry. You're probably bored with Tall Pines gossip."

But when it came to Emily, Colin was hanging on every word. "Ever since what?" he asked.

She smiled the satisfied smile of a storyteller who knows she's got her audience hooked. "Ever since her father died and her mother remarried shortly afterward," she said dramatically. "Her mother told her that she'd sell the place because she was tired of upholding the Stanfield family traditions. There was no way Emily could manage a building that size by herself, but she knew her father would have hated to lose it. So she came up with a plan to use her trust fund and turn it into a hotel."

Colin was riveted. "That's a lot of work."

"I didn't agree with it," his mother said. "It's not the same, having the Stanfield house open to strangers. Paying customers."

"What was she supposed to do?" Colin defended. "Give up and get rid of it?"

His mother wrinkled her nose. "Well, if she'd gotten married to someone rich, she could've kept the house."

Of course marriage would be the solution his mother came up with.

"She was engaged, you know," she added. "Years ago. To Richard Gaines."

"That jackass?"

She glared at him. "Language, please."

Colin fell silent, but he was still shocked. Ricky Gaines was a jerk. A rich jerk, granted, but still a complete waste of space.

"They were engaged as soon as she graduated from Amherst," she said. "But they never did get married. The town was pretty divided on who was at fault."

"So what was your vote?" It was unheard of for Ava Reese not to have an opinion.

"I say he was." She sniffed. "Since he got married and had his first baby a few short months after. Some rich blond girl from Boston. Of course, if Emily had been a bit more attentive when they were dating, he might not have strayed, but that's neither here nor there. Richard and his new family lived here for a year, and it was *very* awkward for Emily."

Poor Emily, Colin thought. No wonder she didn't want to get involved with anybody from town.

His mother put her hand over his. "She's a lovely girl, and I've always felt like the right person might help make her happier. She always seems sad to me, for some reason."

He'd noticed that, as well. "Poor kid."

His mother sighed. "She could use a good husband."

Colin had to change the topic away from marriage—and Emily—in a hurry. "You know," he finally said, "I thought maybe I'd stay here. One last night with you guys." Even though the cot was even less comfortable than the couch, it would probably do wonders for his peace of mind. He'd been fixated on Emily for long enough.

"Oh, we'll miss you, but I think you had the best idea," his mother said breezily. "It's far too crowded here with your brother and your sister and the grandkids. As long as you have the room at the inn, you might as well stay, right?"

"I suppose."

"You know," she added speculatively, "you're right."

Colin's eyes narrowed suspiciously. He knew that look on his mother's face. "I'm right how?"

"Emily *isn't* dating the mayor yet," she said, smiling mischievously.

He saw the light of hope in her eyes…and calculation. *Oh crap.*

Good thing he was leaving in the morning, because one more day in Tall Pines could mean real trouble if his mother decided she'd found him a wife.

"EMILY, YOU LOOK great this evening," Mayor Tim Ryfield said, sitting at the head of the dinner table at his house. "I'm so glad you could make it…especially since we've never had dinner together before."

Emily forced a smile of her own. "A Stanfield has been a guest at the mayor's Christmas party for the past fifty years, Tim," she said. "I'm glad to attend."

There. That showed that she still wasn't really having dinner with him. The last thing she wanted was to date the mayor of Tall Pines, even though she was continually tossed together with him. She wouldn't be surprised if there was some Getting Emily and Mayor Tim Married committee meeting on a monthly basis.

Ava Reese was probably the chairperson. She chaired nearly everything else.

Emily caught herself grinning at the traitorous thought. She blamed Colin's influence. Not that they'd had much interaction in the two days he'd been staying with her. Still, the mere knowledge of his presence had been severely disquieting to her state of mind.

"Stanfields always do their duty," Mayor Tim agreed. "You know, if you'd run against me for mayor, you probably would've won."

"Why would I want to be mayor?" she asked, bewildered.

"I'm not saying that," he corrected. "I'm saying you're a big part of this town. People like you and trust you. They know they can count on you."

She stared at him. "Tim, did you want me to be your campaign manager next year or something?"

He laughed. "That's the other thing I like about you, Em. You're honest and straightforward."

"Honest, straightforward, trustworthy," she muttered. "You're making me sound like a Boy Scout. So spit it out. Why are you buttering me up?"

He looked thoughtfully at his roomful of guests. There were a lot of other people sitting around the large table— the mayor's Christmas party was a long-standing tradition—but everyone else was involved in their own conversations, thankfully. Tim's voice lowered.

"You know how everyone's been matchmaking between us for the past year or so?"

She nodded heavily, feeling pained.

"I've been fighting it, too," he pointed out. "But I've been thinking about it. And maybe, just maybe, they're on to something."

Her eyes widened. "I know you've asked me to dinner, but I've never really thought you've been serious about it."

"I wasn't," he admitted. "But I'm not getting any younger. I've been focused on politics since I was in high school, Em."

"I remember," she said, shaking her head. "You were the only junior I knew who had a press kit."

"It got me this far. And I'd like to go further. To do that, I'm going to need a wife."

Now her eyes bugged out. "Holy crap, you're not asking me to *marry* you, are you?"

As it happened, her statement popped out when there was a lull in all the other conversations. You could have heard a spoon drop. The entire table was riveted on the two of them.

"I'm not asking you to marry me—*yet*," Tim said, eliciting a suggestive chuckle from the other partygoers. "I'm saying maybe we should try going out."

"Oh, Tim," Emily protested, shaking her head. "That's not such a great idea."

"Why not?" He managed to sound reasonable, even logical about it. "I'm not seeing anybody. And you're not involved with anyone." For a fraction of a second he looked tentative. "That is, you aren't seeing anyone, are you?"

She closed her eyes. Unbidden, the image of Colin wearing just pajama pants sprang into her mind. The scent of him, the feel of his hands, his mouth...the wine-edged taste of his kiss.

"No," she admitted, her voice ragged. "I'm not involved."

And whose fault is that?

Not that a one-night stand really equaled involvement. That was the point of it, being one night, after all.

"So there you have it," Tim said as if that was the only barrier to their relationship.

"You're sweet, and we've known each other for a long time," she said gently. "But—"

"You haven't given this a fair shake," he said implacably. "I know I've fallen into nice-guy syndrome with you, but if you give me a chance, I think you'll discover we're quite compatible."

"Come on, Emily," Mrs. Rutledge said from across the table. "You have to admit, you've been pretty chilly about the whole thing."

"No harm in trying," Mr. Rutledge added.

"One simple date is not going to kill you," Mrs. Macnamara said, contributing her two cents.

Emily was appalled. Apparently they'd all ganged up on her tonight. "Let me think about it." She saw that they were ready to ply her with a second assault, so she quickly said, "Oh, and by the way, I hear that there's a big supermarket chain that's trying to buy the Henderson lot."

With that, she set off a tidal wave of debate—which was the point.

Under the cover of the heated rhetoric, she turned to Tim. "Don't ever, *ever* put me on the spot like that again."

"It wasn't entirely my idea," he said mildly. "You're the one who yelped about a marriage proposal."

"Well, I hate feeling cornered. And you're a great guy, Tim, but I just don't feel that way about you."

"What way is that?"

She took a deep breath. "I don't… that is, I'm not… Oh, hell. There's no fire between us. No *passion*."

"Yeah, I know," he said, grinning and taking a forkful of turkey from his plate.

Emily blinked. "I'm not head over heels in love with you is what I'm saying."

"Good God." He sounded horrified. "I'd hope not!"

She finally shook her head. "Okay, apparently somebody slipped acid in my Christmas punch, because I'm having a hard time tracking here. Weren't you trying to date me a second ago?"

"I do think we should date. And if everything works out, I think we should get married," he said as easily as if he were picking an item off a lunch menu. "This is political, Em, not personal. I'm not looking for somebody I'm madly in love with—assuming I could fall madly in love. Which I seriously doubt I'm capable of, by the way."

She tilted her head, surveying him. She'd always seen him as a good guy, maybe a little too ambitious and nose-to-the-grindstone but still overall decent. Now she realized that there was something sort of melancholy about him…something he kept carefully hidden.

"You've never been in love?"

"Thankfully, no," he said. "But you have. And you've been hurt." He smiled, and it was genuinely kind. "I wouldn't hurt you, Em. I'm just saying let's be partners. Give it a try. What have you got to lose?"

She thought about it. What *did* she have to lose?

Again Colin blazed through her mind, almost overwhelming her senses even in the comparative dimness of memory.

I need passion, she thought.

But did she really want to fall madly in love again?

Emily started fidgeting with her linen napkin, crushing it into a wad on her lap.

It was so much easier when all I wanted was sex. She got the feeling that sex with Tim would be…

She wrinkled her forehead, trying to visualize it. Actually, she couldn't even *imagine* sex with Tim. Whereas she could imagine weeklong scenarios of sex with someone far more inappropriate. Like, say, Colin.

Oh, give it a rest, you idiot.

"Trust me. It's a cliché, but passion fades," Tim said quietly. "Good friendships, a relationship based on partnership and mutual goals—now that's got staying power."

"Hmm."

"Man, you're stubborn," he said, leaning back. "You're going to the New Year's Eve ball, right?"

She nodded.

"Flying solo, I'll bet. Well, why don't you go with me? Dinner here beforehand, and then the limo will drive us there and back." He winked. "Don't look at it as a date. Look at it as a ride share with a free meal thrown in."

She laughed. "You're charming, I'll give you that."

"Got me elected two terms in a row," he replied smugly.

She focused back on her meal, but she was still thinking about passion. And Colin.

He's leaving, anyway.

The thought came unbidden. He'd said he was leaving the morning after Christmas, which meant tomorrow morning. She'd only have one more night with him. Then it'd probably be years before she ever saw him again.

Technically he really is an out-of-towner, her subconscious suggested conspiratorially.

So where did that leave her?

"Merry Christmas, everybody!" Tim called out, raising his glass.

"Merry Christmas," she echoed. If she married Tim, this would be her future—formal dinners, companionable friendship, a partnership made with the town in mind. Comfortable, idyllic, picture-perfect. It wouldn't be all that bad, considering.

If you slept with Colin, even if you never felt passion again, at least you'd have an incredible memory to live with.

Emily blinked. Sleep with Colin? Ava Reese's son? The guy Tall Pines loved to gossip about?

Who would ever know besides the two of you?

The thought caused a wave of heat to curl through her. He wasn't even going to see his family afterward if they did spend the night together. He'd just go straight to the airport and that'd be the end of it.

No one would find out.

"There. Now you look happy," Tim said.

She nodded. She *was* happy.

Or at least she would be happy…as soon as she got home.

IT WAS AROUND ten o'clock when Colin got back to Emily's place. He entered quietly, wondering if maybe she was asleep. He wished he were. He was exhausted. He loved visiting with his family, but still, he'd be glad when his cab came and took him to the airport in the morning.

All he needed to do was avoid any contact with Emily, leave her a nice thank-you note and he'd be home free.

The fire was lit, he noticed, and there was a bottle of champagne in an ice bucket. His scented candles were lit, as well, making the room smell like autumn, with subtle hints of pine, nutmeg and cloves.

He glanced around, puzzled. "Emily?"

She stepped out of the bedroom wearing the robe he'd seen her in his first night at her apartment. Her feet were bare, her hair was loose and tumbled wildly around her shoulders. She smiled. "Colin," she said, and her violet-blue eyes were dark with promise. "Merry Christmas."

"Merry Christmas." She looked like a present—waiting to be unwrapped.

"I thought since you'd be missing New Year's, maybe you'd like some champagne." She nodded to the bottle. "If you'd do the honors?"

His gaze went from the champagne to her loosely belted robe, then back to the champagne. Then, furtively, back to her robe, which opened up into a tantalizing V of creamy, exposed skin.

Things were not going to plan.

In fact, things were going to hell in a hurry, and he'd be in too deep in a matter of moments if he didn't take action.

Ah, but what a way to go.

He shook his head, trying to clear it of his prurient thoughts. "Um, Emily...this may not be all that swift a decision."

"What do you mean?" She sat down on the couch, and the hem of her robe shifted to reveal a very shapely leg. Her feet were small with high arches, and her toenails were painted crimson, like ripe cherries.

It took him a second to remember her question. "We've been through this once already, remember?" he said, referencing his very spontaneous—and very rejected—kiss.

She smiled, a slow, deliciously wicked smile. "I'm simply asking for champagne," she purred, leaning back. The motion caused her breasts to press against the robe, forcing the neckline open a few fractions farther. "At least, that's all for right now."

Colin almost knocked the bottle over in his haste to turn away from her tempting display. He opened it and slowly poured two glasses, keeping his back to her.

She's hot, no question. But she's trouble. Remember?

No matter how tempting Emily Stanfield might be, sleeping with her would open a can of worms.

"So," he said slowly, handing her a champagne flute and carefully sitting as far from her as the couch would allow. "I take it you've reconsidered my out-of-town status, then?"

He closed his eyes. He shouldn't have asked, but he was curious as to her change of heart. She laughed, and the sound warmed his bloodstream like brandy.

"The more I thought about it, the more I realized—you *are* an out-of-towner."

He shifted uncomfortably, remembering his early exchange with his family. Emily Stanfield was small-town to her bones. Wholesome values, dedication to her community. Tall Pines to the core.

And you're not.

Her seductive smile slipped, revealing an expression of concern. "You're worried because I turned you down before, aren't you?" she said softly. "I hurt you. I'm sorry."

"No, no," he reassured her, unconsciously moving closer. "It's not that. In fact, I think you were right. We probably *shouldn't* sleep together."

Her eyes snapped, a luminescent blue, fierce as a welding arc. "Why don't you think we should?"

Now she was the one who sounded hurt. He stroked her hair, trying to take the sting out of his statement. "The same reasons you had. I'm not quite out-of-town enough… and the good people of Tall Pines would have a field day if they found out."

"Who were you planning on telling?"

"What?" he asked, startled. "I wouldn't tell anybody."

"Neither would I," she said, and he watched, hypnotized, as her hand trailed down and untied her robe. It fell open to reveal a deep-cherry-red silk teddy edged in white lace. "It's nobody's business but ours, Colin. Nobody else needs to know."

His body went hard in a rush. No Christmas morning had ever held more promise than this moment, with this beautiful woman offering herself up as if she were every toy that he'd ever wanted in his entire life.

But she's not a toy. And he couldn't treat her like one.

"I'm leaving in the morning, Emily," Colin said carefully, even though his voice was rough with desire.

"I know," she answered. Was he imagining it or was

there a thread of regret in her voice? "But we still have tonight."

His body was clamoring for her, his heart beating double time, his cock harder than a steel girder. Were it any other woman, he'd have bridged the distance between them five minutes ago. If she were any other woman, they'd be well on their way to making it a very memorable night indeed.

Of course, if it were any other woman, he'd wake up in the morning and leave without a second thought. But it was Emily—and for whatever reason, he sensed that leaving her would cause a lot more repercussions than that. She deserved better than to be a one-night stand, one on a list of fond memories.

On the other hand, he had the sinking feeling that Emily Stanfield was not the type of woman he'd forget easily. And that caused a whole different kind of problem.

He sat on the couch, frozen in indecision.

She made a small sigh of irritation and then scooted closer, shrugging out of the robe. Emily had freckles on her shoulders, he noticed—a pale sprinkling. She leaned forward. "What time do you have to leave?" she whispered, her breath tickling the sensitive spot just below his ear.

"N-nine," he stammered, struggling against another tidal wave of lust.

"That gives us hours," she breathed, brushing a tiny kiss against his collarbone. He groaned. "Let's not waste any more time."

Colin couldn't help himself. His hands moved forward, his fingertips caressing her long, swanlike neck, then smoothing down the petal-soft skin of her shoulders. His mouth consumed hers in a sensual assault, teasing her for only the briefest of moments before simply devouring her.

He could hear her muffled cries of longing, feel the way her hands bunched in the fabric of his shirt, clutching him as if she couldn't bear to let him go.

Did he position himself on top of her or did she pull him? He felt drunk on the taste of her, dizzy with it. He hazily registered the length of her body beneath his…the way her breasts crushed against his chest, the heat from between her thighs warming his jean-clad erection. Her quick fingers tugged his shirt out of his waistband, then found the naked skin beneath. With a low, unbelievably sexy growl, her hands rubbed up against his bare back, then with gentle insistence she drew her oval nails down his bare skin, causing him to shudder with need. He tore his mouth from hers for a second, gasping for air, fighting for control.

"Oh, Colin," she panted. "No matter what happens after this, *I want you*."

In that second, her statement pierced his desire-soaked consciousness long enough to force him to pause. With superhuman effort he rolled off her, practically falling to the rug. "Damn it," he said, rubbing his hand over his face. "Damn it!"

"What?" she asked, her eyes wide, her voice breathless. "What's wrong?"

"This. Us." He closed his eyes, and a litany of curses rolled through his mind. "You said no matter what happens after this. You *know* this is going to be complicated."

She huffed. "Maybe. But if anything did happen, I'd deal with it." She sent him a shaky grin. "So far, you're more than worth any consequences."

While the compliment only threw more fuel on the fire of lust snaking through his system, he grimaced. "In other words, you don't care what the fallout winds up being if this leaks out."

"Basically."

He frowned. "Wouldn't you resent me for just leaving you holding the bag?"

"Colin, not to be callous," she said, rolling her eyes, "but even if I hated you for it…honestly, what difference would it make? You wouldn't be here to see it. And what are the odds we're going to see each other again so you'd have to deal with them *or* me?"

Now, of all the things she'd said, that stopped him cold. She was offering every man's dream—no-strings-attached, smokin'-hot sex without the need for so much as a phone call after. And he wouldn't make it back to Tall Pines until next Thanksgiving at the earliest, so he would miss any repercussions.

So why did it feel so damned *wrong*?

"I know you think you mean this, Emily," he said as neutrally as possible. "But you've admitted you haven't had sex in a while. And I'll bet you haven't had sex with all that many people in your life, period. Am I right?"

She didn't say anything, just drew her full, pouty lips into a tight line.

He was right. He *knew* he was right.

"I just think," he continued reluctantly, "that when this is all over, you're going to regret saying yes. Maybe for a long, long time."

There. He'd done it. He was listening to his conscience rather than his body, for once in his life.

Emily stared at him, studying him. She seemed to almost crackle with an aura of frustration and need. Then she stood up, stalking back to her bedroom and shutting the door.

He swallowed the rest of his champagne without tasting it. Despite his various love affairs, sex wasn't something he took lightly—and anything related to Tall Pines was a time bomb. He still felt guilty over the stupid stuff he'd done when he was a kid. He wasn't about to compound it by doing stupid stuff as an adult.

He'd probably done the wise thing, although he couldn't help but...

Suddenly the door swung open.

Emily stepped out, totally, gloriously naked.

He stared at her in wonder. Her lithe limbs stretched gracefully from her perfectly proportioned torso. Her waist nipped in before curving out into gently flared hips, and her full breasts were tipped by luscious raspberry-hued nipples that puckered appetizingly with arousal. She stroked one hand over the flat planes of her stomach, stopping just short of the thatch of auburn curls at the juncture of her thighs.

"I *do* want you," she said quietly. "I *do* know what I want. And I *can* make my own decisions, thanks very much."

He was taut as a bowstring, barely registering her words. She looked like an avenging goddess—one that, even if it cost him his life, he couldn't bring himself to look away from.

"Now I'm going to my bed," she said. "I'm waiting for you there. And I can guarantee the only thing you'd regret would be saying no."

She turned, her saucy teardrop-shaped derriere making him groan out loud. Then she glanced over her shoulder.

"And, trust me, you'd regret it for the rest of *your* life." Neatly tossing his words back at him, she disappeared into her bedroom but left the door wide-open.

Colin wasn't made of stone—though it felt like it. And he sure as hell wasn't a saint.

He paused for all of a second before following her soft

footsteps. It might not be the wisest move, but as far as his body was concerned, there was no way he was leaving this place without giving one last, thorough, phenomenal Christmas present to Emily Stanfield.

CHAPTER THREE

EMILY WAS SHAKING by the time she'd made it to her bed. It had taken all her courage to make that dramatic speech. She'd never acted so cavalier about sex before, especially considering Colin had called it right on the money—she'd only had sex with two other people in her entire life. She wanted him, though, and she knew that if she didn't act as if she could coolly handle a one-night stand, he was principled enough and compassionate enough to never touch her. So she'd put on a very convincing act.

Obviously sexual frustration was making her brave, not to mention revealing talents she didn't even know she had. On the other hand, it might also be making her stupid.

Colin stepped into her room and she held her breath.

But this is going to be worth it.

He closed the door behind him. The bedroom was lit with candles, a multitude of votives washing the pale green walls with a warm glow. She had no silk sheets to trot out—her thick comforter and flannel sheets were meant to keep her toasty during the bitter winter nights.

She got the feeling staying warm would not be an issue tonight.

Besides, the last thing he seemed interested in was his

surroundings. He only had eyes for her, and she shivered—
not from any chill in the air but from the intensity of his
gaze.

Emily leaned back on the bed, forcing herself not to
cover up her body with her arms. She felt a delicious rush
of anticipation roll through her and she rubbed her legs together, the friction lessening as her body began to get wet
at the mere thought of him.

He took off his shirt, and she smiled in appreciation of
the purely masculine beauty of his torso. His muscles
bunched and flexed as he removed the rest of his clothes.
When he stripped out of his boxers, she couldn't help but
goggle a little. It had been a while, after all, since she'd seen
a naked man, much less one in all his erect glory.

He smiled. "Stop it. You'll make me blush."

She wanted to toss back some witty comment, but words
seemed lodged in her throat. Instead she put her arms out,
inviting him.

Colin spread out next to her on the flannel sheets, kicking the covers out of the way. He felt like a furnace, and she
warmed herself against him, shuddering at the slide of skin
over skin. He kissed her neck, her collarbone, her shoulder.
His hand stroked gently over her hip before sliding up and
cupping her breast.

She gasped softly as sensation seeped through her like
a hot bath. When he started to pull away, she grabbed his
hand, keeping it on her breast. Moaning, she closed her
eyes, enjoying the sensation as his mouth increased its
pressure on her neck and his thumb gently circled her nipple. She stroked her leg against his, her breathing coming
in soft, sweet exhalations.

"Emily," he murmured, then his mouth found hers and
claimed it with a slow thoroughness. His tongue teased

hers, and she teased back, the back-and-forth a precursor to the joining she really wanted. His other hand found her other breast, and he stroked expertly. Her fingers dug into his firm shoulders in response.

After what seemed like a pleasurable eternity, he released one breast. She whimpered in protest, only to stop when his hand moved lower, reaching between her thighs and dipping into her moist heat. She bit her lip as the sensation overwhelmed her. He gently parted the folds of skin until he found her sleek clit and rubbed it with firm precision. She felt pressure building up in her and she arched her back, trying to bring herself in closer contact with the man who was causing her to react so strongly. He kept working at it, insistently, delicately, until she thought she would explode.

Then he pressed a finger into her, and she couldn't help it. She came, and it was more than an explosion...it was a supernova. She threw her head back, letting the experience rock her.

When she came back to Earth, she looked at him and saw he had a beatific smile on his face. "That was..." She struggled to find a word that covered it and couldn't.

"You're welcome," he said, winking at her. "I wouldn't have pegged you as a screamer."

The blush washed over her entire body. She was sure he noticed, but she didn't care. "I didn't know I was," she admitted. "I don't think I was before."

"You don't say." He moved his head down, sucking first on one nipple, then the other.

Emily still felt desire, but the raw, slicing edge of it had been dulled by her orgasm. Now she was hungry for him, but she wasn't starving the way she'd been before. She could take her time, and enjoy the interplay of their bodies much more intently.

I don't know when I'll have this sort of chance again, she thought. *I'm going to make every moment count.*

She nudged his head up, and he sent her a puzzled look. "Your turn," she said, smiling wickedly.

"Oh?"

She pushed him down against the mattress, enjoying the way his erect cock stood, large and prominent, demanding attention. She pressed a few slow kisses against his chest, then his stomach, her tongue tracing the defined muscles. She was gratified to see his breathing go shallow. Slowly she stroked her hands on his thighs, drawing her nails down the sensitive skin. He drew in a sharp, hissing breath, releasing it in a slow, ragged sigh as she finally encircled his erection with her fingers.

"Your hands are so soft," he marveled, his eyes closing. His hips arched up to meet her as her hands traveled up and down the length of his shaft.

"Think so? Try this," she answered playfully, then took the head of his penis into her mouth.

He groaned loudly. She traced the head with her tongue before sucking ever so softly, caressing the velvety skin with her lips. His breathing increased in pace.

"Emily," he rasped.

His cock was like iron wrapped in satin. She reveled in the clean, masculine taste of his skin, taking him in a few more inches, her fingers stroking the round globes of his balls.

After a few moments, he reached down, pulling her up roughly. "I have to be inside you," he said, his voice coarse with need. "*Now.*"

She smiled, feeling triumphant. He sounded just the

way she'd felt when he'd given her that first orgasm. She liked that she might be able to make this man tremble, mindless with need. "Condom," she breathed, reaching over on her nightstand and getting one of the newly purchased foil packets. She tore it open, rolling it onto him slowly, taunting him with it. He was shaking by the time she was done.

He rolled her onto her back, and she felt the glorious weight of him pressing her into her mattress. He kissed her fiercely, and she responded with equal ferocity, parting her legs so he could fit himself at her snug opening. She felt the head of his cock slide slightly between her wet folds. He reached down, teasing her clit with his hardness until she was gasping with desire, her legs twining around his as she struggled to bring him closer.

"I want you inside me," she said.

Without a word, he finally relented and thrust into her, filling her completely. It felt so incredibly good she could have cried. She circled her hips, instinctively tightened her muscles as she enveloped him in her warmth.

He groaned, withdrawing slowly, and she moaned in return. "Deeper," she breathed, and he returned, with maddening patience, going farther into her. Her legs tightened around his hips, cradling him inside her.

"Colin." She shivered as the first luscious tremors of passion inched through her. "I'm almost there...."

Taking her cue, he increased his speed, his hips moving more quickly as his cock moved in and out of her willing wetness. Emily felt her body start to tighten and she ran her nails down his back as her hips bucked to meet his every thrust.

"Baby, I'm going to..." he groaned, and she cried out in approval. The two of them were frenzied in their joining, as if they couldn't get close enough to each other. He let out a guttural shout as he emptied himself into her with a hard, definitive motion, triggering an orgasm that eclipsed her first. She cried out again, a sound of pure pleasure, as her body clutched around him. To her surprise, he shuddered again as their hips melded together, rocking in the aftershocks of climax.

After long moments, he rolled off her, leaving them both sweaty and breathless. He stared at her, his green eyes like beacons.

"You were right," he said. "I would have regretted saying no to you for my entire life."

She basked in the compliment of his words, even as a small part of her conscious brain registered what he was saying.

This is a one-night stand. She'd just had her world spun on its axis by a man she'd fantasized about for years…but this was it. This was all she was going to get.

Is this going to be worth it?

She glanced at him. In the aftermath of sex, he still looked sinfully tempting. There was no sense of regret, no lingering return of reason that asked her, *What were you thinking?* She knew exactly what she'd been thinking when she decided to seduce Colin Reese. She knew because she was still thinking it.

But what are you going to do when you can't have him again?

He'd made it clear that there was no future. He was leaving, crossing an ocean to get away from Tall Pines. He was certainly not about to return to the small town that he had caused so much grief—and which wanted to return the favor by prying into every minute detail of his now almost famous local-rebel-makes-good life.

So where does that leave you?

She sighed. It left her here, in Tall Pines. Alone.

He leaned over, kissing where her heart beat. "You are going to haunt me," he said softly.

He was going to haunt her, too. But then again, it never could have lasted. She'd been well aware of that going into this little arrangement.

She might settle for the comfort of friendship and a passionless relationship, she thought as his fingers brushed over the surface of her skin, bringing the nerve endings to life. She was a realist. Would she ever find a man she reacted to as strongly as she did to Colin? She could either agonize over the question or simply enjoy the moment.

Tonight was all they had, and she would make the most of it.

"You have to leave at nine tomorrow, you said?" Emily asked.

"Uh-huh."

"We've still got hours," she reminded him, just as she had before, in the living room.

"Really," he drawled. "What shall we do with ourselves?"

She smiled, licking her lips. "As it happens," she said, her voice husky with sexual promise, "I've got a few ideas I'd love to try."

"I SAID, WHERE TO, mister?" the cab driver asked, slowly and carefully, as if Colin were hard of hearing.

Colin guessed that the man must have repeated the question several times. "Sorry," he said. "I need to get to the airport in Hartford."

The cabbie snorted. "I'll give it a shot." The taxi began slowly creeping out of the Stanfield Arms's circular driveway.

Colin stared out the window in a daze. The entire town of Tall Pines was smothered in mountainous drifts of snow, making the whole scene seem oddly muted. It only added to Colin's feeling of surreal displacement.

Did last night really happen?

Yes, it had happened—and in a way was still happening for him, since he'd gotten no more than a catnap or two the entire night. Once he'd given in to his urge and slept with Emily, it was as if he couldn't get enough of her. Fortunately, she'd seemed to feel the same way, because the two of them had feasted on each other for hours, and even now weariness hadn't quite settled in.

They'd made love twice in the bed, once in front of the fireplace, once in the shower and once on the countertop of her bathroom. He hadn't had sex like that for years. His body felt well used, just this side of sore. His mind, on the other hand, kept replaying the more vivid highlights of the previous night—and suggesting new and exciting variations that they might try in a second round.

Pity there isn't going to be a second round.

That was why they called them one-night stands, he reminded himself. One night. He wasn't quite sure where the "stand" part fit in. Although now that he thought about it, the shower...

"You all right, mister?"

Colin refocused on the cab driver. "What?"

"You look sorta out of it," the guy said, peering at Colin from his rearview mirror. "Don't tell me. You had yourself a merry little Christmas, huh? Really tied one on?"

"You could say that," Colin said ruefully, obviously not willing to divulge secrets.

"Hard to believe you could party that hard in a town like this. Tiny little mom-and-pop stores, all those wrought-iron lampposts with holly around 'em. It looks like an old movie or something."

Colin looked out the window as if seeing the place with a stranger's eyes. It was picturesque, he had to admit. The windows were decorated with paint and candles, and the streets were clear of the litter and debris that he was so used to in the sprawling cities he normally worked in. Most of the stores were brick or stone, not concrete. The houses had nice landscaping and everywhere were Christmas decorations, tasteful and old-fashioned.

"I'll have to tell my wife about it," the cabbie continued cheerfully. "She loves this kind of crap. You live here?"

"No," Colin said.

"Just passin' through, then?"

"Yup. Just passing through." The thought brought a pang.

How long is this sensation going to last?

He'd known that sleeping with Emily was going to be trouble even before he'd set foot into her bedroom. Apparently it was going to be more trouble than he'd bargained for...and he hadn't even been away from her for an hour.

"Well, it's cute and all, but it's a pure pain in the ass to get to," the cabbie stated. "Especially with the blizzard."

"Wait a minute," Colin interrupted. "Especially with the *what?*"

"Blizzard. Man, it's been on the news all over the place," the cabbie said. "They've had travel advisories. It's been on the radio and the television and the newspapers. Where have you been?" He shook his head. "That must've been one hell of a party."

"It was," Colin said. "I've got a flight to New York, then a connection to Paris. Any word on airports shutting down?"

"I think there are delays but nothing too bad," the driver reassured him.

"Oh," Colin said. "That's...good."

"Don't sound so enthusiastic," the cabbie joked. "Paris, huh? Ooh la la. Vacation or something?"

"No, I'm moving there."

Without warning, his body suddenly felt exhausted. He wished the cab driver weren't quite so chatty. Maybe it was the thought of a transatlantic flight or maybe it was the thought of leaving, he wasn't sure. Nevertheless, his body abruptly decided to remind him that he hadn't gotten a premium on sleep last night and he wasn't a teenager anymore. Suddenly he was having a hard enough time staying conscious, much less carrying on a conversation.

He wondered absently whether Emily was sleeping. She'd been naked and bundled up in her bedding when he'd said goodbye. She'd smiled, kissed him and turned over so she didn't have to see him leave.

It had been harder than he'd ever imagined to walk out that door.

"Moving to Paris? Wow. The wife would love it, but me, I can't see leaving the States," the cabdriver continued relentlessly.

Colin listened halfheartedly to the cabdriver's cheerful patter. He watched as the town's landmarks moved slowly past them, enveloped in fluffy flakes that almost turned the air white with their abundant barrage. The gazebo in the town square looked like an igloo, piled high with a dome of snow. The statue of the town's founder waded waist deep in a drift, while the Otter Lodge sign was almost completely covered up, revealing only the "Otter."

The cab skidded abruptly, and Colin realized he'd been drifting off. "Whoa!"

"Sorry about that," the cabdriver said. "I've got chains on, but this is nuts. I haven't seen a storm this bad in years."

Colin wondered if Emily was going to be okay. She was up in the attic, after all, and as luxurious as the small apartment suite was, it was awfully close to the roof, which was probably piled up with tons of snow.

He suddenly had a horrible vision of the roof caving in and fought the absolutely irrational desire to have the cab turn around and return him to the inn.

Even if the roof's not strong enough, what were you planning on doing to stop it? Hold the thing up with your arms?

He wasn't sure what he would do. He just knew that he hated the idea of Emily in any kind of trouble. And, if he were being completely honest with himself, some part of him was searching desperately for an excuse to get back to the inn. To *her.*

He knew that it was stupid, but there it was.

Chalk it up to lack of sleep.

"So what kind of business are you in?" the cabdriver asked.

"I'm an architect," Colin said.

"Houses and stuff?"

"Not exactly. My next project is a hotel on the Left Bank, about a stone's throw from the Eiffel Tower."

"Must be nice," the cabdriver said with a low, appreciative whistle. "So, what, they aren't building any hotels on this side of the ocean?"

"Now you sound like my mother," Colin said, and the cabdriver snorted.

"Well, to each his own," he said affably. "You like what you do?"

"Love it," Colin told him, feeling better. "Love the challenges, the new places, the clients. All of it."

"Now you're sounding better," the cabbie pointed out. "That hangover wearing off?"

Colin smiled tightly. "Seems like it."

"I hate hangovers," the cabdriver continued. "Still, every now and then you've got to indulge, you know?"

Colin thought about it. *Indulgence.* That seemed like an inadequate word to cover what had taken place last night. But still, wasn't that basically how Emily was looking at it?

Ten bucks says she isn't mooning about you this morning, pal. She's probably sleeping it off, or getting back to work. The way she'd talked about it, it was the experience she wanted, and the fact that it was with him was incidental. As though he was a stamp in her passport or something.

He didn't believe it at the time, but now, after seeing her in action—honestly, he wasn't sure what to believe anymore.

"So your wife and family going with you or what?"

"What's with the twenty questions?" Colin snapped.

The cabdriver paused. "Sorry, man. Didn't mean to bug you. Some people like to talk, you know?"

Colin sighed. "I'm sorry, too," he said. "I guess that hangover's stronger than I thought. I didn't mean to bite your head off." He paused. "And no. No wife, no kids."

"Huh. Not surprised, actually. You don't really seem like a family man."

Colin sat up straighter, as if someone had smacked him on the back of the head. "Why do you say that?"

"Sharp dresser, goin' off to Paris the day after Christmas, hungover." The cabdriver barked out a laugh. "But, hey, I've seen weirder from married guys, so I wasn't absolutely sure. I remember driving this guy to two of his mistresses' apartments on Thanksgiving, if you can believe it...."

Colin settled back against the cold vinyl seat of the taxi, feeling disgruntled. It all circled back to his family's comments. He wasn't the small-town type. He knew that, had known it since before high school. He'd be the first to say so in most cases. So why should the observation bother him now? Why was he getting so ticked off every time someone pointed out that he wasn't small-town and family-oriented?

You're getting a little tired of being alone.

The thought was so alien Colin actually blinked in disbelief for a second. He'd had lots of relationships, sure. Brief, exciting relationships. But it hadn't occurred to him that he might be lonely.

While he did love his job, there was more to life than work.

Unbidden, the picture of Emily riding him with abandon in the early hours of the morning sprang to mind…causing other things to spring, as well. Embarrassed, he tried to force his unruly body to relax.

Even if you want a relationship, it can't be Emily. For reasons they both understood.

Still, damned if he didn't feel disappointed.

"What's this now?" the cabdriver said, causing Colin to look through the windshield. There was a heavily dressed police officer waving them down with a flashlight. "Is there a problem, Officer?"

The cop nodded. "You can't get to the interstate," he said, his breath coming out in clouds of steam. "The blizzard's gotten too bad."

"But I have to get this guy to the airport," the cabbie protested, "then I have to get home!"

"Not today, you don't," the police officer said grimly. "You'd better find someplace in town to stay, because nobody's leaving Tall Pines. For a few days, if this storm front keeps up. Get off the roads as soon as you can."

The cabdriver grumbled but carefully turned around. "Guess I'd better find a motel," he said. "Where should I drop you?"

Colin paused for a second. He should probably go to his parents' house. They'd be worried about him and they'd love to see him.

But when he opened his mouth, he heard himself saying, "If you could take me back to the hotel, that'd be great."

"The hotel it is," the cabdriver agreed.

Colin sat, silent. He wondered what Emily was up to at that moment. He wondered what he should do when he saw her.

He also wondered what she'd do when he unexpectedly showed up.

"WE'RE STRANDED HERE!" one of the guests was yelling to be heard over the general clamor. "What are we supposed to do now?"

"I only booked the reservation for four days," another guest protested. "You can't expect me to pay for a day that I'm forced to stay here."

"And I have work to do," yet another protested.

"Emily," Sue whispered. "We've got some concerns about the roof, we're running low on towels…"

Emily smiled easily. "Don't worry. Everything's going to be fine."

Sue's eyes narrowed. "How do you figure? It's turning into a disaster!"

Emily didn't stop smiling as she turned to the mob of angry guests. "I'm so sorry for the inconvenience," she said, and although her voice was raised enough to carry over the chaos of multiple complaints, it stayed sweet and pleasant-sounding. That was enough to quiet most of the people milling around the foyer. "The blizzard has caught us all unawares. I can assure you that we are going to do everything we can to make this temporary setback easy and even pleasant for you. I can't offer you the rooms for free," she apologized, ignoring the one customer's irate glare, "but I can offer you a blizzard discount since, as you said, you're being forced to stay here. I'd also like to offer you our breakfast—complimentary, of course—and I can send it to your rooms if you'd prefer." Emily smiled broadly. "If you have to take another vacation day, you might as well take advantage of it, and it's never too late to have breakfast in bed, I always say."

That drew an appreciative chuckle from several of the guests.

"Light up a fire in your rooms' fireplaces, have some cider or wine and enjoy yourself. If there's anything we can do to make your stay more comfortable, please let us know. And if you must work, our business center is open twenty-four hours a day."

The guests wandered away, mollified. Emily turned to Sue. "I've got a call in to Dale Albee to look at the roof, and we'll get some loads of towels going in the basement since the linen service can't get here. And I've already got the French toast in the oven for complimentary breakfasts, so we're set."

Sue stared at her, eyes wide. "Okay, what are you on and where can I get some?"

Emily laughed. "Don't know what you're talking about, but thanks. I think."

"You must have had a great time at Mayor Tim's last night," Sue noted.

"Come on, Sue." Emily sighed. "I thought you of all people would leave me alone about him."

Sue grinned. "Hey, you're single. He's single. And lord knows it's high time you stopped sleeping alone."

Emily quickly turned back to the front reception desk, pretending to look over some bills. She prayed that her cheeks weren't stained with the usual telltale blush.

"Tim's not exactly the type to get a girl hot and bothered. I mean, he's sweet and all, but…"

"I know. But still, those quiet types can surprise you," Sue pointed out.

Colin was a quiet type—the deep, intense, loner type. That had always been a huge draw for her, back when she'd doodled his name on notepaper in high school. He'd seemed like a cross between James Dean and Johnny Depp, with his dark good looks and quirky, iconoclastic behavior. And, yes, he had surprised her.

Heck, she thought with a private smile. She'd surprised *herself* last night.

"I agreed to go with Tim to the New Year's ball," Emily said. "So we'll see how it goes."

"Good," Sue said, and Emily was grateful that her friend wasn't paying that much attention, being so frazzled by the blizzard situation, since she felt as though she might as well be wearing a T-shirt that said *I had fantastic sex with Colin Reese!* Fortunately, keeping busy was helping her stay grounded. "Anyway, I'm really impressed with how you handled all those guests this morning. Honestly, you're a rock. I don't know what we would do if you weren't so unflappable."

Emily shrugged, embarrassed. "You'd manage, I'm sure."

"If you say so," Sue said dubiously. "All I know is you

managed to get that raving mob to back down and go to their rooms, and they've been chewing me out since eight o'clock this morning. I know you were going to take today off, but…"

"Hey, there are no days off for a business owner," Emily said. "Don't worry about…"

Suddenly Sue's statement sunk in.

"Wait a minute. Since eight?"

"Yeah. I know—it was only two hours ago. I shouldn't sound so dramatic.…" Sue saw that her friend was genuinely upset. "Why? Is that a problem?"

Emily did the math. "So the road to the interstate has been closed since…"

"Since about seven this morning," Sue answered. "Some vehicles got in, but they're not letting anybody back out. The roads are too dangerous, they're saying."

Emily felt the blood rush from her face. She sat down.

"Whoa. Are you okay?" Sue was at her side in a flash. "You look terrible all of a sudden. What's wrong?"

"I drank a little champagne last night," Emily said, "and I didn't get much sleep. It must be catching up with me."

All of which was true, as far as it went. But there was one thing she'd left out.

If they weren't letting anyone leave, then Colin was headed back for town.

Emily felt as though her limbs were floating. She felt numb and yet tingly, as if her entire body had gone to sleep but she was still awake.

What were they going to do now?

Her mind instantly supplied a few details of what they *could* be doing…things that sheer physical exhaustion had prevented them from doing the night before. But she'd had her one-night stand. As much as she'd love to spend more time with—and energy on—Colin Reese, she knew that it was a bad idea. There would be talk. His family hadn't realized he'd been staying in her apartment, but they'd probably figure it out if he came back. While the logical, mature side of her argued that she and Colin were adults and what they did was nobody's business but their own, the idea of dealing with Ava Reese, not to mention the whole town just-dropping-in to pump her for information, was enough to make her cringe.

On the other hand, what makes you think he'll come back here at all?

That thought made her feel as though she'd been dropped headfirst in a frozen lake. She was so worried about how to handle seeing him that it hadn't occurred to her—he might not come back. He might not want to see her again.

That was the point of one-night stands, after all.

Emily quickly went downstairs and loaded their industrial washer/dryer with towels, grateful for the physical activity. She probably should sneak in a nap at some point, just to clear her head. But she got the feeling sleep would elude her, especially knowing that Colin was maybe somewhere in town that very minute.

Somewhere, trying desperately to avoid her.

She set her jaw. Well, it had been her idea to have a one-night stand, after all. She didn't need him to hang around. She knew how the game was played. If he couldn't take more than one night, then maybe she'd wrung him out. Maybe he simply couldn't handle another night with her, she thought with a smug internal grin. She'd gotten everything she wanted out of it—a completely memorable night. Even if she never got anything else, she'd cherish the memory. That was enough. It'd have to be.

Emily was so intent on running that mental pep talk through her brain in an endless loop that she ran right into Colin before she registered who he was.

"Hey, there," he said, smiling sheepishly…although his eyes sparkled warmly. "Long time no see."

She couldn't help it. Her heart leaped happily and she felt like an idiot. Her body, in the meantime, was so attuned to him that the mere scent of his cologne was already starting to kick her libido into overdrive—even with her sleep deprivation.

This was one hell of a man.

"I heard about the interstate closing," she said apologetically, trying not to stare at him and failing miserably.

"Got room for one more?" he asked.

His question was completely innocuous, but the tone suggested a lot more. Was he asking for more than one night of what they'd done the night before? Or just for a place to sleep? Should she assume?

He leaned in. "I can sleep wherever you want me to sleep."

Now his tone left no question as to his intent.

Her breasts tightened, and she felt the now-familiar dampness rush between her legs. She smiled at him with invitation.

"I'm sure we can…"

"Sorry to interrupt, Emily," Mr. Albee, the roofer, said, clearing his throat.

"Oh. Yes," she said, and damned if the blush didn't settle into her cheeks. "How can I help you?"

"Your roof's holding up okay. The reinforcements I did over the summer are doing their job, just like I told you they would." He looked from her to Colin, his expression appraising.

"Hello, Mr. Albee." Colin sounded like a schoolboy who had been caught smoking in the bathroom.

"Colin Reese, right?" Mr. Albee smiled slowly. "Didn't know you were staying in town."

"I don't think anybody was planning on staying quite this long," Colin replied. "What with the blizzard and all."

"Well, you'll have to give my regards to your mother and father," Mr. Albee said. "If you get over that way. You're staying here, are you?"

"Just because it's so crowded…" Colin stammered. "What with my nieces and nephews and everything…"

"I was just doing him a favor," Emily supplied.

"Of course you were," Mr. Albee said. "Well, I won't keep you. There's an emergency town meeting tonight, and I'm sure I'll see you there, Emily." He shook Colin's hand. "Nice seeing you again, son."

He left and Emily groaned.

"What's wrong?" Colin asked.

"He's married to Evelyn Albee, remember?"

Colin frowned. "So?"

"So she runs the beauty salon. Which everyone knows is like the CIA and the blogosphere combined," Emily pointed out. "By the time most of the women in this town get their usual manicure and cut-and-color, everyone's going to know we're an item."

"We're not an item, though," Colin said.

She felt a little sting at that. Well, she'd asked for it. "I know. But they're not going to care. And it'll only get worse if you bunk here at the hotel. In my apartment."

"I thought," he said suggestively, "that you weren't going to care about the consequences."

"That was last night," she muttered. "I would have walked over hot coals to have you last night."

He grinned. "Oh?"

"Now I'm about to face the gauntlet at tonight's town meeting," she said. "So it'd be better if you *weren't* staying here."

"You're not telling me to stay at my parents' house, are you?"

She nodded. "That's exactly what I'm telling you."

"So…" His voice was barely audible. "You *don't* want anything else to do with me? It really was just a one-night stand?"

She stared into his eyes and read the hurt there. Emily held her breath for a second, staring at him.

"It ought to be," she said softly. It was going to be trouble, she just knew it. Evelyn Albee, Ava Reese, all the busy women of Tall Pines and their gossip circles…

With a slow, subtle motion, he reached forward and stroked the delicate skin on the inside of her wrist.

She almost melted into a puddle right there in the lobby.

"Okay. Put your bags in my room. We'll figure it out."

Houston, she thought, watching him disappear down the hallway, *we have a problem.*

CHAPTER FOUR

COLIN SUPPOSED HE ought to feel at least a little ashamed of himself for pushing the issue with Emily, knowing that the seeds of gossip were being sown. But as he sat down in the main dining room, helping himself to some pecan French toast, scrambled eggs and bacon, he was having a hard time feeling anything but satisfied.

I get another night with her, he thought. *And maybe more.*

And, as she herself had said, it wasn't anybody's business but Emily's and his. The town might talk, but that's all it would be. Talking never killed anyone.

Sexual frustration probably never killed anyone, either—but he wasn't taking any chances.

"There you are!"

He glanced over and promptly choked on a bite of bacon. "Mom?"

His mother and father and the rest of his family quickly overtook the dining room, helping themselves to the buffet. "We decided to try the breakfast here at the hotel," his mother said innocently. "Especially when you called and told us you were staying here."

"Your mother wants to find out what the inn has that we

don't seem to have at our house," his father added, then winced at his mother's responding glare. "Well, that's what you said in the car."

There were only a few other guests enjoying the buffet—most of the rest were taking breakfast in their rooms, apparently—so his family was able to surround him at the large oak table. "Can we get a look at your room?" his mother asked.

"Uh…" Colin felt his mind go blank. He was hardly going to show them Emily's apartment. "I haven't got a room."

"You don't? Why not?"

"There are a lot of people stranded," he improvised hastily. "And they weren't expecting me to stay, so I think they gave it away."

"Then you can come home," his mother said as if the matter were settled.

Now what? He couldn't offer a logical explanation without revealing his new arrangement with Emily, and that was the last thing he wanted. "I think they'll find a place for me," he said. It sounded lame to his own mind.

His mother's mouth set in a tight line. "All right, son. What's going on?"

"What do you mean?"

"Don't play coy with me. I've been on to you since you took my car the week before homecoming your junior year and went parking with Mary Sue Reynolds—didn't think I knew about that, did you?"

Colin gaped. "Mom!"

"It would've been better if she hadn't left her bra in the backseat." His father snorted. "That was dumb, Colin."

"Why was there a bra in the backseat?" his niece Elizabeth asked.

"Never mind," his mother quickly replied. "Colin, the bottom line is, I know that there's something going on. So either you can tell me or I'll find out on my own."

Colin's mind raced for an explanation. Before he could come up with something plausible, Emily walked in.

For someone who hadn't gotten a lot of sleep, she looked luminescent. Her pale skin glowed in the lights of the dining room's chandelier. She was wearing a plum-colored V-neck cashmere sweater and a pair of black slacks. Her auburn hair was tied back with a matching plum-colored velvet ribbon. Combined with her glasses, she looked about eighteen years old—like a student, maybe headed off to the library.

He definitely had a thing for girls with glasses.

He smiled at her before he could stop himself and he caught his mother noticing his smile. He quickly schooled his expression, trying to redeem the situation.

"Ava," Emily said, smiling genially as she poured coffee into their cups. "It's so nice to see you and your family here."

"I hope you don't mind," Ava said. "We thought we'd enjoy the hotel's restaurant. I've heard good things about your brunch spread."

If Emily were suspicious, she didn't act like it. She looked cool, refined—the perfect hostess. Colin was in awe of her reserve. "We're happy to serve anytime," she answered with grace. "You'll have to try us in the spring. The cook does these fresh strawberry pancakes that are to die for."

"I've also heard good things about the hotel," his mother said, and Colin braced himself. "Obviously it's so incredible my son is hoping you'll find room for him here."

Emily's smile faltered slightly, but so imperceptibly that

Colin felt as if only he would notice. "That's flattering. We're certainly trying to accommodate everyone who's been stranded by the storm." She paused. "It might mean some doubling up, I think...."

Before she could continue, a blond woman walked into the dining room. She was obviously *not* a Tall Pines resident. She had all the look of a big city about her, like New York or Los Angeles. Hell, maybe even Milan. The bright red suit she was wearing, replete with tight skirt and matching heels, looked razor sharp and ready for business. Her makeup was flawless. He would have pegged her as a big executive—he'd run into the type before when he'd started to get some acclaim as an architect. When he'd designed and built a big new art gallery in London, the opening party had been almost entirely populated with women who'd looked like this. This polished, cosmopolitan blonde would've blended right in.

"Good morning, everyone," she said, her voice friendly. "Hey, Emily! This is a great spread. I can't believe you pulled all this together on such short notice. Have I mentioned lately just how impressed I am with this hotel?"

"Hi, Joy." Emily was obviously grateful for the interruption. "These are a few of our Tall Pines townsfolk, the Reese family. Everyone, this is Joy Webster, a friend of mine from out of town."

"Well, *hello*," Joy said when she saw Colin. Her eyes went low-lidded and she smiled. "Always nice to meet the locals."

"I'm not local," Colin was quick to point out.

"Are you staying here in the hotel?" she asked after nodding her hellos to the rest of his family.

"Um...that remains to be seen." He forced himself not to glance at Emily. He was trying to quell gossip here.

"Well, if you need a place to crash, I've got a huge

room." The expression on her face was obviously extending a slightly more intimate invitation.

"Uh, thanks," he said before feeling a sharp kick under the table. "Ow!"

His mother was studiously cutting her bacon and eggs with a fork and knife, pretending she hadn't done a thing. "So how are you enjoying our town, Joy?" she asked, her voice as mild as milk.

"I'm loving it," Joy replied, sounding genuinely enthused. "It's perfect. And have I mentioned how much I adore this hotel?"

"Always nice to be admired," Emily said.

Colin finally looked at Emily. She looked...well, *peeved* wasn't quite the right word, and it was hard to tell behind the smooth facade she seemed to habitually wear. But he could sense there was some kind of irritation hovering just below the surface.

"Seems like the table's pretty full. I'll just take this up to my room, if that's okay," Joy said. "Nice meeting you all. And don't forget—" she smiled privately at Colin "—if you need a place, I'm your girl."

Colin didn't say anything, just smiled back weakly as she left the room. When she disappeared, he felt angry glares aimed in his direction from not one but two women.

"So that's why you're waiting to stay in the hotel," his mother said, with a note of disgust. "Good grief. I might have known that even here in Tall Pines you'd find one of your...your *women*."

"What do you mean, one of my women?"

"Please. I could have picked her out of a lineup," his mother scoffed. "You always like those high-society, high-fashion, high-maintenance types. She fits the description of your usual dates down to a T."

"Hey, I resent that," Colin protested. "I don't have a type."

Emily's eyes had widened at his mother's very thorough diatribe. "I ought to get going," she now said hastily. "Nice to see you again, Ava, Harry. Bring your family by anytime."

With that, she disappeared into the hallway.

Great, Colin thought, glaring at his mother. "I am *not* staying here just to score with Joy," he said, his tone curt.

"What's 'score with' mean?" his nephew asked.

"Language, Colin," his mother warned. "You don't want the kids picking up that sort of thing."

"You're the one that started it!"

"She is pretty," his father noted. "You'll have to give our son that, Ava—he's got good taste."

"Oh, Colin, when are you ever going to settle down?" She sighed melodramatically.

"Okay, *this* is why I'm not staying at the house," Colin declared. "Everything is always about why I won't settle down, why I'm not married, who I'm dating and why I won't move back to Tall Pines!"

The rest of his family fell silent, staring at him. He felt like an ogre.

"I love you guys," he added. "Very, very much. But… I'm doing the best I can, okay? I know you worry about me and you want me to be happy, and I love you for it. But I have to do things my own way."

His mother bit her lip, looking uncomfortable. "I know I can be a tiny bit pushy…."

His father's eyes popped at that statement.

"Harry, not one word," she interrupted, frowning at him before winking. "Okay, I can be *very* pushy. But I really do want what's best for you. If you'd rather stay here at the hotel, I'll understand."

"Thank you," he said gratefully.

They all fell into more comfortable conversation, and he had to admit it was nice to spend more time together as a family, over a delicious meal. When they were done, they all hugged him goodbye.

"I don't suppose you'll be at the town meeting tonight?" his mother asked, hugging him. "It's a special one to deal with the storm."

Colin groaned. "You know I hate those things."

"Okay," she said. "Well, we'll do something before you leave. Good luck in finding a room."

"Thanks." They all left, and feeling a wave of relief, he went to the front desk.

"Excuse me," he said to Sue, the woman running the reception desk. He seemed to remember her from high school. "Is Emily around?"

"No," the woman replied, looking at him suspiciously. "She had to run some errands. Is there anything I can help you with?"

"Uh, no," he answered quickly. "I'll, er, catch up with her later. Thanks." She was still staring at him strangely as he walked away.

He sneaked back up to Emily's apartment, hoping he'd find her there. But for the rest of the day she remained conspicuously absent. It got darker, and by dinner he still hadn't seen her. The cook told him she would be gone until later—she was going to the town meeting.

She was avoiding him, he knew it. He wouldn't put it past her to find someplace else to stay that night just to miss dealing with him. All that talk about Joy, and her blatant invitation, had obviously upset Emily.

Well, he'd have to set Emily straight. They might not have a relationship, but whatever weird thing they did have was pretty special.

And if that meant going to the damned town meeting to tell her... He cringed.

He'd just have to go there and face the fire.

"THANKS FOR HAVING me to dinner, Sue," Emily said, finishing the last of her coffee.

"We love having you," Sue said graciously. "Are you okay leaving Phillip to hold down the fort by himself?"

Emily put her hand in her pocket, pulling out her cell phone. "The apron string he's attached to is now cellular," she answered, knowing Phillip's penchant for panicking. "Besides, he's handled us both being gone for a town meeting before. A little stress won't kill him."

"I'm still surprised you didn't stay at the inn. Especially after you convinced some of those people to double up with the strays."

Emily grinned at the term. "Well, since the highway patrol wouldn't let the poor people leave, the least we could do was put them up."

"Sometimes, I swear, you could sweet-talk the Devil into buying thermal underwear." Sue shook her head. "You're charming, you're persuasive—and yet you're a bulldozer."

"Thanks?" Emily questioned, laughing.

"I meant that in the good way," Sue assured her.

Sue's husband, Vernon, stuck his head into the kitchen. "Honey, if we're going to the town meeting, we'd better get a move on."

Emily swallowed hard. She'd been steeling herself to ask Sue her question since she got to the house, but somehow she couldn't quite come up with a way of making it sound casual. Now it was make-or-break time. "Say, Sue, could I ask you a favor?"

"Anything. What do you need?"

"I was wondering if I could stay here tonight."

Sue looked at her, surprised. "Of course, sweetie. But what's wrong with your apartment?" She rolled her eyes. "Don't tell me. You gave it up to some of the strays, right?"

"One of them," Emily answered, feeling relieved. "I figured it'd be less awkward if I could camp out on your couch."

"We've got the guest bedroom, silly. Don't even worry about it," Sue replied.

Emily felt relief wash through her. Sue was her best friend and had been since grade school. As a result of all those years together, she tended to be frighteningly adept at reading her like a book. Emily had never kept a secret from her about even the smallest thing, much less something of this magnitude.

"Who wound up in your place, anyway?" Sue asked, clearing away the dinner dishes. "The cabdriver? That lost delivery guy?"

Emily briefly considered lying. Instead she decided to try and brazen it out, quickly loading the dishwasher. "Colin Reese, actually."

There was a long pause. Emily deliberately avoided eye contact as she made quick work of helping Sue clean up. When all the dishes were stowed away and she had nothing else to do, she finally met Sue's gaze.

Her eyes had the piercing quality of an Interpol interrogator. "Colin Reese?"

"Yeah." Emily glanced around. "You don't have any cookies left over, do you? I feel like something sweet."

"Colin Reese," Sue repeated, refusing to be sidetracked. "Colin I'm-too-sexy-for-Tall-Pines, guy-you've-crushed-on-since-high-school Reese."

Emily sighed. She should have known she wouldn't get away with this. "That's the one."

Sue let out a frustrated huff. "Weren't you the one that was telling me you want to break your celibacy streak?"

"Colin isn't a candidate," Emily countered. *At least he shouldn't have been.* "Besides, he's just staying in my apartment, that's all."

Sue rolled her eyes. "Don't kid a kidder, Em. You've got a sexy guy in your apartment. Even out of practice, you can't tell me you haven't considered simply seducing the guy."

Emily bit her lip. *I've done more than consider it.* That was the problem. "It's complicated."

"Doesn't have to be."

She frowned. "Remember J. P. Webster? The hotelier that I've been e-mailing?"

"The woman?"

"Yes," Emily said, grimacing. "Well, she offered to share her room with Colin already." She put obvious emphasis on the word *share*. "And apparently she's completely his type, so he's probably going to take her up on it."

"Oh," Sue said. Then her eyes narrowed. "So if he's probably not going to use your place…why are you asking to stay here?"

Emily froze. "Uh…"

"Oh. My. God." Sue let out a squeal of excitement. "You guys *already did it!*"

There was a problem with having a hair-trigger blush reflex, Emily realized. It was like walking around attached to a lie detector. Her cheeks heated, and she braced herself for the onslaught.

"Details!" Sue crowed, tugging Emily toward the kitchen table and nudging her into a chair. "I want details!"

Her husband stuck his head in again. "Honey…"

"Not now!" Sue said. "Emily has dirt to dish!"

Smirking, he retreated.

"I wasn't supposed to tell anyone," Emily said. "And you'd better not say anything to anybody, got that?"

"Of course," Sue reassured her. "So spill. How was it?"

Emily sighed…then smiled. "There are no words."

"So *that's* why you looked so floaty and happy this morning," Sue marveled. "I should've guessed you'd gotten laid."

"I wouldn't quite put it that way," Emily said. Then grinned. "But, yeah."

"How many times?"

Emily's blush intensified. "Er…four." She mentally counted again—her body tingling with each memory. "Wait—five. I forgot the shower."

"In the shower!" Sue clapped her hands girlishly. "And *five* times? What, were you guys popping vitamin E every hour or what?"

"I've been saving up for two years, you know," Emily said wryly. "I don't know what his excuse was, but he certainly didn't seem tired." If anything, he'd been as good the last time as he was the first.

She wondered how he'd hold up a second night.

Not that you're going to find out.

"So what's the deal?" Sue said. "Why aren't you going back there and trying to break your record with six in one night?"

Emily fidgeted. "It was supposed to be the one night, nothing more."

"So what? Tell me that's not the only thing that's stopping you."

"And there was the Joy thing—her inviting him up to her room."

"Did he say yes?" Sue asked, eyes narrowed to slits.

"Well…no." Emily sighed. "But he wouldn't say yes right in front of me, would he?"

"Not if he knows what's good for him," Sue muttered darkly. "So why don't you ask him what he's going to do?"

"I don't want to put him on the spot," Emily said.

"Did he say he wanted to stay with you?"

Emily remembered that morning when she'd tried to turn him away—the look in his eyes, the subtle, sensual brush of his fingertips. "Well, yes."

"So there you are," Sue stated matter-of-factly. "He wants you."

"But Mr. Albee saw us and I think he made some assumptions."

"Evelyn's husband?" Sue let out a low whistle. "Oh. I guess you'll be hearing about that one."

"And Colin's family was at breakfast—and then they jumped all over the Joy thing."

"Oh." Sue sat quiet for a minute.

"So what do you think?" Emily asked, chewing on her lip. "Is it okay if I stay here? I just don't want to deal with him."

"I love you like a sister, you know that," Sue said warmly.

"Thanks," Emily said, feeling grateful.

"That's why I'm not letting you stay here."

"Wait!" Emily said, the grateful feeling evaporating. "What?"

"You're copping out. The guy asked to stay with you, you said yes. Somebody else hit on him, but he didn't take her up on it. So that means he still wants you," Sue pointed out. "And I'm guessing you still want him. Am I wrong?"

Emily slowly shook her head.

"So after the town meeting, go home, find the guy and

enjoy yourself," Sue ordered in a tone that brooked no discussion.

"But what about the gossip?"

"*Screw* the gossip," she said. "There's always gossip. You should be flattered to be considered a hot topic for a change."

Emily paused a moment, stunned. Then giggled.

"I didn't think about it that way," she said, feeling tickled.

"I know. Emily Stanfield, town pillar, yada yada."

The feeling of amusement ebbed. A dim echo of her father's voice reverberated in her mind.

A Stanfield never does anything to cause unflattering discussion.

"Yeah," Emily agreed, feeling bitter. "Town pillar. That's me."

Sue could obviously tell she was still worried. She squeezed her shoulders. "Really—don't worry about it. They might speculate a little, but you've done nothing to give them anything to really talk about."

"And I'm trying to keep it that way," Emily pointed out.

"Em, it's going to be cold damned comfort to have on your tombstone 'She never gave anybody anything to gossip about.' Now head home and boink Colin's brains out."

Emily laughed ruefully. "I have to go to the town meeting. Then I'll decide what to do about Colin."

Sue rolled her eyes. "Okay. It's your life. You've gotta do what you've gotta do."

Emily hugged her. "Still think I should date Tim?"

"Why not?" Sue asked, surprising her. "Colin's a fling. Tim's a keeper."

"Right," Emily said, feeling her stomach drop.

"Hey, there's nothing wrong with a fling, though," Sue

said. "It spices things up before you settle down. In fact, in your case, I strongly recommend a fling."

"Right," Emily repeated, and got her coat to head out to the town meeting.

Colin wasn't a keeper. He was a fling. And she could get one more night out of him, so she might as well enjoy herself.

But she'd already mooned about him all day, and then she was genuinely upset by the idea that she wasn't his type. So what was she going to do if she saw him again? She felt as if she were starting to get addicted. Maybe it'd be better to quit cold turkey.

Emily set her jaw resolutely, driving to the town hall. That was it. He'd probably leave in the next day or two. She'd just avoid him and things would work out fine. She'd barricade herself in the bathroom if she had to, but she wasn't going to get back into bed with Colin Reese, even if they did wind up sharing a room.

It was, as Sue said, cold comfort. But it was probably the smart way to go.

MAYOR TIM STOOD behind the dark cherrywood podium that had been in the town hall almost as long as the town itself had been in existence. He pounded the gavel, bringing the unruly crowd to order.

"It's nice to see so many of you here for this emergency meeting, especially considering the fact that snow is still falling," he said solemnly, the microphone crackling only slightly. "We've got a lot to discuss, but I promise I won't keep you here long."

Emily heard Sue snicker softly. There were perhaps sixty people in the auditorium, a small house by normal town meeting standards, but seeing that the "usual suspects" were present, there was no way that the meeting would be less than two hours, impromptu or not. The people who'd braved the weather were die-hard Tall Pines citizens.

Herself included, she realized with a frown.

"Why don't I start off with concerns from the floor?" Tim said, shuffling a few papers and readying a pen.

There was a cacophony of volunteers. Emily glanced at her watch. Make that three hours.

Suddenly the chaos fell silent as the door to the auditorium opened with a loud, ominous creak. Like everyone else, she glanced over, curious to see who the latecomer was.

Her eyes almost popped out of her head when she recognized Colin Reese, looking cold, irritated and obviously on a mission. He scanned the crowd, who were all staring at him.

"Evening." He spoke casually, as if he'd attended these meetings all his life. "Sorry I'm late."

"No problem," Tim said graciously. "Have a seat anywhere."

Ignoring Ava and Harry Reese's waving hands, he continued looking, his eyes finally lighting on Emily. Her heart caught in her throat.

"Look who's here," Sue whispered in a low singsong.

"Hush," Emily said, snapping her eyes forward. Still, she couldn't help but feel the rush of blood in her veins.

He hated Tall Pines events, especially the free-for-all discussion and endless opining of the theatrical town meetings. He'd probably rather be tossed into a snowbank naked than show up here tonight. But he was here—and he was, from the looks of it, searching for her.

Since Emily had sat toward the back of the auditorium,

it didn't look odd for him to sit just behind them. Sue shot him a quick, mischievous smile before snuggling up against her husband in the adjoining chair. Emily tried hard not to turn and look at Colin.

He leaned forward, his voice only barely audible. "I wanted to talk to you," he said.

She shook her head. "This isn't a good place," she murmured back, still not turning.

"I know," he said. "But you kept hiding out. I figured you'd be here and I thought I'd come to you."

She felt the telltale blush heat her cheeks. She *had* been hiding. But the way he put it made her seem so cowardly.

Damn it. It wasn't as if she had sex all the time so she could be cavalier about these things—no matter how she'd made it sound before she'd slept with him.

You're being silly.

"So you tell me when and where," he whispered, "and we'll...talk."

With that, he fell silent.

She felt the burning intensity of his gaze on the back of her head throughout the next hour as the town discussed the state of the roads, the blizzard, the people stranded here in town, the possible repercussions for the Otter Lodge gift exchange and, most importantly, the annual Holiday Ball. They pondered the problems as seriously as if the world's fate hung on each decision.

As far as Emily was concerned, the conversations sounded like a buzzing monotone. She found it impossible to focus on anything but the presence of the man sitting behind her.

After an hour and a half, Mayor Tim suggested a break for coffee and the delicious snacks provided by Mrs. Albee, which everyone dived for gratefully. Emily looked at Sue.

"I'm going to the ladies' room," she said, more to escape than anything. She exchanged pleasantries without thinking as she threaded through the crowd, making her way to the door that led to the hallway.

She didn't have to look behind her to know that Colin was there, following her, just far enough away not to draw attention.

Once she got out in the hallway, the chill of the air was a welcome relief compared to the heat of all the bodies in the auditorium. The sound of her heels clacking against the old wood floors echoed in the empty air. She headed down the hallway, away from the restrooms, toward the offices.

Within minutes, Colin emerged, looking up and down the hallway. She motioned to him silently and he followed.

She'd been coming to the town hall since she was five years old, when her uncle was mayor. She knew every room in the place. Glancing around to ensure they weren't seen, Emily opened a door marked Boiler Room and took him down a narrow flight of stairs. The door shut behind them.

"This is new," he said when they reached the bottom of the stairs. The room was warm, thanks to the furnace, and was strewn with various cleaning equipment, old cast-off furniture and bric-a-brac. "Do you come here often?"

She shrugged. "I wanted to talk to you and I didn't want anyone else to hear," she explained. "First off, you're right. I *was* hiding today."

"I know."

She rubbed her arms as if cold. This was so hard. "I don't sleep with people often," she said. "And this has gotten a little more complicated than I expected."

He sighed, leaning against the cinder block wall. "I tried to warn you," he said. "Before we did anything. I wasn't sure if you knew what you were getting into."

"I knew what I was getting into…if it was only the one night," Emily countered. "Then you showed up again, and suddenly it wasn't quite so simple."

"Are you sorry we did it?"

His voice was casual, deceptively so. But his green eyes blazed like emeralds in firelight.

She couldn't help it. She touched his face with her hand, stroking the harsh planes of his cheek. "Of course not," she said, and her sincerity rang in her voice.

He let out a breath, and she watched his body relax almost imperceptibly.

"But I wasn't expecting to feel this much," she admitted, and her voice sounded small.

He smiled then, and this time Colin was the one offering comfort. He took her into his arms, wrapping her in his embrace. She felt herself ease against him, enjoying the way his hands stroked down her back.

It felt wonderful. Beyond wonderful.

Soon, though, her body started remembering the night before, and the gentle, reassuring feel of him started to turn to something beyond mere comfort. He leaned his head down, tilting her head with a gentle nudge of his fingertips. Then he kissed her, softly at first, then with growing insistence.

She moaned against his mouth, feeling heat explode through her that had nothing to do with the furnace. Hunger tore at her, surprising her. Her hands slipped beneath his jacket, rubbing against his sweater impatiently. Then, without thinking, she sneaked beneath the waistband of his sweater and felt the hot flesh of his chest beneath her fingertips. He acknowledged her action with a sharp, pleased intake of breath.

He slipped off her jacket, letting it fall to the floor, and he opened the buttons of her blouse, just a few, until her lacy bra was revealed.

Emily knew it was foolish—there was a town meeting going on mere feet away, right up the stairs.

But nobody knows you're here, some wicked part of her mind reassured her, and then all thoughts ceased when Colin leaned down and took her nipple in his mouth, licking it through the lace. She gasped, arching her back to allow him better access. She felt as if she were on fire.

"I've been thinking of you all day," he said, his words burning against her skin. "I can't stop thinking about you."

"I can't stop thinking about you, either," she murmured, forcing his jacket off and rubbing the broad expanse of his shoulders. "You're amazing."

He grinned wolfishly. "I'm staying with you tonight," he said, pausing to see if she'd say no.

She thought about it. This was an opportunity she'd never get again… and one she'd dreamed of. Still, one thing needed to be clear.

"So you're not staying with Joy?" she heard herself ask and winced.

Colin looked puzzled for a second, then chuckled. "You weren't jealous of that lady, were you?"

She bit her lip. "I don't know. This is all new to me." She frowned at his obvious amusement. "And apparently she *is* your type."

He pressed a kiss against her neck, causing her heartbeat to race. "You're my type. You're perfect. Believe me—all I want is you."

She thrilled at the sound of his longing, and she held him tight, rubbing her body against his shamelessly.

"Why, Miss Stanfield," he said, easing off her blouse. "I

never would have guessed you'd be necking with that Reese boy in the town hall."

She felt wicked...and powerful. "That's not all I'm going to be doing," she said, producing a condom from her purse.

He blinked at her, and she laughed to find he was finally shocked. "Here?" he croaked.

She didn't say anything. Instead she unbuttoned her pants, inching the waistband down. "Unless you don't want me."

His eyes gleamed. Then he kissed her, hard, and she felt herself go damp between her legs. She'd never done anything so wanton, or reckless. And, honestly, she'd never done anything that felt so deliriously decadent.

He slipped a hand down her panties, his fingers sliding into her already slick opening, and she whimpered with pleasure.

"I want you," he whispered roughly, unbuttoning his pants and tugging them down. "Seems like I've always wanted you."

Emily knew how he felt. She let her pants and panties drop to the floor, standing there naked in front of him. "Then have me."

Colin groaned as she rolled the condom on his rock-hard erection and then leaned against the wall. He pressed against her, picking her up with his strong arms and hooking her legs around his waist. He entered her quickly, and she leaned her head against his shoulder, reveling in the feel of him filling her. *Fulfilling* her.

"Emily," he moaned, drawing back, then returning, slowly drawing the hard line of his shaft against her clit with deliberate motions.

She made soft sounds of excitement, surprising herself. This was crazy, she thought briefly.

This was *incredible*.

She locked her legs around his waist, pushing him in

deeper, and he started to increase in tempo. She felt the climax roar through her, shocking her with its swiftness and intensity. Emily cried out, and he quickly covered her mouth with his, swallowing her sounds of ecstasy. Shortly thereafter, she did the same as he groaned his pleasure against her, shuddering into her.

Long moments later, he was breathing hard against her neck. Clarity hit her in a wave.

"I can't believe this. We had sex in the town hall," she marveled, feeling a mix of embarrassment and abandon.

"And just think," he said, kissing her, "nobody up there will know."

She closed her eyes. "You bring out the strangest things in me," she admitted softly.

"Run along to the meeting," he told her. "I'm going back to the inn. I'll be waiting for you."

That sentence was a promise. They straightened out their clothes and crept upstairs. Emily could hear Tim trying futilely to get the group back to order. No one saw them leave the boiler room, and Colin shot her one last heated glance before leaving the building. She headed for the auditorium, checked her clothes one more time and went in, wondering if the truth of what had just happened would somehow be stamped on her like an invisible beacon.

To her surprise, some part of her did not care.

"All right, back to business," Tim said forcefully, and the crowd sat down, going quiet.

Sue stared at her quizzically. "Where were you?"

Emily didn't say anything, smiling silently. Through the rest of the town meeting she drifted in a dreamy state, letting the sensual anticipation build…knowing that, whatever else happened, she had at least one more unforgettable night ahead of her.

CHAPTER FIVE

COLIN STOOD nervously in the middle of Emily's living room. He wasn't sure why he was nervous—after all, he'd already had sex with Emily multiple times in the past twenty-four hours. Once in a public place, he thought with a surprised grin. He ought to be relaxed about all of it.

Hell, he ought to be exhausted. But somehow his body kept springing to attention at the mere thought of her.

What is going on here?

It was a question his conscience was raising more and more steadily during his extended stay in Tall Pines in general, and around Emily specifically. He still had a bizarre love-hate relationship with the town: it was adorable, picturesque and still managed to push every one of his buttons. Beyond that, despite the relative brevity of his relationships, he really wasn't all that fond of one-night flings, either.

So why her? And why here?

Colin shook his head. He didn't have any answers, and that worried him.

Instead of brooding, he busied himself readying the apartment for her. They'd left the place a mess after their romp last night—the sheets tangled in a sweaty knot on the bed, the thick down comforter on the floor, food left out on the countertop, empty champagne glasses on the coffee table. He laid a fire in the fireplace, warming the place and giving it the cozy, homey atmosphere he'd soaked up his first night there. He tidied up the kitchen and bedroom, washing the dishes, changing the sheets and turning down the bed. As a joke, he even put small foil-wrapped chocolates on the pillows. It *was* a hotel, after all. Then he considered how he should get himself ready.

Should he be waiting naked? That seemed crass—and even though it was obvious they were going to have sex, for whatever reason he didn't want her to think that was the *only* thing he wanted from her. He genuinely liked her as a person, though what he knew of her was limited to what he'd gleaned from a distance—they had lived separate lives growing up here. She'd always seemed unapproachable: the heiress apparent, the mayor's niece, the golden girl of Tall Pines. He couldn't understand her fascination with the small town. Or how she could manage to please so many people by doing everything so damned perfectly.

But he was starting to discover just how pleasing that perfection could be, Colin thought with a grin. Because last night and this morning—and this evening in the boiler room—she'd been, indeed, perfect. The thing that delighted him was that it had been so unexpected. He'd been reluctantly attracted to her for years, but now that he'd had her, the constant surprise of her, the hidden depths, kept intriguing him.

When she walked in, he was still grinning. "Hi, dear," he joked. "How was the rest of the—humph."

His sentence was cut off as Emily launched herself into his arms, pressing her heated, mobile mouth to his. Her tongue quickly darted out, tracing his lips before coaxing his own into some serious sensual fencing. His cock went from semihard to rock hard in a nanosecond. He pulled back, staring at her in amazement.

Her violet-blue eyes were like crushed wet velvet, deep and dark. She smiled at him. "I'm glad to be home," she said around a sigh.

"I'm glad you're home myself," he said, forgetting for a second that this wasn't actually *his* home.

Her responding look of happiness was like staring into the sun, and for a second he was blinded by her radiance. Then, without hesitation, she took off her glasses and started to strip, letting clothes drop to the floor.

"Whoa," he said, halting her as she had her blouse unbuttoned and was hastily moving to her jeans. "No rush here."

"I know," she murmured, "but the boiler room…well, let's just say it got my appetite going."

He knew how she felt. It had been quick and furtive and intense…and it made him want to do it again, only more slowly and thoroughly. Still, he hadn't thought that she'd simply walk in and they'd pick up where they left off. Not that he ought to be protesting. Maybe he was too tired. Hell, maybe he was getting too old.

Maybe you want to try talking to her. Figure out why she's different.

Colin ignored his conscience's low, insistent promptings. "Maybe I need a little breather." He then cursed himself mentally when her face fell. "Not from you. I'm working on about an hour's sleep and I want to make sure that I do a good job."

Her face eased into a comfortable smile. "Trust me, you're doing absolutely fine."

His muscles bunched eagerly, and he forced himself to

sit and calm down. He patted the sofa cushion next to him. "Come on. Why don't we talk for a bit? Ease into it."

Emily looked surprised but sat as he requested. She did leave her blouse open, though, revealing the delicate white lace bra he'd snacked on a mere hour ago. Her cleavage hung temptingly just a touch below eye level. She leaned against his shoulder, presenting her breasts like a display as her eyes gleamed innocently. "What did you want to talk about?"

Now? His mind went blank. "Uh…what have you been doing since I've been out of town?" he asked finally. "I mean, besides the hotel."

"I went to college," she murmured, moving sinuously so her body pressed against his. She placed a slow, delicate kiss in the hollow of his collarbone. "Got my degree in English Lit."

That schoolgirl thing again. He could picture her in the library, her hair pulled back, glasses low on her nose as she pored over a book…legs crossed in a short plaid skirt. His cock throbbed at the mere thought of it.

Easy, he chastised himself. "Couldn't wait to get back to Tall Pines, huh?" he asked, closing his eyes and reveling in the feel of her hand creeping under his sweater, her mouth brushing a lazy line of kisses along his jaw. He couldn't help it. His arm went around her shoulders, holding him to her, his hand smoothing down the tangled silk of her hair.

She paused in her sensual exploration, and he leaned down, nuzzling her neck in return. "Actually, I really liked college," she said slowly. "I even thought about going to grad school in England."

That stopped him. "Really?" The Tall Pines poster girl going off to Europe? "Why didn't you?"

Her eyes grew clouded. "My father got sick. Mom needed help. I knew where my responsibility was."

She sounded so sad. He cursed himself for bringing up the subject out of sheer ignorance. Still, it brought up another issue, and as long as the mood was already serious… "Then your father died," he said. "I'm sorry."

"So was I," she said, and with that Emily pulled away, closing her blouse with one hand, obviously not realizing what she was doing. Now he really felt like a heel. "Before he died, he reminded me that I was the last Stanfield in the line. I was with him in the hospital when he passed. My mother remarried two months later to a man named Ray, a longtime family friend. They moved to Florida. I'm sure your mother probably told you all about that."

His eyes rounded and he shook his head.

"It was a big scandal at the time," she explained, pulling her knees up to her chest and hugging them to her. "She wanted to sell the house and get the hell out of Tall Pines. Dad loved Tall Pines, and it meant so much to him for the mansion to stay in the family…. Anyway, I kept the house, made it a hotel and, well, here we are."

She shrugged, the sentence succinct and deliberately casual—and obviously covering a world of pain. She smiled, but it didn't reach her eyes.

"Suddenly I don't feel like talking." She put her head against his shoulder.

They sat that way, silent, for a moment. For all their sexual interplay, he'd never felt anything as disturbingly intimate as this moment, with a woman in his arms, quietly embracing him in front of a cheerful crackling fire on a snowy night. It was as if they were the only two people in the world.

Colin didn't know what it was about this woman—and suddenly he didn't care. All he knew was she was special and he was going to stop analyzing and start enjoying.

He tilted her head back, kissing her sweetly. "We were far too rushed there in the town hall," he pointed out.

She giggled, then looked at him solemnly. "Definitely."

"I don't think I can go five times again tonight," he said, "but I think I can make one time really, really memorable."

She pursed her lips, teasing. "I suppose the least I could do is let you try."

He tugged her blouse the rest of the way off, then opened the front clasp of her bra, freeing her lovely breasts. Despite the warmth of the fire, her nipples were puckered and pointed. Topless, she undid the button of his fly, unzipping it and moving her nimble fingers through the gap in his boxers, releasing his cock. Her fingers circled him, and he groaned, pressing forward lightly as a drop of moisture escaped the tip in anticipation.

She leaned down, licking around the head in a tantalizing gesture, then stroked the shaft with steady, gliding pressure. His hips arched again against her palm. "Damn, woman," he breathed. "What are you doing to me?"

"If you don't know, maybe I'm not doing it right."

"Oh, you're doing it fine," he said. "Let's see if I can't catch you up."

He eased off the rest of her clothes, leaving them on a heap on the floor, then rested her against the smooth suede-like fabric of her sofa. "We've already done the floor," he explained, and she laughed. Colin stripped off his clothes and stood naked in front of her, as she parted her legs and waited expectantly.

He shook his head. "Not so fast, remember?" He positioned himself between her thighs but didn't move to enter her. Instead he teased her breasts with his tongue, tracing a wet, winding path around her rib cage and belly button, stroking her nipples with his fingertips. He felt Emily's fingers wind through his hair, heard the way her breathing grew short and choppy. He moved lower, heading for her moist heat, and she tightened her thighs against him.

Slowly he used his fingertips to gently coax her legs apart. She was already wet and ready for him, but her eyes looked nervous. Obviously this wasn't something she'd done very often, and he felt anger on her behalf. She deserved to be lavished over.

He was going to rectify that situation.

He dipped his tongue in, licking at her clit, gently at first, then with growing insistence. Her breathing went ragged and hoarse, her hands bunching into fists against the sofa. She moved against him in jerky, reflexive motions, as if the sheer sensation of what he was doing was more than she could control. Keeping his tongue in motion, he deliberately pressed one finger inside her, then another, searching for the corresponding spot inside.

He knew when he found it. She cried out, a sound of joyous surprise, and she lifted her body to meet his seeking mouth.

He kept up the pace, feeling her pressing against him, tasting the honeyed wash of her response. She was panting, short gasps of sexual exertion. She smoothed her hands over her breasts, exciting him as he watched her obvious enjoyment of her own flesh as well as his tender ministrations.

"Colin," she breathed. *"Colin!"*

He felt her body clench against his fingers, and he almost came on the spot.

When the shudders finished, he clumsily put on a condom, intent on entering her, but before he could, she pressed against his shoulders, surprising him enough to push him on his back. Slick and smooth from her release, she impaled herself on him, and he felt the taut snugness of her envelop him, creating an almost unbearable friction.

Then she started to move, rocking against him with the slightest twist to her hips. Caressing him and carrying him to a frenzy of sensation.

He lost control, plunging into her as she rode him with abandon. He clutched at her hips, drawing her to him, and she pushed back with answering intensity. Before he knew it, the climax roared through him like a wildfire. He sat up, holding her to him even as he buried himself in her welcoming warmth, and she wrapped her legs and arms around him in response.

In the aftermath, they were both breathing hard, clinging to each other like the survivors of a storm…and it was a sort of storm, he realized.

"You do the strangest things to me," he said when he could at last find his voice.

"This is a week I'll certainly never forget." She laughed unsteadily.

And that's when it hit him.

He'd stopped thinking of it as simply a few nights. He was thinking forever. Colin didn't know why or how, but there it was.

I'm supposed to go to Paris, he thought. *I've got a career I love, a building project that's starting, people counting on me. I've got a life that suits me perfectly.*

The last thing he needed was a relationship with a woman who had dedicated her life to a town that he'd spent years trying to escape. Especially when he had no idea how his life and her life could possibly fit together…

* * *

THE OTTER LODGE annual gift exchange was a running joke and one of Emily's favorite town traditions—and considering the buffet of traditions the town of Tall Pines had to choose from, that was saying something. It had all started about twenty years ago—which was recent for a tradition, by Tall Pines standards—when the men of the Otter Lodge had complained to each other about several of the gifts they'd received for Christmas. Seeing that "one man's trash was another man's treasure," they'd devised a "gift exchange" where people could swap, steal, and otherwise have a great deal of fun with small gift items. It was a way of prolonging the holiday and also of celebrating Christmas with friends rather than the small family gatherings that typically prevailed. It was also usually rowdy, liberally doused with the infamous and heavily alcohol-laced Otter punch and, all in all, a rousing good time.

Emily's father hadn't approved of the gift exchange initially, thinking it lacked decorum. It was the one tradition above all others that her mother had refused to attend—even though she'd made a point of bowing to Emily's father's wishes and was a central figure of all the other town functions. But from the first time she was allowed to go, at sixteen years old, Emily had reveled wide-eyed in the spectacle.

She was wearing a pair of black jeans, a burgundy turtleneck sweater and a large paper top hat festooned with a flower.

"What are you exchanging?" the head of the Otter Lodge, John Lambert, asked with a wink.

Emily held up her gift, grinning broadly. Actually, it hadn't been a gift—at this point, people tended to buy the most outrageous "gifts" and concoct stories about them, and that, too, was part of the tradition.

"What have we here?" Phil crowed into the microphone,

causing people to pause momentarily in their carousing. "An adult-size set of full-body pajamas with feet!"

There was a resounding drunken cheer at this. He opened the package, holding it up. Much like an infant's "footie" pajamas, it buttoned up from the crotch to the neck and had slip-resistant rubber soles on the feet. It was baby-blue and looked as if it could fit a six-foot man easily.

"It's even got a back door, folks!" Phil pointed out, unbuttoning the flap that covered the backside. This brought an even louder round of applause. "Now who's going to want *this* beauty?"

Emily grinned as several venerable members of the Otter Lodge quickly went to work bargaining for the pajamas, offering her their awful gifts: a battery-powered egg sheller, chocolate-covered ants and, finally, edible boxers.

"I'll go with the boxers," she said, tucking her exchanged gift under her arm as the seventy-year-old man promptly started to try the pajamas on over his regular clothes, to much hilarity. People started catcalling about her choice, and she made comments back. "Hey! You never know. I might need them!"

"Woo-hoo! Better watch it, Tim!" Phil said. "That Emily Stanfield's a live one!"

Emily blushed, as usual, but more because he'd mentioned Tim than because of the gift. This was why her parents had hated the gift exchange. It was classless, tasteless and often a bit risqué.

In short, it was everything a Stanfield *wasn't* supposed to be.

I wonder if that's why I like it so much?

Emily frowned. Strange, she'd never really thought about it in that light before.

She blamed this latest epiphany on Colin. She felt as though she'd been living on autopilot for the past few years, going through the motions of being a Tall Pines Stanfield without ever really looking at why she was doing what she was doing. She was discomfited now to discover that, even after studying it carefully, she *still* didn't know why she was doing some of the things she was doing. Other than Stanfield duty, of course.

Ordinarily that was enough.

You're just feeling restless.

She smiled. She blamed that sensation on Colin, as well. And thanked him for it.

Her ex-fiancé, Rick, a man of exceptional breeding if not much imagination, had been a nice enough guy but, comparatively speaking, a lousy lover. And her high school boyfriend, Billy Rothchild, had been a virgin, just as she had. What they'd lacked in finesse they'd made up for in sheer enthusiasm…and now that she knew the difference, Emily realized enthusiasm didn't count for a whole lot.

She wasn't in high school anymore. While she liked sex a great deal, she'd managed to go without for two whole years.

I'm glad I waited. It made her experience with Colin that much sweeter.

Of course, he might be leaving any day. The roads were cleared, the blizzard was over. He could be gone by tonight.

Don't think about it. She focused instead on the edible underwear, made out of what looked like pressed dried fruit leather. She would have a great time trying it out on Colin when she got home.

"Emily!"

She looked up to see Mayor Tim flagging her down, with

the Reeses in tow. "Hi, Tim," she replied, then hugged Ava and Harry Reese, feeling guilty.

Hi, I've been sleeping with your son.

"Thank you so much for taking care of our son," Ava said without preamble.

Emily blinked. "Sorry?"

"In your hotel," Ava clarified, and Emily felt her heart start beating again. For a brief second she'd thought that Ava had found out about exactly where Colin was staying in the hotel—specifically their sleeping arrangements. "Especially when you had to put up so many other people. I hate to admit it, but the hotel really has been a success."

Emily laughed. Ava went red-faced.

"That sounded awful, didn't it?" she fussed. "I didn't mean that I wanted you to fail. I just… I mean…"

"It's hard to see things change, I know," Emily said gently. Despite Ava's relentless tenacity, she really was a sweet woman.

"You live in a town like this because it doesn't change. Not really," Ava said, holding her husband's hand and giving it a squeeze. He kissed her temple. For a second Emily was struck by their tenderness toward each other. They seemed like polar opposites—she was talkative and outgoing, he was retiring and wry—but somehow they made a perfect match. "We love it here. We always thought we'd settle down, raise our kids here, watch our grandkids grow around us."

It did sound nice, Emily thought.

"If only Colin saw things the same way," Ava finished with a frustrated gesture. "He didn't stay with that blond woman, did he? That friend of yours?"

"No," Emily reassured her. "I know for a fact that he didn't."

"Has she gone home?"

"No, she's here through the New Year at least," Emily said. Joy had extended her reservation, she was having such a good time.

"Did Colin tell you he's moving to Paris?"

"It did come up," Emily demurred.

"Why so far away, is what I want to know," Ava carped. "When he's got family and comfort and…and home right here."

Emily bit her lip. "Maybe he's looking for something else," she ventured, wondering herself why he hated Tall Pines so much. Sure, it was a little town. And quirky. And it had a lot of traditions. And, yeah, it really was pretty knee-jerk about any sort of change.

Okay. Maybe she *could* see why someone who loved living larger than life might not be so keen on Tall Pines. And he definitely lived on a larger scale, no doubt about it. Even as a teen, the town hadn't been big enough to contain him. The sheer artistry of his elaborate pranks alone had bordered on creative genius. When he'd won a full scholarship to architectural school, the townsfolk had been shocked.

Not Emily. Colin had been destined for great things and had planned to leave Tall Pines if he'd had to shoot himself out on a rocket.

"Something better than this?" Ava asked, astounded. "What else is there?"

Before Emily could answer, Colin walked up, a glass of punch in one hand and a scowl on his face. "I got a Chia Pet." He held up a small clay figurine that looked like a sheep.

"Nice," Emily observed, tongue-in-cheek.

He ran his tongue along his teeth, amused. "It was this or some kind of Super Orgasm hot chocolate. From the *reverend,* if you can believe it."

Emily giggled. "Imagine going to Paris and leaving all this behind."

He grinned reluctantly. Ava pounced on the expression. "See? I told you this would be fun!"

Instantly the grin slid from his face like a blackboard being erased. "Mom…"

"I know, I know," she grumbled. But she didn't look deterred.

"Your mother was thanking Emily for putting you up over at the hotel," Harry Reese said quickly, eager to patch over the awkward break.

Emily blushed. "It's my job."

"Well, you do your job well," Harry said. It might have been the longest conversation she'd ever had with the man with Ava present. "Everyone knows that the hotel is one of the best things to happen to Tall Pines. We don't know what we'd do without you."

Emily had been trying hard not to stare at Colin—and equally hard not to look as if she were trying hard not to stare. Harry's comment surprised her. "Well, I doubt you'll ever have to find out. I imagine I won't be going anywhere."

"Naturally you wouldn't, dear," Ava clucked. "You're the last Stanfield. Where would you go?"

Emily sneaked a look at Colin. The scowl was back in full force. "So, Colin…"

"I'm getting some more punch," he said, sounding truculent. "Then I think I'll walk over to the hotel."

"Are you all right, dear?"

"I have a headache." He turned and walked toward the refreshment table.

Ava huffed impatiently. "He really needs to loosen up more," she observed to her husband. The two of them went off to dance.

Emily waited, then followed Colin to the table. Sidling up next to him, careful not to stand too close, she whispered, "Wait till you see what I got from the gift exchange. It's a lot better than a Chia Pet."

"Listen, I have to get out of here."

She'd been expecting some playful banter, and his serious tone gave her pause. "You okay?"

"Holiday hangover," he said bitterly. "I'm leaving."

Emily frowned. His tone sounded…final. "Are you going to be in my apartment when I get back?" she asked in a soft voice.

He finally looked at her, and his eyes seemed haunted. "Honestly," he replied in an equally soft voice, "I don't know."

With that, he walked away. All she could do was watch him, wondering what had caused the abrupt change…and feeling bereft. Of all the ways for their brief affair to end, this was one she had not anticipated.

WALKING IN THE CRISP, snow-covered landscape, Colin felt like ten kinds of an idiot. There was something about the very air in Tall Pines that seemed to bring out the prime jackass in him, and this vacation was obviously no exception. He had no excuse—and really no idea why he kept succumbing to the bad humors that plagued him whenever he set foot in the city limits, but there it was.

The gift exchange had been sort of fun, and he'd spent some more time with his family without getting into the vicious downward cycle of "Why won't you move home?" He'd been holding up rather well. But when his mother pointed out that Emily would never leave Tall Pines, and Emily had readily and without any thought agreed, he'd suddenly felt a sharp and unbelievable sense of loss—all the sharper because it was so unexpected.

Apparently his subconscious had been working over-time, subversively contemplating a future with Emily Stanfield, even though everything between them had been sexual and deliberately temporary. Even though he'd warned himself not to get involved because to even begin to consider it was the ultimate foolishness.

He lifted his face to the slate-colored sky. It wasn't snowing right at the moment, but the wind was chill and biting, scraping at his cheeks over the edges of his scarf.

"What are you doing out here?"

He looked over his shoulder and saw Emily walking after him. She'd removed the silly paper hat she'd been wearing at the Otter Lodge and now was bundled up in a black leather jacket, a thick black wool hat and matching scarf. Her black leather gloves completed the ensemble.

She looked less like a schoolteacher and more like a hit woman, and he watched her approach with equal dread.

"You can't honestly expect to drop a bomb like that on me and walk away," she said, her voice colder than the wind whipping through the town square.

"You shouldn't be out here," he dodged, stuffing his hands into his coat pockets. "People might see us together, make some assumptions."

"I don't give a damn," she retorted cavalierly, but all the same, he noticed her glancing around. Almost everyone was either still in the Otter Lodge partying or in their houses, safely tucked away from the cold. "We need to talk."

He let out an annoyed huff that came out as a puff of steam. "I shouldn't have stalked off like that," he conceded.

"You think?" Her eyes pierced him like arrows. "I know we're just having a little fling here, but I do think I expected more than a sudden and inexplicable mood swing, starting with you getting pissy and ending with you telling me that I might not ever see you again."

He winced. He *had* done that, hadn't he?

"What is your *problem,* Reese?" she said sharply. "I swear, you act like Tall Pines is Alcatraz and you're building a tunnel. I know you've been all over the world and love your glamorous women, your traveling, your parties and your high life, but what exactly is so damned wrong with living in a small town?"

"Nothing, okay?" Colin barked back, feeling cornered. "There is *nothing* wrong with living in Tall Pines. It's beautiful. The people are nice. They're concerned about each other. When something happens to one person, everyone knows about it."

"So that's the big deal?" she pressed. "You don't like the fact that we've got nosy neighbors? That they can be invasive?"

He rubbed at his eyes, the chill of his own leather gloves dulled by the numbness of his face. "It's not that."

"So what is it?" She crossed her arms like an impatient and demanding goddess.

"It's not Tall Pines. It's *me.*"

She stared at him, looking confused.

"It's perfect here," he said. "It's beautiful. It's what everybody always wanted—ideal, pristine. People care. It's home."

Emily still stared, silent.

"And I never wanted it," he said. "I never, ever fit in here. And I felt like an outcast and a loser for not wanting it."

Her expression softened slightly. "Colin…"

"No, let me finish." He gritted his teeth. "When I was in high school, I didn't have many friends. But the few friends I did have formed a sort of club. We called it the Escape Committee."

She smiled.

"We were so eager to get out of Tall Pines it was almost stupid," he continued. "And we all did get out. I got in trouble a lot, sure, but I always got good grades. Not because I necessarily loved school, but every day I was here I felt more miserable and I knew college was a ticket out."

Colin couldn't look at her, couldn't stand seeing the sympathy shining on her face when he knew there really wasn't any way she could understand. Cold seeped into his bones that had nothing to do with the weather.

"This probably all sounds ridiculous and melodramatic," he said, kicking at a snowdrift with his foot. "But every time I'm home and someone points out to me how wonderful it is here and asks why I don't want to live here, I suddenly seem to revert to being eighteen years old and feeling like a complete and utter freak."

"Colin." She reached out, putting a gloved hand on his shoulder.

He didn't shrug the comforting touch off, but he didn't step closer to her, either. "So that's my story," he said bitterly. "Stupid, huh?"

"Small-town life is not for everybody," she said. "Just because people here think it's perfect doesn't mean it is."

He shrugged, feeling juvenile—and yet still hurting. "Don't *you* think it's perfect?" he couldn't help asking.

She laughed. "Hardly. Everybody here lives in each other's pockets. If I sneeze when I get out of bed in the morning, Hank Salvatore over at the post office usually sends over some vitamin C with my mail, you know?"

He smiled reluctantly.

"And there's always the petty bickering. It's more like being part of a really big family." She shrugged. "It's not perfect, but it's home."

"That's the thing," he said. "I don't feel like it's home."

She stood next to him, silent, for a moment. Then she said, "That's what you're looking for, isn't it? That's why you move around so much." Emily paused. "You're looking for home."

He didn't say anything. He was surprised by her observation—the fact that she'd figured it out and the fact that he never had.

Without glancing around to see if they were being observed, she reached forward and hugged him. Even though her mere proximity tended to bring out a sexual zing, this felt warm...comforting.

Cozy.

He took her proffered warmth, holding her tightly to him.

"I hope you find what you're looking for," she whispered against his ear.

He held tighter for a moment before letting her go. "Let's head back to the hotel. I'm freezing off various parts of my anatomy that I know you've expressed an appreciation for."

She chuckled softly, falling into step next to him, tromping through the thick snow.

As they walked, Colin found himself still drifting in contemplation. "I have to ask," he finally said. "What makes this home for you? How do you feel living here?"

She blinked. "I don't know. I've never really thought about it."

"You love the traditions," he prompted, feeling a weight start to bear down on his chest. "You love the community."

"Some of the traditions, most of the people," she said with a wry smile. "It's a nice town."

But there was something there—some hesitation. He didn't want to pry. Oh, hell, yes, he *did*. He wanted to understand what bound her there.

He didn't want to think about why he wanted to understand.

"I guess the more I lived here, the harder it seemed to picture living anywhere else," she admitted.

That wasn't enthusiasm, he thought, with a creeping feeling of triumph, that was simply *inertia*.

"So," he asked casually, "maybe you'd be happy living somewhere else?"

"I don't know." Now she sounded troubled around the edges of her voice. "Still, what are the odds of my moving?"

They got to the hotel, and Phillip the night manager was there, shoveling the steps. He saw the two of them and smirked knowingly.

"Hey, Phillip," Emily said, either not noticing or ignoring his smugness. "How are things going?"

"The roads are clear," he informed them. "The sheriff dropped by with the latest news. Most of the strays have already gotten into their cars and left." He glared pointedly at Colin, as if to say, *So what are you waiting for?*

Emily and Colin walked into the hotel, going to the elevator and heading for her apartment on the top floor. Emily didn't say a word, but Colin knew what she was thinking.

"I don't have to be in Paris until after the new year," he said carefully. "That's a whole two days away. If you don't mind putting me up until then?"

She smiled. "No," she said quietly. "Two more days would suit me just fine."

With that, she finally kissed him, the heat of her mouth

a jarring counterpoint to the cold of his skin. His blood pumped hot and fierce.

Two more days. Two more nights.

How am I going to leave her when the new year's over?

CHAPTER SIX

IT WAS THE LAST night of the year and the last night she'd be able to spend with Colin. And yet here she was dressing up to go out on a date with Mayor Tim.

Emily suspected that might be ironic somehow. It certainly felt like irony—going out on a date with the man whom it made the most sense to marry before indulging in one last night of ecstasy with the man least likely to be a husband.

She slipped on diamond earrings, checking her makeup in the mirror. Her black long-sleeved dress had a plunging back, looking both elegant and sexy, depending on where you stood. She'd bought it months ago, long before she'd even seen Colin. Or agreed to a date with Tim, for that matter.

She walked out into the living room. Colin was sitting on her couch, looking irritated.

"I suppose it would be selfish of me to ask you to cancel," he said, his voice detached.

"I have to go," she said. "Stanfields always go to the Holiday Ball. It's tradition."

It felt like an excuse. Probably because it was.

"But do they always go with the single, eligible mayor that everyone is trying to marry off?"

The sourness of his tone made her survey him with a quirked eyebrow. "That didn't sound selfish. That sounded jealous."

He grimaced. "You're right. I guess I am jealous."

Even as part of her heart thrilled at that admission, she crossed her arms, mentally schooling herself not to read into the statement. *What's he going to do? Stay here forever?*

Still, the hungry, sad look in his eye melted her heart, and she went over to him, putting her arms around him.

"I can promise you it'll be an early night. This isn't a real date, it doesn't mean anything. He won't even get to first base."

His hand tickled down her bare back, sending a shiver skittering over her nerve endings. "With a dress like this, I'm sure he'll try."

"It's not like that between Tim and me," she said, forcing herself not to curl like a cat against his palm. If she did, she might never get out of here. "It's…I don't know…like we're brother and sister."

"I never wanted to ask my sister out on a date."

She leaned back, feeling irritation warring with desire. "I want you, you know that."

He smiled, warming up. "And I want you."

"But after tonight you're going," she said quietly. "Remem-ber?"

He fell silent.

"I have to live here. More importantly, I'm going to have a life here—without you. I don't know what it is we've got going between us, but whatever it is ends tomorrow. I can promise you I don't sleep around easily and I would never sleep with anyone else while I'm sleeping with you. But I do have to plan for life after you leave."

"And Tim is part of this plan, is he?"

"I don't know," she answered honestly.

"You said he was like your brother." Colin sounded puzzled. "How could you be happy with a life like that? Without passion?"

She stared into his eyes, willing him to understand. "I don't know if I can be. But if the alternative is living alone, waiting for some grand love affair that never shows up—or one who lives thousands of miles away," she said pointedly, "then maybe I can settle for a good lifelong friendship that might shift into something more comfortable."

He looked at her, shaking his head. "That's the other thing I can't stand about this town," he muttered. "You're all against taking risks."

Emily didn't like the way he was suddenly lumping her in with all the things he didn't like about Tall Pines. She stood up, slipping on her high heels with sharp, jerky motions.

"I took a risk with you," she finally retorted.

"Not enough to let anybody know about us."

"Know what about us?" Her voice had raised, and she clamped down on her anger before their disagreement could explode into a full-blown fight. Which, considering she rarely fought with anyone and they weren't even in a relationship, was sort of shocking in and of itself. "Know that I've slept with you without even a date? Know that I was desperate enough to have a fling with a man who can't seem to leave this place fast enough and wouldn't move back with a gun to his head?"

She tossed a lipstick and her keys into a small clutch purse. "You tell me, Colin. Exactly how should I have advertised whatever 'we' seem to have?"

He walked up behind her, tugging her into his arms.

She resisted, anger still burning through her, underscored by humiliation.

My father would be so ashamed of me.

She closed her eyes against the pain of that observation.

Colin was insistent, though, finally holding her in a careful embrace. "I'm sorry," he said softly. "I'm sorry. You're absolutely right. I've got no reason whatsoever to be jealous or to take it out on you. I'm sorry."

She didn't say anything. Instead she leaned her head against his shoulder.

"I might not like the town. But I like you. More than I realized, until tonight. More than I thought I could, especially in such a short period of time."

At that, she laughed weakly. "Well, technically, we've known each other for years."

"Not like this." He tipped her chin up, pressing a slow, gentle kiss against her pliant lips. "It's more than physical. I feel like I've gotten to know you better in the past week than in the past ten years."

"I know," she marveled.

"I don't want you to feel like what we're doing is something you should be embarrassed about," he said, looking deep into her eyes.

She couldn't help it. She looked away.

She heard him growl softly with frustration, and he rubbed his chin over the top of her head as he held her tight. "This is more than just a fling," he said. "You've got to know that."

Emily wanted to believe it. But wasn't that the characteristic of a good fling? Feeling as though it would go on forever—and at the same time that intensity of knowing that it was going to end abruptly?

She'd never had one before, but that was what she'd always assumed—and whatever she had with Colin seemed to be no exception.

"I know it's selfish—and jealous," he said. "But I don't want you to go out tonight. Not out with some other man."

She shook her head, pulling herself gently away. "How many times do I have to tell you? It's not like that. It's not anything."

"It's enough," he argued.

Her phone rang and she answered it gratefully. "Hello?"

"Hi, Em," Tim said cheerfully. "I'm downstairs, ready for our date."

She winced at the term. "Okay. Let me get my coat on. I'll be down in a minute." She hung up, then looked up at Colin.

"I'll be back soon," she said. "And if you still want to enjoy our last night together, then we will. But I'm not putting my life on hold for you, Colin. Not when I know this can't go anywhere."

With that, Emily walked out the door, feeling a lot less sure than she sounded…especially when she had to turn her back on the gorgeous man staring at her each step of the way.

"THIS OUGHT TO BE fun," Joy enthused. "Thanks so much for asking me. I've been dying to check out the town's festivals—and I hear the Holiday Ball is one of their favorite occasions."

"No problem," Colin said, adjusting his tie.

This was probably a bad idea, but he was trying to prove a point. Seeing Emily walk out the door tonight felt wrong. Even though she'd assured him that nothing would happen—and correctly pointed out that it wasn't his business if anything did happen—it still felt wrong.

He wanted a relationship with her. He had no idea how that was going to work, but he knew damned well that it wasn't going to work at all if she insisted on dating other guys. Call him funny, but he felt pretty strongly about that.

"Am I dressed okay?"

He looked at Joy. She was dressed to kill in a midnight-blue velvet cocktail dress that left little to the imagination. Her blond hair was pulled up in a sexy chignon.

"You're stunning," he said. "You'll be the talk of the party."

More to the point, *they* would be the talk of the party, he thought as they walked into the mayor's mansion, where the Holiday Ball was held. The beautiful out-of-towner with the town's notoriously commitment-shy black sheep. It would probably be Tall Pines's juiciest gossip of the night. There was no way Emily wouldn't hear about it.

If she couldn't understand how he felt, then he'd have to give her a taste of her own medicine. She'd see how it felt to watch someone you cared about in the arms of someone else, platonic or not.

"Well, Colin!" Evelyn Albee was working the door, signing people in. "Of all the people I expected to see here, I certainly wasn't expecting you. And who's your lovely companion?"

"This is Joy Webster. She's a guest over at the hotel," he said, paying the entrance fee. "She had nothing to do tonight, so we figured we'd enjoy the party."

"They've outdone themselves this year," she said as she checked in their coats—and took a long, scrutinizing look at Joy's dress—or lack thereof. "You two have a good time."

"We plan to," he replied with a wink.

If that didn't get tongues wagging, nothing would.

He led Joy into the room, and for a split second the sound was reduced to a murmur as they walked in. He felt uncomfortably conspicuous and remembered abruptly why he particularly disliked these town functions. He was a bit of an introvert by nature, and while business had toughened him up, he still didn't love being in a loud and noisy crowd.

Especially now. After the initial surprise, people descended on the two of them like hawks on baby chickens.

"Colin!" This from Mr. Rutledge, one of the oldest and most venerable of the town's citizens. "It's been years! What have you been doing with yourself? And more importantly, who's this pretty lady?"

Colin introduced Joy around, and she was winning, charming and very, very outgoing—something of a relief, since it took the pressure off him. He endured several winks and nudges. Automatically, it seemed, they'd paired the two off. The place was probably ripe with conjecture: Were they having an affair? Had Colin Reese finally fallen in love?

The damned thing being he was pretty sure he *had* fallen in love. Just not with Joy Webster.

"I wasn't expecting to see you here."

He turned at the masculine comment, only to find that the mayor himself had made the comment…and Emily was right there by his side.

"I'm getting that a lot tonight," Colin said, his voice wry. "We didn't have anything else to do and thought we'd drop by."

"Emily, this is fantastic," Joy gushed. "And your town does stuff like this all the time? It's like being transported into a Norman Rockwell painting!"

"So glad we're entertaining," Emily said.

Joy looked taken aback by Emily's chilly demeanor. "I'm not being condescending. I mean it. I love it here."

Her sincerity must have made Emily feel guilty. "I'm sorry," she said. "Sometimes people get the mistaken impression that because we're quaint, we're also hicks, and they write Tall Pines off as a lame small town."

Colin was the one who felt guilty, even though Emily hadn't glanced his way once as she'd made the comment.

"Beautiful, sure. But lame?" Joy shook her head. "What idiot would think this gorgeous little place was lame?"

Now Emily looked at Colin. He cleared his throat, uncomfortable.

"I could live here," Joy enthused, smiling brightly. Colin stared at her, surprised. He knew that she was bubbly by nature, but he hadn't realized just how much she really loved the small town. "This has been just the change of pace I've been looking for…and I didn't know how badly I needed it until I got here." She gave Colin's arm a squeeze.

"Well, I'm glad *you're* having a good time," Emily replied.

There it was again—that tone. This time Joy didn't pick up on it, but Colin felt it like an ice pick in his chest.

"Could you direct me to the ladies' room? I want to make sure my hair's okay," Joy asked Emily, and Emily excused herself, leaving Colin with Tim.

"It's good to see you here tonight," Tim said, taking a sip of his drink. "Your parents are such huge supporters of the town, and I know they miss seeing you."

Colin felt like a world-class jerk. "It's good to be here," he responded, trying hard not to sound like a sham.

"And that's some date," Tim said, letting out a low, appreciative whistle. "Your mom always said you dated supermodels."

"She's an acquaintance," Colin pointed out quickly. "Someone I met at the inn. She didn't have anything to do, so I thought I'd take her out for a bit. Nothing more than that."

Tim's face showed he wasn't buying it. "Must be nice. Living the dream, huh?"

"What about you?" Colin said. "Here you are, mayor for two terms and you're just, what, thirty-six?" He paused. "And now dating Emily."

"Yeah," Tim said, taking another sip. "It's all falling into place. The thing is, she's like royalty around here. Not to mention she'd be a perfect politician's wife."

Colin stared at him, aghast. "You're going to *marry* her?"

The crowd went quiet at that statement. Tim rubbed at his temples with his fingertips.

"Why does everyone feel compelled to yell that particular observation?" he asked, sounding embarrassed yet amused. "I don't know if I'm going to marry her. All I know is we're good friends, I haven't met anybody who fits the bill better and she'd be a great politician's wife. That doesn't necessarily mean she'd be *my* great politician's wife."

"But you're trying it on," Colin supplied, feeling ire bubble through his bloodstream. He strongly repressed the urge to clock good old Tim with a strong right hook.

"No. *She's* trying it on," Tim corrected, and Colin didn't feel any better. "Despite what town gossip spreads, we're just friends."

Colin felt his heart rate slowly calm back down. Until Tim's next statement.

"For now, anyway," he amended. "By Valentine's Day, I imagine, we'll know if it's more than that."

Colin saw red, and it had nothing to do with Valentine's.

Joy returned to them, but Emily was nowhere to be seen. "Where's Emily?" he asked.

Joy looked at them, puzzled. "She said she needed to get some fresh air. I think she headed out for the balcony."

"Fresh air?" Tim sounded aghast. "It's twenty degrees out!"

"Will you excuse me?" Colin said. "I, er, need to...use the restroom."

With that lame exit, he left Joy happily chatting with Mayor Tim, who looked flustered at the beautiful blonde's attentions. Colin quickly went in search of Emily, who no doubt didn't feel the cold. She had fury to keep her warm.

EMILY WANDERED THE upstairs hallway. She'd gone out on the balcony, but without a coat, the below-freezing weather had turned her back. Still, for a second the cold air had been a welcome balm on her burning skin. She wasn't burning with embarrassment, she was red-hot with indignation.

How dare he!

She'd been miserable most of the night, despite Tim's obvious efforts at being a good host and fun date. The problem was she'd felt *guilty* at leaving Colin alone. At treating him like a booty call, some kind of convenient sex toy. She tried to soothe her bruised conscience by telling herself that the arrangement was one they'd both agreed to, the sex was phenomenal, but he was leaving and there was no way they could have anything more permanent.

Nonetheless, she'd still felt lousy.

Then, all of a sudden, she'd heard the buzzing of people around her at the ball, at around the same time she'd been about to plead a headache and head back to the hotel and Colin's supposed waiting arms. Only to find that he had gone and asked Joy Webster, her guest and his "type," to come to the Holiday Ball instead.

Apparently waiting wasn't really his thing.

Jealousy reared its ugly head, but it was dwarfed by the magnitude of her anger at his attempts to manipulate her. The statement he was trying to make was patently obvious: what was good for the goose, aka Emily, was good for the gander. Otherwise known as Colin. And Joy was giving Colin and the rest of the guests a real gander with that dress.

That wasn't nice, especially since she actually *liked* Joy. But she still felt the fires of competition, which was stupid, since it wasn't as if she could keep Colin anyway—he was leaving. Tomorrow, in fact. Therefore, he wasn't even hers to fight for.

She gritted her teeth, rubbing the back of her neck, the base of her skull. At this rate, she wasn't going to have to fake that headache.

"Emily?"

"Oh, great. Just the person I needed to see," she said sarcastically, turning her back on Colin as he hurried toward her. "You didn't abandon Joy, did you?"

"I had to find you," he said. "I needed to explain."

Her eyes widened. "You've got an *explanation* for this?"

"Yeah." He stroked her shoulder. "I'm an idiot."

"I knew that!" She jerked away from him.

"I only asked her because I wanted you to know how I felt," he confessed. "That's small, I know. But I hated seeing you go off with another guy."

She bit her lip. "I didn't like seeing you with Joy," she admitted.

"Thank God for that." He tentatively put an arm around her shoulders, and she didn't move away. He pressed a quick kiss on her temple, and she felt her headache recede. "I ran into Joy in the dining room, and she said that she wished she was doing something tonight, and I thought I'd ask her here.

That way, she'd have something to do, and you'd finally realize why I was so upset when you left with Tim."

Put that way, it didn't sound half as selfish and petty as she wanted to believe it was.

Colin paused, irritation crossing his handsome face. "Did you know the mayor's thinking about marrying you?"

She rubbed at her eyes. "Actually, yeah."

"And you're *okay* with that?" Colin sounded outraged.

"It's only come up the once," Emily said lamely.

Colin stared at her intently. "I want you, Emily."

Her body reacted like a furnace kicking on. "I want you, too," she whispered.

"But more than that," he said, holding her in a loose embrace. "I care about you. I can't believe how much or how quickly…but I do."

Now the heat in her body settled into a strong, steady warmth in her chest. "I care about you, too. It's weird, isn't it?"

He laughed, hugging her. "Yeah. It's pretty strange."

They stood like that, hugging casually. She rested her head against his chest, hearing his strong, steady heartbeat pulsing beneath her ear.

"You did all this just to get even with me," she said, and she heard his low chuckle reverberate through his rib cage.

"I never said I was the sharpest knife in the drawer."

She laughed, too. "Well, it worked. When you walked in with her, I was furious. I've never been so jealous in my life."

He leaned down, expertly pressing a kiss on the nape of her neck and causing her to gasp at the sensation. "Now you know how I felt. The idea of anybody else touching you…"

She hated the thought of it. Of him touching Joy. Or anybody.

For that matter, of anybody else touching her.

You're getting in way too deep.

"You're still leaving tomorrow," she said softly as his kisses grew more insistent, tracing down the exposed flesh of her back. His hands followed the path his mouth took, as if smoothing his kisses into her skin.

"I know." He sighed, pulling away.

"So we've only got tonight."

"I know," he repeated.

She paused. "I was going to tell Tim I wanted to go home."

"I told Joy that I wouldn't stay long," he said. "She said she'd go back to the hotel later without me."

Emily felt a fever of anticipation start to bloom through her, starting with her stomach and radiating outward, pulsing between her legs. One last night. One last, memorable night.

"Let's go, then." Turning to him and getting on tiptoe, she kissed him softly...then with growing urgency.

He growled against her lips, his hands roaming her back. She pressed herself fully against him, her hands jetting inside his jacket and wrapping around his waist, holding him to her. The kiss got out of control quickly, like a match held to dry kindling. It was all Emily could do not to undo some of his buttons then and there.

She'd never responded this way to anyone. It was as if he were a walking, breathing aphrodisiac, and she simply couldn't get enough.

"I don't suppose the mayor's got a convenient boiler room nearby," Colin finally said shakily, resting his forehead against hers. "I'd settle for a broom closet."

"We need to get back to the hotel." Her own voice was unsettled. "In the next few minutes. If not sooner."

"Maybe the cab…" he teased.

She had an image of the two of them in the darkened back of a taxi, their hands roaming under cover of the night. His fingers dipping into her through the slit in her dress. He'd find out soon enough that she was wearing garters instead of stockings, and she'd picked out the underwear with him in mind.…

She moaned softly, biting her lip. As if reading her mind, he grabbed her for one last, long, lingering kiss. She rubbed her pelvis against his, just a suggestion of what she really wanted to do. He groaned, and she felt the hardness of his cock jutting against the fabric of his pants, pressing into her stomach.

"Now," she insisted. "We've got to leave *now.*"

They turned…and promptly bumped into Evelyn Albee.

"I hope I'm not interrupting anything," she said, and from her tone, it was obvious that she'd already witnessed more than they'd intended.

"No," Emily lied, fighting to keep her voice calm and her cheeks pale. If she blushed now, it would probably be the rosy blossom of desire, not embarrassment…but it'd be a close call as to which was stronger. "We were just, er, leaving."

"What were you two doing off by yourselves?"

Colin cleared his throat. "We were catching up," he said, and his voice was casual…although he stood a little behind Emily to try and hide his raging erection. Emily fought a wave of nervous chuckles. "It's hard to hear yourself think downstairs. We thought it'd be easier if we found someplace quiet."

"Really?" Evelyn looked unconvinced.

"Sure. Emily and I go way back."

"I see." And that clearly wasn't all she saw.

"We really were leaving," Emily repeated forcefully. "Come on, Colin."

"I was going to ask," Evelyn interrupted, "how is it that a pretty woman like Joy snagged such a totally devoted bachelor. But I guess that was the wrong question, hmm?" She paused. "And the wrong *person*."

Emily grimaced. She liked many people, but Evelyn Albee got on her nerves. "You're asking if Colin and I are an item."

Eveyln's eyes popped. "Are you?"

"Colin's leaving tomorrow," Emily said.

"And?" Evelyn sounded indecently curious, at the edge of her metaphoric seat.

"And that's it." Emily took Colin's arm, leading him away. Let her chew on that.

"You okay?" Colin said softly.

"I will be," Emily assured him. Assured herself. "Just take me home."

CHAPTER SEVEN

COLIN NOTICED THAT Emily was quiet during the short drive from the mayor's house to the inn. He felt somewhat subdued himself.

This was going to be their last night together—for real this time. Technically, they'd covered this territory before, but this time the ticking clock didn't seem to fan the flames of passion as it had before. It didn't feel like an interlude or an adventure.

It felt like a mistake.

Not being with Emily. As far as he was concerned, it was as if Emily had been made with him in mind, both in bed and out. No, it felt like a mistake to approach the night as though it was going to be their last.

They stepped into her apartment, and a strange awkwardness descended. Emily laughed nervously.

"I wonder if this is so weird because the cat's finally out of the bag?" she mused. "The whole Holiday Ball is probably talking about us right now."

He waited until she'd stripped off her heavy winter coat, then he wrapped her in his arms. It wasn't meant to be sexual. It was supposed to be comforting. Yet, as always with this woman, the heat *and* the comfort were inseparable.

All those years we lived in the same little city, he thought as he stroked her hair and held her tight. *Why didn't I find her before now, when I'm leaving for another continent?*

"Don't think about them," he said, his voice thick. "Just think about us."

"I can't stop thinking about us," she murmured, rubbing her hands up and down his back. "That ought to make this easier, but somehow it's not."

"Don't think about the time frame, either. It's not important. The only important thing is right now. How we feel about each other."

He wondered if she understood what he was saying—how much he felt for her. But he was too nervous to actually try putting his emotions into words. She was the one who seemed to think that the short-term nature of their affair, a "fling" by her own words, was a foregone conclusion.

What if she doesn't feel the same way I feel?

Better to listen to his own advice. Right now was all that mattered. He had to focus on the present and nothing else.

They were slower than they ever had been, even though desire still licked at him with tongues of flame. It was as if he were trying to memorize everything about her with slow precision. He held his breath as she took off his coat and jacket, tugged loose his tie, undid each button with fingers that trembled slightly. He shrugged the shirt off his shoulders, feeling his erection stiffen after simply seeing the admiration in her eyes as her gaze traced over his torso and her catlike tongue wet her lips in a quick motion. He tugged at the hem of her dress, pulling it over her head in a slow, smooth movement.

When he saw what she had beneath, he held his breath, then let it out in a sigh of gratitude.

Emily was wearing a strapless black bra, smooth satin, with a matching thong and garter belt holding up black nylon stockings. Still in her black stiletto heels, she reached up, taking her barrette out of her hair and letting the auburn waves cascade around her shoulders. Her full lips were crimson, her violet eyes even larger and smokier than usual.

She looked like a sexual fantasy brought vividly to life. She looked like the type of woman men would sell their souls to be able to possess.

Hell, if there were a dotted line in front of him, he'd sign in blood for the chance to keep her.

She unbuckled his pants, her full lips curving into a slow, inviting smile. Colin groaned as she slipped the pants down to the floor, leaving him only in boxers. He kicked off his shoes and socks, leaving them both in their underwear, there in the living room.

"Nice," he said, pointing to her ensemble.

She stroked her hand over the front of his boxers, where his erection was emerging. "I thought you'd like them." Her lips quirked in that quicksilver smile that never failed to pump adrenaline through his system. "And I must say, they seem to be doing their job nicely."

She reached into his boxers, drawing out his cock and rubbing her fingers gently up and down the shaft. They also fell to the floor. He groaned again, leaning forward against her soft, warm palm.

"Still, I think we can do better," she said, her voice teasing. With that, she knelt down, taking him into her mouth.

All rational thought fled in the face of the overwhelming sensation of her wet, warm mouth caressing him. His fingers tangled gently in her hair, his body twitching slightly as the rough silk of it brushed cool against the heat of his cock. She suckled softly but insistently, and he went harder than he'd even thought possible.

"Emily," he moaned, closing his eyes. Colin felt himself losing control and he tugged her up to her feet. "I need you," he said, his voice thick with desire. "Now."

"You can have me," she responded, her eyes gleaming. "Whenever you want."

Then I want forever.

He didn't say it. Instead he kissed her roughly, feeling the satin of her panties rub the length of his shaft before his cock rested against the smooth plane of her stomach. He lifted her into his arms, carrying her with haste into the bedroom and placing her carefully on the bed. She looked at him, eyes bright with invitation and desire.

For a moment he paused. He didn't want to simply take her. It was more than just sex, no matter how brief their relationship had been up to this point.

He stretched out next to her, taking off her bra, panties, garter and nylons. She looked at him, curious.

"Don't you like it?" Her voice sounded unsure. "I wore them for you."

"They're great," he said, stroking a wayward lock of hair out of her face. "But I don't need them. I don't need anything else to make me want you. And tonight I want it to be just us."

He hoped she understood.

She still looked slightly puzzled, but she nodded. Then she seemed to melt against him, her skin feeling even softer and more sensuous than the satin had felt.

He murmured incoherent words of passion against her skin, touching her like a blind man, tracing every curve and hollow. She kissed his shoulders, his chest, his abdomen. He slid over her, capturing first one nipple, then the other with delicate intensity, laving each until they were rosy and erect. He cupped her breasts carefully, kissing her cleavage, delighting in the way the tempo of her breathing increased.

He saved the best for last. When his fingers finally dipped inside her entrance, stroking her thighs intently, he found she was already wet and slick, ready for him. Slowly he rolled on a condom, then went back to kissing her as if they had all the time in the world to consummate what they'd aroused in each other.

She sighed against his lips. "Colin," Emily breathed, and the word was filled with emotion.

Smiling, he finally positioned himself between her legs, sliding into her like a key into the perfect lock.

For a second he stayed still, relishing the snugness of her, the way she accommodated him so incredibly. But the tightness of her, the way her passage enveloped him and clenched against him, soon made staying still impossible. Nevertheless, he took his time, retreating carefully, maximizing each stroke for the most pleasure possible. Their breathing quickened, and despite his efforts, they moved faster, cycling into the inevitable build of passion. They clung to each other, so close that they seemed to be one person as he filled her and she rose to meet each thrust.

"Colin!"

He felt the clutching tremors of her climax, and they triggered his own orgasm. Oblivious to everything but the sensation of her, he shuddered against her, feeling her thighs tighten around him as his cock pressed deeper and deeper into her welcoming flesh.

When it was over, and his consciousness returned, he couldn't help it. He smoothed his fingertips over the light sheen of sweat on her long-limbed body and pressed kisses against her temples, her high cheekbones…even the bridge of her nose. She smiled at him.

"I…" Her eyes held the faintest trace of tears. "I don't know what to say to you."

Tell me you love me.

He blinked. Was that what he wanted?

Yes. He wanted her. He wanted love. He wanted the whole package.

He rolled next to her, stunned by the revelation.

"You mean a lot to me," he finally said, his tone cautious. "More than I thought."

That didn't sound right. He frowned.

"You mean a lot to me, too," she said.

The silence that fell was a huge chasm, so much that despite the fact they were skin against skin, it felt as if the Grand Canyon lay between them.

"I…" He cleared his throat. "I don't know when I'm going to be back in town, but…"

To his surprise, she put a finger to his lips, hushing him.

"Right now is all that matters," she said, throwing his words back at him. "Remember? I'm not worried about later."

He frowned again. "But…"

She snuggled against him and he was thrown off. "Just make love to me again," she said. "It'll be enough."

He held her, feeling her heart beat against his chest.

It's not going to be enough for me, he thought. But he was leaving the next morning and he didn't know when he was going to be back. It wasn't fair to ask her to wait for him, was it?

He didn't know what to do. So he did as she said—he focused on the present, making love to her as if it was all they were going to have. Because for all he knew, it was.

* * *

EMILY FELT BLEARY-EYED and exhausted. She hadn't gotten any sleep the night before, and it wasn't because of her activities with Colin—although they'd both done their best to make the night memorable. When he had fallen asleep, she'd found herself staring at his face...the way his long eyelashes rested on his cheeks, the way his hair tousled itself against her pillowcase.

She was falling in love with him. She wasn't sure how or why, but it was a fact. Just like the fact that he was on a plane, headed for Europe, and she wasn't sure when or if she would see him again.

She swallowed. She had a few too many facts to deal with.

Emily wandered down to the front desk, thinking that the hotel itself might provide her with a respite from her wayward feelings. A few hours dealing with the day-in-day-out running of the inn ought to be a comfort. But when she got there, she noticed that the front lobby was way more crowded than normal—and that most of the people were definitely not guests.

She recognized Evelyn Albee and her stomach twisted into a knot. "May I help you?" she asked, forcing her voice to remain casual.

Evelyn had been chatting with two other women with her, and they all huddled conspiratorially around Emily. "We were talking this morning, and it struck us how long it's been since you've visited the salon," Evelyn said, in a peaches-and-cream voice that was at odds with the almost predatory gleam in her eye.

"It's been ages!" one of the other women, Shirley Hayworth, agreed heartily.

"So we decided to treat you to a full day of pampering." This from Evelyn's second in charge, Madge Tyler. Madge handed Emily a gift certificate, hand-lettered.

"Thank you," Emily said. A full day of pampering would have sounded nice if she didn't know Evelyn's motive. People tended to find the salon comforting, almost therapeutic—and therefore turned the beauty technicians and fellow customers into a sort of "spa therapy" group. As a result, the salon was a hotbed of gossip and a place for solicited and unsolicited advice from the women of Tall Pines. "I'll see when I can fit it into my schedule."

"Oh, but the roads are cleared," Evelyn said smoothly, smiling at Sue, who was manning the desk and looking apologetically at Emily. "Most of your guests have gone, and Sue was just saying the holiday rush was over for a few weeks at least. So…"

Emily bit back a sigh. "The guests might be gone, but business still keeps grinding along." She tried to keep the annoyance out of her voice. "I've got inventory to do, ladies, but I appreciate the gift certificate. Thanks so—"

"Is Colin still here?" Madge's comment shot out like a bullet.

"Madge!" Evelyn looked incensed. She might be there trolling for gossip, but she wasn't about to be *that* obvious, apparently.

"Well, you said they were making out at the Holiday Ball!" Madge was fiftyish and recently divorced. For her, gossip was more than a hobby, it was a lifeline. "Is it true? Are you and Colin Reese…you know?"

"I don't know what you mean," Emily said, her voice cool.

Evelyn sneered. "I *told* you not to say anything directly!"

"In all fairness, Evelyn, I wouldn't have told you anything at the salon, either," Emily said. "Sorry, Madge."

"It's not fair," Madge grumped. "Colin's like a celebrity. After all those big, crazy buildings he designed, he's been in big magazines. *Newsweek. Time.* Even *InStyle*." Madge gave a beatific grin; as far as she was concerned, getting your picture in *InStyle* was tantamount to being royalty. "You've heard Ava talking about the women he normally goes with. Models, actresses, flashy businesswomen…"

Emily blanched. Women not like her, in other words.

Of course, now he's got plenty of opportunity to get back to his "type."

"He also has a reputation for leaving them," Shirley said, her voice more quiet than the other two. "How are you holding up, sweetie?"

Emily should have been surprised, but Shirley was about sixty or so and considered herself a sort of universal den mother. Although it wasn't the older woman's business, she accepted Shirley's pat on the shoulder with a wan smile. "I'm hanging in there," she found herself saying.

"Oh, Emily," Madge said, and there was real outrage in her voice. "You, too? All men are *dogs,* honey. Just *dogs.*"

"Well, you knew his reputation," Evelyn admonished, and in that second Emily could have smacked her.

"Excuse me, Emily?"

Emily turned, wondering who was going to be grilling her about her love life now. To her surprise—and relief—it was Joy.

"I don't mean to interrupt," Joy said, "but Emily and I have a business meeting right now."

Evelyn's eyes narrowed. "Aren't you the woman that Colin took to the Holiday Ball last night?"

Emily wished that the earth would swallow her up. "Joy is a friend and a guest. And also in the hotel industry. We were going to discuss, er, some ways to improve the hotel."

"But the hotel's perfect, sweetie, just the way it is," Shirley assured her. "You run the place like a top."

"If you'll excuse me?" Emily said, feeling an edge of desperation to her words.

"Fine, fine." Evelyn was obviously unsatisfied. "But don't forget about that gift certificate, all right?"

"You deserve it," Madge added. "*Dogs.* The lot of them."

Emily watched the retreating figures of the three ladies, then dropped the gift certificate on the desk like a hand grenade.

"Wow. That was like something out of Stars Hollow."

"Excuse me?" Emily rubbed at the back of her neck. She should've stayed in bed—except her sheets smelled like Colin's cologne, and she couldn't face a whole day surrounded by reminders of him. Of *them.* "Stars what?"

"It's the small town in that TV show *Gilmore Girls,*" Joy explained. "Very cute, if a little overbearing."

"That's one way of putting it," Emily said ruefully.

"Do you have time? For a meeting, I mean."

Emily started to say no but then saw another wave of townspeople heading toward the lobby—with obviously no intention of renting rooms. "Certainly. Why don't you come with me to my office."

She led Joy to the room she'd converted for office use. Joy whistled. "This is gorgeous," she said, looking at the dark maple furniture. "I've worked in multibillion-dollar hotel chains that didn't look half as good. You've done something special here, Emily."

"I try," Emily said, sitting at at a small occasional table and gesturing to Joy to sit next to her. She poured them both a cup of coffee from the coffeemaker on her credenza. "I didn't know how much went into running a hotel, but I've always been a quick study."

"And you're amazingly good at it," Joy said, taking her

own seat. "But, you know, with a few strategic improvements, you could make this place even bigger."

Emily smiled tiredly. "Yeah, if I had a billion dollars and a cast of thousands at my beck and call…"

But Joy's expression was serious. "I hope you don't think this is out of line," she said hesitantly, "but I drew up some numbers and some strategy ideas." She slid a piece of paper over the surface of the table.

Emily looked at it. The strategy was clear, precise, in Joy's neat handwriting. Then she looked at the income expectations. The number took her breath away. She closed her eyes, rubbing them, then read the number again.

It was still the same. She had thought that fatigue was making her hallucinate.

"You wouldn't necessarily see those profits first year," Joy said easily, as if they were simply swapping recipes instead of discussing a huge change in Emily's business. "But with the right combination of management, marketing and some key overhauls, you could quadruple your profits in under five years, easy. With that much money, you could start hiring that cast of thousands to help you."

With that much money, she might not want to keep working, period, Emily realized. "This is more than I could have sold the house for by itself."

"Tall Pines is going places," Joy said and her voice lit with excitement. "It could be the next big bedroom community for larger cities, and it's getting a good reputation as a tourist attraction. If you really pursued it, you could help put Tall Pines on the map."

Emily's head swam. In her sleep-deprived state, it was too much to contemplate.

"I know you think I've been patronizing, gushing about

this place," Joy said. "But this isn't a joke, Emily. If I know one thing, it's how to make a hotel a success."

"But…this is my home," Emily said, feeling dumb-founded. "The changes you're suggesting…"

"I know," Joy said, and her voice was rich with sympathy and what sounded strangely like envy. "It's a lot to think about. But do you really want to keep struggling at this level for the rest of your life?"

Emily thought about it. She wasn't hand-to-mouth any-more, granted, but it was hard, managing the hotel. More money would make her life easier. Wouldn't it?

At the same time—did she *want* to manage a hotel for the rest of her life? She'd only taken it on so she wouldn't lose the house. On the other hand, giving up the hotel would effectively take the Stanfield house out of her family for good…an idea her father had vehemently disagreed with.

Realizing Joy was still there, waiting for a response, Emily bit her lip. "Sorry. This is all so sudden."

"I'm staying through the end of the month," Joy said. "I know how emotional the whole thing is for you. Think it over, take your time. If you decide to move ahead, I'd be happy to help you plan, get financing, whatever."

With that, Joy started to get up and leave the office. Before she could stop herself, Emily blurted out, "Why did you go to the Holiday Ball with Colin?"

Joy turned. "I was bored," she said easily. "Trust me, if I'd known, I wouldn't have gone anywhere near him."

"Known what?"

Joy's eyebrow quirked up. "That you two were in-volved."

"We're not." Emily felt the burn of the lie on the tip of her tongue. "Not exactly," she amended.

"If I knew the two of you were *anything*, I would've

stayed away from him," Joy said. "He's gorgeous, but this is business. And I'm all business."

With that, Joy winked and left the room.

Emily held up the paper with its imposing financial figures on it.

The hotel had been her life for years. The house had been her father's legacy. The town was already up in arms about outside business coming in and changing things too rapidly. It would cause enormous upheaval and disappoint a lot of people.

She folded the paper, unable to bring herself to throw it away.

What would I do if I didn't have this place? she asked herself.

To her surprise, her mind changed one word in the sentence.

What could *I do if I didn't have this place?*

She'd never thought about that before.

Sue popped her head in. "Everything all right?" she asked.

"Yeah. Everything's fine." Emily tucked the paper into her desk drawer. "Let's do inventory. It's sort of early, but I'd rather stay away from the public today."

Besides, counting towels and bed linens would keep her mind occupied enough to stop thinking of losing Colin—and now possibly leaving the inn.

COLIN WAS SITTING at Heathrow Airport in London, feeling more disoriented than usual. He tried to chalk it up to jet lag, but he'd had jet lag before. It was different than this overwhelming sensation of displacement—that no matter where he was, it was the wrong place.

He'd only been gone for a day and a half, and as he'd feared, thoughts of Emily crowded his brain incessantly.

He'd stopped himself from dialing the inn's number a dozen times in the past twenty-four hours, mostly because he had no idea what he would say. If he had no intention of having a relationship with her, it seemed unnecessarily cruel to both of them to keep intruding on her. Better to simply move on to his new life and let her move on with hers.

He pictured Mayor Tim and gritted his teeth.

She deserves to move on to something better than that, though.

He credited Emily with more common sense than to enter a loveless marriage with a guy who was looking for a "practical" wife. But then, most people probably would have credited Emily with more common sense than to take up with a commitmentphobic drifter like himself, too.

Instead he jotted down more notes on the office he'd be opening. He'd already done a ton of work on the plane while his fellow passengers had been napping. Now he was buzzing on a caffeine high and lack of sleep.

He'd get to Paris, buckle down and bury himself in blueprints for a while. His work was one thing he'd always loved, and he'd gotten so caught up in the holidays and Tall Pines that he'd practically pretended it didn't exist.

Face it—you got tangled up in Emily. And you still are.

His cell phone was in his hand, and he found himself tracing her number one more time.

Only this time, as if it had a mind of its own, his thumb hit *Send.*

He heard the ringing and considered hanging up—but she'd know he called. By now his number was probably showing up on caller ID. He winced, trying to think of what he'd say.

"Hello?"

Emily's voice sounded rough with sleep. Suddenly he

remembered he didn't know what time it was in London, much less Connecticut.

"Oh God, I'm sorry. It's late, isn't it?"

There was a pause. "Early, actually," Emily said, sounding much more alert. "How are you?"

He paused, too, trying to frame a reply. "Tired," he answered honestly.

"Me, too." He heard the smile in her voice. "Although I'm glad you called."

"Maybe I should call back," he said, wincing. "I didn't mean to…"

"Why are you calling?"

That one caught him flat-footed. "Honestly? I don't know." He ran his hand through his hair in a gesture of frustration. "Yes, I *do* know. I miss you. That's nuts, isn't it?"

She laughed. "No. It's nice." The warmth in her voice was clear as crystal even over an intercontinental cell phone line. "I miss you, too."

"So what are we going to do about this?" His voice was almost demanding, and he toned it down. "I've never felt like this. It's confusing and uncomfortable, and damned if I know what to do next."

"Well," she said slowly, "it probably would've been better to have this conversation when we were, say, two feet away from each other instead of several thousand miles."

He chuckled. "I know. That is, I know that *now*."

"So I don't know what to tell you," she continued. "You're there. I'm here. That makes a lasting relationship hard."

"But not impossible, right?" He blinked. Had he really asked that?

She seemed surprised, as well. "Is that what you want?"

"I think…yes." He sighed. The loudspeaker was announcing that his connecting flight to Paris was boarding. "I have really lousy timing."

"Sort of," she admitted. "I really care about you, Colin."

"I care about you, too," he confessed, feeling his heart expand in his chest. "I meant to tell you when I was there, but I chickened out. And I didn't know where it would lead, anyway. Where it *could* lead."

"I still don't know that it can lead anywhere." Emily spoke softly. "The bottom line is, we had some wonderful nights together...."

"You can say that again," Colin said, his body going taut at the mere memory.

"But we only spent less than two weeks together. That's hardly enough to say one way or another how we feel."

"I know how I feel." *I'm falling in love with you.* Sudden or not, he was certain of that.

"Well, no matter how you feel, the bottom line is you didn't feel strongly enough to stay here and discuss it with me face-to-face."

He grimaced. She did have a point there.

The announcer broadcast his flight again. He'd have to hurry if he was going to make it. "Listen, I have to catch this plane. Can I call you back at a more decent hour?"

"If you want," Emily replied noncommittally. "But... Colin, think about what you really want with me before you do. Because I...I wasn't expecting to feel the way I feel about you. And, to be honest, it's starting to hurt."

He felt guilt crash on him like a wrecking ball. "I never meant to hurt you."

"I know," she assured him. "I know you didn't."

But if he was only going to string her along, he'd be hurting her anyway. Colin heard what she wasn't saying as clearly as what she was.

"Listen, I should've said all this back in Tall Pines. I know that now."

"You've got to catch a plane," Emily said. "Call me when you get to Paris and…I don't know, Colin. I can't promise anything."

"Okay," he said weakly. *Tell her! Tell her you love her!* "We'll talk soon."

"All right," she agreed. "Good night, Colin."

"'Night." He hung up the phone, then stared at it.

Minutes later, the announcer was calling out his name. "Is there a Colin Reese? Colin Reese. We're looking for passenger Colin Reese. Your flight is awaiting departure."

Colin rushed up to the desk. "I'm Colin Reese."

The flight attendant smiled thinly. "You're late, Mr. Reese. You're our last passenger. We've been looking for you."

"I'm sorry," Colin said. "But I have to change my plans."

Her eyebrows went up. "Beg pardon?"

"I have to get a flight back to Connecticut. How can I arrange that?"

CHAPTER EIGHT

"I'D LIKE A MANICURE and a facial, please. I'm using your gift certificate."

Emily said the words clearly enough to be heard over the chattering of the crowded beauty salon. As she'd expected, the whole place fell silent when they recognized her voice.

"Certainly, certainly." Madge ushered her over to a manicure station. "You sit right here. How are you doing?"

How was she doing? It had been two days since Colin had left, and she couldn't remember feeling quite this way before. Missing him was like a dull ache, countered only by feelings of foolishness and confusion. When he'd called, she had felt excited at hearing his voice and then abruptly depressed by reality. Would that be their relationship from then on? Long-distance phone calls and maybe the occasional transatlantic flight for a weekend of passion? Maybe a whole week if they were lucky? Would that be enough?

Then again, considering the big, bleak romantic desert of her life, was she being too damned picky?

She realized Madge was still waiting patiently for an an-

swer and quickly cleared her throat. "Sorry. I'm fine, really. I've just been sort of out of it lately."

"Oh, no problem," Madge said easily. "Cynthia? Could
you do a manicure for Emily here?"

Cynthia was about twenty-three. Emily had babysat for
her in high school. She quickly started to soak Emily's
nails. "Man trouble, huh?"

Emily straightened her spine. She'd decided to simply
brave the lion's den rather than hide in the inn. "No," she
said. "No trouble."

"I don't blame you," Cynthia said sympathetically. "That
guy Colin was *seriously* yummy."

Emily cringed. She remembered when Cynthia used to
watch *Sesame Street,* for pity's sake. Hearing her call
Emily's lover "yummy" was disturbing.

"I'm fine. It's fine."

"So dish." Cynthia's youth and enthusiasm bubbled
through her like some high-sugar, high-caffeine soda.
"What was he like?"

"Um, I don't think I'm comfortable discussing my love
life in graphic detail," Emily said. "He was a dear friend and
we…considered having a relationship, but the reality is,
he's living in Paris and I'm living in Tall Pines and it simply wasn't feasible, so…"

She let the words trail off. She'd been crafting that careful public announcement for two days. Now she understood
why celebrities sent out cautiously worded press releases
when they had high-profile breakups. It made things easier all around.

Cynthia made a face. "You sound like a banker. Wasn't
the sex any good?"

Emily goggled. She'd expected questions but nothing
quite this blunt.

"Good grief, Cyn," Madge said, smacking her lightly on the shoulder.

"What?" Cynthia looked bewildered. "Don't tell me you're not wondering, either. A guy that gorgeous you don't dump unless there's a big problem."

"And the fact that he's living a whole other continent away isn't what you'd consider a big problem?" Emily asked sarcastically.

Cynthia shrugged. "There are planes, aren't there?"

Emily blinked.

"So you dumped him because he's not living here in town?" Cynthia made a *tch-tch* sound in her throat.

"Who's saying I dumped him?"

"Well, you wouldn't be here acting all mopey if you hadn't."

It was hard to refute the logic of a twenty-three-year-old, Emily thought with a wry smile. After all, they knew everything. She certainly had when she was twenty-three.

"We parted amicably," Emily said, remembering the party line.

"Yes, but was it his idea?" Madge pressed.

Emily realized that, for the moment, she was the center of attention at the salon. Women had even shut off their dryers to hear her commentary. She sighed.

"No. It was my idea."

They collectively gasped at that bit of news.

"Well, what was I supposed to do?" Emily finally broke down. "He lives in *Paris,* for pity's sake. If I'm lucky, I could see him, what, a couple of times a year?" She shook her head. "I don't think that would work."

"I guess you're right. I mean, long-distance relationships have, like, a twenty percent success rate," Cynthia said sagely, buffing Emily's nails. "I read that in *Cosmo*."

"There's also more of a chance that you'll get cheated on," Madge interjected darkly. "All that temptation, and you're miles away."

That comment hit Emily like a fist in the gut. She focused on the tray of nail polish colors as if her life depended on it, trying not to picture Colin with some other woman—probably some stylish Parisian woman with no body fat and a fabulous wardrobe.

The more she tried not to see it, the more vivid the picture became.

"Well, at least you got back up on the horse," Evelyn said...then promptly burst out laughing.

"Oh my God." Emily tried to cover her face with her hands, but Cynthia had already applied the base coat of polish, and they were still wet. Cynthia giggled.

"I think she meant that more *figuratively,* hon," Madge clarified helpfully. That was the straw that broke the camel's back, apparently, because the entire salon joined in, laughing raucously.

If Emily's face got any hotter, they could toast marshmallows in front of it. Brave the lion's den, huh?

This was such a bad idea.

"Come on, come on," Evelyn said, and she gave Emily a small half hug around her shoulders. "If you can't talk to the girls at the beauty shop, then you can't talk to anyone. Besides, I think a big part of your problem is that you bottle things up, sweetie."

"I didn't know I had a problem," Emily said. *Boy, could this get any worse?*

"Hmm. That's also part of the problem." Evelyn seemed to size her up, then nodded, as if making a decision. "You know what? We ought to get you drunk."

Emily choked. *"Excuse me?"*

Cynthia clapped her hands together. "Ooh! And hire a stripper!"

Madge poured herself another cup of coffee. "Just tell me when and where," she declared, "and I'll be there."

Emily glanced around. Mrs. Rutledge, who had been at the mayor's Christmas dinner and was seventy-four if she were a day, was placidly reading a *People* magazine, her hair covered in foil from her dye job. "Mrs. Rutledge, I'm so sorry," she said. "This is so inappropriate."

Mrs. Rutledge didn't even look up. "That's all right, dear," she responded. "Considering my neighbors are swingers, I suppose I'm harder to shock than most."

Emily's eyes bugged out. *"The Carltons are swingers?"*

"Not those neighbors." She sounded appalled. The Carltons were somewhere in their eighties and pillars of the community. "The Smiths. Good grief, girl, they've been wife swappers for years," Mrs. Rutledge said disdainfully. "Where have you been?"

"This is what happens when you don't make your regular hair appointments," Evelyn added.

Within the next hour Emily went through an eye-opening epiphany. She also became best friends, it seemed, with every woman in Tall Pines. Or at least every one that was a customer at the Magnifique Beauty Salon…which was actually pretty much every woman in Tall Pines. By the time she'd gotten herself talked into a haircut and style *and* a pedicure, she'd divulged her entire brief sexual history and relationship woes.

"After Rick," Emily found herself saying, "I didn't want to hurt like that again. So I figured I'd focus on other things. Running the hotel was hard enough."

"Emotionally, too, I'll bet." Mrs. Rutledge was long done with her hairstyling, but had stayed on for the conversation. "It was a big change turning the mansion into a hotel."

Emily nodded. "I wasn't sure whether or not my father would've approved," she admitted. "I'm still not."

"Now, now," Evelyn said. "You know, as much as we all love your family, sometimes you can be awfully…"

Emily looked at her as she trailed off. "Awfully what?"

"Well, stiff." Evelyn frowned. "Hmm, that's not the right word, either. But sometimes you're a little too proper."

"The whole town didn't like the hotel at first," Emily reminded her.

"Maybe not," Evelyn agreed. "We're sort of stuck in the mud sometimes ourselves. But we always liked *you*."

Emily grinned. It was that kind of support that made her love Tall Pines. She suddenly felt better than she had since Colin left. In some ways, better than she had in years.

"So now that Colin's gone," Cynthia said, "I guess you're going to date Mayor Tim, huh?"

The women surveyed her eagerly.

"After everything I've told you," Emily replied, "I don't know. I don't think I can go from someone like Colin to someone like Tim."

There were some mixed comments after that statement.

"There's more to life than passion," Evelyn said sagely. "I love Dale, but let's face it—he's no male model." She grinned wickedly. "Of course, he *does* have his moments."

Hearing about the "moments" Dale Albee had was more than Emily could handle right now. She cleared her throat. "Well, I'm not going out with Tim again. And as for Colin, I can't honestly believe there's a future there. And now that I know what I'm missing, I don't think I want to settle for anything less."

The women around her cheered.

The door opened and everyone turned to welcome the new arrival.

Emily's eyes bugged.

"Hi, Emily," Colin said quietly. "Sorry. Sue said I could find you here. She was expecting you back hours ago."

"You're supposed to be in Paris," she said, feeling dumbstruck. "What are you doing here?"

He stared at her for a second. Then he smiled. "Do you have to ask?"

"Oh." Madge dabbed at her eyes. "This is like something out of a movie."

"Are you done?" The question was a plea as he shifted uncomfortably under the intense scrutiny of the women.

"Have fun, dear," Mrs. Rutledge said with far too suggestive an edge for a septuagenarian.

Emily stood up, going for her wallet.

"It's all on the house, dear." Evelyn shooed her money away. "It's more than worth it. We'll be discussing this for weeks."

Emily put on her coat and walked out with Colin, hearing the explosion of conversation as she shut the door behind her.

He cleared his throat. "Was it bad?" he asked.

"Was what bad?" Missing him was bad. Thinking he was gone for good—that was bad.

"The grilling." He sounded worried. "I'm sure they were terrible."

"They actually weren't that bad," Emily said, smiling. "I'm glad you're back."

She wrapped her arms around him, giving him a long, lingering kiss.

He growled, pulling away from her. "You can't do that

in broad daylight," he said, his eyes gleaming. "Not unless you want to shock some of these fine townfolk."

She grinned, remembering the wife-swapping tidbit. "They're harder to shock than you think." Then she frowned. "Wait. That's not why you're back, is it?"

"I couldn't leave you to face the fire alone."

She felt her stomach clench. It wasn't the reason she'd been hoping for. Still, he'd flown all the way back, so that had to say something. And he *did* care for her.

It wasn't going to be clear in one day, she thought resolutely. "Come on," she told him. "Let's go over to the hotel."

As usual, she'd enjoy whatever time she had. However long—or short—that was.

FUNNY, HOW HIS exhaustion seemed to disappear the minute he saw her. And walking into her apartment was more like coming home than walking into any of the residences he'd rented in the past five, ten years, he realized as he hung his coat up on her coatrack. It had been excruciating walking into the beauty salon, surrounded by all the town's busiest bodies but at the same time he'd found that he simply couldn't wait for her another minute.

That tells you something, doesn't it?

They would have to figure this out. He had a job, a life to get to in Paris. He couldn't keep jetting back here to Connecticut just because he couldn't function without her.

She turned to him, cheeks rosy from the cold, eyes sparkling like gems. "I can't believe you came back," she repeated for the tenth time.

"I'm having a little difficulty believing it myself." He took her into his arms. "We need to talk."

She kissed his jawline. "Right this second?"

In a snap, his body went taut as a bowstring. "Well...wait. Yes." He wasn't going to get sidetracked by his body. He'd flown thousands of miles and postponed moving into his new apartment to get back to this woman. They had a few things to straighten out. Namely what the heck they were going to do about this...this *thing* that was going on between them. "We definitely need to talk."

"All right." She played up a pout, looking kittenishly sexy. Then she sat down on the couch, patting the space next to her.

He thought about it. Sitting that close to her would definitely make conversation difficult. "Why don't we stand," he suggested. "In the kitchen." So far, that was the one place that they didn't have any sexual memories. Besides, kitchens reminded him of home, family gatherings—intrinsically nonsexy memories. That ought to be some kind of insurance against getting sidetracked.

She smiled, obviously amused, and walked over to the kitchen. "Mind if I fix myself a snack?" she asked.

"Sure." He paused. "If you don't mind, I'm kind of hungry—starving, actually. All I've had is some snacks and airplane food in the past forty-eight hours."

"Poor baby," she said, stroking his face, and for a second he felt like saying *to hell with conversation* and dragging her over to the bed. They had plenty of time to talk, didn't they?

He clamped down on the instinct. They had plenty of time for the physical stuff, too...and the talk, at this point, was more important.

"So what did you want to talk about?" she asked over her shoulder, opening her well-stocked fridge.

"This. Us," he clarified. "What's going on with us?"

She leaned against the refrigerator door, looking puzzled. "Honestly, I have no idea. But I am enjoying it."

"So am I," he hastily assured her. "But... hell. I'm moving to Paris. We're going to have an ocean between us."

"That *did* cross my mind," she said, bringing out cheese, meat, croissants and an assortment of fruit. "This okay?"

"Fine," he answered absently, watching as she arranged the food attractively on a platter. He leaned up against the counter. "So if we're going to be thousands of miles away from each other, where does that leave us?"

"I don't have an answer to that," she admitted. She handed him a croissant sandwich, and he wolfed it down. "Maybe we should approach this from a different standpoint. What do you want to happen?"

I love you and I want you to be with me.

Colin frowned. He'd never lived with anyone in his life—his relationships had been far too brief, and he'd never been comfortable sharing that much of his space and his time. And that would mean turning her entire life upside down. Was that what he wanted? And was that something he had the right to ask for after, what, two weeks?

What if she moved to Europe, and hated it? And you?

He winced. No, that wasn't a good solution.

"I'm not sure," he prevaricated. "All I know is I think about you all the time and I love being with you."

There. He was creeping toward the *L* word. Maybe it was hasty, but he wanted to lay the groundwork.

She jumped up, sitting casually on the countertop of her kitchen island, next to the platter of food. She picked out a chocolate-covered strawberry, dipping it in a bowl of whipped cream and taking a slow, thoughtful bite.

His mouth went dry.

She put the stem down on her plate. "I love being with you, too," she said, her voice low and musical. She picked up another, this time licking it slightly before biting it. He wondered if it was deliberate, as his cock hardened just watching the fruit tickling those full lips of hers. "Are you saying you want a relationship?"

"Yes," he said, watching as she licked some stray chocolate from the corner of her mouth. "That's exactly what I'm saying."

She frowned. "Long-distance relationships don't have a really high success factor," she stated, then grinned ruefully. "If *Cosmo* is to be believed, anyway."

"I wouldn't want it to be long-distance." He couldn't help it. He picked up another strawberry, holding it out to her. Emily smiled, then delicately bit into it, some juice dribbling down her chin. She laughed.

That was his breaking point. He leaned forward, licking the stray juice from her. She sighed happily.

"So what would you want?" She looped her arms around his neck, kissing him slowly.

"I want to see you all the time." He nuzzled her neck, and she wrapped her jean-clad legs around his waist. He could feel the heat of her burning him. "I feel like I'm going crazy when I'm not with you."

Her breathing sped up and he kissed her hungrily. "I know," she moaned. "I feel the same way. I've never felt like this before in my life."

"Me, neither." The food was forgotten—they were practically clawing at each other with need.

She reached down, undoing his pants, and he did the same, their mouths never separating. She kicked off her shoes, and he tugged her pants and panties off, leaving her gasping. He barely took the time to pull down his own briefs and roll on a condom before he was entering her, right there in the kitchen.

She threw her head back, panting loudly. "Oh, this feels so *good…*"

He leaned his head on her shoulder. The countertop was the perfect height for them. She wrapped herself around him and he pushed into her, rocking against her. His body fit hers perfectly. He withdrew, leaving her whimpering with desire, then he plunged in, devouring her cry of pleasure.

"Emily," he murmured against her lips as his body increased its tempo. *"Emily."*

"I love the feel of you inside me," she whispered back, her hands digging into his shoulders, pulling him as close as possible to her.

They moved as one, straining against each other. When the climax hit, it hit them both simultaneously—and it hit like a freight train.

When it was over, he leaned against her, holding her as if he were too weak to stand on his own. They were both breathless.

"You know," he panted, "I used to have enormous self-control before I met you."

She giggled. "I never needed self-control before I met you."

They wound up stripping off the rest of their clothes and eating a more substantial meal naked in front of the fire. Colin couldn't remember the last time he'd felt this relaxed and comfortable—and he knew it had nothing to do with the cozy nature of Emily's home but more with the nature of Emily herself. The way she laughed. The way she listened, no matter what he was saying. The things she thought about.

He was fascinated with her.

"I've known you for years—well, known *about* you for years," he ventured, leaning against her couch as she rested her head against his shoulder. "I can't believe we never... you know. Before now."

She nibbled on his earlobe, simultaneously stroking his chest with one warm palm. "It wasn't for want of trying, believe me."

That surprised him. "You wanted me?"

"Are you kidding?" She laughed. "The hot, mysterious, lone-wolf Colin Reese? I wanted you since the moment I was old enough to understand what wanting was."

He felt pride and excitement bubble up from his chest. "Where the hell was I?"

She punched him lightly on the shoulder. "As I recall, having sex with most of the senior-class girls before importing a few from out of town."

He chuckled. "Trust me, my reputation was vastly overrated." He recalled his senior year fondly. "Well, maybe not that vastly—*ow*."

She punched a little harder but grinned. "Anyway, what would you have seen in a nerdy, type-A sophomore?"

He stroked her cheek. "The same thing I see now," he said softly. "Someone thoughtful and sweet and beautiful."

She stared at him, her eyes misting slightly with a sheen of tears. He kissed her tenderly.

"What can we do?" she asked finally.

It took him a second to see that she had looped back to his initial conversation—the one he had meant to focus on solely before getting sidetracked, as always, by his intense desire for this woman. He stroked the hair away from her face, then kissed her shoulder.

"I think there's only one thing *to* do."

She frowned, puzzled.

He sighed. "I think I need to take you home to meet my parents."

* * *

EMILY HAD BEEN TO Ava and Harry's house dozens of times over the years, so in a way it felt ridiculous to feel so nervous now. But then she had been a guest, either for a committee meeting or Ava's Secret Santa party or the book club. Now she was coming as an entirely different entity: their son's girlfriend. Although *girlfriend* felt like a shallow and frivolous word for what she felt for him—and, considering they'd only been together less than a month, it was at the same time a bit of an overstatement.

She was confused enough when it was just the two of them.

"Hi, honey," Ava said, hugging her son before turning to Emily. "He's never brought *anyone* home for dinner, much less somebody that he jumped on a plane from Europe for!"

"Ava," Harry warned, before giving Emily a hug. "Nice to see you, Emily. Hope you like ribs—I've spent the morning making up a whole batch."

"Are you kidding? Your ribs are famous." Emily grinned. She liked Harry. He had a way of making her feel comfortable. "I remember them from the firehouse barbecue last year."

"Well, these are oven-cooked rather than grilled," he said critically, "but they ought to do all right. I guess."

Ava frowned. "I told you—ten degrees is way too cold for you to be grilling, Harry."

Emily laughed, then turned to Colin, who was looking skittish and unnerved. "You okay?" she murmured.

"Just dandy," he replied in a low voice, taking her coat.

She bit her lip. She knew this was going to be a high-pressure event for him. His parents, darling though they were to her, seemed to be a big part of his aversion to Tall Pines. This was probably harder for him than braving the beauty salon had been for her.

"I heard you got a gift certificate for the full-day beauty package over at Evelyn's shop," Ava called from the kitchen before emerging with a tray full of appetizers. "Sounds like you had quite the afternoon."

Emily winced. Suddenly she felt as uncomfortable as Colin looked. She took a shrimp puff from the tray Ava offered. "I got my nails done," she said inanely. "And, er, got a facial. And a cut and style."

"Well, you look great," Ava said, although her eyes glinted mischievously. "And then Colin walking in, looking for you…"

"Need help in there, Dad?" Colin said, then fled the living room, heading for the kitchen. Emily was left with Ava, who gestured to their large sectional sofa.

"Have a seat, dear. Make yourself comfortable."

Emily had sincere doubts that she'd be feeling overly comfortable during this intimate get-together and abruptly wondered why she'd thought it was a good idea when Colin suggested it.

"So, now that the men are out of the way—" Ava put her tray down on the coffee table "—I can't tell you how happy I am that you're together with my Colin!"

Emily looked down at the floor. "I'm happy, too."

"I mean, I love my other two kids, but Colin has always been…troubled." Ava sighed. "I've been wishing and praying for him to find some nice girl to settle down with. I had no idea you two would hit it off so well. And so quickly!"

Emily fought against the blush that threatened. "Neither did we," she admitted, taking a few more shrimp puffs and a small pig in a blanket. They really hadn't eaten much today. "But…well, here we are."

"So," Ava said, folding her hands in her lap. "When is he moving home?"

Emily choked on a puff. "I'm sorry?"

Ava glanced at the door to the kitchen, then lowered her voice conspiratorially. "I've never seen him like this. And, like I said, he's *never* brought a girl home. You're special. I think he's in love."

Emily felt her chest expand, like a large bubble blowing up inside of her, filled with happiness.

I hope so, she thought, *because I think I'm in love with him.*

"And for him to fly all the way back? Well, that means something," Ava pronounced with authority. "He's serious about you."

"What does that have to do with him moving home?" Emily asked in an equally low voice, hoping that Colin wouldn't hear.

Ava looked surprised at the question. "Well, he can't marry you if he's all the way in Europe, now, can he?"

"Marriage?" Emily put the rest of her appetizers down on the coffee table, her appetite suddenly waning. "We've only been together for a couple of weeks. Don't you think you're jumping the gun there?"

Ava frowned. "He wouldn't have brought you here if he wasn't serious." Her tone said, *At least he'd better not have or he's in serious trouble.*

"I'm not saying he's not serious," Emily backpedaled. "But…we aren't sure how we're going to work all this out yet."

Ava's face smoothed out in relief. "Oh, well, I'm sure you'll figure out a way," she said, leaning over and patting Emily's hand. "You'll get him to see that what he needs is a wife and a family and a home. I hate seeing him so rootless."

"It seems to work for him," Emily pointed out. "He likes

seeing different things, doing different things, having adventures."

"Well, sure, that's fine when you're young," Ava said dismissively. "But he's going to be thirty-five this year. Time to start thinking of settling down. He's had enough adventures."

Emily found herself frowning. She was only thirty-two, about to turn thirty-three, but she didn't think she had had enough adventures. Actually, she hadn't had *any* adventures—which was, she realized, a big part of the chain of events that led her to Colin and, consequently, to here.

"What are you two talking about?" Colin asked, bringing Emily a mug of hot spiced cider.

"Oh, nothing," Ava lied breezily, winking at Emily. "Girl stuff."

He looked suspicious—and nervous. *And he's right to,* Emily thought, considering the topic of their conversation.

He sat next to Emily and then took her hand. She felt some of the tension that had been tightening her muscles slowly unravel.

"Oh, there, now don't you two look cute?" Ava gushed, and the tension snapped back into place.

"Ava, where did you put the big platter? I want to get these ribs out on the table," Harry called from the kitchen.

Ava shook her head, smiling at Emily and Colin. "I swear, that man would lose his head if it wasn't attached to his neck. I'll be right back."

When she disappeared into the kitchen, Colin let out a long, beleaguered sigh.

"Why did you think this was a good idea again?" Emily whispered.

"Because you're important to me," he answered, not taking it as the joke it was meant to be. "We're in a relationship. This is something you do when you're in a relationship."

Emily thought about that. *Wouldn't it be more important to decide logistics...like how often you'll fly here or I'll fly there or whether or not one of us is supposed to move?*

"Besides, I wanted to see what this was like," he added.

"This?"

"Bringing you home," he said. Then paused. "Being around my family."

"Oh." And suddenly it did make sense.

He's trying to see if he could live here, this close to his family. In his own way, he was figuring out logistics.

Suddenly the dinner took on an element of pressure that she hadn't even believed was possible.

They sat down to eat, and as usual, Ava did all the talking, chirping happily. Emily tried to steer the conversation to safe topics, something that should have been easy to do since she and Ava actually had a lot in common. The more they discussed Tall Pines community stuff, however, the more Colin seemed to withdraw. Emily felt his discomfort like rippling waves, buffeting her without meaning to.

"And, of course, there's the Easter egg hunt coming up in April," Ava said, pausing only long enough to pass the mashed potatoes and make sure everyone had a second helping of her "world-famous" corn bread. "The little ones are always so cute wandering around the lawns of the square." She winked. "You two might be enjoying that pretty soon, hmm?"

"Mom," Colin said warningly.

Emily quickly turned to Harry. "These really are fantastic ribs."

Ava refused to be deterred. "After all, you're not getting any younger...."

"*Really* good ribs," Emily interjected. "You know, I heard about a rib recipe recently..."

"And Emily here loves kids..."

"It had maple syrup in it, and, er, nutmeg," Emily continued desperately.

"And you know, Colin," Ava said thoughtfully, "I've always known you'd make a wonderful father...."

"And, er, chocolate syrup, as well," Emily blinked. "Wait. That's not right."

"Sounds intriguing, though," Harry said, chuckling. "Ava, you're making our guest white as a sheet. They've only started dating. Would you let them mail out wedding invitations before you throw the baby shower?"

Ava smirked self-consciously. "Maybe I *am* jumping the gun a tiny bit."

"You think?" Colin muttered.

Emily struggled her way through dinner. Ava meant well, she really did—but she was so intent on her picture of a perfect family that she was like a heat-seeking missile, unable to go off course once she'd locked on to a target. Her other children and their families lived in neighboring towns, just twenty minutes or so away. Colin was the one element of her perfect picture that didn't fit...and now she saw a way to get him to finally come back to the fold.

Watching Colin endure his mother's machinations actually made Emily queasy, forcing her to refuse the "world-famous" key lime pie that Ava had prepared.

"So how long are you going to stay in town?" Ava asked as they got ready to leave.

"I'm not sure," Colin said. "That hotel's not going to build itself, so probably not longer than a week."

Emily's heart sank. She'd known it wouldn't be much time, but a week? Would they be able to come up with a conclusion by then?

Especially since it looks like it'll be a cold day in hell before Colin moves back to Tall Pines. No matter how strongly he felt about her, she'd gotten the feeling that he was a wild animal caught in a trap as they'd sat through dinner.

"Well, come back anytime," Ava said expansively, hugging Emily. "I'm so glad, dear. So very, very glad."

Emily smiled wanly, then left with Colin. He let out an explosive breath as they got into the car.

"I thought that would *never* end," he burst out.

She laughed, a weak sound compared to her usual laughter. "Yeah. I love your mom, but she's pretty intense, huh?"

"She was adopted," he said as they drove back. "She's obsessed with family being close by. I love her, too, but…"

He let the sentence trail off and he looked pained.

"But you've got to be you," Emily said.

He stroked her shoulder. "You understand me," he said. She nodded.

"Emily…"

"Don't," she interrupted. "We've still got a few days to figure something out. But I think I've had enough thinking for one night."

He was silent for a moment, then made a monosyllabic noise of assent. "Yeah, I understand that one." Then he grinned. "So what shall we do with the rest of our evening?"

She pulled the car into the driveway, looking at him beneath lowered eyelashes.

"Surprise me," she said huskily.

They'd worry about the future tomorrow. Right now, the confident and relieved smile on his face was all she could ask for—and the most she could handle.

CHAPTER NINE

COLIN HID HIS wince of discomfort as he and Emily walked through the door of Halloran's, a family-style diner that represented some of the only nightlife the town of Tall Pines had to offer. It was, as usual, packed to the rafters full of regulars. Everybody who was ambulatory, it seemed, hung out at Halloran's, either eating dinner, having monster ice cream sundaes or enjoying whatever sporting event was playing on the big-screen TV over the bar. It was loud, boisterous and crowded, just as he remembered.

He had to be crazy to take Emily here, of all places. But there was at least a method to his madness this time around.

"Are you sure about this?" Emily asked, pressing close to him, her breath brushing against his ear as she struggled to make herself heard over the strains of the jukebox. He reveled in the feel of her compact body molding itself against his for a second, then nodded.

"If we're going to do this," he said, his lips tickling her earlobe, "then we might as well dive in."

There was more to it than that, though. He knew exactly what was going to happen. They would be seated, then everyone in town would take the time to greet them, interrupting their dinner to not only ask about whether or not they were a couple but probably to weigh in on their relationship. Emily would then be forced to see just how problematic living in Tall Pines could be if they were going to be together. She knew it logically; she'd mentioned it when they first got together, after all. But he thought that a real-life demonstration of the small-town fishbowl that would be their dating atmosphere might be a more effective argument. He'd also see just how much he could take.

He wasn't betting on much. After one night, he figured he would remember exactly why he couldn't move back to Tall Pines...as if his entire visit hadn't been reminder enough.

And after tonight, when she was frustrated and distracted, he'd ask her if maybe she wouldn't mind visiting him in Paris for a few days. Maybe a long weekend. From there he'd show her the vast contrast between her life in Tall Pines and the glory of living out in the world. He'd show her adventure. New sights, new sounds, new people, all the things he loved about his job. He felt confident that she'd be won over.

Then he'd work, slowly but surely, on convincing her to stay with him and leave Tall Pines behind.

"Emily!" Mr. Halloran yelled from behind the bar. "And...good grief, is that Colin Reese?"

Just like that, the whole restaurant miraculously went quiet, except for the belting lyrics of "What'd I Say?" by Ray Charles. Colin watched as Emily blanched.

"Long time no see," Colin said easily, watching as Mr. Halloran came out from behind the bar to give Emily a big hug. To his surprise, he gave Colin a burly hug, as well.

"What, you get too accustomed to ritzy food that you can't come back to Halloran's?" he asked Colin, giving him a punch on the shoulder that actually stung a little. Not as much as the guilt, Colin realized. Mr. Halloran managed to make him feel about twelve years old. He half expected the large older man to put him in a headlock and give him a noogie, rubbing his knuckles across Colin's skull, for staying away so long.

"Whatever, it's nice to see you—both of you," Mr. Halloran declared expansively. "Hey, Janie! Look who's here!"

Janie, his wife, smiled broadly, hugging them both, as well. "I can't believe it," she gushed, as conversations started again around them.

"I do leave the inn occasionally," Emily said, blushing. "I mean, I love the burgers here...."

"No, no, not that," Janie said, ushering them through the crowd. "I can't believe you two came *here*. You just started dating, right? I would've expected you to want a little more privacy." She wiggled her eyebrows. "If you know what I mean."

Now Emily's blush was scarlet. Colin coughed. "Uh, we thought we'd come up for air and sustenance," he joked. This was working out better than he'd thought.

Janie laughed raucously. "Here's the best table in the house for you two love birds." She gave them a booth far from the music and the bar. It was relatively quiet and se-cluded.

"Thanks," Emily said, her voice ringing with apprecia-tion. She took the seat that didn't face the room. Colin au-tomatically sat across from her. "Maybe this wasn't such a good idea," she added when Janie walked away after leaving them with menus.

"If we're going to be a couple, we might as well get used to being seen together, right?" Colin asked mildly, looking over the menu. It hadn't changed one bit since he'd left.

"Are the fries still as good as I remember? And the milk shakes?"

Emily nodded, distracted. "About being a couple..." she started, her voice tentative.

He gripped the menu a little tighter, but kept his voice steady. "Yup?"

Before she could continue, Evelyn Albee and her husband, Dale, came up to the side of their table. "How cute are you two!" Evelyn gushed, clasping her hands together. "Aren't they cute, Dale?"

"Adorable," Dale said, rolling his eyes. "How should I know?"

"Honey, honestly, you can be such a man sometimes," she said with a dismissive *tsk* noise. "Colin, all the ladies are still going on about you coming all the way back from Paris."

Colin shifted in the vinyl booth. This was exactly what he'd wanted to happen, but that didn't make it any more comfortable. "Emily's worth it," he said. And meant it.

"*Awwww.*" Evelyn's eyes misted. "That is so precious."

"Evelyn." Dale nudged her. "You promised, remember?"

"Hmm? Oh, yes," she replied, straightening. "Anyway, we girls at the salon were talking..."

Colin braced himself.

"And we came to the decision that we really need to let you alone for a while."

It was like running off the edge of an escalator. Colin felt off balance. "What?"

Emily smiled gratefully. "Thanks, Evelyn. That's very kind."

"It can't be easy to start a relationship in this town," Evelyn said, shrugging. "Sure, watching people fall in love is something of a spectator sport here, but that doesn't mean that we can't respect some boundaries."

Colin blinked. This was not what he had been expecting.

"We figured that Colin hasn't been here in a while and he's probably having some trouble adjusting," she continued, speaking directly to Emily. "Madge said that you don't want to scare him off. After all, he's never really felt comfortable here anyway."

"Uh, hello, I'm sitting right here." Colin waved, nonplussed.

"Colin, you never *have* felt comfortable here, have you?" she repeated, turning to him with eagle-eye scrutiny.

He didn't know how to answer that. His mouth worked wordlessly, like a fish flopping on the deck of a boat. She laughed.

"Don't worry," Evelyn reassured him, laughing. "We'll make it nice and easy for you. It might take a little work, but I bet you'll be surprised at how quickly this place grows on you. Especially now that you're not a rebellious teenager. You've lived around the world and gotten a lot of that stuff out of you. Now maybe you can appreciate what you had growing up."

Colin stared at her, aghast at her observation. Was that what she thought? Was that what *everybody* thought? That it wasn't them—it was *him* that was the problem?

"Anyway, you kids have a nice dinner," Evelyn said, leaning over and hugging Emily, then patting Colin on the shoulder. "How long are you in town for, anyway?"

Colin was still stunned, so Emily answered. "We're not sure. He's going to have to go to Paris pretty soon. Maybe a week?"

"A lot can happen in a week." She winked at Colin, who

gaped at her. "Have fun." With that, she linked her arm in Dale's and the two walked away. Colin noticed that everyone else in the restaurant was studiously avoiding looking over at him and Emily. Evelyn wound up talking to almost everyone before finally taking a seat at a table with Dale.

"Wow," Emily breathed with a deep exhalation. "How about that?"

"How about that," Colin echoed weakly.

"Are you all right?" she asked. "You look sort of nauseous."

"Huh? No. I'm fine."

But he wasn't fine. His mind was suddenly racing, turning over Evelyn Albee's words in his mind, testing them for validity. Feeling completely and foolishly unsure.

Emily didn't seem to notice his reticence as they ordered Halloran's Famous Patty Melts, French fries and milk shakes. "See them?" she said, nodding at a young couple holding hands at their dinner table. "That's Bobby Rothchild. His dad's younger brother was my boyfriend in college. Everybody was shocked when Billy started dating Molly Rutledge...."

He listened as Emily pointed out various people in the restaurant, marveling at the fact that he knew most of them or at least their families. Instead of being bored, he found himself laughing as Emily painted the portraits of what had happened to each, illustrating the history of the town since he'd moved away to college. He'd tuned his mother out so often he didn't realize how much he'd been missing...or how much he would actually enjoy catching up. The food was even better than he remembered, and he was surprised to discover that instead of putting up with his surroundings, he was slowly and inexorably being charmed by them.

It's because of Emily, he thought. With Emily, every-thing was brighter, sweeter. Better.

The jukebox started playing a slow tune, something bluesy and yet still romantic. Colin stood up, holding out his hand. "Want to give 'em something to talk about?" he asked, wiggling his eyebrows.

"Why, Colin," she said, batting her lashes outrageously. "Are you asking me to dance?"

"That's not all, if you're lucky."

Her eyes widened. "Here at Halloran's?" she whispered, sounding scandalized.

He laughed out loud, noticing several people turn at the sound, eyes wide. Was he that taciturn that people were shocked by his laughter? He shook his head. "I meant later at the inn," he clarified. "Dance first."

She smiled, putting her hand in his, and they headed to the postage-stamp-size dance floor. Merging with the crush of people, Colin put his arms around Emily's waist, smiling to himself as she rested her head on his shoulder. He breathed in her vanilla scent, nuzzling the crown of her hair.

"This is nice," she murmured against his chest.

They swayed easily, back and forth, while the other dancers cleared a path for them, keeping a respectful distance. He noticed people smiling warmly at him, and for the first time in his memory he felt like a part of the small town. Embraced by them. He held Emily tighter, enveloping her in his arms.

"I could get used to this," she added.

He leaned down, nudging her chin up with his finger-tips. Without another word, he kissed her, long and slow and thoroughly.

They must've been that way a long time, because he slowly surfaced when the sound of whistling, applause and good-natured catcalls drowned out the music. He pulled away, blinking.

"Good one, man!" the teenager, Bobby, said, whistling loud enough to hail a cab. His date was applauding wildly. Evelyn and Dale were also clapping. Others joined in. Mr. and Mrs. Halloran were looking on proudly, beaming as though they were new parents.

"Wow," Emily said. "Maybe we should move to the 'later' portion of the program." She waved, then put her arm around Colin's waist, leading him toward the door.

He put his arm around her shoulder in response, marveling at the smiling faces surrounding them.

He'd been so convinced that it was horrible living here. Now, as he walked outside into the pristine winter night with Emily, he started to wonder if he'd been wrong, if it had just been teenage perception that had colored his view of the town and its inhabitants.

If that's the case, he wondered silently, *how am I going to convince her to leave with me?*

He closed his eyes as an even more disturbing thought pierced his mind.

And what if that's not the best solution?

"Thanks for coming to this staff meeting," Emily said, sitting in the cramped office at the inn the next afternoon.

"No problem," Sue said, leaning back in her chair. "What's going on? I figured you'd be too busy, er, entertaining guests to get bogged down in inn details," she added with a mischievous grin.

Phillip made a sour face. "I don't think that's necessarily appropriate," he said sternly to Sue. Then he looked at Emily hesitantly. "Besides, her…uh, *guest,* is going to be leaving soon, anyway. Isn't that right? Which means we'll be getting back to business as usual." He looked smug at this observation.

Emily looked at the ceiling for a moment. She loved Sue, and Phillip had been a good employee for the few years that the inn had been open. But the fact that they were so close did make it difficult to discuss business without personal stuff getting mixed into it.

Which was going to make this discussion that much harder.

"Let's focus here," she urged instead. "Financially, according to the bookkeeper, we're doing okay, keeping afloat. A few more years like this fall, and we'll be doing well enough to make some improvements. Maybe even get a raise or two, add some staff."

Sue cheered at this. Phillip preened.

"The hotel has had some rough years, and we've all tightened our belts," she continued slowly. "But we've always had lots of potential, and I think that we're not the only ones to see it."

Now Sue and Phillip looked confused. "You're losing me," Sue said. "What's this about?"

Emily took a deep breath. "I've been…kicking around some options. About the future of the inn." She paused. "About my future."

Sue's eyes widened. "You're talking about Colin, aren't you?" Before she could continue, Phillip broke in, his voice irate.

"You're talking about getting rid of the inn and leaving, is what you mean," he said sharply. "Putting us out of jobs, no less!"

Now Sue looked concerned. "Really, Em?" she asked, her eyes troubled. "We'd lose our jobs?"

"I didn't say that," Emily quickly reassured them, cursing Phillip mentally. "But I am thinking of selling the hotel. In a general, vague sort of way."

She didn't cushion the blow as well as she'd hoped. Sue looked at her as if Emily had run over her cat. Phillip, on the other hand, looked as though Emily had run over *him*.

"You can't do this to us," Phillip pleaded, his voice more impassioned than she'd ever heard him. "You can't do this to Tall Pines!"

"How would you even start going about doing something like that?" Sue sounded bewildered. "I mean, it's not like you can just put it for sale on eBay or something."

Emily leaned back in her chair. "Like I said, it's tentative," she said, keeping her voice strong. Then she slumped a little. "But, er…I was thinking of asking J.P.—I mean, Joy. She's run hotels for years."

Sue turned white. Phillip turned purple.

"You've already looked into it?" Phillip shouted with outrage.

"Okay, you need to calm down, Phillip," Emily told him sternly. "We're friends, but I'm still your boss, and it's my inn besides. Quit yelling at me!"

He crossed his arms, his expression sullen, but he did fall silent. Sue looked near tears, so Emily focused on her next.

"I'm not making any decisions on short notice. You know me, Sue. I wouldn't do anything without giving it a lot of thought."

"You've been thinking about it for a while," Sue accused. "You weren't sure you wanted to turn the place into a hotel in the first place, but you were afraid to get rid of it. Afraid of letting down your dad."

Emily's mouth snapped shut as Sue's words stung her heart. "I love this hotel," she said, tears forming at the corners of her eyes. "And I told you that in confidence. *As my best friend.*"

Phillip pounced. "If you sold the hotel, they'd change the name. You could say goodbye to the Stanfield Arms forever."

Another pang, one she hadn't expected. Emily bit her lip hard, blinking to keep the tears from falling. "I said I haven't made any definitive…"

"They'd bring in new people," Sue said, anguished. "You know they would. I don't have any experience in the hotel business. They wouldn't want me to be a manager!"

"You've got five years of hotel experience," Emily said, exasperated.

"No, I don't!" Sue wailed.

"You've got the experience *here,* you goof! Remember? Worked here for five years?"

"Oh." Sue sat back, momentarily put off stride.

Emily felt the muscles in her back and neck tense into knots. This was going much, much worse than she'd expected.

"But they'll have better people," Phillip pointed out, making matters worse. "They'll want people who have outside experience. They'll probably bring in their own staff."

"Phillip, would you stop that?" Emily snapped. "Honestly. It's like you're yelling 'Fire!' in a theater. You're just trying to get Sue riled up, and I don't appreciate it."

If he weren't a grown man, Emily would've sworn the guy was pouting. No, she was right. He *was* pouting.

"Nothing would happen overnight," she promised, enunciating clearly and tapping her finger on the tabletop with each syllable. "And I still haven't made any firm decisions. Can we repeat that together? I'm not going anywhere."

"Not yet," Phillip muttered.

She glared at him and he shut up.

"Okay, that wraps it up for our staff meeting," Emily said, standing up. "Phil, you'd better go work the front desk." She waited until he left, then turned to Sue. "Are you okay? I thought you'd be surprised, but I didn't expect you to get so unhinged."

"I'm sorry." Sue sniffed. "It's not your fault. It's just...I think I'm pregnant."

Emily's eyes widened, then she rushed over to her friend, giving her a hug. "That's great news!"

"Thanks," Sue said, hugging her back. "But it's made me crazy emotional. I never know how I'm going to react to anything. Besides, I hate the thought of you going away."

"How many times do I have to say this? I haven't—"

"—Made any firm decision," Sue repeated with a watery grin. "Yeah, yeah, you said. But you're thinking about it. And you've got a six-foot, gorgeous reason to leave waiting upstairs in your apartment."

Emily felt the heat of a blush on her cheeks. "This doesn't have to do with him."

Sue stared at Emily in utter disbelief.

"Okay. It doesn't have to do with him *completely*," Emily amended, embarrassed even further.

"I'm glad you're getting back into the dating pool," Sue said seriously, clasping her hands together. "And I don't want you to think I'm a lousy friend. I want what's best for you."

"Thanks." Emily relaxed, feeling relief for the first time since she'd called the staff meeting.

"But I'm not sure that Colin and Paris and selling the inn is really what's best for you," Sue continued slowly. "You're small-town, Emily. You love this place. And I know you. Could you really forgive yourself if you gave up your father's house?"

Emily winced. That cut to the heart of it pretty much.

"I've got a lot to think about," Emily said slowly.

"Yeah, you do," Sue agreed. "There's a lot of excitement and passion in an affair, Emily, but it's not a marriage."

She stiffened. "What do you mean?"

"I mean, did it ever occur to you," Sue said slowly, "that Tall Pines is your longest relationship? You're married to this town. You're married to this life."

"I wouldn't say that," Emily said, completely disconcerted.

"You wouldn't say that?" Sue laughed ruefully. "You, the woman who's been on almost every town committee since she was fourteen years old? The girl voted most likely to have a statue erected to her in high school? Are you kidding me?"

"There's more to me than that," Emily protested.

"That's not the point," Sue countered. "The point is it's a big part of you. Too big a part for you to just walk away from."

With that, Sue walked out, leaving Emily alone and confused in her office. She unconsciously headed back upstairs to her apartment, her body numb, her mind churning.

Is that all people see of me? Is that what they think?

It disturbed her. Sue was her best friend, but apparently even she couldn't see Emily moving out of the small town. They saw it as a betrayal.

Is it such a bad thing to want to grow?

Colin was sitting on her couch watching TV when she walked in. She sat next to him on shaking legs.

He quickly shut off the TV. "Are you okay?" he asked, his voice rich with concern.

She tried to nod, but wound up tilting her head to hold back the tears instead. "Do you think that I'm small-town?"

His eyes widened. "It depends on how you define *small-town*. Do you mean unsophisticated, closed-minded, a hick?" He shook his head emphatically. "In that case, absolutely not. But if you mean warm, open, friendly and compassionate, then yes, you have some definite small-town elements."

She hugged him, feeling comforted by his heat, his strength. "Do you think that I'll never leave Tall Pines?"

She felt him go quiet, every muscle freezing in place beneath her hands. "No," he said, his voice sounding oddly strained. "I don't think that."

"Really?"

"Really." He kissed her temple, his hands starting to stroke down her back in delicious, lazy glides. "I think that you might have lived in Tall Pines all your life, but you've got the soul of an adventurer. And given the opportunity, I think that you'd leap at the chance to try something new."

She grinned at him. He always knew just what to say. She leaned up, kissing him softly at first, then with growing passion.

"Speaking of trying something new," she said, feeling a streak of mischievousness shoot through her, "I was thinking…have you ever had chocolate-covered strawberries?"

He shrugged. "Sure."

She tugged him toward the kitchen, shedding clothes as she did. "Not like this, you haven't."

COLIN WALKED INTO the town hall with Emily on his arm and lovemaking on his mind. The woman was right—he'd never had chocolate-covered strawberries presented in quite so exotic a fashion. She'd melted some dark chocolate, warm and liquid in a glass bowl, with cut strawberries presented on a plate…and herself naked on the dining room table. He'd never had so enticing a platter to eat from before. He'd painted her nipples with the chocolate, licking them off with a slow thoroughness, then placed a strawberry between her thighs, amusing himself by nibbling it out, then lapping up the sweet strawberry juices that had drizzled into the soft folds of her labia. She'd licked chocolate off his cock, taking him in deep, circling the flesh of his blunt head with her curious tongue. Sticky, coated with fruit juice and chocolate, they'd taken a shower and then made love standing up under the pounding water, so turned on they could barely stand it.

He could never get enough of Emily, he knew that. If he was willing to put up with a Tall Pines town meeting, it had to be love.

"Colin?" his mother said, astounded. "What in the world are you doing here? Oh, you're with Emily. Of course! Why don't you two sit here by us?"

Colin looked at Emily, who smirked at him. Apparently Evelyn Albee's Mafia-style assurances that the town had agreed to leave them alone did not apply to his parents. He wasn't really surprised, but he *was* disappointed. Emily sat next to him on one of the uncomfortable wooden folding chairs.

"I'm sure it'll be a short meeting," she reassured him, her eyes glowing. She took his hand, lacing her fingers in his. Her smile reminded him of the dining room table and their "dessert."

He swallowed, leaning over. "Don't suppose you want to take a quick tour of the boiler room?" he croaked.

She laughed, but for a second her expression turned devilish. She'd considered it, he felt quite sure.

He grinned back. The town meeting always had an inter-mission after an hour. He could always change her mind then.

"All right, all right," Mayor Tim said, pounding his gavel against the hardwood podium, looking serious. Colin had largely overcome his jealousy for the man now that things had worked out. Mayor Tim might want a passionless mar-riage of convenience with Emily, but Colin knew firsthand that there was no way Emily could live without that flash and burn of desire. He stroked the delicate skin on the in-side of her wrist, his eyes never leaving the front of the room. He heard her gasp softly and smiled secretly to him-self. That was a pleasure point for her, he'd discovered—much like the soft bend of her inner elbow and the dimple just under the curve of her buttocks. It was like charting un-explored territory, each new spot a treasure trove of plea-sure and suspense.

She was one of the best adventures he'd ever pursued.

"We've got a lot to cover. Can't we start, for once, on time?" With that grouse, Tim managed to get a lot of the chat-tering citizens of Tall Pines to quiet down. "We've got a short agenda, and it might be nice to leave after two hours. So let's move briskly. First item—the upcoming Valentine's dance at the Otter Lodge—"

"Wait a second," a man's voice yelled from the back of the room. "I thought that you needed to ask if there was any new business first! That's always the first item!"

Colin noticed that Emily stiffened, whipping her head around to look at the loudmouth. He glanced back.

It was Phillip, the manager at the inn. The pain in the ass who always gave Colin a dirty look.

"Who's running the inn?" Colin asked, surprised.

"Sue, I guess," Emily said, sounding puzzled...and nervous. "But she's not supposed to be. Phillip's never been interested in town politics before. He lives for the inn."

Her palm turned moist in his hand, and Colin realized she was sweating. "What's wrong?" he whispered.

Before she could answer, Tim cleared his throat. "Well, yes, but I thought we'd skip it tonight. I don't think anybody has any new business. At least nobody mentioned anything to me this week…"

"Well, *I* have new business," Phillip continued imperiously. "Business that affects this whole town."

"And you are?" Tim asked, amusement clear in his voice.

Phillip gave him a withering stare. "You *know* who I am, Tim. I lived down the street from you for eight years!"

"Let me rephrase that," Tim said easily. "What exactly has happened to *you* that is so earth-shattering we've got to introduce it as new business and dedicate God knows how long to dealing with your problem?"

Colin smothered a grin. Now that he wasn't in competition with the guy, Tim seemed pretty cool.

Phillip's expression was one of supreme distaste. "Well, I thought that it might concern the town that one of their leading landmarks would be sold to outside interests," he proclaimed, his voice ringing through the auditorium like a Shakespearean actor's. "But I guess it's *far* more important for you to discuss the Valentine's dance."

"Sell a landmark?" This from Mrs. Rutledge, who sounded outraged. She got to her feet, frail but still an imposing presence. "Who's selling what to whom?"

Tim's frown was deep. "I have no idea what you're talking about, Phillip," he said, impatient. "Want to cut the theatrics and explain yourself?"

"Maybe you should ask *Emily*."

Emily went pale. Colin clutched her hand. What was going on here?

"Emily," Tim prompted. "Do you know what he's talking about?"

She stood up, and the auditorium went silent as a tomb. All eyes were on her. Colin still held her hand, feeling her tremble slightly beneath his fingers.

"What he's talking about," she retorted, her voice betraying only the slightest tremor of nerves, "is not of any concern to the town. It was a *private* conversation, an *internal* conversation, and it was just in passing besides."

Everyone looked confused by this, and Colin watched as Emily turned a poisonous glare at Phillip. Phillip stood his ground.

"I don't think it's private or internal," he countered, "if you're thinking of selling a building that's been in this town for over three generations."

Colin heard everyone in the meeting gasp collectively and he winced. *Oh crap. Here we go.*

Emily wilted under the scrutiny, slumping slightly. He squeezed her hand, trying to give her some comfort.

"Is this true, Em?" Tim asked, sounding scandalized. "You're going to sell the inn?"

"I hadn't made any decision about it," she said. "I was just thinking about it and I discussed it with Sue and Phillip. I didn't think it was anything that the town needed to know about yet."

"Well, it affects all of us, missy," Mrs. Rutledge replied sharply. "You can't throw around an idea like that and not expect it to ruffle some feathers!"

Sell the inn? Colin was gobsmacked…and heartened. If she was willing to entertain the idea, then she was already thinking of leaving the town. Hopefully to be with him.

He smiled to himself, cheered immensely by the thought.

"Like I said," Emily repeated, "I'm not sure…"

"You couldn't possibly sell the Stanfield house," Ava Reese interrupted, looking distraught. "It's been in your family for so long. Your father would be heartbroken!"

"Mom," Colin whispered fiercely, seeing Emily's stricken expression. "For God's sake."

"What? It's true!"

"You're upsetting her," he said a little louder than he'd intended.

"What do you have to do with this anyway, Colin?" This came from old Mr. Carlton, a well-respected member of the community. "You're not even a part of this town! Haven't been for years!"

Colin turned, surprised at the vehemence in the man's voice. "Emily's my concern."

"Obviously you're her concern, too," Phillip said snidely, "since she never considered selling the place before you showed up and *moved into her apartment*."

Colin's jaw clenched, and the muscles in his arms bunched. That was hitting below the belt. He suspected that Phillip had a thing for Emily, and now that Emily was connected with Colin, Phillip was lashing out in the only way he knew how.

Unfortunately, his verbal assault was doing its damage. Emily looked sick, and she held on to the back of her chair for support.

"That's none of your business," Colin barked. "And it is *not* fodder for the town meeting."

"Colin," Emily said, shaking her head.

"What?" he asked, confused. "It isn't. We're adults. And our relationship has nothing to do with anything in Tall Pines."

"She's talking about selling the Stanfield house," Tim said, his voice mild even though his expression was dismayed. "It's one of the oldest houses in the town, on one of the biggest parcels of land. Which she got rezoned for commercial." He sighed heavily. "I hate to say it, but it *does* affect the town. If she sells—or if she's even considering selling—it's a matter of public debate."

"She said she wasn't sure," Colin prevaricated. He looked at Emily. "You're not sure, are you?"

She looked pained. "No."

"There you have it," he said. "Now leave her alone...."

"This is all your fault!" Phillip shouted, undeterred. "You never gave a damn about what happened to this town. You just wanted to get out as soon as you could. This place could burn to the ground for all you cared! So don't pretend that you've got any say in what she does or doesn't do. You don't belong here. *You never did.*"

"Will you *shut up?*" Colin growled.

He glanced around at the faces staring at him. He saw it then—the sentiment that Phillip had shouted so crazily echoed in their expressions.

He didn't belong here. He was jeopardizing the town by affecting one of its leading citizens and convincing her to not only leave but to possibly destroy one of their most famous homes. He was changing things.

He might be grown-up, but he was still Hell-Raiser Reese, the troublemaker. The kid that didn't fit in.

He grimaced. "Come on, Emily," he said, pain and alienation slamming through him like a freight train. "I don't think I'm wanted here."

"I'll be there in a moment," she replied, looking at him imploringly. "I'll meet you back at the hotel."

He stared at her, then nodded curtly. He turned on his

heel, stalking out of the auditorium, feeling every pair of eyes watching his exit.

In that moment he'd never felt more like a stranger. And without Emily, he'd never felt more alone.

CHAPTER TEN

EMILY'S BLOOD WAS pounding in her temples as she watched Colin walk out of the auditorium, surrounded by the judgmental gazes of the townspeople that she'd considered her friends for so long.

She had been quiet, the model citizen, for her entire life. But in one moment something inside her had snapped.

"How dare you?" she demanded, addressing the group at large. "What gives *any* of you the right to discuss my private life this way or to talk to Colin Reese that way?"

"Now, Em," Tim said, trying to get control of the situation. "We're just—"

"No, Tim," she said, walking up to the podium. She felt as if electricity were sizzling through her skin as she grabbed the microphone, tugging it down to her chin. "You ask me if I'm going to sell the hotel. Say that it's something I'd need to discuss with the town. Well, the thing is, if I had decided to sell, I would have told each and every one of you. I would have brought it up at the town meeting and at Evelyn's salon and at the post office, the grocery store and every committee meeting. You all know me and you *know* I don't do anything lightly."

There was a general murmur of assent. "Which is what

makes this all the more disappointing, dear," Mrs. Carlton said, sounding confused.

"Yes, it *is* disappointing, Mrs. Carlton," Emily retorted. "Disappointing that because of one…one *loudmouthed butthead,* you all decided that I somehow have impaired judgment and believed that I'd hurt the town. You believe that not only do I have a responsibility to disclose every detail of my private life, you actually think that *you've got a right to interfere with it.* And, finally, you believe that because I'm sleeping with Colin Reese that somehow *he's* the one to blame!"

Tim had the grace to look shamefaced. Ava and Harry Reese simply looked shocked. Phillip still looked angry but also a little nervous. Not as nervous as he should be, Emily thought acidly, but it was a start.

"Well, you know what? I'm *tired* of being the town's golden girl." She slammed her palm down on the podium, punctuating her statement with all the passion of an evangelical preacher. "I've loved living here, so I've put up with the interference and the gossip and the meddling. But I am not going to watch you righteously stomp all over me and hurt Colin simply because you feel like I'm not doing what's best for the town."

"What are you saying?" Mrs. Rutledge said, sounding aghast.

"I'm saying that the hotel is mine," Emily replied. "Selling it is not a matter of public debate. You can gossip about it, you can be disappointed with it, but none of you has a say in what I decide."

"And I suppose *Colin* has a say?"

She looked at Phillip, noting the undisguised hatred in his eyes, the fury in his voice. "It's my decision," she shot back. "Just like this one—Phillip, you can consider yourself fired."

Phillip finally looked stunned.

"Now, Em." Tim stepped in. "Let's all calm down here. Things are getting out of hand. You're acting too emotionally and you're going to say and do things that you'll regret later...."

"That's the thing, Tim," Emily said, her voice clear and even. "I'm not. I've thought about selling the place a million times since I inherited it, but I never said anything. I worried about what my father would think or what you would think or what would happen to the town. But now I know that you all think that what happens to the town is more important than what happens to me. And I don't agree with that."

"Come on, Emily." The mayor crossed his arms. "That's not fair."

"No, it isn't," she agreed. "Mrs. Carlton, did you once think that it might be hard for me to run the hotel by myself? That some months I've had trouble making ends meet? That I can't afford staff and I did a lot of the work myself, starting out?"

"Well, no," Mrs. Carlton said.

"And Mrs. Reese, you say that my father would be heartbroken if I sold the place. Wouldn't you think that he loved me enough to want me to be happy?"

Ava didn't say anything. She just looked away, embarrassed.

"None of you know me," Emily said. "Not the way I'd hoped you would. The fact that you think it's okay to jump into my life like this...well, let's just say *I'm* disappointed in *you*."

With that, she stepped away from the podium, heading down the aisle and walking toward the door.

Phillip stepped in front of her. "You don't mean that,"

he said. "I know it was wrong of me to say all of this in front of everybody, but I just wanted to shock a little common sense into you, that's all."

"Well, surprise," she said, trying to sidestep him. "You betrayed me and made an ass of yourself. Oh, and lost your job. Congratulations on that."

"I only did it because I care about you," he protested, sounding desperate. He put his hands on her arms. She tried to shrug them off, but his grip was tight. "I've been in love with you since I started working at the inn. Longer. You just never saw me!"

She should've suspected—there were plenty of clues. The way he always volunteered to work late. How he'd sometimes deliver dinner to her apartment, staring as if he were waiting to be invited in. It had made her a little uncomfortable, but he'd been such a good manager, and she'd needed the help…maybe she just hadn't wanted to see. She shook her head.

"I don't feel that way about you," she relented. "And I'm sorry. But you had no right to do what you did tonight."

"You're making a big mistake with Colin," he said, sullen as a child. "I've stood by you, just like this town has. He doesn't have any loyalty. He's just in it for himself."

She stiffened. "And you're the prime example of loyalty in Tall Pines?" she asked. "Get your hands off me."

"Emily…"

"Now."

He released her. She walked out the door.

There was a light snow flurry, fat flakes dancing out of the dark blue sky. She walked carefully toward the inn, letting the cold air clear her head.

Emily felt heartsick at what had just happened. How could

it have gotten so out of control so quickly? She knew how much the inn meant to the town, but she had no idea that they thought they could actually dictate to her what she should and shouldn't do. She wasn't a child. And as much as she loved the town, it wasn't her family.

She wasn't going to keep worrying about what people would think. She was making this decision on her own.

She walked into the hotel. Sue was at the front desk, looking concerned. "You all right?" she asked.

"No," Emily answered. "I need you to work some extra shifts."

"Uh, okay," Sue said uneasily. "For how long?"

"Until I can find a replacement for Phillip."

"You *fired* Phillip?"

"Yes. I'll tell you the whole thing later," Emily said, cutting off Sue's barrage of questions. "Right now I've got some things I need to do."

She left Sue wide-eyed and shocked. Instead of going up to her apartment, she headed to Joy Webster's room.

Joy answered her knock. "Hey, there," she said. "What's up?"

"When we talked before, you mentioned financing," Emily said. "Do you know people who might buy a hotel?"

Joy looked surprised. "Well…yes. But are you sure you want to sell?"

Emily took a deep breath. "I'm not positive. But I do want to get the ball rolling."

Joy nodded. "It's such a lovely place. I haven't had this relaxing a vacation in I don't know how long. I am in love with this town."

I'm not, Emily thought but bit back on the urge to share her current bitterness. "It's got its moments," she said instead. "But I've lived here all my life and I'd like to explore some new options."

"My father buys hotels." Joy rubbed her chin slowly. "He'd snap up this place in a heartbeat. But... I don't know that I can recommend that."

"Who else might buy?"

"I'm not sure," Joy answered. "I could look, but it'd take some time."

"But your father would buy it in a hurry," Emily echoed.

Joy nodded, looking unhappy.

"I know it's a big favor, but would you contact him?" Emily paused, her expression pleading. "I'll even give you a finder's fee."

"I'll do it for free," Joy said. "But...are you *sure?*"

Emily closed her eyes.

"Yeah," she said. "Yeah, I'm sure."

"All right, then. I'll get the ball rolling."

Emily suddenly felt dizzy. "I appreciate it."

"I was going to pack up and leave tomorrow," Joy added, "but I guess I'll hang out for a while longer. See how this deal goes. I don't have anything pressing and I enjoy it here, anyway."

Emily nodded, barely hearing what Joy was saying. "I have to go," she said finally. "I will call you." She left in a rush, heading upstairs to her apartment. She opened the door to find Colin pacing in the living room in front of the fireplace. His face was like a storm cloud.

"What happened?" he asked. "Are you all right?"

She smiled. He was angry, and rightfully so—but not because of how they'd treated him. He was angry because he was worried about her.

He always put her first.

She threw her arms around him, kissing him fiercely.

After a moment's surprise, he kissed her back with the consuming passion she'd grown accustomed to. When they parted, she rested her forehead against his broad chest.

"I'm selling the inn," she murmured. "At least I think I am."

"You don't have to make any decision tonight," he reassured her, stroking her back.

"Can you get me out of here?" she said, curling into his arms like a cat, enjoying the comfort of his touch. "I just...I want to get out of town for a while. I want to feel better."

He smiled at her. "Sure, sweetheart," he murmured. "I think I've got just the place."

"COLIN, THANK YOU," Emily breathed. "It's so beautiful. I had no idea."

Colin looped an arm over her shoulders, breathing in the crisp winter air as they walked together. They were crossing one of Paris's many gardens, the Tuileries, and had spent the morning in the Louvre after having a breakfast of coffee and pastries in an open-air café. They'd wandered through the city for the past two days. Emily wanted to go everywhere, see everything. More importantly, Colin wanted to show her.

She'd asked him to take her out of town, so he'd taken her on a long weekend...to France. With any luck, it would be a short jump from convincing her to take a vacation, to convincing her to stay.

"What else do you want to see?" Colin asked, feeling like a conquering hero. "Anything. The city's your oyster."

"Actually...I'm getting tired," Emily said, looking embarrassed. "Would it be all right if we went back to your apartment for a bit?"

"Sure, sure," Colin said quickly, feeling badly. "Jet lag?"

She made a noncommittal noise. "I don't know. Haven't flown this far before."

He was so used to flying around the world, he'd forgotten how tough it could be for other people. She hadn't gotten her clock adjusted to European time.

He brought her back to his apartment, just off Saint-Germain-des-Prés. It was three stories up, an older building with an irregular circular staircase and a great view of the street. She stood at the window, wrapping her sweater around herself while he made them espresso.

"I made these strong," he said, handing her a small cup and saucer, "but if you'd rather nap, maybe…"

"No, no," she said, taking the coffee. "I need to get used to Paris time."

She sipped at the drink, still staring out the window.

He sighed to himself. She wasn't content—and it had nothing to do with Paris. She was still feeling guilty about the hotel and the sale. She'd already spoken with Joy Webster several times since they'd arrived in Europe. She wasn't backing down, but she obviously wasn't happy.

He wasn't sure how to feel. On the one hand, he loved the idea of her being free to move as she liked, especially since he wouldn't mind having her stay with him for a while to see where things would lead. But on the other hand, she was obviously having seller's remorse. She had been hurt by Phillip's accusations and the small town's knee-jerk response to any sort of drastic change. He didn't know if she wanted to keep the hotel, but he knew that deep down she didn't want to sell it like this.

He rubbed her shoulders. They were like slabs of ice, cold and stiff. She moaned softly as he worked out the knots of tension.

"That feels wonderful." She sighed, leaning back against him.

"I offer full massage services," he murmured against her ear. "You'd have to get naked, of course."

"Well, if that's the only way," she teased, then put her cup down and followed him to the bedroom.

Emily stretched out on the bed, pulling off her sweater, then unbuttoning her prim white blouse. She tossed both to the floor. Then she undid her jeans, sliding them off her legs, taking off her socks with them. She was left in matching underwear, a black bra and French-cut panties. "Completely naked?" she asked innocently with a gleam in her eyes.

He rubbed his hands together. "'Fraid so."

She chuckled low in her throat, then reached back and unhooked her bra, tossing it by her sweater. Then she inched the panties down, slipping them over the long length of her legs before kicking them also to the floor. "Ooh, it's chilly," she said, tugging back his covers and crawling under. "Turn the heater on."

"All right," he said, doing as she asked, "but trust me— in a minute you won't need the heater."

She pulled the covers up to her chin. "Why, what do you mean?"

He took off his clothes, then dived into bed with her. She laughed as they tussled briefly beneath the covers. "This isn't a massage!" she cried, shrieking with laughter.

"It's better," he huffed, playfully wrestling with her. "Hey, you want to get relaxed or not?"

The two of them collapsed in a heap, laughing madly. Then he settled himself on top of her, his naked skin covering hers, and all humor ended. He kissed her slowly and tenderly, his lips nipping at hers. He captured her full lower

lip between his teeth, sucking softly, and she gasped, her
nipples turning into hard pebbles, raking against his bare
chest. His cock went hard, pressing against her stomach,
and the kiss turned more serious.

"Emily," he murmured, his breath hot against her skin.
He sucked at her neck with gentle pressure, and she gasped,
arching against him. The edges of her nails clawed down
his back gently, and she scooted up so his erection was nes-
tled between her thighs, cradled against her moist heat.
"Wait a second. Let me get a condom...."

"No, wait," she said, twisting under the covers. She
reached down, taking his cock into her soft, smooth hands.
Then she angled herself downward, moving him from her
palms to the wet heat of her mouth. When she started to
suck, he groaned, moving on his own toward the juncture
of her thighs. With all the concentration he could muster,
he parted the auburn curls at her opening, pressing his fingers into her slowly, his penetration eased by her growing
dampness. She moaned around his penis, the sound
stroking him as softly as her tongue. Colin leaned forward,
exchanging fingers for his mouth. He caressed her softly,
first with his teeth, then by flicking his tongue and tasting
her honeyed wetness. She gasped and bucked against him
in surprise, then her thighs eagerly parted to give him better access. He continued tracing her clit with his tongue as
his finger moved in and out slowly, pressing inside her,
searching for the elusive spot of her pleasure.

She hummed, increasing her speed slightly, taking him
deeply into her mouth, her hands cupping his balls and tracing them with featherlight delicacy. He almost came then
and there but fought his way back from the edge, moving
his mouth and fingers in careful orchestration. She was moving more frantically now, and he struggled for self-control.

She pulled away, her breath coming in short, panting gasps. "I want to feel your cock inside me," she said.

She didn't need to ask twice. He grabbed the condom, rolling it on hastily with shaking hands. She pressed him against the mattress, tossing the covers aside, then lowered herself inch by inch onto his hard, eager erection. He groaned softly as she enveloped him in her wet softness. "That feels so good," he muttered through gritted teeth. She lifted herself up, then slid back down even more slowly, her thighs clenching together, her body tightening around him. He lifted his hips, burying himself deeper inside her. She swiveled slightly, and his world went gray around the edges.

"Emily," he murmured, clutching her hips, grinding her against him. She twined her legs with his, her breathing turning shallow and quick as she moved with force, sliding her clit along his cock, rubbing it where the shaft met his body. She made soft little cries of pleasure every time their bodies met, when he was buried in her fully.

"Oh, right there," she purred, sliding with purpose against him.

He was close to the edge. "I want you to come, baby," he murmured. "I'm close. I want you there."

"Yes," she breathed. "Oh, *yes*…"

She moaned as he lunged inside her. He clutched at her hips, holding her flush against him, burying himself fully, and she covered his hands with her own, urging him to hold her tighter, grip her harder, go even deeper. The feeling was intoxicating. He found himself moving to the ever-changing rhythm she set.

"*Yes!*" she screamed, and he felt the force of her orgasm spasming around his cock like a vise.

Just like that, he was forced over the edge. He thrust into

her over and over, emptying himself inside her. She met his every movement, impaling herself on his hardness, making tiny mewling cries of ecstasy that matched his groans of release. Afterward, she collapsed on top of him, both of them breathing hard.

When they recovered, Colin cleaned himself up, then went back to bed next to her. He kissed her softly. "Now I need a nap," he said, yawning.

She shook her head, smiling. "I do feel more relaxed," she admitted, propping herself up with one arm. "So I guess you did your job."

He studied her face. Unfortunately, the smile didn't reach her eyes.

His heart fell. If their lovemaking couldn't cheer her up, what could? "You're still upset," he noted, his voice low.

Her eyes widened. "No, I'm not."

"You think I can't tell?"

Emily looked as if she was going to argue the point, then she let out a long exhalation. "No," she said. "I won't bother. I am still upset."

"Does staying there mean that much to you?" He steeled himself for the answer.

"No," she replied, and he let out a breath he didn't know he was holding. "I've daydreamed about leaving tons of times. Long vacations, sabbaticals. Early on, when I was having so much money trouble, I used to dream about the place burning down," she said, looking sheepish. "That was just stress, though. But I still love the place. And the town." She twirled an auburn lock of hair around her fingers, nibbling at the end. "Guess I want to have my cake and eat it, too, huh?"

Some of his guilt subsided. "If you're just selling it for me," he declared, "then don't."

She looked as if he'd pinched her. "What?"

"I mean it," he said slowly with more bravery than he was feeling. "Because if you move here and live with me, I want it to be because you genuinely want to...because you're excited to be with me and you're thrilled with the adventure of it all. Not because I railroaded you into it. Certainly not because the people of Tall Pines pissed you off." He sat up, cupping her face in his hands. "If you move here for any other reason, then it'll always hang between us, and I don't think that's a good way for a relationship to start."

She stared at him silently. He stroked her cheek, then put his hands down by his sides. He wondered if he'd said too much. Had he scared her off? Been too aggressive? Too brutally honest?

When she still hadn't said anything a full minute later, worry turned into paranoia. "You're killing me here," he finally muttered. "What are you thinking?"

She closed her eyes. When she opened them, they were rimmed with unshed tears.

"Oh, jeez," he said, appalled. "I didn't mean..."

"You're asking me to live with you?"

He blinked. "Well, yeah. I thought that was obvious."

"You thought it was obvious," she echoed, shaking her head and laughing. "We may want to work on our communication a bit."

Then she kissed him, a slow, lingering kiss that only had the slightest hint of sadness to it. When she pulled away, she looked at him with wonder.

"You want to try that again?" she said with a small grin.

"Huh? Oh." He cleared his throat. "If you're going to sell the hotel anyway..."

She frowned.

He started over. "No matter what, I want you to move to Paris. I want you to live with me. I want you to enjoy a whole new life. I want to share my adventure here with you."

"Very nice," she said, snuggling against him.

"So what's the answer?"

"I don't know," she said.

"You don't know?" he yelped. "But…"

He looked down at her face and he could see her confusion…and pain.

He closed his eyes, counted to ten. Then opened his eyes. "All right. You take your time."

She kissed him sweetly, lingeringly. "I love you," she whispered.

He felt a zing through his system like a power surge. "I love you, too," he murmured. Then Colin held her tight and hoped against hope that everything would work out for the best.

"ARE YOU SURE YOU can't stay longer?" Colin called from the kitchen.

"I'm stretching my vacation as it is," Emily said ruefully, stepping out of the bedroom. It was Wednesday, and she'd only meant to stay till Tuesday at the latest. "I have to be back by the end of the week. Sue is probably frantic without Phillip there. It's not fair to her."

"You're right." He sighed, putting a plate of pastries out on the table. She'd gained five pounds in the few days she'd been here, easily. Or at least she would have if they weren't walking for miles every day.

"You've got to have stuff to do," she said, wondering again if she was preventing him from focusing on his work.

"I'm meeting with the building crew next week as well

as the owner. So I guess I will be pretty busy." He sat down next to her, rubbing her shoulder. "But I'm going to miss you every second you're gone. You know that, right?"

She warmed under his attention like a flower facing the sun. No one else had made her feel this cherished, this incredibly special before.

"At least stay till Sunday," he murmured, nuzzling her neck.

"Colin," she protested weakly.

He made doe eyes at her, trying hard to look harmless. She laughed at the attempt.

"Let me call the hotel," she relented. "If Sue's swamped, there's no way I can stay."

He grinned like a little boy on Christmas morning. She laughed again, then picked up the phone. With effort, she dialed the international code and the phone number of the inn.

Sue picked up on the fourth ring. "Stanfield Arms," she said, sounding frazzled.

Emily immediately felt guilty. "Hey, Sue," she greeted her. "How are you holding up?"

"Oh, hey, Emily," Sue replied, some of the stress vanishing from her voice. "I'm hanging in there, but I gotta tell you, I am going to be *so* happy when you're here where you belong. When's your vacation over again? Tomorrow?" She sounded hopeful.

"Er, I was thinking maybe Sunday," Emily said tentatively.

"Oh, hell." Sue let out a long breath.

"But I can come back sooner," Emily quickly added. "Friday okay?"

"That'd be great," Sue said gratefully.

Emily bit her lip. "I shouldn't have fired Phillip before

leaving," she said, then amended her statement. "I mean, I *should* have fired Phillip. I should not have left immediately after."

"Phillip wouldn't have helped, I don't think. You know how much he depended on you. He would have freaked out when he had to make all the decisions." Sue paused. "Honestly, I didn't know how much *I* relied on you being here to run the place."

"I'm sure you're doing a great job," Emily reassured her. "It's good that I left, I think. Now you know you can handle things without me, and it'll be that much easier next time."

"Next time?" Sue repeated, aghast. "You've leaving *again?*"

Emily's heart fell. "Not immediately," she said. "But I was hoping…"

"We really need to talk when you get back," Sue interrupted.

"What about?"

"About finding a replacement for me as well as for Phillip," she said with a hiccupy little sob.

"Oh, Sue." Emily cradled the phone. "Are you all right?"

"I can't do this all by myself," Sue said. "I never realized how much you handle until you left, and if you're going to be leaving a lot…well, with being pregnant and everything, it's more than I think I should deal with right now."

Emily nodded even though Sue couldn't see her. "I thought you needed the job, though."

"When Vernon found out about the baby, he took that higher-paying job in Hartford," Sue informed her with evident pride. "He said he wanted me to stay home once the baby's born. So you'll definitely have to replace me, no matter what."

Emily felt flabbergasted.

"But you're going to sell the place anyway," Sue continued, "so I figured it wouldn't matter. You can find someone temporary to fill in for Phillip, and I'm sure I can ride it out until the sale goes through."

"There's that," Emily agreed, nibbling at her thumbnail.

"So it's all working out," Sue said. "There's a stack of paperwork that Joy left for you. Whoever she lined up to buy the place is apparently really, really hot to close the deal."

Emily felt as though she was in freefall. In one short week she'd gone from staid local innkeeper to European jet-setter who was about to sell her childhood home and unload her business in one fell swoop. It was all a bit dizzying.

"Want me to fax it over?" Sue asked, interrupting her mental ramblings.

"Uh, no," Emily replied. "I'll be back soon enough. I'll deal with it then."

"By the way, Tim's been calling every day," Sue said. "He's frantic, but he won't say why. Do you mind if I give him Colin's number in Paris? He's saying it's an emergency."

Emily squinted, thinking hard. What could possibly be an emergency that Tim would want to discuss with her? Hopefully it wasn't anything personal, like the fact that his "potentially perfect political wife" Emily was slipping away. "I suppose it's all right," she finally answered slowly.

"Great. Thanks, Em. Oops, customers. I'll see you on Friday!"

Sue hung up the phone.

Colin walked in the room, then stopped. "You okay?"

"I'm not sure," Emily said, recounting the conversation with Sue.

"Well, then, it's all working out," Colin said, sounding satisfied. "I'm sorry you can't stay longer now, but the sooner you sell the hotel, the sooner you can come here and live with me." He made it sound simple, like ordering a latte.

Emily shivered. "It's all happening faster than I imagined."

Colin sat down next to her, rubbing her shoulders. "Seller's remorse?" he asked seriously.

She closed her eyes. "A little." Then she opened them, looking deeply into his. "But it's not that bad. I'm sure whoever buys the hotel will take care of it, probably better than I can. They'll be able to modernize it and make adjustments that I haven't been able to afford. Maybe even hire a few more people from the town." She smiled. "Who knows? It's probably going to be the best thing that ever happened to Tall Pines."

"More importantly," he declared, taking her thumbnail away from her mouth, "it's probably going to be one of the best things that's ever happened to you."

She grimaced, embarrassed. "I haven't bitten my nails in years."

"You're nervous," he said comfortingly. "It's a big change."

He could say that again. There was so much to deal with. Selling the hotel. Moving in with Colin. Moving to Paris. She didn't even speak French, at least not beyond rudimentary high school classes.

Her stomach clenched nervously.

On the other hand, her visit had been beautiful. She'd

quickly and irrevocably fallen in love with the city and despite the jet lag, she'd also fallen in love with the idea of
being Emily the adventurer. She knew that the only thing
marring her good experience was residual guilt over her last
angry words to the town at the meeting. She'd been too
harsh. She'd fix that when she got back, as well. She'd
make sure that the new owners got fully acquainted with
all the locals and would do anything she could to make the
transition as painless as possible. She'd also visit a lot,
Emily thought with a smile.

She felt the knot of tension in her stomach release inch
by inch and she reached for a chocolate cream puff, sighing with pleasure as the sweet cream filling overwhelmed
her taste buds like a vanilla cloud.

Oh, I could get used to this.

"Now that's more like it," Colin said, leaning forward
and kissing her. "You're not leaving until Friday, right?"

She nodded, licking her lips to get any stray wisps of
cream.

"Well, then," he said, reaching for her and tugging her
out of the chair, "we'd better not waste any time...."

Before he could continue, the phone rang.

"Saved by the bell." Colin wiggled his eyebrows at her
and she laughed. He picked up the phone. *"Bonjour."*

Emily watched as his eyes widened with surprise, then
narrowed with suspicion. "This is unexpected," he said in
a cold voice. "I see. Hold on a second."

He turned, then held the phone out to her. "It's Mayor
Tim for you."

"Oh, sorry," Emily whispered. "I forgot to tell you—Sue
said it was an emergency, so I let her give him this number."

Colin crossed his arms. "This better be good," he said,

not leaving the room. "After everything that happened at the town meeting, the guy's got a lot of nerve calling you while you're on vacation."

Emily felt the same, and the briskness of her voice reflected it. "Hello, Tim," she said. "What do you want?"

"I've been trying to reach you for two days," he complained. "Em, I know that after the meeting fiasco you're probably still ticked with Tall Pines in general, but I don't think that you actually hate us. Not enough to go through with this."

"This is your emergency?" she asked with disbelief. "You're calling me from three thousand miles away to let me know that you think I'm making a mistake in selling the hotel?"

"Hang up," Colin suggested, his expression stormy.

"Don't hang up," Tim pleaded, obviously hearing. "I don't care if you want to sell the hotel, Em. I don't care if you want to move away from Tall Pines and never hear from us again. I don't care if you want to marry Colin, have twenty kids and live in a frickin' shoe on the outskirts of Amsterdam, for pity's sake!"

Emily smiled reluctantly. "Now, there's an image."

"The point is, you don't know who you're selling to," he said. "Have you done any research at all on the group who's interested in buying the inn?"

Emily felt the first skitterings of uneasiness. "Not yet," she hedged. "But they're recommended by Joy, and I trust her judgment. She's taught me a lot about being a hotel owner and she comes from a family of hotel magnates."

"That's the thing. It's *her* family," Tim continued, his tone ominous. "They're rich, powerful and bloodthirsty. Anywhere they can make a profit, they *will* make a profit."

Emily chuckled nervously. "Come on, Tim," she said.

"It's a small hotel in the middle of a small town. It's not like they're going to be making a killing by running what's basically a glorified bed-and-breakfast."

"You're right there," Tim said. "That's why they're going to tear the place down."

"What?" she practically yelled.

"They're already inquiring about demolition contracts, building codes, parking and traffic," Tim informed her. "They're judging how best to use the land."

"But…you could stop them, couldn't you?" Emily asked. "I mean, can't you turn them down when they try to get it rezoned?"

"You already got the place zoned for commercial," Tim pointed out. "I could give them the runaround as far as building permits, but they've got money and lawyers, and if nothing else, they'd have the land. They're looking to gut the Stanfield Arms."

Emily felt sick. This wasn't what she'd had in mind at all.

"You're not going through with it, are you?"

Emily swallowed. "I'll be back as soon as I can," she promised, then hung up.

Colin looked at her. "What happened? What did he want?"

"The buyers just want to buy the inn to level it," she replied.

Colin nodded thoughtfully. "That doesn't surprise me."

His answer surprised *her*. "You knew that would happen?"

"I'm an architect," he said. "I know buildings and land. Big businesses have been trying to get into Tall Pines for years. If I were buying the inn I'd probably turn it into condos or a corporate-housing hotel. Something bigger and more modern."

"That's my home," she said, anguished. "And the town would never be the same!"

Colin sighed. "I'm sorry, sweetie. I thought you knew."

"I have to go. I have to fix this."

The only problem was, she had no idea *how*.

CHAPTER ELEVEN

"IT'LL BE ALL RIGHT," Colin said to Emily as he drove her to the airport.

She stared out the window disconsolately, not responding.

He felt terrible about how everything had worked out. He knew that he'd set off the chain of events that had led her here to this painful dilemma. He wasn't sorry that he'd asked her to live with him, but he was sorry that she was going through all of this in order to do so.

"I wish I could go with you," he added.

"Me, too," Emily said softly, not turning from the window.

"But I've put off starting this building project long enough," he continued, feeling like a heel regardless.

She finally turned to him, her blue eyes full of understanding. "I know, Colin," she reassured him with a smile. "I don't want to take you away from your work any more than I already have. You've got enough on your plate."

"Like you don't?" He let out a frustrated huff as he negotiated the Paris traffic. "I want to make things easier for you, but I don't know how."

"It's all right, really," she said, and he knew she was trying to comfort him. That made him feel even worse. "I've managed on my own this long."

"That's the thing," he said. "You shouldn't have to figure all this out by yourself. You had to turn your home into an inn so you wouldn't lose it and disappoint your father. Then you decided to sell the inn so you could be with me. Then everybody you trusted turned on you and said you were being some kind of traitor because you didn't put their needs first!"

"Then the people I decided to sell to turned out to be greedy corporate land pirates," she added. "I knew the whole recap, but, hey, when you put it that way, I *have* had a hell of a holiday season, huh?"

Colin let out a short laugh. "You're amazing."

"I'm practical," she corrected. "I still want to be with you. But I'm not going to ruin the town to do it."

He nodded. "I wouldn't expect anything less." He might not care if the town got a big new shopping mall, but he knew that Emily loved Tall Pines too much and was far too loyal to allow anything like that to happen. And *he* loved that about her—that fierce loyalty.

"I figure they're not the only buyers in the world," she said. "I'm sure I can find someone interested in buying and keeping the Stanfield Arms the way it is."

Colin was less confident, but he didn't say anything.

"It might take a bit longer," she admitted, "but I'll do what it takes."

He felt his heart drop. It might take years, he thought with an edge of disappointment.

She glanced at him. "Would you wait for me?"

He thought about it. They'd only been together for a few weeks. But in that time frame he'd asked her to change her whole life. He'd agreed to change *his* life by moving in with her. Would he wait for her?

"Yes," he answered, his voice clear and strong. "Absolutely. But I am going to be selfish enough to hope the whole thing happens quickly. I'll miss you too much."

"You can always come and visit," she said, stroking his leg.

He smiled as heat curled through his system. "Every chance I get," he agreed huskily, then shook his head. "Unfortunately, I don't know how many chances I'm going to get in the next year. The owner is under a tight deadline."

Emily went silent and her expression was thoughtful. He distrusted the undercurrent of sadness he was sensing. They arrived at the airport, and Colin slowly made his way through the concrete multilevel parking garage, heading for the top level to avoid any hassles fighting for a spot.

"What are you thinking?" he finally asked.

"This is real life intruding," she replied, her voice rueful, almost resigned. "It was different when it was a holiday fling. Now we've got lives to deal with and businesses to run." She took a deep breath. "Do you think we can make it, Colin?"

He pulled into a spot on the isolated floor, then leaned over and kissed her, hard and passionately.

"I *know* we can make it," he whispered against her lips. "If we want to make it work, then we'll find a way."

"Oh, Colin," she breathed, hugging him tightly and kissing him back wholeheartedly.

He held her close, his mouth moving over hers, his tongue tickling hers slightly. His body was aflame for her, but it was more than that—it was always so much more than that.

After long moments, he pulled away, breathing heavily. "Unless you want me to take you here, in a very tiny car in a public parking lot," he warned, "we'd better stop."

He expected her to kiss him, then get out of the car. He was in for the shock of his life when her eyes gleamed.

"There's no one around," she said in a low voice, her hand rubbing over the fly of his slacks.

His jaw dropped. *"Emily!"*

"Don't tell me you've never made love in a car," she teased, her rubbing increasing in pressure, slowly caressing his semierect cock to full hardness.

"Not at the airport," he said in a strangled voice. "And certainly not in a car this size."

"It'll be a challenge." Her voice was rough with desire.

He glanced at her, suspicion running through him. "I wondered why you were wearing a skirt for a flight. Seemed impractical."

"Like I said, I'm very practical," she replied, laughter hidden in her voice. "You just need to know what I'm going after. Can that seat scoot back a bit?"

He glanced around, making sure that there really wasn't anyone there. It felt illicit…exciting. Even as Colin knew it was foolish, he wanted her too much to protest overtly. The fact that it was her idea only made it that much more appealing.

He pushed the seat all the way back, reclining it. She slid her panties down her legs, then unzipped his fly, nudging his pants down enough for his cock to spring free. She pulled a condom out of her purse, smiling as she opened it, then placed it on the tip of his cock.

Then she leaned over, rolling it over his engorged flesh with her mouth.

He groaned, his head lolling back against the seat's headrest. The feeling of her moist, tight mouth circling him was incredible.

She sat up, smiling, then clambered over clumsily, cov-

ering him with her skirt. He felt his penis nudge the opening of her, wet and slick already with arousal. "You're
soaked," he marveled. Then all talking ceased as she slid
down over him, her body covering him like a snug, warm
glove. She let out a long, satisfied sigh, her thighs tightening on either side of his hips. "You feel unbelievable."

"We have to hurry," she said, but her body worked at
odds with her words, slowly gyrating against him, stroking
his penis with leisurely, graceful movements. She bit her
lip, her eyes closed.

He reached up, cupping her breasts through her thin
shirt. He was sorry that she wasn't naked, but as he looked
at their surroundings, the fact that they were both clothed
added even more of a thrill to it. He held her hips, jerking
her down to him, and she gasped at the roughness before
smiling with wicked abandon.

"That's it," she murmured, moving faster.

The pressure building was incredible. He buried his face
in her breasts, his arms wrapped around her as she increased both speed and pressure, bucking against him with
a steady rocking motion. She started to pant, her fingers
clawing down his back as he thrust up against her. His
knee hit the steering wheel, but he ignored the pain in the
face of the mind-blowing pleasure that was pumping
through his system. He leaned up, kissing her, and her
tongue plunged into his mouth, mating with his in a rough
frenzy.

He angled his hips, aiming his cock so his shaft rubbed
against her clit and the head targeted the elusive spot of
pleasure, high and forward in her pussy. She threw her head
back in a shriek of ecstasy, and he knew he'd found what
he was looking for. He drove up inside her as much as the
small confines of the car would allow, and she gripped the

back of the seat and his shoulder, riding him like a bronco, her thighs gripping him like a vise.

"*Colin!*" Her voice rippled with the sound of her orgasm, and his name was an explosive shout of release.

He felt the strong contractions rocking through her, milking him, and he gave in to the sensations battering him. His answering orgasm shuddered through him, and he clung to her, jerking against her as she ran her fingers through the hair at the nape of his neck and rocked her hips to meet his every thrust.

When it was over, he caressed her, whispering unintelligible murmurs of love and longing against her thundering heartbeat. She stroked his shoulders, not speaking, simply pressing kisses wherever her mouth could reach.

"We'd better get going," he said with regret. "Somebody might come."

They laughed as they clumsily maneuvered their way out of the car, making sure they were fully and respectably dressed before exiting.

"How do I look?" she asked, smoothing down her skirt and then twirling for him.

He did a quick visual survey. Her eyes were bright, her hair slightly mussed, her lips full and bruised-looking.

"You look like you just had sex," he said hungrily, which earned him a playful swat. "Damn, I'm going to miss you."

He grabbed her bag out of the trunk, rolling it for her. "Get things handled as soon as you can," he ordered, putting an arm around her waist. "Then come back to me."

She leaned into him, resting her head against his shoulder. "Find a break in your work schedule," she ordered back, "and visit when you can."

With those commands, they kissed one last time. Then

he handed her the bag and watched her walk through the glass doors of Charles de Gaulle Airport and out of his life.

Not for long, he comforted himself. But some sinking premonition told him it would be longer than either of them wanted.

EMILY TOOK THE sheaf of escrow papers from the top of her desk, handing them to Joy, who was seated across from her. "I'm sorry for wasting your time, Joy. I'm not going to sell."

Joy nodded, folding up the papers and putting them back in her briefcase. "Doesn't surprise me," she said. "When you asked me if I knew of a buyer, I thought of my family, but I wasn't sure if that's the route you wanted to go."

"Why didn't you warn me?" Emily asked, feeling shaken.

"I tried to, but you were in such a hurry," Joy answered, shrugging. "I figured once you had a little time to clear your head, you'd change your mind—and if that didn't do it, then you'd definitely back out once you did some due diligence and found out what the plans were for the inn."

"I feel like such a fool," Emily groaned, leaning back in her chair and rubbing at her eyes with the heels of her palms. "I've created this tempest in a teapot, and all for nothing."

Joy made a sympathetic sound. "It's not that bad," she said. "No harm, no foul."

"Actually, I fired one of my managers, and the other one's quitting," Emily said ruefully.

"Ooh." Joy wrinkled her nose. "I'm sure you can find people to replace them."

"Not here in Tall Pines. Remember when I first started taking your course? I had just hired the two of them. I can't afford someone from out of town. And, frankly, nobody *in* town has the experience I need."

"But I thought the inn was doing well," Joy interjected.

"It is," Emily said. "But it's going to need some over-hauls, and I put all my money into keeping this place afloat. Now I won't have the money to make any changes or improvements. I'll barely have money for the necessary stuff, especially if I have to shell out for an increased salary or two to replace Sue and Phillip." She sent Joy an apologetic expression. "I'm sorry again, Joy. This isn't your problem. I don't know why I'm dumping on you this way…especially after you stayed, hoping for a finder's fee."

"I stayed because I'm sort of at a crossroads right now," Joy said, her voice earnest. "I've been teaching hotel management, true, but they're online courses. I can teach them anywhere. I haven't run a hotel in about a year and a half. My family's been pressuring me to rejoin their business, but, frankly, it hasn't been appealing."

"Why not?" Emily asked, thinking that their high-priced, fast-paced lifestyle was probably right up Joy's alley.

"I don't approve of how they do business," Joy said primly. Then she sighed. "And, to be honest, I'm burned out."

Emily stared at her. "I never would have guessed," she said. "You look so…together."

Joy's smile was bright, but now that she was looking, Emily could see the tightness in her expression. "I've been hiding it for a while. It's not hard to keep up a front if you practice."

Emily thought about her years in Tall Pines, being the perfect Stanfield. "I hear you," she said with feeling.

"So what's next?" Joy asked, and Emily got the feeling she was changing the subject.

"I'm going to look for another buyer. I can't keep doing this by myself. I'm burning out, too."

Joy looked shrewd. "And there's the little matter of a gorgeous guy waiting for you in Paris, huh?"

Emily laughed uncomfortably. "Been listening to the gossip, huh?"

"I got my hair done at the salon." Joy chuckled. "It was better than watching a rerun of *Desperate Housewives*."

"I would like to get back to Colin," Emily said. "But I have to handle all this first."

"Have you ever thought—"

Sue knocked on the door, one quick rap, before opening it up. "Emily?" she said, looking excited. "Tim's here. Sorry to interrupt, but he said it was important."

Emily looked at Joy, who stood up. "No problem. I'm staying through the end of the week anyway, if that's okay."

"We love having you," Emily said, and she meant it. She might have spent less than a month with the woman face-to-face, but she'd known her for years online. Besides, it was nice to have someone she could talk shop with, someone who understood the ins and outs of the hotel business. "If you're not busy, maybe we could grab dinner at Halloran's."

"Sounds great." Joy bumped into Tim as he burst into Emily's office. "Excuse me."

"Sorry," Tim muttered, giving Joy a quick, nervous once-over…then a double take. Joy was dressed to kill, her usual getup, and apparently Tim appreciated it. Then he must've remembered who she was—and who she represented. "Hope I'm not interrupting any important business," he said with a slightly disapproving tone.

Joy grinned brightly at him. "Just girl talk," she replied with a flirtatious wink that obviously threw the mayor off. "See you at dinner, Emily."

Emily shook her head. The woman might say she was burned out, but she certainly put on a good act.

Tim waited until Sue shut the door behind Joy, then he sat down in the chair she had just vacated. "You can't sell the inn," he said bluntly.

Emily gritted her teeth. Admittedly, she'd come to the same conclusion, but the hackles on the back of her neck still rose at the town's dictatorial stance. "Tim, you can't just tell me what to do."

"After what I told you about them bulldozing the Stanfield Arms to the ground and bringing in a huge chain supermarket or building cookie-cutter condos or whatever, you're still up for entertaining the offer?" He sounded shocked and appalled.

"I didn't say that," she replied. "I'm just saying…Tim, you're a good guy, and Tall Pines is a good town. But the whole reason I pursued selling the inn in the first place was because you all got too pushy."

Tim's handsome face went pink. "We were a little heavy-handed," he admitted in a low voice. "The whole town meeting got absurdly out of control, and I apologize for that."

Emily leaned back in her chair, feeling mollified. "To answer your question, I am not going to sell to the Webster Collective," she said—and she saw Tim slump in his chair with relief. However, there was something in his expression that made her uneasy.

"Thank God," he said, making a gesture of wiping off his forehead. "That's a bullet dodged, huh?"

Emily closed her eyes briefly, thinking of her issues with the hotel…and the fact that Colin was three thousand miles away. "I'm still going to look into selling," she told him earnestly. "I know it's a disappointment to you and to the town, but it's what I want."

Now Tim looked really uncomfortable. "But won't you miss it all?" he asked, a note of pleading in his voice. "You love this town. You love this house. Can you really just sell it and move away for good?"

Emily felt a pang. "I will miss it. I still love Tall Pines. And, yeah, I love the hotel. But it's getting to be too much for me to handle, Tim. I can't keep slogging away by myself."

Tim shifted in his chair, his expression pained. "I'm sure you can hire some more people.…"

"With what money, Tim?" She shook her head. "No. I'll try to find someone who will keep the inn the way it is, hopefully someone who has enough money to turn it into the showplace I know it can be. And I'll come back to visit. Heck, I'll probably even stay here for old times' sake," she said, with a slow grin. "But I'm going to sell the inn, Tim. There's no question about that."

He looked dejected. "Actually…er, there is some question about that."

She looked at him, not comprehending. "What are you talking about?"

"The Stanfield house has been here for four generations," he explained, his pale gray eyes begging her for understanding. "It's one of the oldest buildings in the town. It belonged to one of the founding fathers of Tall Pines. It's mentioned in the town charter and any number of documents in the town records. It's even in old letters that we have in the historical section of the main library."

"I still don't understand," Emily said. "I already know how much the house means to the town. But you know my reasoning."

"Em," he said, "we were really worried that you were going to sell the place to a monster land developer, somebody who would crush the spirit of the town that we've been working hard to preserve."

"Well, I'm not," she pointed out, irritated. "Damn it, Tim, what's going on?"

"While you were gone," he said slowly, "we had an emergency town meeting."

Emily felt a cold chill ball in her stomach. "Somehow I'm not shocked." It was probably the hottest gossip they'd had in years. "Other than discussing how terrible I was for three hours, what conclusions did you come to?"

"We don't think you're terrible," Tim said quickly. "We thought you were...upset. And that Colin—"

"Don't even bring Colin into this," Emily snapped. "Not unless you want me to kick you out right now."

"Okay. No Colin," he agreed.

"Just get to the point, Tim."

He took a deep breath, and his face was hangdog ashamed. "You can't sell the inn, Emily."

Emily growled. "I know you don't want me to, all right? I got that. And if that's all you came here to—"

"No, you don't understand," Tim clarified. "You *can't* sell the inn. Not without the town's written permission."

Emily stood up. "What?"

"We had the Stanfield house turned into a historic landmark while you were in Paris," he said in a low voice. "We made it so you can't sell the inn to anyone."

Emily stared at him, agog. "You won't let me look for buyers."

"That's about it." At least he sounded apologetic, and he stood up, reaching for her to give her a hug.

"Get away from me," she said, her voice cold.

Tim sent her one last sad look, then left.

She sank back down in her chair, her head in her hands.

She had no help, no money to make improvements and now she couldn't even look for sympathetic buyers. The town had found a way to keep their golden girl there, possibly forever. She wouldn't be able to take a vacation to Paris in the next few years, much less move there.

Tall Pines. Her childhood home. For many years her favorite place on Earth.

She felt the tears start to crawl down her cheeks.

And now I'm trapped here.

THE PHONE RANG IN Colin's apartment. He looked up from the blueprint he was going over on his drafting table, answering it automatically. *"Bonjour?"*

"Hey, Colin."

"Emily," he said, smiling and relaxing for the first time in days. "I was just thinking of you. Haven't stopped, as a matter of fact."

"That's nice," she said. "I haven't stopped thinking of you, either."

That's when he heard it—the little catch in her voice, the tiniest tremor. She was upset. "What's wrong?" he asked quickly, bracing himself.

"I can't sell the hotel."

"Well, not to those people," Colin said, confused. "There's a big world of investors out there, though, and I'm sure you—"

"You don't understand," she interrupted. "I didn't at first, either. The town declared the inn a historical landmark while I was gone. Now it's political. I can't sell the hotel without the approval of the town."

Colin felt his blood run hot with fury. "They *what?*"

"They declared the Stanfield house a historical landmark," Emily said, her voice drowning in fatigue. "I couldn't believe they could move so fast, but I guess when they all really, really want something…"

"So what does that mean?" Colin asked, trying not to let his anger get out of control.

"It means I need to get permission from the town council and the mayor's office to put the house up for sale. They need to approve anybody who buys it, making sure that they uphold the usage and preserve the monument for future generations."

"It's a nice inn, but a monument?" Colin said, flabbergasted.

"Yeah, I know," Emily answered. "I doubt they'd think of it as a monument if they knew what I know about the plumbing in room five. Not to mention the attic."

He clutched the phone until his knuckles turned white, the only thing that prevented him from throwing it in a fit of anger. "I can't believe it," he said slowly. "No. I *can* believe it. Those bastards."

"Wait a minute," Emily said slowly. "I felt upset at first, too, but I'm trying to stay positive about all this."

"Positive?" Colin yelped. "They're just looking out for themselves and their interests and making sure that not a damned thing changes in their perfect little Americana world."

"Come on. Don't you think that's a little harsh?"

"Are you actually defending them?" he replied. "You're the one they're screwing over. They've taken away your right to determine what you do with your own business and your own house. They've basically *chained* you there." He realized he was close to yelling and clamped down on his wayward emotions, forcing his voice to level out. "After all that, you're just going to let them get away with it? You're going to try to convince me that it's okay?"

"It's not okay," she said sharply. "But I know why they did it. Now nobody can tear the place down and build some corporate megalith here."

"And you can't leave," Colin added.

"I'm sure that wasn't the point." But Emily didn't sound sure at all.

Colin ground his teeth together, hard enough for them to rasp. He growled in frustration. "What about us, Emily?"

There was a long pause. "I don't know." She sounded lost.

"Damn it!" He knew he shouldn't be losing it this way, but he'd been thinking of her almost every moment since he'd dropped her off at the airport. Especially after their stunning goodbye in his car. He couldn't drive it without thinking of her, a precarious development. "I'm sorry, Emily. I just…"

"I know," she said, and her voice was ragged. "Believe me—nobody's more disappointed than I am by this turn of events."

"I think I could debate you on that," he said. "There's got to be some loophole. Some way to get out of it."

"I'm still looking into it. But with Sue quitting on me, I'm swamped with stuff that needs to be done in the hotel. By the time I get a minute to research the details of the landmark decree, I'm usually blurry-eyed and exhausted."

Colin thought about it. "You could just abandon it," he suggested.

"Sorry?" she said. "Did you say…abandon the hotel?"

"They're the ones that put you in the position." He had a sinking feeling. "It would serve them right to deal with what you've had to deal with all this time."

"I know that what they did wasn't right," she said in a placating tone. "But screwing them over just because they screwed *me* over doesn't feel right."

He exhaled loudly, trying to relieve some of the tension skittering through his system. "I knew you were going to look at it that way," he groused. "So, again…where does that leave us, Emily? What are we going to do?"

She laughed weakly. "I don't suppose you've got a vacation coming up? I've got a bed waiting here at the inn for you."

His stomach turned. "I can't go back to that town knowing what they did to you. What they're doing to *us*. It's pure selfishness and small-mindedness, and as far as I'm concerned, they can rot in their cozy little houses, for all I care."

"You don't mean that."

"I can't begin to tell you how much I mean that," Colin said, his voice curt. "Emily, I know you're a good person, and I admire you for turning the other cheek. But you got *reamed*. You can't just sit there and take it."

"It's my decision." She exhaled sharply. "You're not the one who's trapped, I am. And I'll deal with it my own way."

"Fine," he said. "But you can't expect me to go there and put on a good face for all those people. I won't do it, Emily."

"Are you kidding me?" she yelped. "Like I don't have enough problems, now you're refusing to visit me?"

"As long as you're going to roll over and play dead while they stomp on you, yes!"

Another long pause. "I don't need this," she said softly.

"If you're choosing to submit to them without even a token fight," he replied, "I can't go along with it. You have to see my point."

"It's official. I have snapped. I have completely *had* it with all of you," Emily yelled.

"So do something about it," Colin said, warming up.

"I am." Emily took a deep breath. "It's been real, but we've had our run."

He blinked. "Wait a minute. You're breaking up with me over this?"

"I've had enough ultimatums in the past week to last me a frickin' lifetime," she said. "I don't know what I can do about the town, but you were supposed to know me, and love me. You, of all people, were supposed to back me up."

"I can't help you if you won't help yourself," he countered, feeling uneasy.

"I am doing the best I can," she stated.

"Well, when you come up with an answer…"

"I thought I meant more to you than your animosity for Tall Pines."

That took him aback. "You do."

"Not that I've noticed." Her words were bitter, acidic. "You're so interested in punishing them and showing that you're a bigger moral force that you're willing to let the woman you supposedly love just twist in the wind all by herself. Just so you can be right."

"Emily," he said, stricken.

"No. I'm done." She was crying. He could hear it in her voice. "Have a good time in Paris—or Borneo or wherever your damned buildings take you. I'll still be here in Tall Pines."

With that, she hung up. He heard the buzzing European dial tone and slammed the phone into its cradle.

"Damn it!" he repeated, punching the air ineffectually. How could one small town make him so crazy? Why couldn't they let Emily sell the hotel and move on with her life?

Why couldn't she see why he was right—that they were blackmailing her and she couldn't give in to them?

Colin closed his eyes. He'd made a mistake, obviously. She was too set in her ways, too small-town. She'd rather put up with them than stand up to them once and for all. Well, at least he'd found out now rather than when she'd moved all the way to Paris to be with him.

He swallowed hard, feeling emotion choking his throat. *I love her,* he thought. *I miss her. I want to be with her.*

He closed his eyes. So this was what real heartbreak felt like. It sucked something awful.

He turned back to his plans. He'd focus on his work and not think about Emily or Tall Pines or any of it.

CHAPTER TWELVE

"So ARE WE ALL agreed?" Ava Reese said, rapping her water glass on the Formica tabletop. "Instead of the usual red and pink hearts and streamers for the Valentine's dance at the Otter Lodge, we're going to go with silver, black and gold balloons and confetti, tealight candles on mirrors for centerpieces and the big black-and-white movie posters of romantic couples? I think it'll be striking—and not so cliché."

There was a general murmur of assent from all the ladies present, and she cheerfully checked it off her list.

Emily sat in the living room at Janet Cunningham's house, surrounded by the twelve members of the dance committee. Valentine's Day was only two weeks away. They were behind on the planning, and all the women were scurrying around, gossiping lightly, complaining about how they were still recovering from the holidays.

Emily was still recovering from other things. Sue was hanging on, trying to help even though her stomach now showed the beginnings of a bump. In the meantime, Emily was interviewing candidates, running through numbers and doing whatever she could to ignore the fact that it had been two very long, very painful weeks since she had heard from Colin.

"Can we take a break?" Mrs. Rutledge asked. "We've been here for an hour, and I'm starving. I brought some fresh-baked banana bread."

"All right." Ava was clearly reluctant to give up the floor.

"Come on into the kitchen," Janet invited. "I've got plenty of food, tea, coffee. Help yourselves."

Everyone but Emily and Ava stood up. Emily noticed that most of the women either avoided looking at her completely or sent her the occasional look of confused apology mixed with disappointment. Emily didn't react to either the sentiment or the avoidance. She didn't react to anything anymore, it seemed.

Mrs. Rutledge came back to the couch, a piece of banana bread on a small paper plate in one hand, an earthenware mug of coffee in the other. She put the mug on the coffee table, then turned to Emily with determination. "I understand you've recently gotten back from Paris," she said, her tone casual. As if she'd never said anything at the town meeting, much less accused Emily of betraying the town's trust. "How was your trip?"

Emily stared at her for a second. She hadn't let go of the situation, not entirely. But Mrs. Rutledge was old, and it wasn't going to change Emily's situation at all to be bitchy to a woman she'd known all her life. She decided to take the high road. "Paris was nice," she offered.

It was a small olive branch, but Mrs. Rutledge grabbed it. "Paris is so lovely," she enthused. "Even in the winter."

Emily nodded. "It was one of the most beautiful cities I've ever seen."

There. Easy, comfortable conversation.

Then Mrs. Rutledge studied her with scrutiny. "Will you be visiting again anytime soon?"

Emily stiffened. She wasn't asking about vacation plans. She was asking about Colin.

"Not in the foreseeable future," Emily said, her voice frosty. "I'm far too busy with the inn."

"Ah," Mrs. Rutledge said, sipping her coffee. "I don't suppose you're expecting any visitors, then?"

Mrs. Rutledge was subtle, at least—or tried to be. Emily had to give her that.

"No, no visitors," Emily answered. It was as if they were speaking in code. "Joy may drop by—it seems she's fallen in love with the town. But otherwise I'm not expecting anyone."

"I see." Mrs. Rutledge nibbled at her cake, obviously weighing her next words. "I know you're busy, dear, but you shouldn't let your correspondence fall behind. It's a nice thing to keep in touch with the people you love, especially the ones who are so far away."

Emily didn't know what to say to that, so she didn't say anything.

"And do send letters," she added. "E-mails are so terse and common. Letters, on the other hand, are a lost art."

"When I think of what to say, perhaps," Emily hedged.

Mrs. Rutledge smiled knowingly. "Perhaps."

Ava stared at Emily throughout the whole exchange. "You know, I have something for you out in the car," she said, getting to her feet and nudging Emily. "Walk with me?"

Emily started, feeling dread. She hadn't been alone with Colin's family since before she'd left for Paris. She couldn't think of any reason to say no, however, so she got up, accompanying Ava. They stepped out Janet's front door into the chilly air. "I should have brought my jacket," Emily said inanely, wrapping her arms around herself. "If you…"

"I'm so sorry, dear."

The statement brought Emily up short. "For what?"

"The town meeting. The landmark decision. Colin." Ava looked miserable. "Everything."

"It wasn't your fault," Emily demurred, feeling off balance. Then her eyes narrowed. "What exactly about Colin are you apologizing for?"

"I thought it would be wonderful for him to fall in love with a girl from Tall Pines," Ava said. "He'd finally understand what it means to settle down and…oh, I'll admit it, I was selfish. I'm adopted, did I ever tell you?"

Emily blinked. "I seem to remember something…."

"I was raised by my aunt and uncle, the Stewarts. They were wonderful to bring me in, but…" Ava frowned delicately. "They weren't really children people, if you understand."

"Oh," Emily said, feeling uncomfortable. What could you say to a statement like that?

"At any rate, I've always had this vision," Ava shared wistfully, "of having all my kids around me, a big, happy family." She went quiet for a minute. "When Colin went off to school and then made it clear that he wasn't coming back, my heart broke. I knew my son—when he sets his mind to something, he does it."

Now, *that* Emily could relate to. She patted Ava's shoulder awkwardly, trying to comfort her.

"When he brought you home to dinner, I was beyond thrilled," Ava finally said. "It never occurred to me…"

The sentence petered off, and Emily prompted her, "Never occurred to you that what?"

"That he'd break your heart, too."

Emily felt tears sting at her eyes, completely without warning. She turned away, keeping her eyes wide to keep them from spilling over.

"He cares about you," Ava said, and now she was the one offering comfort. "I think he may really love you. But he's never coming home to Tall Pines, dear. I've finally accepted that."

The cold felt insubstantial now. Emily had lost all feeling in her body, and it had nothing to do with the weather. "You think he's staying away because he hates the town?"

Ava looked startled. "He's hated Tall Pines since high school. He wouldn't change his opinion of it for his family, so I thought…"

"He's not coming back because of what the town did to me," Emily said with a slightly hysterical laugh.

Now Ava looked shocked. "I know that the decision to make the hotel a historical landmark was a disappointment, but I didn't think it would bother you that much," she said, sounding puzzled. "You love it here. Besides, it was in the best interest of the town."

"I know." Emily wiped at tears with the backs of her hands. "But the town didn't care what it did to me. I was expected to fall into line, no questions. When I tried to do something for myself, you all called me a traitor."

"Now, now, that was just in the heat of the moment," Ava said quickly. "You know how Martha Rutledge is during a town meeting. She's incorrigible."

"I don't care." Emily raised her voice. "All I know is I'm drowning under the obligations of the inn. I've been able to keep it afloat and I'm not hurting for money, but at the same time, I can't rest. When the inn was all I had, I didn't care. But now I've found someone I love and a life I want to pursue…and I *can't*. Because of Tall Pines." She sniffled loudly, cursing herself for losing it.

Ava looked stricken. "I didn't know," she murmured. "None of us knew. Why didn't you say you were in trouble?"

"Because I don't see it as being in trouble," Emily said. "Or at least I didn't. I don't want to complain and I'm not expecting anybody to save me. But when I tried to take care of myself, all I got were accusations, and then you went behind my back and forced me to do what you wanted. Did it ever occur to any of you that I'd never betray this town?"

Ava shook her head.

"Why didn't you trust me?" Emily's throat hurt. "Why didn't you…oh, why am I bothering? It doesn't matter."

"And Colin…?" Ava said slowly before Emily could walk away.

"Colin is sick of all of you." Ava winced at the comment. "He can't believe I'll still defend you and that I'll stay here after how Tall Pines treated me. So instead of helping me or comforting me, we wound up breaking up because I can't do what he wants, either."

Ava looked green.

Emily closed her eyes. All the emotions she thought she'd successfully walled off were now bubbling out of her like lava from a volcano. "I have to go," she said, going back into the house.

Janet stared at her. "Why, Em, honey, what's wrong?"

Emily didn't say a word. She grabbed her jacket and her purse, ignoring the other women's words of concern, and left the house. She stumbled through the snow blindly, heading for the inn.

"Emily?" Sue asked, bewildered, when she stumbled past her in the lobby.

Emily kept walking, heading straight for her apartment. When she locked the door behind her, she sank onto her couch, feeling the floodgates of emotion start to break.

It'll get better. It'll get better. She chanted it in her head. But she kept on crying.

* * *

"HI, EMILY," Joy said a few days later, standing in Emily's apartment doorway. "What did you want to talk to me about?"

"Come on in," she said, gesturing to her couch.

Joy came in, sitting down, then studying Emily's face carefully. "You okay?"

"I am now," Emily answered with determination. "I see you're going to be leaving tomorrow."

"It's been a long vacation," Joy answered. "Longest I've taken in my life. I was hoping to get a few things figured out."

"And did you?'

Joy nodded thoughtfully. "I know I don't want to go back to my family's business. That's for sure."

"Uh-huh." Emily poured them both a cup of coffee.

"At the same time, I don't want to go back to teaching," she said, sipping from her cup. Joy shrugged. "Anyway, I'm sure I'll figure out something. I'm just glad I stayed here. It's been wonderful."

"We're happy to have you. And I can't thank you enough for pitching in."

Joy smiled. "Don't worry. That wasn't work—that was fun. So how about you? Have you figured out what you're going to do?"

Emily's responding smile faltered. "I think so," she murmured. "But it depends on a few things." She took a depp breath. "I've been looking at that piece of paper you gave me. The ideas. for building up the inn's business."

Joy looked embarrassed. "Oh, that was before, you know, everything happened," she said. "I wouldn't expect you to do all that by yourself. Especially not now."

"I think you're right," Emily agreed. "I think it could work."

"It would mean added money," Joy protested. "And more managers."

"I know," Emily said. "But I've got an idea…"

THE WALK ALONG THE left bank of the Seine River was like something out of a movie: the sky gently overcast, the water rippling with the gusts of wind, the ancient stones beneath his feet all picturesque. In fact, it was like living in a black-and-white French film, complete with lovers kissing under bridges and monuments like Notre Dame popping into the frame every time you turned around. Ordinarily Colin liked Paris. He'd chosen this project with his fondness for the city in mind, hadn't he? The place he was going to spend the next two years? He loved the food, the architecture, the style, the flair.

But now he seemed to walk endlessly, restlessly. And, yes, he wasn't stupid enough to pretend he didn't know why.

I miss Emily.

He headed over to the temporary office that was right across from the future building site. He'd spent more time there than in his home, it seemed. Despite her brief stay, the apartment was now inextricably linked to Emily. In a fit of despair one night, he'd even considered moving in an effort to get away from the memories each stick of furniture seemed to evoke.

"*Bonjour,* Colin," Francois, the owner, said, adding, in lightly accented English, "You're here early, yet again."

Colin was glad that Francois's grasp of English was nearly flawless.

"You're here, period," Colin responded, grinning slightly.

"*Oui,* but then I am going to Germany, then Monte

Carlo," Francois countered. "Besides, I love when buildings are just starting. So much potential!"

Colin shrugged. "We're off to a good start, but we've got a long way to go."

"*C'est bon,*" Francois said easily, clapping him on the shoulder. "It is beyond good, in fact, my friend. Your reputation is well deserved. In fact, everything I heard about you was true and more...except for this rumor of your constant partying." He laughed. "I expected to see you cavorting with some scantily clad women, dashing in front of the Moulin Rouge with a topless dancer. But, no, you come here early, you stay late and otherwise you wander around the streets with an expression like this." Francois demonstrated an exaggerated dour face.

Colin smiled. "Maybe I'm a brooding poet."

"Ha," Francois scoffed. "You're a man in love."

"Really?" Colin tried to sound amused. "How can you tell?"

"I'm French."

Colin waited, but Francois seemed to think that was all the answer required, so he let it drop.

"Who is she?"

Colin winced. "I like you, Francois," he said hesitantly. "I mean, you're a great guy. But you're also my client, and...well, this is sort of personal...."

"Of course it is," Francois said. "Which is why I asked now, before any of your crew got here."

"No, I mean it doesn't have to do with business." Colin wondered if maybe there was a language problem after all.

"I know what you meant," Francois said with a dismissive wave of the hand. "But I beg to differ. You are working far too hard, my friend. I know how you Americans are. You're driven by the clock, shall we say?"

Colin shrugged. "I thought that was why you hired me."

Francois grinned. "*Oui,* there is something to be said for someone who believes in pushing to get things accomplished. Not to disparage my countrymen," he added hastily. "But while I appreciate your dedication, this is not mere work ethic. This is mania." His forehead furrowed. "I am concerned, Colin."

Colin fidgeted with his watchband. "Don't worry," he said. "I won't let it affect work."

"It affects *you,* Colin. It affects everything."

Francois was a nice guy, affable, charming in the way that only Europeans seemed to pull off. But he was also a tank. Colin got the feeling that Francois would not budge on the issue until he had an answer.

"Yes, there is a woman," he muttered, feeling foolish. He felt even more foolish when Francois nodded sagely.

"As I knew," he said, rubbing his beard. "Where is she? What happened to make you so unhappy?"

"She…" He was about to say, *She left me,* but saying it would hurt too damned much. He opted for a classic instead. "We agreed that the relationship was not going to work, so we broke up."

Francois looked puzzled. "Why wouldn't it work? You love her, don't you?"

"Yes."

"She doesn't love you, then?"

"She does love me," Colin protested reflexively.

Francois nodded sympathetically. "She's married, then?"

Colin choked. "No!"

Francois frowned. "So what is the problem?"

"She lives in the United States," Colin said heavily.

"Ah." Francois said the word with exquisite delicacy. His frown deepened and he gestured with his hands. "And…?"

Colin rubbed his face. "It's complicated."

"I would assume." Francois paused. "Certainly we don't know each other well enough to share confidences, but you must know me enough to realize I am going to give you advice whether you want me to or not."

Colin let out a short, surprised bark of laughter. "Shoot."

"Would you really rather have this job than the love of this woman?"

"Are you firing me?" Colin asked. The French were romantics and all, but this seemed excessive.

"*Non, non,* of course not. I did not mean to give you that impression," Francois said hastily. "Your work is very much appreciated. But it's obvious to me that if you're willing to let an obstacle like an ocean get in the way of your love for this woman, then perhaps she was right to break up with you."

"I didn't say she broke up with me!"

Francois' smile was condescending. "Colin, please."

"Right. You're French," he said, fighting not to roll his eyes. "It's not that easy, though."

"It's not that hard, either," Francois countered. "At least it doesn't need to be."

"She's living in a tiny town in Connecticut—the town I grew up in—and she won't do what it takes to leave and be with me," Colin said. "If she's not willing to make the effort to defend herself or fight for us, then I can't stand by and watch her get hurt."

Francois' expression turned sad. "It's better, then, to let her suffer her hurt all alone?"

Colin fell silent, stunned as if Francois had hit him with a brick.

"Perhaps she needs your love and your understanding. If she is in a difficult situation, you might want to give her time."

"What are you, France's answer to Dr. Phil?"

Francois frowned. "Who is this Dr. Phil?"

"Nothing. Bad joke. Never mind." He rubbed at his temples with his fingertips. "Aren't you a little tall to play cupid?"

"Aren't you a little old to be so obstinate?"

Colin grimaced. "Point taken."

"You've been moping around here for two weeks, working like a demon, and I was beginning to wonder when you would burn out," Francois said briskly. "I thought I would find out what was happening. Love is a specialty of mine, incidentally. This is my city, after all."

"Huh?"

"Paris. The city of love, *oui?*"

"I thought that was just for the travel brochures."

"We do get a good number of tourists," Francois admitted. "Listen now. I would not say this to anyone else. I hired you because I knew that you were the best. I am selfish enough to want to keep you that way rather than lose you to overwork and stress halfway through the project. If this woman makes you happy, then we must do what we can to keep you happy. You see?" He grinned mischievously. "It's completely practical."

Colin shook his head. "I don't know how to fix things."

"Don't you have the saying 'Love will find a way'?" Francois grinned broadly, leaning back in his chair. "So. We find a way."

He grimaced. He was still angry with the town of Tall Pines for how it had treated her—how it had treated him. "I swore I'd never go back there," he found himself saying.

"What, to the town this woman lives in? Why?"

"Because they don't accept me."

"Does she accept you?"

Colin thought about it. "Completely."

"Then who gives a damn?" Francois shook his head. "If this is all that's been keeping you from this woman, I will be very disappointed in you, my friend. Old ladies and nosy neighbors are no reason to break up a perfectly good love affair."

Put that way, Colin felt like an ass. "The commute's a bitch," he said.

"Computers, phone and fax. Come into the office as often as you can, but you're in charge of this project," Francois pointed out. "You can be here or not, as you like. I trust you."

Colin tapped his fingertips together, something he normally did only when working on a particularly difficult design.

"It'll take some planning," he muttered, reaching for a piece of paper. "The logistics…"

"There you are," Francois said, his tone imminently satisfied. "You see? Love finds a way when you let it."

"And when I stop being a butthead," Colin muttered, glancing at his calendar.

"Yes," Francois agreed, stepping out the door. "That, also."

"SETTLE DOWN, SETTLE down," Mayor Tim said plaintively at the next town meeting. "Do we *really* have to do this every single time? Really?"

The crowd reluctantly hushed, slowly coming to order, with pockets of rebellious chatter here and there. Emily didn't sit in her usual seat but, rather, sat hunched in the back. She didn't want to be there in the first place, but Sue had cajoled her.

"Don't give 'em the satisfaction," Sue had said, and after everything, Emily realized she was right. She was tired of being a wounded duck about all of this. If they were going to box her into a corner, then she was still going to come out swinging.

It was going to be a town meeting to remember, that was for sure.

"So," Mayor Tim said, straightening his tie. "Any new business before I go through the agenda?"

Emily stood up. "I have some new business."

There was an expectant rustle through the crowd, which fell silent far more quickly than when Tim pounded his gavel. All eyes turned toward her.

"We're here to listen," Tim said. "What's on your mind, Emily?"

"While I was away on vacation, the town council saw fit to declare my building a historical landmark. Without consulting me. They somehow thought they had the right to dictate what I did with my family property."

Tim reddened. "Now, Em…"

"I love this town," Emily said, her voice throaty with emotion. "But I have to say I was very disappointed by the lack of trust that action showed."

There was a rumble of throat clearing and embarrassed coughing, but otherwise the room remained silent.

"I still love this town," Emily continued. "But it's not fair for you to dictate what I'm supposed to do with my building without giving me any funds to take care of it."

Tim's eyes bulged. "Give you…funds?" He looked at the council sitting in the front row. "We don't have the budget.…"

"Barring that," she said, "I do not need the town's approval to get investors. I have other interests and I no longer wish to be sole owner of the Stanfield Arms. I may need your permission to sell the place outright, but you can't dictate my choice in partners."

"No, we can't," Tim agreed.

"So I'm taking on as a partner..." She gestured, and Joy stood up. "Joy Webster."

There was a low outcry. "You're partnering with the group that would've flattened your house?" Evelyn Albee said, sounding scandalized.

"No, she's partnering with me," Joy said, and her smile was like sunshine. "I'm not working with my family on this one."

"Joy is going to be a hands-on partner from now on," Emily explained. "She'll be taking over the management duties for a while, then we'll be hiring more people as we get some more cash inflow." She crossed her arms. "And when we finally get enough money...I am leaving."

"No," Mrs. Rutledge said, her voice sad.

"I've stayed here long enough," Emily continued. "I love you all, but...it's..." She choked up and pressed her hand to her lips.

"It's time for you to move on," Ava Reese said, surprising her. "Try new things. Have an adventure or two."

Emily nodded, smiling a little even though tears threatened at the corners of her eyes. "Exactly."

"How much money would you need?"

Emily blinked. "Uh...I'm still working the numbers."

Ava looked around. "She's right, you know. Our behavior was terrible. She's been one of our best and brightest for years, and we yelled at her, accused her and then put her under house arrest."

"You're just saying that because she's hot for your son," a heckler yelled.

Ava stood regally, her stare withering. "Scott McPhee, do you really want me upset with you?"

Scott slumped in his chair. "Uh, no, Ava. Sorry."

Ava nodded. Emily would've laughed if she wasn't so blindsided by the events taking place.

"It seems to me like the least we could do is help her out," Ava continued. "I've got some money put aside. And I've been looking for an investment opportunity."

"Whoa, wait a minute," Emily protested. "I didn't mean..."

"We owe you," Ava said, waving away her hesitation. "You've done so much for our community. We can all pitch in to help out one of our own, can't we?"

"Count me in," Mrs. Rutledge said, smiling. "I've felt terrible, dear. And I've got gobs of money. It'll be fun."

"Uh..." Emily quickly saw their helpfulness spiraling out of control. It was bad enough that they had dictated what she could do when she wasn't there. What would they do when they were *investors?*

Ava seemed to read her mind. "Not to worry, dear. We'll help out if you need us to, but we won't expect to run the inn. That's still up to you. And your new partner there," she said, smiling at Joy. "We'll just be silent partners. You know, the type that gives money." She winked. "Although if you want to give us a break and let us host a few things in your ballroom, I wouldn't say no."

Emily felt the anger and resentment that had been brewing inside her dissipate like steam in front of a fan. When she looked around the room, she saw the love and support she remembered—the reason she'd always loved Tall Pines.

"I'd love your help," she said and the crowd cheered.

"I'll get it all set up," Ava said briskly in her businesslike way. "We'll be the Tall Pines Investors' Club. Ooh! Fun!"

Emily shook her head. The woman was unstoppable.

"Now, once you have the money," Ava continued, "I imagine you're going to have some plans."

Emily felt her cheeks heat with a blush. "I was considering moving," she said slowly.

"Moving?" Tim repeated. "What, to Paris?"

"Paris?" Scott McPhee piped up. "Why so far?"

"Because of Colin, idiot." Madge rolled her eyes. "Don't you know anything? He went there because he had some big building thing to take care of and now she's going to move in with him."

Emily blinked. "Are you guys bugging my apartment or something? You're worse than the FBI."

"I like to think of it as being well-informed," Madge said. "Besides, I did Ava's hair last week, and she said so."

Ava made a quick *ahem* noise, and Madge fell silent. Emily grinned. If Emily was the princess of Tall Pines, then Ava was definitely the queen.

Ava turned to address the crowd. "I've been more interested in preserving our town's history and traditions and its home-like feel than pretty much anyone else here," Ava declared. "But I've recently become aware that we can't have everything picture-perfect no matter how we try to control things. Sometimes we have to take some risks and let things change."

The crowd let out a muted wave of confusion and dissent.

"I didn't like it, either," Ava added with a small, self-mocking grin. "But there we are. So, if we really love Emily—and I love her like she was my own," she said, smiling at her warmly, "then we have to let her go. It's the right thing to do. It's the only thing to do."

The crowd slowly quieted down, still murmuring.

"And anybody who has a problem with Emily's decision," Ava finished firmly, "can discuss it with me."

The crowd went silent at last. Nobody in his right mind crossed Ava Reese if he could help it.

"Well, then," Mayor Tim said slowly. "I guess congratulations are in order." His tone turned gentle and he sent Emily a lopsided grin. "I'm sorry about everything, Em. We might have been heavy-handed and short-sighted, but I hope you know we've always cared about you."

Emily felt tears hovering and smiled back.

"Good luck in Paris," Tim finished. "We're going to miss you."

With that, there was a slow eruption of applause, gradually growing into a thunderous echo in the meeting hall. Emily was shocked—and touched. Joy handed her a tissue, and Emily realized she'd started to cry.

Ava hustled up to her, hugging her. "You take care of that son of mine," she said, her voice thick with emotion.

"I'm not going to Paris for your son," Emily said under cover of the applause.

"Sure you're not," Ava agreed, her voice turning businesslike. "If you're going to move to Paris, you'll have a million things to do. What do you need help with? Moving? Packing? A ride to the airport?"

People heard Ava's comment, and there was an outbreak of helpful offers. It was a whole kind of new business—something they could really help with.

"Dale would be happy to crate up any breakables," Evelyn said. "I can pack up your china myself."

"I'm an expert at packing clothes," Madge said proudly.

"I'll help out with the paperwork," Mayor Tim volunteered. "I owe you big-time. Might as well make some use of my bureaucratic position, huh?"

"Well, I don't like your leaving," Mrs. Rutledge conceded. "But if you're going to go, I do hope you write me some letters." She sniffled. "Why is it the wife swappers stay when the good people leave?"

"You leave the Smiths out of this," Ava reprimanded, and Emily coughed.

"Man," Joy marveled, "I am going to love living here."

"I did," Emily said, her voice rich with emotion.

But she got the feeling she'd love living in Paris just as much…if she could just solve the Colin problem.

CHAPTER THIRTEEN

COLIN WAS EXHAUSTED. It had taken a few flights and a lot of strings, but here he finally was—at the Stanfield Arms, on Emily's doorstep. Armed with a laptop and all the accoutrements necessary for telecommuting, he planned on staying for at least two weeks this go-round—which ought to be enough to fix things with Emily and figure out how they were going to negotiate the rest of the year.

Not to mention, hopefully, the rest of their lives.

He wasn't looking forward to doing this much traveling indefinitely, he thought as he tromped up the steps of the hotel and headed for the front desk. But he had high hopes that, by the end of a year or two at the most, they'd come to a more workable solution. The important part, at this point, was seeing Emily.

He couldn't wait.

He lugged his baggage to the front desk. Joy smiled at him broadly. "Hello, and welcome to the Stanfield Arms. How can I help you?"

He blinked. "You're working here?"

"Working, nothing," she said. "I'm part owner."

"Owner?" Obviously a lot of stuff had happened while he'd been away.

"I'm here to see Emily," Colin said, wondering what else he might have missed. He'd felt fortunate to not run into any townsfolk when he got in, but now he wished he'd caught up on the gossip. "Could you tell her I'm here?"

Joy smiled, revealing deep dimples. "Actually, I can't."

He leaned forward, his voice beseeching. "I imagine you're being loyal. She probably told you about our fight, and you probably think you're doing the right thing by blowing me off," Colin said slowly, trying to remain reasonable despite his exhaustion. "But let me put it this way—I have just been on three connecting flights after being up all night packing. I've put off I don't know how many meetings and run up all kinds of air-phone charges, all so I could be here, with the woman I love. If that doesn't earn me some kind of brownie points, I don't know what will. In short, I don't know and don't care what the hell your problem with me is. Now, please, *go get Emily*." Colin's voice meant business.

"Colin, what are you doing?" Emily's friend Sue rushed up, and Colin sheepishly turned from the amused-looking Joy.

"He wants me to go get Emily," Joy said, her voice almost rippling with humor.

"She won't tell Emily I'm here," he said.

"No, Colin," Sue clarified, looking more flustered than amused. "I meant what are you doing *here?*"

"I'm here to—"

Before Colin could finish, a gaggle of women trooped into the lobby of the inn bearing a large number of cardboard boxes, tape and twine. His mother was heading the group, he noticed.

"Colin!" she said, eyes wide. "What are you doing here?"

"Why is everyone asking me that?" he snapped, lack of

sleep and frustration at not seeing Emily making him doubly irritable. "Could somebody *please* go get Emily?"

"Well, no, actually," his mother said. "We can't."

Colin stared at her. "*Why not?*"

"Because she's not here, dear," his mother answered, chuckling. "You know, this is like that story *Gift of the Magi*. Do you remember that one?"

"Mom, I love you, but right now I'm at the end of my rope," Colin pleaded as the other women laughed amongst themselves, chattering away. "Would somebody please tell me what the heck is going on here?"

"Emily's gone," Sue said.

"Gone?" He stared at her blankly. "Gone where?"

Now everyone laughed. Colin was beginning to feel furious.

"Paris," his mother finally answered.

"Paris?" he echoed.

"She wanted to surprise you for Valentine's Day—which is tomorrow, I might remind you," his mother said, grinning.

"I know," he said. "That's why I came here. To surprise her."

"That *is* ironic," Joy said.

Colin gave her a warning glance. She merely smiled back at him cheekily.

"Well," he said, sighing, "I'm glad that she's forgiven me. And hopefully she won't have to travel so far to visit me from now on. At least not for a few weeks out of the month."

"What do you mean, dear?"

Colin took a deep breath. "I mean I'm moving back to Tall Pines. Sort of."

"*What?*"

"I'm going to be telecommuting," he said. "I'll still have to be in Paris a lot, and it means a lot of traveling, but...well, I was stupid for a while, but slowly I figured out that I don't want to live without Emily, no matter what. So I'm doing what I have to to stay with her."

"Oh," his mother said, putting her hand on her chest and smiling wistfully.

"That's the most romantic thing I've ever heard," Evelyn Albee added. "Almost as moving as Emily's speech at the town meeting before we all became investors."

"What?" Colin felt distinctly at a loss with this whole conversation. To make matters worse, he really didn't have time to straighten it out. He needed to get on a flight and see if he could catch Emily before she got to an empty apartment....

Suddenly the boxes and the women's grins pierced his thoughts. "Wait a second," he said, suspicious. "What are all of you doing here?"

"We're packing Emily up," Evelyn said, her voice smug. "She's moving."

Colin rubbed at his temples. He was really not up to this conversation. "Moving where?"

"*Paris*," Evelyn said. "Where have you been? We just told you she wanted to surprise you."

He stared at them, the whole thing seeming too surreal to be believed. Then he put down his bags and leaned against the counter. "Okay. From the top. Mom, could you explain to me what exactly is going on here?"

His mother smiled. "Emily decided that she's had enough and that she wants to be with you. So she sold most of the Stanfield Arms and she's moving to Paris." She cleared her throat. "Of course, I think she was planning on visiting and then telling us when we should ship things—

and where," she added, staring at him meaningfully, "but in the meantime, the whole town's volunteered to help her move."

"Apparently she loves Paris so much she's going to move there whether you want her to or not," Sue said, with a gimlet smirk.

Colin felt as though he'd been hit by a train. "Why didn't she call me?"

His mother crossed her arms. "Why didn't you call her," she asked logically, "before you decided on your grand plan to telecommute?"

Colin could've sworn he was blushing. "I feel like an idiot," he admitted.

"Well, it's touching that you two care enough about each other to make such big sacrifices," his mother said, stroking his cheek. "I only have one request. I know you love Europe and all, but will you at least come home—I mean *here*— for the holidays?"

He hugged her. "Fair enough."

All the women went *awwww* and Colin shooed them away. "Now I just have to make sure I beat Emily to Paris," he fretted.

Joy sprang into action. "I've got her complete itinerary in the office." She rushed to get it.

"We'll get you to the airport," Evelyn said.

"I'll see if there's some way to contact her," Ava volunteered.

Colin smiled, touched. For the first time in a long time he felt as if he was a part of the whole Tall Pines dynamic. In a way, he'd miss it. He wouldn't even mind coming back for the holidays.

But the most important thing right now was that he wanted to give Emily a Valentine's Day she never forgot.

* * *

EMILY LANDED AT Charles de Gaulle airport feeling excited, nervous and jet-lagged. She staggered through the throngs of people, tugging her roller bag behind her.

I should have called. It was a bit late now for that sentiment.

She never should have listened to Ava Reese. "Whatever problems you two have had, it's not going to get solved if you don't get face-to-face and talk about it," she'd said authoritatively.

"I don't know," Emily had protested nervously. "We had a really, really bad fight."

"Honey, there were times when I wanted to brain Colin's dad with my Mixmaster," Ava said with a broad grin. "But we always talked it out."

Privately Emily suspected Ava had simply talked the poor man into submission. She, too, had found herself getting carried along by Ava's voice and sheer enthusiasm. Before she knew it, Ava had raised a very substantial sum, Tim had started the paperwork for the investors' fund and they'd gotten her a ticket for Paris on Valentine's Day. Business class. She was in the air before she was even fully cognizant of what she was doing.

Surprising Colin for Valentine's Day had seemed like such a great idea back at Tall Pines. They did need to talk, after all, and she loved him. The thought of seeing him had been even more compelling than all of Ava's arguments put together.

But leaving had been her idea—and they hadn't really communicated clearly since.

How did I imagine this was going to work out? she thought, wrung out with fatigue, suddenly hoping that he wasn't upset or angry. Or worse, hoping that he hadn't moved on to some model-skinny Parisian woman named Monique.

She was so intent on her nervous thoughts that she walked right past the limo driver holding up a sign: Emily Stanfield.

Wait. Was that my *name?*

She backed up, staring. Well, it wasn't as if Emily Stanfield was all that uncommon a name. Still…

"Mademoiselle?" the limo driver said, tipping his hat. "Are you Emily Stanfield?"

She nodded. "Well, that's my name," she admitted. "But I didn't…"

"You're coming from…" He rattled off her flight number.

The odds of two women named Emily Stanfield on the same plane were pretty slim. "Yes, that's me," Emily said, feeling mystified. "But…"

"Come with me, please." The driver started to grab her bag.

"Whoa! Wait a minute," she said, tugging the bag from him. "I didn't get a limo. Who sent you?"

He smiled. "This is your Valentine's Day surprise," the limo driver explained. "From a Monsieur Colin Reese."

Colin. Feeling floaty and disoriented, she allowed the limo driver to take her bags and she followed him to the waiting car.

Somehow it wasn't a surprise. Colin knew she was coming—even knew what flight she was on. How had he managed that? Obviously he'd called the hotel and someone had told him. Probably Sue, Emily thought with a smile. It would be like her.

It took almost an hour, but the driver took her from the airport to the city, cruising through the picturesque streets. She felt a growing bubble of excitement.

This is going to be my home, she thought. *With Colin.*

After a long time, they finally wound their way up a hill. "*Voilà.* Here we are, *mademoiselle*," the limo driver said with a flourish.

"Where is here?" she asked, getting out of the car and stretching slightly.

"*Montmartre*," the limo driver answered. "Home of artists, poets…lovers. Enjoy!"

She wandered to a set of stairs where people were sitting enjoying the sprawling view of all of Paris below. It was breathtaking. Emily hugged herself.

Suddenly another pair of arms covered her own, hugging her to him. "Hey, you," Colin's voice whispered in her ear.

She turned—and saw a completely bedraggled, disheveled Colin. He had about two days' growth of beard, and his eyes were bloodshot.

"What happened to you?" she asked, concerned.

He laughed. "You would not believe what my last forty-eight hours have been like," he said. "By the way—we need to talk."

She stiffened. "About what?"

"No, I mean we need to talk more than we do," he said, kissing her with a chuckle. "Do you know how many people are swarming all over the Stanfield Arms as we speak? It's like a packing convention over there."

"I know," she agreed ruefully. "I hadn't even decided yet when I was going to move or where, and next thing I knew I…" Slowly his statement sank in. "Wait a minute. You *saw* them?"

"I just got back from Connecticut," he said, kissing her again. "I've been on more planes than I care to think about and I had to pay outrageously to beat you here. I just landed, myself."

She burst out laughing, hugging him. "We're idiots."

"Yeah," he agreed. "But we're in love. That's got to count for something."

She felt warmth bubble through her. "I got some investors."

"I heard." He hugged her tighter.

"Joy's running the place—better than I ever could," she said, her words tumbling out in a rush. "I'm still an owner, but I don't have to be there anymore. The place stays in my name, and I still can go back whenever I like, but Joy has my apartment. I'm moving here to Paris." She bit her lip. "I was hoping I could live with you. That we could work things out."

"That's the funny thing," he said. "I'd just set up a tele-commuting arrangement so I could be with you."

The warmth expanded, enveloping her in its comforting glow. "You would've done that for me?"

"I would have done more." He stroked her hair. "I'm so sorry I wasn't more supportive. I was so intent on all my old hang-ups with Tall Pines that I didn't see you were having trouble keeping your head above water. I was so focused on what *I* would've done," he said, kissing her softly, "that I didn't pay attention to what you needed."

Emily smiled. "It took a while, but I finally figured out that I was hiding in my past," she confided. "I was trying to please everyone. The only important thing was making sure that I was doing what I really wanted to do. And as much as I love Tall Pines, I need to grow. I need to try new things." She nuzzled his chest. "I need *you*."

They kissed deeply. Then they turned to look at the city laid out like a present before them.

"Welcome to your new life, Emily Stanfield," Colin said.

She turned to him, eyes glowing.

"I can't wait."

EPILOGUE

One Christmas later

"JOY'S REALLY DONE wonders with the place, hasn't she?" Emily surveyed their room. It was redecorated in shades of brick-red, deep forest-green and copper and looked like a sumptuous autumn landscape.

"Yeah. The whole town couldn't stop talking about it at the Secret Santa party tonight," Colin said, slipping out of his clothes and climbing on the bed. "Seems like since almost everybody kicked in money for the Investors' Club, they all feel like they're owners now."

Emily felt her heart warm with pride. "I love Paris," she said expansively, "but I have to say, I'm glad to be back."

Colin wore a crooked, bemused smile. "You know," he said with wonder, "so am I."

She grinned. "What did you get tonight, anyway?"

"A six-foot-tall set of footie pajamas," he said, laughing, and she joined him. "I think I've been regifted."

"You won't believe what I got," she began.

"You can tell me in the morning," Colin interrupted, and she noticed that his cock had gone hard and dark. "I've got plans for you tonight, Ms. Stanfield."

Her heart thrilled, and she felt the familiar stirrings in her body. After a year together, they still couldn't get enough of each other. "You'll like this," she said with a mysterious smile. "Just wait there a second."

She went to the bathroom, pulling the odd gift out of its bag and changing into it with lightning speed. She grinned at her reflection in the mirror as she pulled on the matching hat.

"Em, honey, I don't care if somebody got you the Hope diamond on a chain," he called, "I can't wait to…"

His words died on his lips when she stepped into the room.

"What do you think?" she said, doing a little turn in her high heels.

"Sexy Mrs. Santa?" He looked torn between laughter and desire.

"Just like the outfit you decked out my poor great-grand-father's statue in—can you believe it?"

"It looks better on you," he said with admiration, his green eyes alight.

She did a little strut, the short fur-trimmed skirt bouncing high enough to show off the bright red thong. She wore white lace-trimmed thigh-high stockings, and the corset-style top propped up her breasts to their best advantage. "What do *you* want for Christmas?" she asked with a sly wink.

"Come here." He reached for her, and she laughed as they tumbled on the bed.

She was still chuckling when he kissed her, but when he tugged down the top of her dress and started sucking on each breast in turn, she turned serious, focusing on the pleasure he was giving her. She shivered as he pushed aside the thin strap of material covering her pussy, stroking her clit with knowing fingers. "Colin," she breathed, leaning her head back until it hung over the side of the bed. Her hat fell to the floor unnoticed.

He pressed his fingers inside, spreading her wider. "You're all I want for Christmas," he said and he replaced his fingers with his long, hard cock. "You're all I want forever."

"Oh, Colin." She felt his hard length slide inside her slowly, filling her. She wrapped her legs around his waist as he entered her with measured thrusts, cupping her breasts so he could tease her nipples with his thumbs as he rocked his hips against her.

She arched her back, squeezing him with her thighs, tensing her muscles so her pussy clenched around him snugly. He groaned. "I love it when you do that," he said through gritted teeth.

"I do, too," she murmured.

Their lovemaking was graceful, easy…incredible. After all this time, each time was just as exciting as the first—and at the same time amazingly cozy.

She felt the pressure begin to build, and her breathing went shallow, speeding up. He took the cue, his thrusts becoming harder, deeper. She gripped his hips, meeting his every plunging motion as his cock hit her special spot. She let out a rippling cry as the orgasm rolled over her. Moments later, he shuddered against her, whispering her name as he trembled.

"This is the best Christmas ever," he gasped, when he could finally speak, and Emily laughed.

"So where are we going to go next year, when the Paris project's over?" she asked, curling against him as they righted themselves on the bed.

"There's a project in Tokyo that they're offering me," he said thoughtfully. "Or Sydney. What would you prefer?"

She thought about it. "I'd love to see either city," she said. "As long as we can still visit here once in a while. What do you think?"

He smiled at her, and she felt warmth bubble up through her chest.

"I think," he said, his eyes full of tenderness and love, "that whenever I'm with you, I'm home...wherever we are."

She opened her arms. "Then welcome home, Colin," Emily said and kissed him.

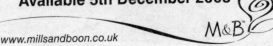

FROM INTERNATIONAL BESTSELLING AUTHOR DEBBIE MACOMBER

Childhood sweethearts and unexpected romance...heading home for the holidays could lead to three winter weddings!

Available 5th December 2008

To marry a sheikh!

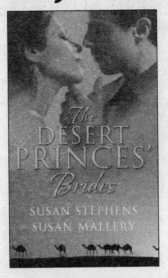

The Sheikh's Captive Bride by **Susan Stephens**

After one passionate night, Lucy is now the mother of
Sheikh Kahlil's son and Kahlil insists that Lucy must
marry him. She can't deny her desire to share his bed
again, but marriage should be forever.

The Sheikh & the Princess Bride by **Susan Mallery**

Even though beautiful flight instructor Billie Van Horn
was better than Prince Jefri of Bahania in the air,
he'd bet his fortune that he was her perfect match
in the bedroom!

Available 19th December 2008